Dancing In the Dark

Cover design: Christopher Kantz
Interior Design: Christopher Kantz

ISBN: 979-8-9916268-0-4

For more information visit :

www.chriskantz.com

For Levi and Sofia:
All of the information is there,
except for the information that isn't there.

For Marisa:
None of this would have been possible without you. You mean
everything to me, and I love you more than words can express.

UT IN OMNIBUS GLORIFICETUR DEUS

Dancing In the Dark

by
Christopher Kantz

Table Of Contents

<u>Introduction</u>

In 2007, on my last day living in Italy, I found myself standing in the foyer of my home, looking up for the first time. It was one of those moments when time seems to stand still, and you realize that you're part of something much bigger than yourself. As I soaked in the surroundings, my eyes were drawn to a Latin inscription above:

"Ut in omnibus glorificetur Deus"—*"That in all things, God may be glorified."*

That phrase struck a chord deep within me, resonating with something I had always felt but could never quite put into words. It was in that moment I knew it had to be part of the book I was destined to write. I had always been told that I should write a book, and that day, the seed was truly planted. I began crafting what I called a *libello*—a little book of ideas, reflections, and observations. Over time, that *libello* evolved, expanded, and transformed into what you now hold in your hands.

Writing this book has been a journey in itself, one that has spanned over a decade. During this time, my ideas grew and shifted, much like life itself. I've always been inspired by the works of writers like Jack Kerouac, Hunter S. Thompson, Haruki Murakami, and Whitley Strieber—authors who challenge the status quo and explore the depths of the human experience. Their influence, along with my own life experiences, has shaped the narrative and themes within this book.

But my journey wasn't just about writing a story—it was about creating something meaningful, something that could offer guidance and insight to those who read it. After falling ill in 2023, the urgency of this task became clear to me. I wanted to leave something behind for my children, something they could learn from, something that would help them navigate the complexities of life.

As I wrote, I found that the act of putting pen to paper became a mirror—reflecting my own fears, hopes, and beliefs. What started as a personal endeavor transformed into something much larger, something that, I hope, will resonate with anyone seeking to find their way in life.

"*Dancing In The Dark*" is more than just a story; it's a repository of knowledge and insight, woven into a narrative through allegory, metaphor, and symbology. My goal was to distill as much wisdom as possible into these pages—an attempt to explain the history of the universe and everything that might ever happen, an ambitious endeavor to find certainty amidst the uncertainties of life.

This book is divided into twelve chapters, each one telling a part of Alex and Eden's story. At the end of each chapter, you'll find a lesson that ties into the narrative, along with an activity designed to help you apply these ideas in your own life. These lessons are not just for my children—they're for anyone who picks up this book, because I believe that no matter how much we know, there's always something new to learn.

This book is designed to help anyone who is willing to learn. It offers practical solutions to everyday problems, guides you in making the best decisions, and encourages you to become the best version of yourself. Whether you are seeking guidance, inspiration, or simply a good story, I hope you find something valuable within these pages.

Life is an earthbound experience, full of imperfections and uncertainties, and we're all just trying to make sense of it as best we can. My hope is that through Alex and Eden's journey, you'll find reflections of your own experiences and discover new ways to grow, adapt, and thrive. I encourage you not to skip the lessons or activities, even if they seem simple at first glance. They're meant to be practical tools for living a more balanced and fulfilling life.

Though this book is complete, my journey as a writer is far from over. I have many more ideas from my *libello* to explore and stories to tell, which I hope to share in future books. But for now, I invite you to step into the world of *Dancing In The Dark*—a world where love, life, and meaning intertwine, offering you not just a story, but a guide for living well.

Prologue

That in our wake, we shall find that
which we desire the most, and after finding it,
we lose it, only to remember its joy.

Sigh.

One day I was thinking,
And my thoughts became words.
Every word became a common shape,
Until the world of which I thought,
I knew, became a surreal text.

It started with "Once upon a time," and ended with, "Sigh."

Once Upon a time,

In the darkness surrounded by emptiness.
Ages have passed, we slowly drifted apart.
Though our time together seemed forever,
Everything began to start.

Our joy echoes endlessly,
Energizing and electrifying the space between us.
Light begins to flash.
Colors and shapes move in all directions.
Joy becomes ecstasy, and then we perceive,
That what we had lost would soon be found,
And it would only be better this time around.

I begin to condense, then hear,
see, then touch,
smell, then taste...
Live a life create.
I can imagine and believe,
Laugh and play.

There is no hurry when you have an eternity.

> "We must be willing to get rid of the life we've planned, so as to have the life that is waiting for us."
>
> -Joseph Campbell

Chapter 1: A Mysterious Encounter

"Wake up, wake up." The urgent voice cut through the haze of Alex's dreams, pulling him reluctantly from slumber. He groaned, rolling over and burying his head deeper into the warmth of his blankets.

But his mother was persistent. "Alex, if you stay in bed any longer, you'll end up missing trick-or-treat tonight," she warned.

That snapped Alex to attention faster than a bolt of lightning. With a sudden jolt, he sat up, rubbing away the remnants of sleep.

"Wait, what? Tonight's Halloween?" he exclaimed, his voice sounding with disbelief.

His mother nodded. "Yes, it is. And you wouldn't want to miss out on all the fun with your other eleven-year-old friends, would

6

you?"

As the realization sank in, Alex scrambled out of bed, his heart pounding with excitement. Halloween in Everbrook was like no other night of the year, filled with magic and mystery.

With a newfound energy coursing through him, Alex hurried to get ready for school, eager to immerse himself in the enchantment that awaited in his beloved town of Everbrook later in the day.

Everbrook was the kind of quaint, close-knit town where imagination and curiosity were encouraged from a young age. Alex embodied this adventurous spirit, growing up fascinated by all things supernatural and mystical.

His parents, George and Cindy, were high school sweethearts who had lived in Everbrook their whole lives. They embraced their community's freethinking and creative spirit.

Alex's dad was an eccentric high school English teacher who filled their home with books and hung dream catchers and crystals in the windows. His mom was a nature-loving social worker who taught Alex about plants, foraging, and holistic medicine. They didn't bat an eye at Alex's interests, letting him decorate his room with star charts, monster posters, and strange artifacts.

Alex also had a sister who was two years older than him, named Sarah. She loved to perform pretend rituals and seances with him in the woods. She would help him create haunted houses in their basement each Halloween, using homemade props and costumes. Even though she was a singer and musician at school, Sarah never judged Alex for being different. She stood up for him when kids teased him about his strange obsessions.

The whole family would join in Alex's imaginative play, embodying characters and acting out his magical stories. Their warped sense of humor and playfulness allowed Alex's creativity to thrive.

Alex's room was his own personal supernatural lair. The shelves were crammed with weathered books about myths, monsters, magic spells, and more. His prized collection on ghost phenomena took up an entire corner.

Posters covered the walls, showing images of werewolves, vampires, and zombies. Intricate charts mapped out constellations of mythical creatures and symbols. Strange artifacts he had found in the woods sat on display, from bones and feathers to crystals with mystical auras.

His best friend, Gabriel, one year older than him, took Alex's interests seriously. They had bonded in elementary school over a shared love of fantasy stories about dragons. While the other kids played games at recess, Alex and Gabriel imagined epic adventures fighting off evil villains and outwitting sorcerers.

When taunts and teasing started, Gabriel became Alex's staunchest defender. He understood Alex wasn't like the other kids. Where their peers only saw strangeness, Gabriel saw wonder, creativity, and a compelling way of viewing the world.

With his backpack slung over his shoulder, Alex dashed down the stairs, the anticipation of Halloween coursing through his veins. His mother was waiting for him in the kitchen, a warm smile on her face as she prepared breakfast.

"Ready for school, my little man?" she asked, handing him a plate of eggs and pancakes.

Alex nodded eagerly, devouring his breakfast in record time.

As he gulped down the last bite, his mother gave him a knowing look. "Don't forget, after school, we're going to drop you guys off at Mach Pizza for dinner. I have to work late tonight, and your dad is helping out at the festival."

A smile spread across Alex's face. Mach Pizza was a local favorite, known for its delicious slices and jubilant atmosphere. It was the perfect way to kick off this evening's Halloween festivities.

"Thanks for the reminder, Mom!" Alex exclaimed, grabbing his backpack and rushing toward the door.

His mother followed him, giving him a quick hug before he stepped outside. "Have a great day, sweetheart. And remember, no matter how busy you get, don't forget to have fun tonight."

With a wave goodbye, Alex barreled down the front steps, excitement bubbling inside him as he made his way to the bus stop. Today was going to be an unforgettable Halloween, filled with laughter, adventure, and, of course, plenty of pizza.

●

In contrast to Alex's quaint hometown, Eden, also eleven years old, was raised in a bustling Big City where schedules and structure ruled over spontaneity. Her parents, Maria and Antonio, both teachers at her private school, kept a strict schedule for Eden and her younger brother, Leo. They valued academic pursuits over imagination.

"How was school today?" Eden's mom asked as they drove to their apartment. "Learn anything interesting?"

Eden shrugged, gazing out the window. "It was fine. We learned about volcanoes in science."

"Fascinating! What can you tell me about how volcanoes form?" her mom continued enthusiastically.

Eden sighed internally. Chosen for her academic prowess, her parents always expected detailed reports of scholastic activities. Emotional check-ins were rare.

While Eden's parents supported her introverted tendencies, they wished she was more outgoing and ambitious, like the other city kids. Books and observing people from afar were Eden's escapes. She often wandered the rooftop alone, finding nooks to read in and watch the world go by.

An avid analyst, Eden filled notebook after notebook with her inner thoughts and insights about others. She could spend hours studying someone's posture or expression, imagining their life story, inner world, and motivations.

Her overactive imagination and reflective nature made her feel out of place among her fast-paced, achievement-driven peers. She found joy in the quiet moments she carved out for herself, cultivating her rich inner world through reading, people-watching, and journaling her ideas. Eden's introspective personality developed as she learned to embrace the freedom of her own mind among the crowded streets.

At home, each night involved homework checks over a healthy dinner, followed by showers and early bedtimes. Eden's parents meticulously planned out their weekends too, packing their calendar with physics lectures, art gallery visits, and scholarly meetups.

Eden admired her parents' intellect but often felt stifled by their regimented lifestyle. She yearned for more freedom and spontaneity. With the constant shuffle from one strict routine to the next, Eden found escape in books and her own private thoughts.

After school, Eden's mom shuttled her to piano lessons, tennis practice, tutoring sessions, and other enrichment activities depending on the day. Eden would stare out the car window, imagining herself in faraway lands instead of wherever she was being dropped off for that day.

At night, Eden often curled up in bed with her younger brother, Leo. She would read aloud from his favorite fantasy novels, doing funny voices to make him laugh. Cuddled against her shoulder, Leo hung on every word with wonder-filled eyes.

With Leo, she could be playful and imaginative without judgment. Their bond allowed her sensitive self to emerge in ways she hid from the world. She wished her parents could see this side of her, the side that longed for nurturing and acceptance.

Eden would often spend time with her neighbor, Maya, who was a couple of years older and attended public school.

Despite the age gap, the two girls bonded closely over shared interests like music and movies. Maya acted protective of Eden, offering her younger friend advice on navigating school and relationships.

Though sometimes left out of older activities with Maya's friends, Eden appreciated having such a mature, caring confidant. When they spent afternoons chatting and giggling together, their age difference seemed to fade into the background.

Eden's bedroom was filled with books, art supplies, and cozy reading nooks. The walls were painted a deep purple and decorated with framed sketches Eden had drawn of fantasy creatures and scenic landscapes.

A desk displayed Eden's sketchbooks, colored pencils, markers, and half-finished drawings. The closet overflowed with elegant clothes reflecting her refined tastes. White Christmas lights hung above the bed, providing a cozy glow for late-night reading or journaling. She could spend hours in her room, getting lost in one of her many books, filling pages with her thoughts, or working on a new sketch. It was a perfect spot for her to relax and escape from the rigidness of her day-to-day life.

Eden spread a map out on her bedroom floor as Leo and Maya sat closer to take a better look. It was a neatly hand-drawn map of the nearby town of Everbrook, where they would be trick-or-treating tonight.

"Alright, team, tonight's mission is to beat our candy record from last year," Eden announced, pointing to the map. "With some strategic routing, I know we can hit more houses than ever."

She began tracing out the streets, explaining the town's layout to her companions. "The main part of town is set up in a grid, with North, South, East, and West Streets intersecting at the central Town Square. That's where the parade will be later tonight."

Eden circled a street on the east side. "Here, on East Street, is where the haunted fun house is located. We'll have to budget our time carefully to get through there and still have enough time for trick-or-treating."

Next, she pointed out the bakery in the town square. "This is where Mom and Dad said to meet them before the parade. The surrounding streets are filled with tons of great houses for trick-or-treating," Eden explained, "but we can't waste time criss-crossing back and forth. I've mapped out the most efficient route to maximize our hits."

Leo's eyes lit up as Eden gestured to the streets fanning out from the square. He imagined each one decorated with spooky inflatables, cobwebs, gravestones, and more. She traced a looping path down the streets on her map.

Maya nodded thoughtfully. "This is great. We'll save so much time not backtracking all over."

"Exactly," Eden replied. "Now, the key is this graveyard shortcut." She indicated a path cutting through the cemetery on the south side. "If we take this, it shaves off nearly fifteen minutes between these neighborhoods. It's the fastest way to get to the fun house from Maple Street for prime trick-or-treating time-saving usage-analysis."

Leo looked uneasy. "Those big words confuse me. Is the graveyard safe at night though? It seems kinda creepy..."

Eden waved off his concerns. "Don't be a scaredy cat, it'll be fine. Maybe a little spooky, but it's the best route. The gravestones and mausoleums will get us in the Halloween spirit!"

Maya agreed enthusiastically. "I'm not afraid of some old graves. It's the perfect shortcut, let's do it!"

With their route decided, the kids felt confident they could beat their candy record tonight. All that was left was the execution.

"This is going to be epic, you guys," Eden said as she rolled up her map. "Tonight, Everbrook won't know what hit it!"

They high-fived and then rushed to get into their costumes before Eden's parents arrived to drive them to Everbrook. As Leo adjusted his wolf mask in the car, Eden grinned, thinking through the route one more time. In just a little bit, they would launch their plan to collect more candy than ever before.

•

The houses and stores of Everbrook were decorated with jack-o'-lanterns, spiders, and fake cobwebs. The streets buzzed with activity as townsfolk readied themselves for a night of tricks and treats.

Alex could hardly contain his excitement as his parents pulled up to Mach Pizza in their station wagon. He and his sister, Sarah, had spent their time after school preparing their vampire costumes, complete with capes lined with satin scarlet cords. His friend, Gabriel, had come over earlier to finish his zombie makeup and ripped clothing.

"Now, you three stay out of trouble tonight. Work hard, but not too hard!" Alex's dad said as they climbed out of the car. "And meet me at Cosimo's Italian Restaurant at the square for the parade later!"

"We will, Dad," Alex promised, adjusting his vampire fangs.

His mom smiled, reaching back to straighten his crooked cape. "Have fun! And stop by the hospital if you need any help."

"We will," Sarah said. "See you later!"

The three friends waved as Alex's parents pulled away, ready to take on the excitement of Halloween night. Lively music and laughter poured out of Mach Pizza, the fastest pizza shop this side of the Mississippi. The walls were painted in bold reds, yellows, and greens with a black-and-white checkered floor.

Weaving their way through the crowd of costumed kids and parents, the savory scents of pizza dough and melted cheese filled the air. Classic rock music played over the speakers, complementing the retro vibes.

"Ew, what's with all the flies?" Sarah said, swatting them away as they walked to their booth. Gabriel looked around, noticing flies buzzing over tables and landing on abandoned pizza crusts.

"Must be something attracting them in here," he said.

Alex waved away flies gathering around a nearby soda. "Yeah, not very appetizing. Hopefully, they clear out so we can actually eat."

They grabbed a booth and scanned the room, taking in the decorated windows and arcade games. The tables featured glass bottles of ketchup and Parmesan cheese shakers in the shapes of mushrooms.

Along one wall was a long counter where customers could watch their pizzas being freshly tossed and topped. Alex felt a rush of excitement looking around at all the creatures emerging on this magical night—zombies, vampires, ghosts, and more.

"I'm going to grab some tokens for the games," Sarah said.

"We've got to play Zombie Shooter!" said Alex.

"Good idea!" Gabriel replied with a grin.

Just then, a group of eighth-grade bullies crept over to their booth. Alex looked over at the group of bullies, whom he nicknamed Moldy Mike, Pumpkin Boy, and Handsome Tom. The three bullies had always picked on Alex for as long as he could remember. Though cruel, Alex knew their meanness came from their own insecurities and home lives.

Moldy Mike's dad was an overly strict military man who was never satisfied with his son's grades and punished failure harshly.

Pumpkin Boy came from a poor family and got made fun of for his tattered hand-me-down clothes.

Handsome Tom secretly felt isolated as the only child in a family that didn't understand his sensitive nature.

Alex's sister, Sarah, had a secret crush on Handsome Tom. She sensed a sweet side under his tough facade. Sometimes, she would catch Tom looking back at her in class with a hint of a smile. Both were misunderstood kids seeking connection.

"Well, if it isn't Count Weird-ula and his sidekick, Zombie Turd! That cape is lame even for a baby vampire like you," Moldy Mike sneered. "What's with the weird symbol necklace, creature freak? Something from your creepy cult?"

The bullies laughed. Alex gripped his soda cup tightly, trying to ignore their taunts.

"Why don't you losers hit the road," Pumpkin Boy chimed in. "This booth is for cool kids only."

Gabriel stood up defiantly. "Seriously, get lost," he said, though his voice wavered slightly.

Handsome Tom shoved Gabriel back down into the booth. "Or what, zombie boy? You gonna put a hex on us?" he mocked. The bullies erupted in laughter.

Just then, Sarah returned with the tokens. "Back off, creeps," she said, stepping between them and Alex. She turned to Handsome Tom. "I expected better from you," she added quietly.

Handsome Tom shuffled his feet, avoiding her gaze. "Come on, guys, these wimps aren't worth it," he muttered. The bullies begrudgingly started moving away.

Sarah watched Handsome Tom walk away with an admiring gaze as she sat down next to Alex. "You alright?" she asked.

Alex let out a relieved sigh. "Thanks, big sis," he said to Sarah, but they knew the bullies would be back to bother them again soon.

Frank, one of the older high school kids who worked at Mach Pizza, came over to their table. "Hey, sorry you guys had to deal with those punks," he said sympathetically. "I used to be one of them before I realized being a bully doesn't make you cool. Trust me, guys like that are just insecure. They put others down to feel big," Frank continued. "But there are better ways to handle them."

He glanced around, then said in a low voice, "In thirty minutes, meet me behind the shop for a deal you can't refuse. I've got a plan for you guys that will teach those bullies a lesson they won't forget."

Alex, Sarah, and Gabriel looked at each other eagerly. "We'll be there," said Alex.

After eating pizza and playing some games, the trio snuck out the back exit of Mach Pizza into the alley, where Frank was waiting with a mischievous grin. In his hands were bags filled with supplies—bottle rockets, slingshots, stink bombs, a few boxes of fly paper, and more.

"Here's the deal..." he began, laying out the pranking materials. "I got my hands on some of these goodies and thought maybe you could put them to use. Those bullies won't know what hit them."

Eagerly peering into the bags, Alex, Sarah, and Gabriel huddled together, whispering and scheming about how to creatively take the bullies down.

With Frank's assistance, a new surge of confidence flowed through Alex, and he declared with determination, "Let's blow this popsicle stand!" Tonight, he was prepared to stand up for himself and turn the tables on the bullies.

●

Costumed kids and parents gathered in Everbrook's Town Square as the sun began to set on Halloween night. A cool autumn breeze rustled the festive corn stalks and hay bales which decorated the area. At the center of the square stood a tall, distinguished man in a suit and tie with an oak tree pin. He tapped the microphone and welcomed the crowd.

"Greetings, Everbrook! I'm Executive Oakmaster John Wilson from the Tall Oaks Organization. We're so pleased you've all joined us tonight for the annual Fall Festival and Halloween celebration. Please enjoy a fun night of trick-or-treating throughout the neighborhood. Be sure to stop by the elaborately decorated houses and support our local businesses here around the square. Later, return here for the big finale—our Halloween Parade and Fireworks Extravaganza! It's sure to be a thrilling show. Now, let's get this night started! Happy haunting, Everbrook!"

As he stepped down from the stage, the families dispersed to begin trick-or-treating. Eden grabbed Maya and Leo, triple-checking the optimal route on her map.

Meanwhile, Alex and Gabriel adjusted their zombie makeup and vampire fangs, ready to hit the streets. The hunt for candy was on!

Laughter and excited chatter filled the air as the costumed kids fanned out into the neighborhood streets. Overflowing cauldrons of candy awaited them as the fun holiday night got into full swing.

The full moon began to glow over the street as Eden, Leo, and Maya set out into the neighborhood. Shadows danced across the sidewalk from the flickering flames inside illuminated jack-o'-lanterns. Cobwebs waved from trees and shrubs, faintly stirring in the autumn breeze.

Eden relished the holiday atmosphere. It was a perfect night for tricks and treats, just crisp enough to need a light jacket but not freezing. The group's costumes helped keep them cozy too—Eden as a witch with a feathered hat and cape, Leo as a wolf in fuzzy paw gloves, and Maya as a mummy wrapped in gauze.

Their first stop was a house draped in purple and orange lights. A plastic skeleton hung from the roof, its bones clinking in the wind. Inside, cauldrons bubbled with candy as a speaker blasted creepy sound effects.

"Trick or treat!" the kids yelled when the door creaked open. A cackling witch presented them with heaping handfuls of sweets.

"You look boo-tiful!" she said, patting Leo's wolf ears. The kids giggled and breathed in the scent of fresh popcorn balls as they continued down the street.

Meanwhile, Alex and Gabriel were having a blast scaring each other between houses. They jumped out from behind trees, faking bloody injuries or undead groans. Sarah just rolled her eyes at their antics.

Up ahead, the bullies were up to no good as always. They streamed toilet paper around a tree and threw eggs at a house that gave out toothbrushes. Sarah frowned, watching their vandalism, but Alex and Gabriel remained unfazed, determined not to let anything ruin their fun night.

As the groups went door to door, the streets came alive with activity. Kids marched along proudly showing off their costumes and comparing candy hauls. Parents with flashlights peered out from under capes and masks, keeping watch over their mini superheroes and princesses. The neighborhood felt like one big party. Sparkling cobwebs and smoky fog machines created an otherworldly atmosphere. It was a night for mischief, imagination, and community spirit.

Eden was in her element, perfectly executing their route between top candy houses, making sure to prioritize houses that gave out full-size candy bars. At each door, she would conjure up an elaborate witchy persona. The homeowners ate it up, heaping more and more candy into her bag.

After hitting up Maple Street, it was time for their secret weapon —the shortcut through the cemetery. The trio stood before the imposing iron gates of the cemetery, hesitant to pass through.

"Are you sure about this?" Leo asked nervously. Eden just cackled a witchy laugh.

Eden took a deep breath, trying to maintain her matter-of-fact composure. "This shortcut through the graveyard will shave fifteen minutes off our route. The record is within reach if we keep up the momentum."

The friends reluctantly passed through the gates, instantly feeling as if they had crossed some threshold into another realm. The gravel pathway crunched beneath their feet as they navigated the rows of weathered headstones. Carved names and epitaphs were barely legible in the dim moonlight.

As they maneuvered deeper into the graveyard, an eerie fog

rolled in, obscuring the path ahead. They could barely see a few feet in front of them. A wolf's mournful howl in the distance made them jump. Leo grabbed Eden's arm nervously.

"I don't like this, let's turn back," he pleaded. Eden shook him off, but her voice quavered as she replied,

"Quiet! We just have to keep heading straight." She quickened her pace, doubts creeping in.

The fog swirled thickly around their feet, disorienting them. Grotesque statues seemed to leer at them as they passed. Maya shrieked as a raven cawed overhead. What was that shadowy figure moving behind the crypt? Eden's heart hammered in her chest. Leo gripped her hand tightly, his palm sweaty. A bone-chilling breeze brought goosebumps to their skin.

The dark tombs pressing in around them hid untold dangers. Terrible thoughts raced through Eden's mind about lurking creatures and disturbing mysteries. She imagined ghostly hands reaching for them through the gloom.

"This was a mistake," Maya whispered through chattering teeth. Eden shot her a harsh look, betraying her rising panic. But staring into the cemetery's gloomy depths, she knew Maya was right. They never should have entered this frightening realm so unprepared.

"C'mon, let's move faster," Eden whispered, picking up the pace. The fog swirled around their feet as they hastened down the path, eager to get through to the other side.

But as they maneuvered deeper into the graveyard, the path diverged in different directions. Unsure of which fork to take, they huddled beneath a stone angel statue, peering into the shadows surrounding them.

"We're lost, just admit it," Maya said with a quiver in her voice. Eden studied the graveyard map, not wanting to concede their predicament. But the reality of the situation soon became clear—they were lost and alone.

Suddenly, a loud boom echoed from the direction of the Town Square, making them jump. It sounded like a firework.

"The parade must be getting ready to start!" Eden said. "Oh no! We're running behind."

Another mysterious, loud boom could be heard in the distance.

"I told you we shouldn't have come through the graveyard," Leo said anxiously.

"Come on, we have to get back to Main Street!" Eden yelled. The group broke into a run toward the booming sounds, their trick-or-treat bags bouncing at their sides. Decorated mausoleums blurred past as they sprinted through the graves.

Meanwhile, on a neighborhood street nearby, Sarah explained the plan one more time to Alex and Gabriel. "Those bottle rockets we just heard mean Frank has the trap set up at the haunted Fun House," she said.

Alex nodded, adrenaline pumping in anticipation. "So, now we just have to get the bullies to chase us there," he said with a grin.

"Exactly," Sarah replied. "Then they'll stumble right into Frank's trap and get a taste of their own medicine."

Alex picked up his slingshot from his trick-or-treat bag, his eyes staring down through the slingshot. "Time to stick it to 'em..."

The stage was set. As Eden's group raced through the graveyard, Alex and his friends prepared to execute the ultimate Halloween prank on the cruel bullies.

Eden, Leo, and Maya burst out of the graveyard and arrived at the Fun House entrance. But Frank suddenly appeared and blocked their path.

"Sorry, kids, we're closed for a bit for a special, uhhh, event. But the parade's starting soon, you can go that way if you want to watch it!" he said.

Eden was frustrated but nodded. No time to argue. She hurried her group back onto their trick-or-treating route. They had to make up for lost time!

On South Street, Gabriel spotted Pumpkin Boy egging a house. "Hey punk! Come get some!" Gabriel yelled.

Pumpkin Boy whipped around angrily and said with a grin, "Trick or trick? Hahaha!" He threw two small pumpkins and started chasing Gabriel, who led him toward the Fun House.

Meanwhile, on West Street, Sarah spotted Handsome Tom throwing toilet paper at a tree. "Hey handsome, over here!" she called out teasingly. Handsome Tom turned and saw Sarah waving at him. She playfully blew him a kiss.

"Ooooh, I'm so scared of the big bad bully," Sarah taunted. "Come and get me, dweeb!" She took off running down the street.

Handsome Tom grinned, ripping the toilet paper from the tree and chased after her. "You can't get away from me that easy!" he yelled as he pursued Sarah.

She glanced back with a smile as they raced at full speed toward the Fun House. Handsome Tom was falling right into their trap.

At the same time, Alex was on North Street launching stink bombs with his slingshot at Moldy Mike, who took off after him, shouting curses. Alex raced away, Moldy Mike hot on his heels.

All three groups were converging rapidly on the Fun House on East Street. Inside, Frank did a final check of all the traps. It was go time!

Eden, Leo, and Maya raced down the sidewalk, the crinkling of candy wrappers in their bags egging them on. They had lost time in the graveyard, but Eden was determined to break their candy record, even if by just a few pieces.

Out of breath, they dashed up to a cheery yellow house just as the distant sirens signaled the end of trick-or-treating in Everbrook. The porch light flicked off.

"Wait!" Eden yelled desperately. The door creaked open and an elderly woman peered out.

"You kids are just in time," she said with a smile, dropping generous handfuls of sweets into their bags.

Eden quickly counted their haul—538 pieces. "We did it!" she cheered, high-fiving her friends. Their strategy had paid off.

As they headed toward the Town Square, fire trucks rolled past, signaling that the parade would start soon. Eden smiled proudly, their candy mission accomplished. They arrived at the bakery where Eden's parents greeted them with a smile.

On the other side of town, Alex, Sarah, and Gabriel approached the Fun House. Alex glanced at his watch—the parade would start in about thirteen minutes. They had to get the bullies trapped fast.

Boldly, they entered the Fun House. Moldy Mike, Pumpkin Boy, and Handsome Tom caught up to them.

"Well, well, well, if it isn't the loser squad," Moldy Mike sneered. "You freaks looking for more trouble?"

"Maybe you're the ones who are in trouble," a voice said from the shadows. Frank emerged from a haze of smoke. "The name's Frankystein, and you just stepped into my trap."

Frank snapped his fingers. The doors slammed shut and the room went pitch black. The bullies shouted in surprise. Eerie sound effects and strobe lights switched on, revealing a hallway lined in cobwebs.

"Try getting out of this haunted maze," Frankystein cackled. He nodded at Alex and his friends, who took off down the exit path Frank had shown them earlier.

"Come back here!" Moldy Mike yelled. The bullies charged clumsily into the maze, arms outstretched. The cobwebs stuck to their faces and clothes, slowing them down.

They turned a corner and were met with a hallway of doors and mirrors. Handsome Tom tore each one open only to find more cobwebs and spooky lighting effects.

"It's just a stupid fun house," Pumpkin Boy said nervously. But he didn't seem convinced. After several misdirects, the bullies stumbled into a large room. A sign read "The Bully Trap." Before they could react, the floor shifted under their feet with a snap.

The lights flashed on—they were caught in a massive web of flypaper! The more the bullies struggled, the more stuck they became. Laughter echoed from a speaker.

Frank emerged with Alex, Sarah, and Gabriel. "Not so funny now, is it, boys?" Frank said.

The bullies shouted curses but couldn't free themselves. Shaking their heads, Alex's group turned and left their tormentors helplessly trapped.

"Very funny, now let us out!" Moldy Mike yelled after them. But the pranksters had disappeared.

Pumpkin Boy ripped in vain at the flypaper. "This really sucks," he grumbled.

"Yeah, this stuff really works, man. Too bad it isn't pretty girl paper," Moldy Mike said jokingly. The bullies groaned, consigned to their sticky fate.

Meanwhile, Alex and his friends ran outside and made it to Cosimo's Italian Restaurant just as the parade started. They exchanged exhilarated smiles. The bullies had finally gotten a taste of their own medicine, thanks to a little creativity and teamwork. It was a Halloween they'd never forget.

Crowds lined the sidewalks as the Halloween Parade made its way down Main Street. Parents held costumed toddlers on their shoulders while kids of all ages jostled for front-row views. Upbeat music filled the air from a marching band dressed in skeleton outfits, their shiny instruments glimmering in the streetlights.

Elaborate floats rolled by each decked out in Halloween

splendor. Giant spiders crawled over fluffy webs, witches stirred bubbling cauldrons, and zombies emerged from flower-adorned graves. People "ooohed" and "ahhed" at the creative designs.

On the sidewalk, Alex stood with Sarah and Gabriel, each filled with excitement as they pointed at the elaborate Halloween floats. Nearby, Alex's dad smiled and waved, happy to be enjoying the festivities together.

Across the street, Eden held her brother Leo's hand tightly so he didn't get lost in the bustling crowd. Their parents craned their necks to glimpse the floats over the rows of spectators. Though tired from trick-or-treating, Eden was enthralled by the community event.

As the parade passed, volunteers began throwing handfuls of candy from buckets marked "Tall Oaks Fall Festival." Kids of all ages scrambled to grab the flying sweets, their treat bags open wide.

Alex dove to grab a chocolate bar. At the same time, a hand reached from the other direction. Their fingers briefly collided before landing on the treat.

Alex looked up, finding himself staring into the eyes of a mysterious girl dressed as a witch. For a flickering moment, they were locked in surprise as the crowds moved around them.

There was something intriguing about this girl that made Alex linger. A curiosity and spark of wonder that reminded him of himself. He studied the witch's hat, askew on her head, wondering who she was.

Eden also felt a sense of familiarity looking at the messy-haired boy in his vampire costume. His exciting energy felt similar to her introspective spirit. Their gaze held for a second too long before embarrassment crept in.

They simultaneously withdrew their hands, the chocolate bar dropping back to the street. Alex rubbed his neck awkwardly while Eden adjusted her hat. A friendly smile teased at both their lips.

Before either could speak, voices called them back. "Time to go, Alex! We need a good view for the fireworks."

At the same time, Eden's dad waved to her from across the road. "Eden, Leo, Maya, over here! The show's about to start."

Soon the sky exploded in dazzling bursts of color and light as the fireworks show began. Fizzling rockets burst into glowing spiderwebs and jack-o'-lanterns overhead. Crowds gasped at the extravagant Halloween designs filling the sky.

Alex's eyes widened with wonder, reflecting the shimmering colors. He loved seeing the ordinary world transformed by holiday magic.

Across the street, Eden snuggled Leo as they tilted their heads skyward. Crackling bat signals morphed into candy corn high above.

As the grand finale erupted in a flash of purple, green, and orange sparkles, the crowd erupted in cheers. The lingering smell of smoke and a sky full of stars were the only remnants of the day's splendor.

Later that night at his farmhouse window, Alex sat staring at the sky, replaying the epic events. He felt a new sense of confidence after standing up to the bullies with his friends. They had turned the tables using creativity and teamwork.

Alex traced invisible lines between the stars, connecting dots into daring tales of warriors and mythical beasts. Each constellation represented an epic saga, a testament to the infinite playground of his imagination.

Meanwhile, Eden gazed out her rooftop window at the starry night. For once, a glow of optimism stirred within her as she thought about the events that evening. Breaking out of her rigid routines had awakened something.

In that graveyard, facing fears became thrilling instead of crushing. The starry sky shone brighter when she wasn't viewing it through a telescope's calculated lens. Eden realized she could cast off expectations and simply enjoy life's moments.

She pictured herself back in the crowd, reaching for candy beside that imaginative vampire boy. Eden smiled, knowing that the world held more surprises if she opened herself to spontaneity.

Tomorrow she would add some personal touches to her carefully planned schedule. But tonight, Eden basked in the lingering Halloween magic, excited for what freedom tomorrow might bring.

She looked at the stars and traced the figures of star-crossed lovers, elegant dancers, and whimsical characters, each one a story of love, beauty, and grace. The stars became an open book of timeless tales, whispered only to those willing to listen.

As the night deepened, a sense of peace settled over them. They closed their eyes, the day's memories flickering like the stars overhead.

※

<u>**Lesson 1:**</u>
<u>**Discovering Your True Self**</u>

Our journey starts with one idea: "Discovering Your True Self." This idea shows us that we are all on a profound journey of self-exploration and self-realization. It is an invitation to delve deep within and unravel the layers of conditioning, societal expectations, and external influences to uncover the authentic essence of who we truly are. We must find out who we are and what we truly want to start making real and lasting changes within our lives and the lives of those around us.

At its core, this idea speaks to the inherent desire within each of us to live a life aligned with our true nature, values, and passions. It is an exploration of the depths of our being, seeking to understand our unique identity, purpose, and inner truth.

To embark on the path of discovering your true self is to embark on a quest of self-discovery. It requires introspection, self-reflection, and a willingness to question the beliefs, narratives, and patterns that have shaped our lives. It is about peeling back the layers of societal masks, expectations, and past conditioning to reveal the authentic self that lies beneath.

As we progress, we will continue to define who our "True Self" is. We are constantly changing, and so is our concept of self. The journey begins with a deep dive into self-awareness. It is an opportunity to explore your thoughts, emotions, desires, strengths, and weaknesses with curiosity and compassion. It involves examining the stories you tell yourself, the beliefs you hold, and the fears that may be holding you back from embracing your true self.

"Discovering Your True Self" is not a destination but an ongoing process of self-exploration and growth. It is about discovering the values that resonate with your soul, the passions that ignite your spirit, and the purpose that gives meaning to your life. It is about cultivating self-acceptance, self-love, and authenticity in every aspect of your being.

As we immerse ourselves in the experiences of Alex and Eden throughout this book, we will witness their growth, resilience, and the power of self-discovery. We will witness their courage to confront their inner demons, the healing that comes from embracing vulnerability, and the liberation that follows as they step into their authentic selves.

As you embark on your own journey, I hope that you find the courage to peel back the layers, the wisdom to listen to your inner voice, and the joy that comes from living a life in harmony with your true self. The best place to start is the beginning. Let's go there.

Uncovering Childhood Experiences

What is your first memory? Is it the smile of a parent, the sound of laughter, or your first step? Our memory is a fundamental process in human cognition and is essential for a wide array of functions, such as learning, problem-solving, and adapting to new situations. In the vast landscape of our lives, our childhood holds the key to understanding the roots of our beliefs, behaviors, and patterns.

Uncovering our childhood experiences is like embarking on an archaeological dig, excavating the layers of our past to reveal the treasures that have shaped our present selves. Our childhood memories are not mere fragments of the past; they are portals to a world that once defined us. They contain the imprints of our earliest encounters with the world around us—the moments of wonder, joy, pain, and confusion that have left an indelible mark on our souls.

As we embark on the journey of uncovering our childhood experiences, we open ourselves to a deeper understanding of who we are and how we have come to be. It is a voyage of self-discovery, guided by the recollections and fragments of our past that reside within us.

Each memory shapes our identity. From the vivid recollections of family vacations to the quieter moments spent under the covers with a favorite book, our childhood experiences have shaped our perceptions, beliefs, and values in ways we may not fully comprehend.

Uncovering our childhood experiences requires a willingness to dive into the depths of our memories, to revisit the stories that have shaped us, and to embrace the emotions that surface along the way. It is an invitation to reconnect with the innocence, curiosity, and vulnerability of our younger selves as we seek to understand the impact of those formative years on our present lives.

Through this process, we may unearth not only the joyful and idyllic moments but also the wounds, traumas, and challenges that have left their mark. It is in acknowledging and honoring the full spectrum of our experiences that we gain a better understanding of who we are.

Uncovering our childhood experiences is not about assigning blame or dwelling in the past; it is about reclaiming our narratives and understanding the seeds from which we have grown. It is an act of self-compassion and self-awareness, empowering us to release old patterns that no longer serve us and cultivate new ways of being that align with our true selves.

As we delve into the realm of our childhood experiences, we may discover hidden strengths, resilience, and wisdom that have accompanied us throughout our lives. We may encounter tender memories that bring forth a renewed sense of gratitude, or we may face painful recollections that require healing and forgiveness.

The journey of uncovering childhood experiences is a deeply personal one, unique to everyone. It is a path that invites us to embrace our vulnerability, celebrate our resilience, and honor the complexity of our lives.

Understanding Family Dynamics

Family plays a fundamental role in shaping our identity and influencing our beliefs, values, and behaviors. Understanding the dynamics within our family system is essential for personal growth and developing healthy relationships.

In every family, there exists a unique set of dynamics that govern the way members interact, communicate, and relate to one another. These dynamics are influenced by a variety of factors, including cultural background, values, traditions, roles, and relationships between family members.

To delve deeper into understanding family dynamics, we must first acknowledge that each family is a complex web of interconnections, with each member playing a distinct role. These roles can vary widely, ranging from caregivers and nurturers to mediators, leaders, or the responsible ones. By recognizing and exploring these roles, we can gain insight into how they shape our perception of ourselves and others.

Furthermore, the patterns of communication within a family greatly impact the dynamics. Communication can be open and supportive, fostering trust, understanding, and healthy conflict resolution. Alternatively, it can be closed off, lacking in emotional expression, or marked by frequent conflicts and misunderstandings. By examining our family's communication patterns, we can gain awareness of how these patterns have influenced our own communication style and our ability to build meaningful connections with others.

Family values and traditions also contribute to the dynamics within a family. These shared beliefs and practices shape the family's identity and provide a sense of belonging. Understanding and evaluating these values allows us to examine how they align with our own values and whether they have positively or negatively influenced our personal growth.

In exploring family dynamics, it is crucial to recognize that each family is unique, with its own strengths and challenges. While some families may have experienced harmony and stability, others may have faced adversity, conflicts, or dysfunction. Understanding these dynamics enables us to empathize with our family members and develop a deeper sense of compassion and acceptance.

To better comprehend family dynamics, it can be helpful to put on paper and visually map out family relationships and patterns across generations. This allows us to identify recurring themes, unresolved conflicts, and intergenerational patterns that may have shaped our family's dynamics.

Ultimately, by gaining awareness of our family's patterns, beliefs, and communication styles, we can break free from negative cycles, heal past wounds, and create healthier, more fulfilling relationships both within and outside of our family unit.

Nurturing Individuality

Honoring your distinctive qualities and embracing your authentic self allows you to live a fulfilling, values-based life. Self-awareness and self-acceptance are key to nurturing your individuality. Take time to appreciate the unique combination of strengths, passions, and perspectives that make you who you are. Recognize that everyone has imperfections, so treat yourself with compassion and understanding.

As you nurture your individuality, continuously reflect on your core values, and make choices aligned with them. Express your genuine thoughts, feelings, and desires, whether through creative outlets, personal style, or sharing your perspectives. Surround yourself with supportive relationships that encourage you to be your true self.

View life as a journey of ongoing self-discovery. Seize opportunities to learn, grow, and explore new facets of yourself. Embrace taking risks and pushing your boundaries in the spirit of personal expansion. With an openness to change and a commitment to authentic self-expression, you can nurture your individuality every step of the way.

Make the conscious choice each day to honor your uniqueness. Celebrate your original qualities and engage in practices that reveal your inner truth. By nurturing your individuality, you can cultivate a profound sense of freedom, confidence, and fulfillment.

Nurturing individuality is a lifelong journey that requires self-awareness, self-acceptance, and a commitment to personal growth. By embracing your uniqueness and expressing your true self, you create a life that is aligned with your values, passions, and aspirations. Celebrate your individuality and let it shine brightly in all that you do.

This activity will help you gain a deeper understanding of yourself and celebrate your unique qualities. By exploring your childhood memories, embracing your strengths, and reflecting on your family's influence, you'll uncover valuable insights about who you are and how your experiences have shaped you.

Read all the steps first before you begin the activity.

1. Remember Your Childhood: Find a quiet and comfortable space. Close your eyes and think back to your childhood. Allow memories to come naturally, without judgment. Think of both happy and challenging moments.

2. Reflect on Feelings: As memories come to mind, try to recall how they made you feel. Were you excited, scared, or happy? Don't be afraid to explore different emotions. Write down your reactions.

3. Embrace Your Strengths: Take a moment to think about what you're good at. These could be skills, talents, or personal qualities that make you special. Write them down and be proud of your strengths.

4. Think About Family: Consider your family and how they influenced you. Think about the good times and any challenges you faced. It's okay to acknowledge both positive and negative experiences. Write down your observations.

5. Connect the Dots: Look for connections between your childhood memories, strengths, and family experiences. How do they relate to who you are today?

6. Set Positive Goals: Use your newfound understanding to set positive goals for yourself. Focus on using your strengths to grow and overcome challenges. Write down your goals.

Embrace Your Journey: Remember that self-discovery is a lifelong journey. Be patient and kind to yourself. Celebrate your progress and use your insights to become the best version of yourself.

By reflecting on your past and embracing your strengths, you've gained a better understanding of yourself. Remember that you are unique, and every experience has shaped the person you are today. Embrace your strengths, set positive goals, and continue to learn and grow. You have the power to create a fulfilling and meaningful life.

●

In this lesson, we went on a journey of self-discovery. We explored our childhood memories, family relationships, and unique qualities. Revisiting childhood moments showed us how early experiences shaped who we are today. By digging into our past, we better understand what influences our beliefs and values now.

Examining our family dynamics was eye-opening. We realized how much impact our loved ones have on how we see ourselves and the world. Looking inward helped us understand our family bonds better. Embracing our own passions, quirks, and strengths was empowering. We learned to accept ourselves for who we authentically are. We found power in nurturing our individuality.

This first step of self-reflection guides us forward. Looking inward takes courage, but it's worth it. The more we know ourselves, the better we can live with purpose and confidence. As we continue our path of self-discovery in the next chapters, we'll keep building on what we learned here. This is just the beginning of our journey toward self-love and living freely.

Chapter 2: Together, We'll Meet...

It was a typical noisy night at the Oakwood University cafeteria. Students chattered and laughed, clearing their trays into the pie-hole bins with a clatter. In the steaming dishroom, Steve grimaced as trays came flying in faster than he could wash them.

Over his many years working at Oakwood, Steve had seen it all: food fights on Taco Tuesdays, clogged drains from spilled milkshakes, and more than a few cockroaches scurrying around. He didn't love the job, but it paid the bills.

Lately, though, some of the rowdier students had been intentionally slamming their trays into the bins extra hard. A few times, the metal edges even crashed into Steve's back, leaving bruises. He knew they were doing it on purpose to mess with him.

30

Tonight, as Steve was scrubbing ketchup and noodle remnants into the sink, a tray hit him sharply on the shoulder blade.

"Hey, watch it!" he yelled. Laughter echoed from the cafeteria.

That was the last straw. Steve ripped off his rubber gloves and burst through the dishroom doors. A group of loud guys was cheering as another wound up to launch his tray.

"Cut it out!" Steve shouted, his voice booming across the cafeteria. Everyone froze and stared. "I've had enough of you disrespecting me. Grow up!"

The manager came rushing over. "Steve, get back in the kitchen. I won't have you talking to students this way."

"No, these pricks need to learn some manners," Steve yelled as he began chasing one of the guys through the cafeteria. The manager shook his head sternly and told Steve he was done. Just like that, after years of service, he was fired.

Steve stormed out to the parking lot, anger swirling with sadness and disappointment. How had he let his temper get the better of him? But he refused to be pushed around any longer.

Steve drove off into the night, hurtling down the highway. The roar of the engine drowned out the war inside his head. His foot pressed heavy on the accelerator, the speedometer creeping past eighty, then ninety. He glanced down at the phone in his lap, thinking about his wife and kids at home, and how he had let them down.

The highway signs whipped past in a blur. His mind swirled with memories of his past, every lingering thought drenched in regret. It would never get better. The darkness had slowly become his default state.

As he drove, his vision obscured by tears, Steve's trembling hand clutched his phone, grasping for connection. In the blink of an eye, reality crashed into his consciousness as his vehicle collided with the car in front of him. Metal screeched, glass shattered, and the world spun in a dizzying whirlwind.

Steve's car flipped and tumbled, a twisted ballet of destruction. The front end crumpled inward, obliterating the windshield. Everything went black. Inside the chaos, Steve's battered body fought for survival.

Slowly, Steve regained consciousness, the metallic taste of blood in his mouth. Though injured, Steve was miraculously alive. But the car in front of him had not fared so well. Its twisted wreckage was engulfed in towering flames. There would be no survival for whomever was inside.

Later that night, across town, the phone rang in Eden's house. Her mother, Maria, answered the phone, her usual cheer fading as the officer on the line relayed the tragic news. She looked over at her children, Leo and Eden, happily playing a board game together in the family room while the TV played mindlessly in the distance. How would she find the words to explain their father wasn't coming home tonight?

Overwhelmed, Eden's mother sank to her knees with a heart-wrenching sob. The children rushed over, their game forgotten. They had never seen their strong mother crumble this way. Maria took a deep breath and gathered them close.

Choking back tears, she finally managed to say, "There's been an accident. Your father... he's going to be with the angels now."

The children broke down, the loss hitting them in waves. Their mother held them tight as grief filled the room. She didn't know how they would cope, but they had each other. Rocking her children, she whispered a prayer for the strength to carry on.

•

The late afternoon sun cast long shadows across the fields as Alex trudged up the gravel driveway, the familiar crunch under his shoes bringing a sense of comfort. He saw his dad, George, sitting on the porch steps, a stack of papers in hand and a look of deep contemplation on his face. Alex's mom, Cindy, joined him with a cup of coffee, her expression a mix of worry and hope.

"Hey, sport," George called out as Alex approached. "How was school?"

"It was fine," Alex replied, dropping his backpack by the door. He could sense the tension in the air and knew something was up.

"Alex, we need to talk," Cindy said gently. She patted the space beside her on the steps, and Alex sat down, glancing between his parents.

George cleared his throat. "I got a job offer today. It's a big opportunity for us, but it means we'll have to move to the city."

Alex's heart sank. He loved their small town, the open spaces, the sense of community it provided.

"Why can't we stay here?" he asked, his voice barely above a whisper.

Cindy placed a comforting hand on his shoulder. "The company your dad will be working for is in the Big City. It's a significant career move, and it will provide us with more stability and opportunities. Plus, the company offers better healthcare benefits, which is something we really need for you and your sister."

George nodded. "I know it's hard to leave everything behind, but this job will allow us to have a better future. It's not just about the money, Alex. It's about giving you a chance at a better education, more experiences. The city has a lot to offer."

Alex looked down at his hands, trying to process the news. He knew his parents were right, but the thought of leaving his friends, his school, and the countryside he adored was overwhelming. "When do we have to leave?" he asked, his voice trembling.

"In a few weeks," George replied. "We'll have time to say our goodbyes and pack up everything. It's going to be an adjustment, but we'll get through it together."

Cindy hugged Alex tightly. "We're a family, and we'll face this new adventure together. It won't be easy, but we're here for you, always."

As the weeks passed, the reality of the move set in. Alex spent his days helping pack up their home, saying goodbye to friends, and taking long walks through the fields he loved. Each step felt like a farewell to a chapter of his life he wasn't ready to close.

Finally, the day arrived. The countryside faded into the distance as their car sped toward the Big City. Alex, now fourteen, pressed his forehead against the cool glass of the car window. The familiar fields and forests of his childhood blurred into a tapestry of green, slowly giving way to the gray sprawl of the Big City.

Up ahead, skyscrapers loomed like giants guarding the skyline. Even from afar, Alex could sense the frenetic energy of the traffic zipping along the bustling streets. It was a stark contrast to the sleepy country town he had called home his whole life.

In the countryside, Alex was used to waking up to the gentle chorus of birds chirping and sunlight streaming through his bedroom window. The air carried the sweet scent of grass still wet with morning dew. Now, with his dad's new job in the Big City, the sounds of car alarms and shouting woke him up from his gentle sleep.

The towering skyscrapers and never-ending hustle felt like a lonely maze. The blaring noise of car horns, sirens, and the constant rush of people became a jarring assault on his ears. The vibrant mix of cultures and individuals, once an enchanting allure, now seemed alien and daunting. Surrounded by the teeming masses, Alex struggled to find his place. His rural upbringing had instilled in him a sense of simplicity and connection to nature, which now seemed at odds with the fast-paced urban lifestyle.

The city's concrete jungle offered little relief for his desire for open spaces, green landscapes, and the serene tranquility he once cherished. As Alex tried to navigate the intricate web of city life, he felt like an outsider, a lost soul drowning in a sea of strangers. The relentless energy of the city seemed to swallow him whole, leaving him feeling invisible and insignificant. The vibrant lights that adorned the streets at night felt empty, devoid of the warmth and familiarity he had left behind.

Loneliness crept in, taking hold of his spirit. The connections he had once treasured, the laughter shared with childhood friends, and the comforting embrace of his tight-knit community felt like distant memories. At school, Alex sat alone, keeping to himself. The blare of voices and the chaotic clamor of the hallways made him yearn for the quiet he had once taken for granted.

After school, he wandered the city streets, exploring the alien environment. He slowly discovered tiny pockets of nature tucked between concrete buildings: a flowering tree, a miniature park, and the calls of birds passing overhead. These traces of his old life brought some comfort, reminding him that even in the heart of the city, fragments of his past could still be found.

One afternoon, as Alex sat on a bench in a small park, he watched a group of children play, their laughter ringing out above the noise of the city. For a moment, he closed his eyes and imagined he was back home, lying in the grass, the sun warming his face. When he opened his eyes, the city seemed a little less daunting, and the path ahead a little less lonely.

●

Eden's father, Antonio, had always been there for her, cheering her on, guiding her through life's challenges, and filling their home with his infectious laughter. He was the one who had introduced her to the wonders of the city, from the intricate labyrinth of streets to the quiet corners that held whispered tales of the past. Together, they explored museums, attended street festivals, and wandered through parks—his presence a constant source of joy and security in her life.

The suddenness of his death a few weeks prior left a gaping hole in Eden's teenage world, casting a long shadow over her once-vibrant existence. She could still vividly remember the moment her life was irreversibly changed, the numbness that took hold as she struggled to comprehend the loss of her father.

Maria was also a portrait of sorrow. Her once sparkling eyes were now glassy, her radiant smile reduced to a mere memory. She did her best to support Eden and her brother, but the grief was too overwhelming, creating an invisible wall between them. Maria tried to maintain a semblance of normalcy, but the pain was always there, lurking beneath the surface, making it difficult for her to connect with her children the way she used to.

Eden drifted through her life like a ghost. She attended a prestigious private school on the opposite side of the Big City from Alex, but the academic pressures and social dynamics felt trivial compared to the void left by her father's absence. She participated in extracurricular activities, but the joy of living seemed to have evaporated, leaving her going through the motions without any real enthusiasm.

Maya, her older best friend who had recently moved to another part of the city, attempted to comfort her over the phone, but her words seemed distant and hollow. Maya meant well, but her life, untouched by the grief that consumed Eden, made it difficult for her to truly understand the depth of her sorrow.

Though they talked for over an hour, with Maya offering kind words and funny stories to try and cheer her up, Eden felt lonelier after hanging up. She missed the days when Maya could wrap an arm around her shoulders and simply sit with her in silence when needed. The distance prevented Maya from being the comfort she once was to Eden.

Every day, Eden would visit the park outside their apartment where she and her father used to spend their evenings. She would sit on their favorite bench, staring at the spot where they used to fly kites and have picnics—now an empty space filled with memories.

Sometimes, she would talk to him, hoping that somewhere, somehow, he could hear her. She poured out her heart, sharing her struggles, her triumphs, and her deepest fears, seeking solace in the familiar surroundings.

In the days and weeks that followed, Eden found herself oscillating between anger, sadness, and a yearning for her father's presence. She longed for the stability of their strong family bonds, the sense of security that had been shattered by his sudden departure. The vibrant city that once felt like a playground now seemed cold and uninviting, each street and building a reminder of what she had lost.

Eden's journey through grief was a lonely one, but she clung to the hope that, with time, she would find a way to navigate this new reality. She sought comfort in the memories of her father, drawing strength from the lessons he had taught her and the love he had shown. Slowly, she began to piece together a new version of herself, one that honored his memory while forging her own path forward.

<u>...In A Dream</u>

Late one night, while reading, Alex drifted into sleep to the steady, rhythmic patter of rain against his window. In his dream, the familiar city streets and tranquil country hills faded away, and he found himself instead in a dense, humid jungle. Towering trees blotted out the sky, their thick branches casting deep shadows that moved with the subtle sway of the wind. Unfamiliar sounds surrounded him—rustling leaves, the low hum of insects, and the distant calls of creatures hidden in the underbrush.

The air was thick with the earthy aroma of damp soil and trees that had sheltered his people for generations untold. As he inhaled deeply, the familiar scent grounded him. The soft symphony of birds greeting the dawn brought a sense of calm, their melodies weaving through the gentle rustle of the waking jungle. His community was just beginning to stir, preparing the morning meal, smoke curling lazily above the simple thatched huts they called home. This isolated pocket of the world, untouched by time or civilization, had been Alex's only reality. He had never imagined there could be another way to live—until that fateful day.

He had just sat down to enjoy his breakfast when the jungle erupted into chaos. The peaceful chorus of birds and the gentle sway of trees were abruptly swallowed by panicked screams and the unsettling hum of machines. His heart slammed in his chest as he leapt to his feet, eyes wide as he watched his people scatter in terror. Mysterious figures, emerging from the mist that clung to the trees, moved like shadows, dragging his family and friends into the jungle's depths.

Before Alex could make sense of the unfolding nightmare, two men—dressed in strange, shiny black suits with smooth, emotionless masks—grabbed him. Pure terror surged through his body, locking his breath in his throat. He fought against their grip, his limbs thrashing wildly, but their hold was iron. His mind reeled, struggling to comprehend the chaos around him. The lush, colorful jungle he had known all his life—the place that had always protected him—was now marred by destruction and violence. The harmonious life he had lived only moments ago had been torn apart in an instant.

Thrown into a sleek silver vessel, Alex found himself surrounded by harsh, bright lights that reflected off the cold, metallic surfaces. He blinked rapidly, his vision blurred, trying to adjust to the sterile surroundings. He had never seen anything like it before. There were glowing screens, buttons that blinked and hummed—things he had no reference for in his simple life. His skin prickled with unease, but beneath the rising panic stirred an odd sense of fascination with this utterly foreign world.

The silver doors closed with a sharp hiss, sealing him inside with his captors. Alex flinched as one of them pulled out a slim, unfamiliar device, slowly waving it over his body. It emitted a low hum, scanning him, though for what purpose he couldn't fathom. The masked men communicated with rapid, clipped rhythms, their voices distorted by the dull gray masks that hid their features. The language they spoke was alien to Alex, their words a strange melody of unfamiliar tones and clipped syllables.

His heart hammered violently against his ribs as the floor beneath him began to vibrate. The vessel lifted off the ground with a deep, resonating hum. Alex's gaze locked on the window as his homeland shrunk beneath him, the jungle disappearing into a patchwork of green. The vivid blue sky above was vast and endless.

His jaw dropped, terror mixing with awe. What sort of dark magic was this? Where were they taking him, and why? The questions burned in his mind, but his captors gave no answers, their emotionless masks betraying nothing.

Feeling utterly helpless, Alex closed his eyes and retreated into the safety of his memories. He clung to the sound of his people singing and dancing around the fire, the sweet taste of jungle fruits exploding on his tongue, the nights spent lying beneath a sky full of stars, listening to the village elders pass down ancestral wisdom. In his mind, he could hear the familiar notes of the tribal guitar, each note a thread pulling him back to the harmony of his old life. It calmed him, if only for a moment, as the vessel soared through foreign landscapes, far from anything he had ever known.

As the ship ascended higher, his fear began to transform into something unexpected—a surreal sense of wonder. The vast expanse of the jungle, once his entire world, now seemed like a mere patch of green amidst an endless sea of unknown territories. His mind swirled with questions, emotions warring within him. Yet, through the storm of fear and uncertainty, a quiet determination took root. Whatever lay ahead, he knew he had to find the strength to face it. His people needed him, and no matter how far he was taken, he carried their resilience and spirit within him.

●

That same evening, as Eden sat in her father's study, she discovered his guitar tucked away in the back of a closet. Her father, Antonio, had loved music, often filling their home with the soft strumming of melodies from that old instrument. Now, as her fingers grazed the strings, a wave of sadness washed over her. The rich, resonant tones echoed through the room, mingling with the soft patter of rain against the window.

The sound wrapped around her, filling the empty space, each note heavy with memories. She strummed slowly, and with each chord, she felt a pang of familiarity—an ache, as though the music reflected her own tangled emotions. The melody carried her back to a time when life brimmed with endless possibilities. She remembered the dreams she once had, like any other young girl: dreams of becoming a beautiful princess, of finding her own happily ever after. But those dreams felt distant now, and reality pressed down on her like a weight she couldn't lift. The tightness in her chest deepened, each second making the lump in her throat harder to swallow.

The rain outside became a steady hum, drowning out her whispers of discontent. She longed for escape, for the vibrant colors that once painted her world to break through the dullness that had taken hold. Her eyelids grew heavy, and the guitar, now resting loosely in her hands, slipped from her grip as she drifted into sleep—a sleep that carried her into a vivid and overwhelming dream.

In the dream, Eden stood before the majestic spires and winding canals of the great city of Lumina. Its glittering architectural marvels stretched toward the sky, once filling her heart with hope and inspiration. Generations ago, Lumina's founders had transformed this remote Atlantic location into a paradise, using advanced harmonic technologies to sculpt stone like clay and manipulate the earth's energies.

But Lumina's brilliance had dulled. The city that had once cured diseases, facilitated instant interdimensional travel through resonating gates, and allowed communication across vast distances —achievements that had improved countless lives—now trembled under the weight of rising threats. The mood in the streets had shifted from ambition to uncertainty. Uprisings from fringe elemental mystics, combined with violent fluctuations in the planetary energy grid, had begun to unravel the city's very core.

Ominous auroral storms swirled on the horizon, casting an eerie glow over Lumina as Eden maneuvered past armed City Guardians on her way to the famed Institute of Technology, nestled deep within the central island. Inside its shimmering towers, elite engineers, alchemists, and arcanists worked feverishly to uphold Lumina's legacy of progress. But the pressure was mounting. Groups of top scientists raced against the clock, developing defensive measures to shield the city from impending upheavals. Failure meant the unthinkable: the unraveling of civilization itself, sending them back thousands of years.

As Eden disembarked from the tram, she flashed her clearance badge and passed through checkpoints leading to the Institute's inner sanctum. As the lead scientist on Project Radiance, Eden had devoted years to researching interdimensional energy as a way to stabilize the planetary grid. But lately, something had shifted. Data pathways were being restricted. Experiments, once routine, were abruptly suspended. Whispers of strange humanoid specimens with glowing tattoos being transported to isolated labs had reached her ears, and Eden's instincts screamed that something deeper, darker, was at play.

Determined to uncover the truth, Eden pored over ancient texts, her mind swirling with references tied to the glowing symbols she had heard rumors about. Her research became relentless, driven by an unyielding desire to understand. Bit by bit, she connected threads spanning mythic tales, technical diagrams, and redacted archaeological reports. What she uncovered left her breathless—the "Chalumuk Glyphs," ancient symbols from a lost civilization that had mastered planetary energies through a unique biological-spiritual symbiosis.

The specimens in the labs—beings with those very Glyphs etched into their skin—held profound secrets. But were they the key to stabilizing Lumina's future, or were they a terrible weapon, controlled by the city's most corrupt leaders? Eden didn't know, but the stakes had never been higher. The future of Lumina hung in the balance, and the weight of that responsibility pressed heavily upon her. She would not rest until she found the answers that could either save her city—or expose the darkness lurking within its highest echelons.

●

Meanwhile, in the sterile confines of Laboratory G, Alex endured another round of painful scans and experiments. The scientists were relentless, analyzing his bioenergy channels linked to the pulsating Chalumuk Glyphs imprinted on his skin since birth. The lab was cold and impersonal, its gleaming steel surfaces and humming machinery offering no comfort. Technicians in white coats moved efficiently around him, their faces masked by detachment, focused solely on their tasks.

Alex's mind, however, was far from the lab. His thoughts raced back to his village. What had happened to his people? Were others like him trapped in this strange complex? His heart twisted with fear, the contrast between his serene homeland—full of warmth and nature—and the harsh, mechanical reality of the lab deepened the ache inside him.

As these questions gnawed at him, Alex noticed new guards arriving. They wore insect-like armor, their bodies marked with glowing symbols eerily similar to his own. The sight sent a shiver down his spine. The symbols... Were they connected to him? A flicker of recognition danced in his mind, chased quickly by dread. What did it mean? The implications terrified him.

The scientists' behavior had become more urgent and secretive. Their interest in the Glyphs had turned obsessive. He overheard snippets of conversation—fragments about "Project Radiance" and "interdimensional energy stabilization." Though the words were foreign, the tone was unmistakable: whatever they were planning, it was monumental—and dangerous.

Alex knew he had to escape soon. If he waited too long, he'd be no more than a pawn in Lumina's increasingly ominous schemes. But how? The guards were ever watchful, and the facility felt like a labyrinth, each door locked, each corridor stretching into unfamiliar darkness. Over time, Alex began memorizing the guards' routines, noting the lab's layout. Weaknesses, even small ones, might offer a sliver of hope.

Then, one night, everything changed.

During a particularly painful scan, something in Alex snapped. As the machine's whirring filled the room and the scientists leaned in, scrutinizing data, he felt an unfamiliar resonance with the Glyphs on his skin. A surge of energy, stronger than anything he had felt before, pulsed through him. The pain remained, but now it was accompanied by a strange, growing power—a connection to something much greater.

In that fleeting moment of clarity, Alex realized the Glyphs were not just markings. They were a part of him, a deep well of potential he had yet to tap. He focused on them, willing the symbols to respond. The energy within him began to pulse in time with the machine, causing it to flicker. The equipment faltered, lights dimming and screens blinking out. The scientists scrambled to regain control, but Alex knew this was his only chance.

With the lab in chaos and the guards momentarily distracted, he made his move.

He bolted from the table, his body moving with newfound agility and strength. Every step felt more precise, his muscles infused with power from the Glyphs glowing brighter on his skin. Urged forward by a force he could barely comprehend, Alex charged toward the exit. The halls of the laboratory blurred as he sprinted through them, his thoughts a whirlwind of freedom and urgency. Every turn, every door passed was a victory over his captors.

As he rounded a corner, one of the bug-like guards stepped into his path. Before the guard could react, Alex instinctively summoned the energy from his Glyphs. A pulse of light flashed from his hands, and with a single, swift motion, he incapacitated the guard. The glowing symbols guided his movements as if they had always known what to do.

But just when freedom seemed within reach, a blaring alarm ripped through the air. The facility erupted into chaos. Reinforcements arrived within seconds. Despite his strength and the energy coursing through him, Alex was outnumbered. The soldiers overwhelmed him, their armor deflecting his desperate attacks. He fought with everything he had, but it wasn't enough.

A sharp sting hit his neck—tranquilizers. His vision blurred, limbs growing heavier with each passing second. The world around him tilted and faded as the chemicals took hold. The last thing he saw before darkness claimed him was the harsh, sterile ceiling of the lab.

When Alex awoke, he was back inside the complex, lying on the cold floor of a small, dimly lit holding chamber. The walls, thick and reinforced, seemed to close in on him. The once-bright Glyphs on his skin were dim, their power drained by the tranquilizers. He lay there, his body limp, his mind swirling with frustration and despair. He had come so close, only to be dragged back, defeated.

Outside the chamber, he could hear the faint, muffled voices of the scientists. They were discussing new precautions, more intense experiments. His fate was sealed, it seemed—trapped within the sterile walls of the lab, a prisoner to their dark plans. The walls, once mere barriers, now felt like a crushing weight, smothering any spark of hope.

But deep within, a small ember of determination remained. Even in the darkness of the holding chamber, Alex clung to it. He couldn't give up. He wouldn't. The Glyphs—his Glyphs—were still a part of him. Their power, though dimmed, was not gone. He just needed time to understand it. To harness it.

For now, all he could do was wait and plan. Another chance would come, and when it did, Alex would be ready. He would find a way to escape, to fight for his freedom, and to protect his people— no matter the cost.

●

Analyzing the star charts and almanacs laid out before her, Eden uncovered a complexity of celestial cycles. Through meticulous research, she discerned that certain patterns repeated within larger cycles, allowing her to grasp the precise timing of these interconnected cycles with near perfection. The ancients, whom she now knew as the 'Chalumuk,' harnessed the symbiotic bioenergy properties of the glyphs imprinted on select members of their kind. Through this biological-spiritual harmony, they stabilized the energetic chaos that otherwise resulted when cosmic and terrestrial forces aligned.

Without the Chalumuk's maintenance, great floods and epic planetary disasters inevitably followed, restarting civilization's clock as scattered survivors tried to piece together lost knowledge from the ashes. Eden realized in horror that the next cataclysmic alignment was imminent, and the original Chalumuk had been extinct for millennia—or so the top scholars of Lumina had thought, until recent discoveries. But the newly discovered specimens represented a vital thread back to the past. Eden knew she needed to make contact with the humanoid specimens, and together unveil Lumina's plans before the planet itself acted against them all.

Eden pored over the Institute archives, digging deeper for clues as to where the remarkable humanoid specimens were being held. References to a remote field research outpost named Laboratory G piqued her interest. If she could convince the Director to allow her access under the pretense of comparative harmonic analysis, Eden might uncover the prime source.

She submitted formal travel orders to the mysterious jungle location, holding her breath in apprehensive anticipation. The documents processed with unusual speed, and the Director's seal seemed almost impatient. Eden had her clearance pass, and within hours she departed swiftly as paranoia and curiosity warred within her mind.

The journey stretched endlessly into unfamiliar waters, well off any established aquatic transit lanes. Eden was accompanied on the ominously quiet boat by an armed entourage who rebuked any conversation attempts. The tropical night breeze carried the briny scent of the surrounding ocean. What had she stumbled into, and could she still turn back?

As the boat rocked gently on the waves, Eden steadied herself against a supply crate, her mind racing with thoughts of the discoveries that lay ahead. She knew the significance of the Chalumuk Glyphs, and the potential they held for preventing the looming disaster. But as the island drew closer, her apprehension grew. The dense jungle and the imposing research facility loomed ominously, casting long shadows over the water.

Alex lay awake in the sterile holding cell, his mind unable to silence itself for sleep despite overwhelming exhaustion. The glowing glyphs on his skin now felt like brands marking the unknown fate that awaited him. He stared through a window at a strangely colored and unnaturally round moon which sat among unfamiliar constellations.

As Alex scanned the moonlit horizon beyond the guarded perimeter of the research base, he noticed lights breaking through the smooth darkness. Squinting, Alex made out a sleek vessel cutting through rough waves. It seemed to ride strangely high atop the shimmering surface.

Just as the vessel became fully silhouetted, warning sirens blared in the distance. Alex watched chaos unfold as personnel mobilized defenses in the distance. Where had this strange boat appeared from and what havoc did it bring? His mind spinning with possibilities, he looked down at his arms noticing subtle, glowing pulses quickening in his tattoos.

Eden steadied herself against a supply crate as an explosion rocked the research transport boat, sending shrapnel flying in all directions. The deafening blasts disoriented her as she tumbled to the floor. She stood up and clung to the railing, trying to stay upright amidst the turmoil. The metal hull groaned under the pressure, and cracks appeared along its surface.

Panicked shouts from the guards could barely be heard above the roaring rush of oncoming water. They were under attack... but by whom? Eden had no time to ponder the implications as the frigid ocean spray engulfed the tilting deck.

Without a moment's hesitation, Eden dove into the tumultuous waters, leaving the boat behind. Her lungs burning, she finally breached the churning surface water, scanning for the shore while fighting hyperventilation. The attackers had dealt a crippling blow, and the once imposing vessel was now sinking. Eden channeled reserves of inner resolve and began to swim against the current.

Stroke by difficult stroke, the island inched closer. Eden collapsed onto the sandy shore, her heart pounding wildly. She struggled to catch her breath as lingering adrenaline mixed with shock coursed through her veins. The smoldering ruins of the research transport continued sinking into murky depths behind her. Eden shivered at the thought of a similar fate awaiting her if she didn't quickly regain her strength.

Unzipping her hydro-pack, Eden found an emergency blanket which she swiftly wrapped around her exhausted, aching body. The smart fibers radiated warmth while gently compressing Eden's limbs to accelerate circulation.

As warmth seeped back into her bones, Eden gazed up the beach to the looming outline of the research base. As she walked, she hugged the shadows behind cargo crates and pipes along the perimeter, and then she slipped unnoticed into a side access tunnel.

The base seemed eerily empty, only the distant throb of generators penetrating the stillness within. Following discarded food wrappers and transient heat signatures, Eden felt fate pulling her deeper through the sterile passageways.

Pausing at a junction to scan her surroundings, Eden's gaze locked onto familiar glows emanating from an observation room ahead. There, hovering before her, lay the mysterious humanoid specimen emitting those same radiant Glyphs she had read about back in Lumina.

Without hesitation, Eden rushed to the thick glass barrier. Just as the extraordinary captive turned to meet her stare, explosions ripped through the night as the base erupted into a glowing fireball. Eden dove for cover as chaos upended the base. She watched in astonished relief as the humanoid's holding chamber took a direct mortar hit, shattering his restraints and providing an escape route through an exposed wall.

Shrapnel rained down as explosions continued to rock the research facility. Seeing his restraints torn open, Alex seized the opportunity and slipped unseen into the chaotic corridors. Alarms drowned the shouts of troops rushing outside to defend against the mysterious assault. Guided by his glowing glyphs, Alex navigated through the base and descended into a drainage pipe.

As Eden regained her bearings, she glimpsed flickering glows disappearing down a partially collapsed utility tunnel. Desperate to uncover the truth, she gave chase, descending into the maze of halls not knowing where it led.

She emerged coughing minutes later into humid jungle air. Pulling vines aside, Eden spotted the humanoid bounding ahead between the trees. Determination surged within her as she raced to close the distance, calling out appeals for unity against the forces seeking to destroy them both. But her words were lost in the sounds of snapping twigs and rustling leaves.

Alex scrambled up a crumbling stone pathway, the glowing glyphs tugging him urgently onward. Their eerie luminescence illuminated the opening to a small cave nestled into a cliff side. He paused briefly, feeling an inexplicable importance about this place. Glancing back, Alex saw the strange scientist still pursuing him tirelessly. He went inside the cave, which provided a defensive choke point to finally confront this mysterious follower.

Eden climbed faster, her eyes locked upon the glimmering entrance her target had disappeared through. She knew answers awaited within about Lumina's plans and the humanoids' role. The threats they faced mattered more than any rivalry.

As Eden passed the cliff into a crystalline cavern, she saw the specimen waiting, radiant markings slowly pulsing in resonance with her heartbeat. As Alex and Eden moved slowly toward one another, a plume of violet mist swirled in hypnotic currents and quickly filled the space between them. Though no words passed their lips, a magnetic attraction conveyed a sense of intimate familiarity that instantly transcended their vastly different origins. Both knew with certainty that fate had fused their paths.

As the violet fog thickened, ethereal ribbons wrapped the nearly embracing couple, transporting them into an endless starscape. Alex and Eden floated lightly, scarcely touching hands. The starscape around them shimmered with vibrant colors, a visual symphony of the universe's hidden harmonies.

Then, suddenly, their dreams ended abruptly! Traffic horns

sounded loudly outside. Disoriented, Alex found himself at home in the Big City, a book fallen at his side. The rain no longer sprinkled against the window. The details of city life emerged as the glow of sunlight came through his blinds. Faint shouts came from early morning pedestrians on wet sidewalks below.

Meanwhile, Eden woke abruptly in her father's study, the guitar she had idly strummed now lying on the carpet. As consciousness returned fully, the implications of her extraordinary dream experience gripped her fiercely.

Alex sat up slowly, rubbing his eyes. The vividness of the dream lingered in his mind, leaving him with a sense of awe and confusion. He could still feel the strange connection to the girl he had encountered, as if the dream had bridged some unseen gap between them. He glanced out the window, the city's morning hustle beginning to stir, but his thoughts remained on the dreamscape and the intense emotions it had stirred within him.

Eden, too, was lost in thought as she stared at the ceiling of her father's study. The dream had felt so real, so significant. The boy with the glowing markings was more than just a figment of her imagination. She felt a strange, almost magnetic pull, urging her to understand what the dream meant. Her heart ached with a mix of longing and curiosity.

Both children pondered the dream for a few minutes longer. Was it just a dream or a memory? It almost seemed as if they had lived that life once before. They couldn't shake the feeling of mystery it presented and how real it was. Even though they were awake, the dream had left an indelible mark on their hearts.

Eden lay there in the early morning light, thinking to herself, "Together, we'll meet again, if only in my dreams."

※

Lesson 2:
Harnessing the Power of Your Mind

Our thoughts have immense power, shaping the experiences we attract into our lives. When we focus on positive thoughts and emotions, we tend to draw in positive experiences. On the flip side, negativity often leads to more negativity. In this lesson, we'll explore the role of emotions in our lives and how we can harness their power for personal growth and well-being.

Emotions are a fundamental part of being human. They influence our thoughts, actions, and how we experience the world. By understanding and managing our emotions, we can lead a more balanced and fulfilling life. Emotions act as signals, giving us valuable insights into our needs, desires, and reactions to different situations. When we recognize and acknowledge our emotions, we gain a deeper understanding of ourselves and our environment.

Consider the physical sensations that come with different emotions—how your body feels when you're happy, sad, angry, or confused. This awareness helps us better understand and identify our emotions, which is the first step toward managing them effectively.

Managing our emotions is key to harnessing their power. Throughout life, we develop strategies for regulating our feelings, ensuring they don't become overwhelming or harmful. Think about a time when you felt intensely sad or overjoyed. How did you manage those emotions?

Practices like deep breathing, mindfulness, and self-reflection help us navigate our emotions with greater ease. Seeking happiness and positivity, even in challenging situations, can steer your life in a more positive direction.

As you read this lesson, take time to reflect on your own emotional experiences. Becoming more attuned to your emotions enhances self-awareness and offers valuable insights into your thoughts, behaviors, and overall well-being.

Ultimately, mastering the power of our emotions leads to a more harmonious and fulfilling life. By managing our emotions and how we respond to others, we can make better choices, build healthier relationships, and face challenges with resilience and adaptability.

The Basics of Emotions

Think of emotions like the colors of a rainbow—each one is unique and beautiful in its way. We've got the classics: happiness, sadness, anger, fear, surprise, and disgust. These are our primary emotions, and everything else is just a mix of these core feelings. For example, happiness can range from contentment to euphoria, while sadness can vary from mild disappointment to deep grief. Understanding these basic emotions helps us decode our more complex emotional experiences.

Just like colors can be light or dark, emotions can be mild or intense. Imagine a slider that moves from "a bit annoyed" to "furious" for anger or "content" to "ecstatic" for happiness. This spectrum helps us understand that emotions aren't binary but exist in varying degrees. Recognizing where we fall on this spectrum can guide our responses and help us manage our feelings more effectively. For instance, feeling slightly anxious before a presentation can be motivating, but overwhelming anxiety might require coping strategies.

Here's a fun fact—emotions aren't just in our hearts; they're in our brains too! Different parts of our brain light up when we feel different emotions, and hormones like adrenaline and dopamine play a big role in how we experience these feelings. The amygdala, for example, is crucial for processing fear and excitement, while the prefrontal cortex helps regulate our emotional responses and decision-making. Neurotransmitters like serotonin and oxytocin also influence our mood and social bonding. By understanding the biological foundations of emotions, we can appreciate their complexity and learn to manage them better.

The Role of Emotions in Daily Life

Ever made a decision because it "felt right"? That's your emotions at work! They help us decide what to do, from choosing what to eat for breakfast to making big life choices like changing careers. Emotions provide valuable shortcuts in decision-making, helping us navigate complex situations quickly. However, it's also important to balance emotional insights with rational thought to avoid impulsive decisions. For instance, while fear can protect us from danger, it might also prevent us from taking beneficial risks if not properly managed.

Emotions are the glue that holds our relationships together. They help us connect with others, understand them, and show empathy. When we share our joys and sorrows with friends, it strengthens our bonds. Empathy, the ability to feel what others are feeling, allows us to support loved ones in times of need. However, emotions can also create misunderstandings and conflicts. Learning to navigate these emotional waters can improve our relationships and make them more fulfilling. By practicing active listening and expressing our feelings honestly, we can build stronger, more resilient connections.

Our emotional health is tied to our mental health. Being aware of our feelings can help us stay balanced and happy. Suppressing emotions can lead to stress, anxiety, and even physical health problems. On the other hand, acknowledging and addressing our emotions can promote mental well-being. Regularly checking in with ourselves and seeking support when needed are crucial steps in maintaining good mental health. Engaging in activities that promote emotional health, such as meditation, exercise, and socializing, can enhance our overall well-being.

Understanding and Managing Emotions

The first step to mastering our emotions is to know what we're feeling. It's like being a detective—pay attention to your feelings, give them a name, and understand what's causing them. Journaling, mindfulness, and meditation are excellent tools for building emotional awareness. By regularly reflecting on our emotions, we can identify patterns and triggers, helping us respond more thoughtfully in the future. For instance, if you notice that you often feel anxious before meetings, you can prepare strategies to calm yourself beforehand.

Sometimes our emotions can get a bit wild. Learning how to calm down and stay cool is key. Try things like taking deep breaths, going for a walk, or even dancing it out! Techniques such as cognitive reframing, where we challenge and change negative thought patterns, can also be effective. Developing a toolbox of strategies to manage our emotions ensures we can handle whatever life throws at us without becoming overwhelmed. For example, practicing deep breathing can activate the body's relaxation response, reducing stress.

Bottling up emotions is like shaking a soda can—it's going to explode eventually. Find healthy ways to let your feelings out, whether it's talking to a friend, writing in a journal, or creating art. Expressing emotions constructively can prevent them from building up and causing stress or conflict. It's important to communicate our feelings clearly and respectfully, ensuring our needs are met while also considering others' perspectives. For instance, using "I feel" statements can help express emotions without blaming others.

Using Emotions to Better Ourselves

Think of your emotions as messages from your inner self. What are they trying to tell you? Use them to gain insight and grow. Reflecting on emotional experiences can reveal underlying beliefs and values, helping us understand ourselves better. For instance, feeling jealous might highlight insecurities we need to address, while joy can point us towards what we truly value and enjoy. Regular self-reflection can guide personal development and help us align our actions with our goals.

Every emotion, even the tough ones, are a chance to learn and improve. Embrace them, learn from them, and keep moving forward. Adopting a growth mindset means seeing challenges as opportunities rather than obstacles. When we view emotions as tools for growth, we become more resilient and adaptable, better equipped to handle life's ups and downs. For example, viewing failure as a learning experience rather than a setback can foster perseverance and innovation.

Being emotionally intelligent means understanding your feelings and those of others. It's like having a superpower that helps you navigate life's ups and downs. Emotional intelligence involves empathy, self-regulation, motivation, and social skills. By cultivating these abilities, we can improve our interactions, make better decisions, and lead more fulfilling lives. For instance, practicing empathy can enhance our relationships, while self-regulation can help us stay calm under pressure.

<u>Activity: The Emotion Exploration Challenge</u>

1. Morning Check-In
   - Start your day with a brief meditation or deep-breathing exercise.
   - Take a moment to note how you're feeling. Are you excited, anxious, calm? Write it down in a journal.

2. Emotion Log
   - Carry a small notebook with you or use a note-taking app on your phone.
   - Throughout the day, jot down any significant emotions you experience. Note the time, what you were doing, and what might have triggered the emotion.

3. Emotion Wheel
   - Draw a circle and divide it into sections labeled with different emotions (happy, sad, angry, scared, etc.).
   - Color in the sections that match the emotions you logged throughout the day.

4. Reflection Questions
   - What triggered each emotion?
   - How did you respond to it?
   - What could you do differently next time?

5. Evening Reflection
   - At the end of the day, review your emotion log and wheel.
   - Write a short summary of your emotional journey. What patterns did you notice? How did your emotions influence your actions?

Share your findings with a friend or family member. Discuss what you learned about your emotional patterns and how you can use this insight to improve your emotional well-being.

By dedicating a day to exploring your emotions, you'll gain valuable insights into your emotional landscape and learn practical strategies to manage your feelings. Happy exploring!

The journey of emotional awakening, though often overlooked, holds profound lessons for leading a fulfilling life. Through the experiences of Alex, Eden, and those around them, we've gained invaluable insights into nurturing emotional awareness, intelligence, and resilience within ourselves.

This exploration revealed that emotions hold the key to unlocking our innermost truths. Understanding their power is the pathway to self-knowledge and authentic living. Alex and Eden's journey taught us the wisdom of viewing emotions as guides, providing deeper insights into our needs and desires. Their stories instilled a newfound reverence for the treasures hidden within our emotional landscape.

This journey reveals that emotions offer a gateway to inner truth and wisdom. Learning their language allows one to decode their core needs and desires, empowering conscious, values-aligned living with authenticity. Just as a compass points travelers on the right direction, emotional awareness provides vital orientation toward purpose and meaning.

The resilience displayed by Alex and Eden in navigating adversity serves as a beacon, reminding us that we too can emerge stronger from life's tribulations. Their responses to pain and heartache showcase that healing and growth are always possible with wise engagement in the challenges before us. Instead of breaking us, hardships can expand our capacity for understanding and grace.

As we turn the page on this chapter, the focus shifts to the art of setting powerful goals and harnessing our potential for personal transformation. While the destination remains unseen, Alex and Eden have illuminated the path for the next step ahead, guiding us toward a future of continued growth and self-discovery.

<u>Chapter 3: The Midnight Bakery</u>

Eden took a deep breath as she looked herself over one last time in the floor-length mirror on her bedroom wall. Today was graduation day—the culmination of years of late-night studying and long hours in after-school programs. She had worked hard for this day, earning a 3.69 GPA, and reaching 3rd in her graduating class at the ultra-competitive Evergreen Academy private school.

Smoothing out her royal blue gown and adjusting the graduation cap atop her neatly pinned-up blonde hair, Eden couldn't help but grin. She still couldn't believe she was about to graduate near the very top of a class full of Ivy League-bound students. A wave of excitement and nostalgia washed over her as she headed out the door.

In the school auditorium, Eden took her seat alongside the other honor students toward the front. Looking out at the sea of graduates behind her, she spotted her best friend Monica waving excitedly. Eden waved back, reflecting on all the fun times she and Monica had these past four years.

The graduation march began to play as the students quieted down. This was it—in a matter of minutes, Eden would walk across that stage as a high school graduate. As the headmaster began calling names, butterflies swirled in Eden's stomach. She glanced over two rows at her boyfriend, Nate, grinning as they locked eyes.

Nate mouthed, "Congrats, babe!" and gave her a thumbs up. They had plans to go out for a fancy dinner with their families after the ceremony to celebrate finishing high school together.

Finally, Eden heard the headmaster call out, "Eden Ambrosia!" She strode across the stage confidently, shaking the headmaster's hand as he pressed the diploma into her palm. Out in the audience, Eden spotted her family cheering loudly, partly standing up to snap a picture.

"Way to go, Eden!" her brother Leo yelled loudly. Her mom was dabbing her eyes with a tissue. Eden smiled wide as she took her seat again, diploma safely in hand.

The graduation march concluded thirty minutes later as the last students returned to their seats. Eden looked down, admiring the diploma in her lap. Four years of dedication had led to this singular moment, and now her future at college awaited. She sighed contentedly, tightening the royal blue gown around her shoulders.

The headmaster concluded, "I present to you this year's graduating class of Evergreen Academy!" A roar went up from the audience and students alike as they tossed graduation caps skyward in celebration.

Hugging her friends, Eden let it sink in—high school was over. A bittersweet sensation for sure, but she tingled with excitement about what came next.

The graduation fanfare died down as Eden headed out of the auditorium, arm in arm with Nate. She spotted her mom and brother waving her over, beaming with joy.

"Honey, we are so incredibly proud of you," her mom gushed, pulling Eden into a tight hug. "I can't believe you graduated third in your class!"

"Thanks, Mom," Eden replied. "I really worked hard for it."

Leo put a strong hand on her shoulder. "The world is yours now, Eden. With those grades and test scores, you could go to any college you want."

Eden nodded, "Thanks, little bro, I appreciate it!" She felt almost overwhelmed by the big decision facing her. She had applied to and been accepted at colleges across the country. But now she had to pick one.

On one hand, she desperately wanted to attend BCU, a highly acclaimed biology program only a few stops north on the city subway. They had offered her a substantial scholarship and attending with Nate and Monica so they could all stay together was a big draw too.

But Eden had also gotten into top-ranked medical programs a little farther away. She envisioned herself in a white coat, saving lives. The path was longer, but it might be worth it.

As everyone gathered for dinner, the gravity of choosing a college weighed on Eden. She knew it would impact everything that came after graduation. Excusing herself to the restroom, she stared at her reflection—the future doctor or biologist? Cause and effect hung in the balance, decisions had to be made.

Eden gripped the sides of the bathroom sink, staring into her own eyes with an intensity she rarely felt. Choosing between a college close by with Nate or chasing her dream of medical school was proving more difficult than she imagined.

She thought of the long talks she and Nate had over late-night cups of cocoa, dreaming together about breezing through college packed with parties, football games, and adventures together. The campus at BCU was gorgeous too—she could picture herself strolling the streets to class with Nate, hand in hand.

But Eden also imagined herself confidently diagnosing patients, caring for the injured, and maybe even discovering new lifesaving techniques. She had idolized groundbreaking doctors since she was young, and the medical program at Everbrook's Center for Medicine was one of the best in the world.

The voice of her high school biology teacher floated into Eden's mind then. "Eden, you have a singular talent for medicine," Mrs. Beasley had told her. "I know you have a lot of tough decisions to make. But if you want to change lives, go where your talent takes you."

Eden took a deep breath, straightening her dress in the bathroom mirror. Maybe she didn't have to choose between true love and following her dreams. If her bond with Nate was real, it would last across however many miles lay between their campuses. They could still chat daily and meet up on breaks. This was her future at stake.

Eden knew then exactly what she wanted to choose as she pushed open the restroom door. With the sounds of the restaurant flooding back in, she saw Nate across the room laughing with her family.

Eden set her shoulders and walked towards him. She had made up her mind and decided where her talents would take her. The possibilities made her dizzy with anticipation.

●

Eden double-checked the student registration site just to be positive—all of her classes for the semester perfectly matched with Nate's. She had managed to get into the same sections as him for Biology 101, English Literature, and even the same gym class.

"We are going to be together nonstop!" Eden said to Nate excitedly over the phone. "Just try not to get sick of me," she added with a laugh.

"Never," Nate said. "It's going to be so much fun tackling it all side by side with you next week. Especially intro biology—it's supposed to be intense."

Eden grinned, envisioning herself and Nate handing in lab reports together, flashing smiles at one another across the lecture hall, and dashing through the quad to make it to classes on time. Even with a mountain of studying, having Nate there with her every step of the way would make college amazing.

The first day of classes arrived in a whirlwind. Eden spotted Nate waiting outside her dorm to walk with her to their back-to-back classes. With his familiar hand clasped in hers, Eden strode toward the biology building, ready to take on anything college could throw at them.

The first few weeks of classes flew by in a flurry of lectures, lab reports, pop quizzes, and lots of late-night coffee runs and study sessions with Nate. Eden was thrilled to be experiencing it all with her best friend by her side the whole time.

They fell into an easy routine together—Nate would quiz Eden on anatomy terms while they waited for the morning coffee shop rush to die down. Eden prepped Nate for literature exams while they took sunny afternoon walks around campus.

At night, they usually ended up at the library, huddled together over textbooks until the wee hours. Eden would rest her head on Nate's shoulder when her exhaustion peaked, her long blonde hair tangled. He always seemed to know exactly when she needed an encouraging pep talk or a quick break to blow off steam.

Before she knew it, Eden was deep into the semester with Nate. College was everything she had hoped for—mostly thanks to having him there. Her mom kept telling her to enjoy this special time together. As far as Eden was concerned, the blissful college days would never end.

As the first year of college neared its end, Eden noticed with unease that her perfect schedule with Nate had fallen out of sync. With finals looming, they no longer spent long afternoons wandering the quad or popping into town for unplanned dates.

Most days, Eden rushed straight from her last class to the science library, only emerging once the sun had set to walk, exhausted, back to her dorm. She kept meaning to talk to Nate, but usually ended up cramming in more study time instead.

When they did meet up to review biology notes at their favorite campus café, Eden sensed Nate growing more distant. He was often distracted, checking his phone frequently and providing only one-word responses to Eden's questions about properties of enzymes.

One humid night in April, as finals came to an end, Eden asked Nate if he wanted to join her for a late-night study session. She had to finish memorizing the circulatory system for her anatomy final.

"Oh, uh... I can't tonight," Nate replied, eyes darting away from Eden's. "I picked up an extra shift at work. Gotta make that money, you know?"

Eden sighed but said she understood. As Nate hurried off, she felt a knot forming in her stomach. She stood there frowning for a minute before slowly turning toward the library, alone.

The next day, Eden dragged her feet walking back from her exhausting final anatomy exam, dreaming of the nap she planned to take now that all of her tests were done. She couldn't wait to enjoy a relaxing summer with Nate after surviving freshman year.

As Eden approached her dorm building, she spotted her friend Monica sitting alone on a bench, staring at her, then toward the ground. Eden could tell that Monica had been crying.

"Monica! What's going on?" Eden asked worriedly, rushing over. Monica and Eden had grown closer during their first semester but rarely hung out anymore.

Monica glanced up, her puffy eyes awash in guilt. "Eden, I'm so sorry..." she said faintly, a fresh tear trickling down her cheek.

Eden felt her stomach drop as she sat beside Monica. What did her friend have to apologize for? She took Monica's hand, bracing herself as Monica took a quivering breath.

"It's about Nate," Monica whispered. "We've been... we've been seeing each other for a few weeks, but..."

Eden jerked backward, dropping Monica's hand. No. It couldn't be. The words echoed numbly in Eden's mind. Nate and Monica? Her Nate? The Nate she had just endured freshman year alongside?

Eden leapt off the bench, fighting back tears. Ignoring Monica's pleas, she broke into a run toward Nate's dorm, praying it wasn't true. Eden felt suspended in a nightmare as she sprinted across campus toward his dorm. There was no way he could have betrayed her trust and their relationship like this. Her breath came in ragged gasps by the time his dorm building emerged, but she couldn't slow down.

Bursting through the front door, Eden took the three flights of stairs to Nate's room two at a time. She pounded fiercely on his door, calling Nate's name. A long minute passed before the door creaked open. Nate stood before her, confusion fading to guilt as he registered Eden's tear-stained face.

"Tell me it didn't happen, just tell me," Eden pleaded, searching Nate's eyes desperately.

Nate slumped against the door frame. "Monica told you... I'm so sorry, Eden. I never meant..." His voice trailed off miserably.

Eden just shook her head as a sob escaped her lips. "How could you?" she choked out. Nate stepped toward her, but she recoiled from his touch. A toxic wave of anger, betrayal, and sorrow crashed down on her.

Without another word, Eden whipped around and sprinted down the stairs, away from his dorm, and away from this campus that now harbored such painful memories. She ran, half-blinded by tears, back across the quad, unsure where she was headed except away from the source of her heartbreak.

Eden ran until she reached a secluded courtyard garden on campus, nearly empty this time of year. Crumpling onto a stone bench, she finally let the floodgates open fully, choking out heaving sobs. She wrapped her arms around herself and rocked gently, willing away the searing ache in her chest.

As her crying subsided into sniffles, Eden pulled out her phone with trembling hands. There were three missed calls from Nate and a few panicked texts. She swiped them away angrily before scrolling to Maya's name.

Maya had been Eden's closest friend all through middle school before moving across the city to attend a public high school. They talked fairly often but rarely about anything too meaningful. Now, though, Maya lived across the city at another college, and Eden desperately needed Maya's familiar, comforting presence.

She tapped out a text: "My world collapsed today. Can I come stay on your couch for a bit? Need to get away."

Within a minute, Eden's phone pinged with Maya's shocked reply, urging her to come straight over. Her dorm had an extra couch with Eden's name on it. Eden exhaled, the tiniest bit of the weight on her chest lifting. She stood from the garden bench on shaky legs, determined to make it across the city to Maya's place. As Eden took a step, though, she wavered slightly. Maybe Nate deserved a conversation at least. But rage flared up again inside Eden, and she walked on. She needed Maya now more than ever.

●

Eden stepped off the bus into the bustling city center where Maya's dorm room was. She felt numb as she navigated the crowded streets, dodging business people ducking into cafés and tourists consulting maps outside souvenir shops.

Three more blocks to Maya's place. Eden tensed as she noticed a handsome guy about her age striding toward her on the sidewalk, his head wavering, glancing in her direction. He looked vaguely familiar, though Eden couldn't place him.

They walked towards each other, and both glanced up at the

same moment, briefly locking eyes before passing on the narrow sidewalk. Eden paused, feeling she somehow knew his kind eyes and wavy brown hair. But the moment slipped away, their shared moment together now a memory.

Eden stepped inside from the darkening night into the dorm lobby, harsh fluorescent lights reflecting off scuffed tile under her feet. The old creaking elevator shuddered slowly upward. Cheerful fliers advertising drama groups and yoga sessions taped to its walls jarred Eden's gloomy mood.

Walking down the long hallway, she spotted the flower garland Maya had playfully tacked to her door. Behind it, the cheesy melody of pop radio filtered out around the door frame. Hearing the upbeat tune despite the cheap speaker quality lifted Eden's mouth unconsciously as she began to quietly sing.

She knocked lightly three times, a shuffling movement erupted, followed swiftly by Maya swinging open her door, bracelets sliding down her wrist, and the smell of lavender incense in the air.

Though her bright grin wavered slightly seeing Eden's raw eyes, she swept her friend inside. The snug dorm was filled with glimpses of Maya's frenetic style, piles of strewn clothes and textbooks laid randomly on the floor.

Perching on the lumpy dorm futon, Eden picked at a loose thread rather than meet Maya's sympathetic gaze. In broken words stitched together between shaky breaths, Eden fought back tears as she explained about her friend Monica confessing to her after class that she and Nate had been secretly seeing each other for weeks.

Eden described hysterically racing across campus to Nate's dorm to beg impossible denials from his red, guilt-ridden face. The lost and aimless feeling now clouding any ability to picture tomorrow poured out of Eden as Maya listened intently, periodic head shakes punctuating each wounding detail.

When emotion wrung Eden dry of words at last, Maya reached over to grip her hands tighter. "First, we cut ties with those backstabbing cowards immediately. Consider me your loyal filter for all their future calls." She flashed a hint of a crooked smile before her expression shifted more earnest.

"But tonight... let's go out and hit Sanctuary, a classy new club downtown! DJ Astrus is playing, and he's the hottest thing right now. I had plans to go out with my boyfriend Tyler and his friends. We'll dance, laugh, and shake this crappy cloud off! Whaddya say, babe?"

Eden hesitated, throat tightening at the thought of bearing her raw heartbreak beneath the pulsing lights and prying gaze of strangers at some ultra-trendy club. The idea of changing out of her sundress and into flashy going-out clothes felt exhausting. Still, seeing Maya's hopeful smile start to slip, Eden nodded weakly.

"I guess a quick stop wouldn't hurt..." Eden managed. Maya squealed excitedly, already leaping up to fling open her closet doors and start rifling through clothing options.

"Ooo, try this crop top—it'll go gorgeously with your eyes!" Maya held up a shimmery emerald tank top and black mini skirt that made Eden's stomach lurch. But her friend's enthusiastic momentum felt hard to obstruct.

Ten reluctant minutes later, Eden shuffled awkwardly in a pair of Maya's strappy heels while her friend artfully pinned back silky strands of her hair. Maya whistled approvingly, steering Eden by the shoulders toward the streaked mirror on the back of her door.

"Dang, girl, supermodel status!" Maya winked as Eden looked at the unfamiliar bombshell staring back behind expertly brushed mascara and eyeshadow. A few short moments later, they grabbed their purses and stumbled, giggling, down the three flights of stairs toward the crisp spring sidewalks to meet up with Tyler and his friends.

•

Alex arrived at the Midnight Bakery as the sun began to set, the aroma of freshly baked bread filling the air as he prepared for his last overnight shift before departing on a year-long trip to foreign countries.

The Midnight Bakery had become a second home to him over the years, and tonight marked the end of an era. He felt abuzz with excitement to share with Emmanuel, the bakery owner, details of a magical encounter he had experienced just minutes before on his walk over.

"Emmanuel, I've got to tell you about something that happened just before I got here," Alex began, excitement and nostalgia mixing in his voice. He recounted the story of a chance encounter on the street with a captivating girl who caught his eye.

"Once upon a time, on a beautiful April evening, just a few short minutes ago... as the sun cast its final glow upon the narrow streets, I found myself strolling along, lost in the twilight of my thoughts.

Suddenly, the perfect girl approached me from across the street. She may not fit society's conventional standards of beauty, but her allure was undeniable to me. Her appearance didn't jump out at me right away, yet there was an undeniable magnetism that drew me toward her. The gentle curve of her lips, the way she carried herself with grace—it was enough to make my heart tremble and my mouth grow dry.

I've always had my own unique preferences when it comes to the ideal girl. Whether it's a particular physical feature like slender ankles, enchanting eyes, or a laugh that hypnotizes the soul, I've always been captivated by these subtle details. But the perfect girl cannot be confined to a preconceived notion or a checklist. Yet, what remains etched in my memory is the supernatural feeling that she is the one, the girl meant for me.

As we passed each other this beautiful April evening, her heading east and I heading west, a pleasant breeze brushed against my skin, the setting sun deep in the distance. The scent of roses filled the air, carried by the dampness of the asphalt. I longed to engage her in conversation, to spend just half an hour unraveling the intricacies of fate that led us to this moment. I yearned to share our stories, to reveal the secrets that lay dormant within us, like an antique clock that held the warmth of a bygone era.

She crossed the street ahead and began heading directly toward me. I began to daydream and imagine that we would share a delightful lunch sometime, perhaps watch an old movie or find ourselves drinking coffee at a local café. And if destiny smiled upon us, our connection might blossom into something more intimate, transcending the boundaries of mere words.

Yet, as we walked, the gap between us closing to a mere twenty, maybe thirty feet, I found myself at a loss for words. How could I approach her? What could I say to capture her attention, to convey my feelings in a way that would resonate with her?

'Good evening, miss. Would you spare some time for a little conversation?' I contemplated, but it felt contrived, like a spam call asking if my car warranty was ending soon. Perhaps the simplest approach would be the most genuine. 'Good evening. You are the perfect girl for me.'

But doubts whispered in my mind. Would she believe such a bold declaration? And even if she did, what if she couldn't live up to my expectations? Rejection lingered as a perceptible fear.

She began to slow down as we passed by a charming flower shop. She held a tiny purse in her right hand, its rugged surface tempered over the course of time. The evening breeze ruffled her blonde hair as she approached. Her choice of attire reflected her charming simplicity and let off an air of understated elegance.

She donned a flowing sundress, decorated with a subtle floral pattern that seemed to mirror the smell of fresh roses in the air. The dress, in soft pastel hues, draped gracefully over her figure as she moved. A light cardigan rested gently on her shoulders, ready to embrace her in cold weather.

As she walked by with an air of quiet confidence, her feet embraced the cobbled pavement in comfortable sandals. A dainty necklace graced her neck, its subtle elegance drawing attention to her collarbones. A simple bracelet decorated her wrist, capturing the soft glow of the setting sun as it gently caressed her skin. Her hair, softly styled, cascaded over her shoulders in natural waves.

With each stride, the gap between us grew wider, until I turned my head, hoping to steal one last glimpse of her. But she dissolved into the crowd, swallowed by the bustling ebb and flow of life. Our connection slipped through my fingers, leaving an ache of what could have been. My mind conjured impractical ideas, as is my tendency..."

Sigh.

A steady silence stood between them briefly. Emmanuel studied Alex, then replied gently, "My friend, let this vision kindle your creativity. One day the unsung words in your heart will find their audience. In any case, congratulations are in order for you, my friend," Emmanuel exclaimed, extending his hand to shake Alex's. "You've come a long way as my apprentice, and I'm proud of the skilled baker you've become."

Alex beamed with gratitude. "Thank you, Emmanuel. It's been an incredible journey working here. I've learned so much, not just about baking, but about life."

Emmanuel nodded knowingly. "Ah, life's lessons are often baked into the dough, my boy. Now, tell me about this grand adventure you're embarking on."

With no hesitation, Alex explained, "Well, as you know, today marks my last day here, Emmanuel. I'll be leaving a little early tonight. I've saved up enough money, and early tomorrow morning, I'm catching a plane to travel overseas."

Emmanuel's eyes widened with a mix of surprise and pride. "Ah, foreign lands across the sea! That's quite a journey, Alex. What inspired this decision?"

Alex reached into his backpack and pulled out a worn-out book titled *The Wonders of the World*. He opened it to reveal pages filled with images and descriptions of iconic and mysterious places across the globe.

"This book, Emmanuel. I want to see these wonders for myself, experience different cultures, and learn about the world beyond these kitchen walls."

Emmanuel studied the book with a nod of approval. "A quest for knowledge and adventure. It warms my heart to see you embracing the call of the unknown. Travel has a unique way of shaping a person."

With a genuine smile, Emmanuel continued, "You've earned this journey, my boy. Take in the sights, embrace the unknown, and return with stories that will enrich not just your life but the lives of those you meet." Emmanuel disappeared into the back room, returning with an older camera, its black leather casing showing signs of age.

"I'm a photographic genius! If I do say so myself," he said, snapping a picture of him and his apprentice. "This picture will always bring back the fondest of memories," Emmanuel remarked as he handed the developed photo to Alex with a smile.

"Keep this as a reminder of where you come from, Alex. The Midnight Bakery will always be here, a home for you, no matter where your adventures take you."

Touched by the gesture, Alex carefully placed the picture in the *Wonders of the World* book. "Thank you, Emmanuel. This means the world to me." With a final glance at the familiar surroundings, Alex donned his apron, ready to tackle his final night baking. The familiar rhythm of the bakery came alive as they kneaded dough, shaped loaves, and prepared pastries, their shared passion for baking lighting up the room despite the impending farewell.

As Eden and Maya's heels clicked down the lamp-lit streets, laughter echoed ahead from Tyler's dorm party. Eden's phone jangled with a familiar ringtone from inside her tiny purse. Nate's charming grin flashed onto the outer screen.

Eden hesitated, thumb hovering as nervousness and resentment churned within upon seeing his face again. Maya nodded in encouragement, giving her space to sort through the sudden complex wave of emotions. Did she owe Nate an explanation after all they had weathered and dreamed together?

Decision made, Eden passed the jangling device to Maya, both girls' mouths set in silent solidarity. Maya answered the phone, and in brief, concise terms, confirmed that Eden's choice to move forward was for her own peace and accord. Eden watched Maya's face harden as she heard Nate's immediate pleading tone, her rebuttals gaining conviction with each "But Eden loves me still!" uttered.

With a tone allowing no pushback, Maya firmly reiterated Eden's resolve before wishing Nate well and decisively clicking the phone off.

Linking their arms, Maya proclaimed to Eden, "Nate is now just somebody you used to know!" She promised to gather Eden's things herself so no more words would need to pass between her and Nate. Eden exhaled with relief, feeling grateful and supported.

They strode forward with excitement toward Tyler's dorm up ahead. Watery reflections from the dorm courtyard fountain glittered across Eden as she and Maya approached the boisterous group spilling out of the propped-open double doors.

Eden counted at least six guys in letter jackets hovering around Tyler in the pulsing light, their raucous laughs and impromptu wrestling punctuated by periodic swigs from suspiciously dented cans.

Eden lingered at the edge of the fray as Maya slipped gracefully to Tyler's side. Though still floating in relief from the closure of the call, being the only girl minus a boyfriend as arm candy made Eden suddenly self-conscious again.

As several guys detached from jousting matches to meander tipsily over with obvious opening lines, she readied herself with stinging comebacks and wit.

"Nice shoes, wanna make out later?" slurred a bold, smug guy as he tripped over his own feet.

"Nice opening line, been striking out since middle school?" Eden retorted dryly.

Another popped up offering unwelcome consolation about breakups leaving "smokin' singles" newly available.

"Tempting. Though a pity pledge night clearly already scrapped the talent pool bottom..." Eden trailed off pointedly as his jaw dropped. She knew wit was her sharpest armor against these dim-witted jocks.

While the group relaxed in the dorm, engaged in lively sports debates, Eden observed Maya sitting close to Tyler on a small loveseat. Her smile disappeared as he grumbled, clearly irritated.

Eden edged subtly closer, straining to hear Maya reply gently, "Oh c'mon, I couldn't just leave her to mope..." while Tyler snorted derisively about plans being ruined with her tagging along tonight.

Eden felt her cheeks flush, wondering if she should discreetly slip out and leave the couple to smooth things over. But Maya caught her hesitating glance, giving a subtle, reassuring head shake as she turned back to sweet talk Tyler's attention away from an engrossing game on the TV.

Tyler shrugged casually, which made Maya feel ignored and discouraged. Withdrawing into her own thoughts, Maya sought comfort while Eden watched the scene, becoming increasingly sad and confused.

The friendly and comfortable atmosphere of the evening seemed to fade away, and an unexpected tension took its place. Eden struggled to understand why this had happened, questioning if she had made the right decision to come.

As the group left Tyler's tense dorm room, Eden trailed behind Maya and Tyler toward the trendy new club, their crisp words punctuating angry footsteps down the lamp-lit street.

"I just don't get why B-rad has to come too... you know we don't vibe," Maya hissed, voice saturated in fresh annoyance toward Tyler's linebacker roommate, lumbering tipsily behind.

"He's my buddy, and I already said he could roll with us tonight," Tyler bit back without turning around, indifference clear. Eden watched Maya cross her arms tightly.

Eden felt despair oozing, wondering if saying something awkward might salvage their strained dynamic. Before she could open her mouth, the pulsing club entrance swarmed startlingly into view.

Velvet ropes unclipped, the heavy oak door before Eden gave way to strobe lights flickering wildly over the tightly packed Friday night crowd. Thick humidity from swaying bodies hit her instantly as the club's throaty bassline hummed up through the soles of her strappy heels.

This was Sanctuary—the hottest new downtown spot where students flocked for dancing and delirious detachment from any collegiate cares nagging come Monday.

Out on the central dance floor, though, a sea of strangers flowed seamlessly together under the pulsating DJ sets. Feeling an urge to step fully into the rhythmic energy swirling ahead, Eden pivoted decisively toward the neon-lit dance floor, despite Maya dropping back while bickering with Tyler.

She began gently pushing through outer rings of giggling friends gathered for pictures, bypassing circles of dancers and couples embracing. Weaving adeptly inward, closer to the DJ, Eden felt her sense of adventure rising. Soon, she was surveying her new vantage point, pleasantly anonymous amid the beautiful cross-section of young dancers.

Eden closed her eyes, letting the lyrics about embracing change wash over her as she surrendered to the music. Her hips began swaying slowly, tentatively at first, then gaining confidence as the drummer's familiar beat reverberated through her body in textbook perfect rhythm.

She twisted smoothly on the polished floor, her unease melting rapidly into a sly smile. She had missed being this sure of herself, owning her style. It reminded her of secret dance parties in Maya's apartment after her parents went to bed.

They would beam flashlights across sleeping bags to illuminate silly magazine trivia quizzes before huddling under a blanket fort, whispering secrets and dreams as their favorite pop divas sang reassuringly on the radio all through the night.

As the melody commanded her hips' swaying approval, she basked in nostalgia's glow, spreading warmth through her heart, once badly bruised. Gliding through the bustling dance floor, she welcomed the admiring gazes keeping a shy distance.

Just then, Maya appeared, her sparkling black curls bouncing atop an enormous grin as she shimmied up alongside Eden, seamlessly matching her blissful rhythm. Reunited intuitively, they let themselves get lost like countless times before.

Suddenly, screams pierced the music. Whipping around, they glimpsed Tyler across the floor, jaw clenched, jabbing his finger into another guy's chest. People nearby parted as shocked words caused the leaner student's face to darken. Friends restrained Tyler as he unleashed another vicious insult.

The damage was done—boiling tempers crossed a line. Security forced the pair swiftly outside. Friends rushed after to try calming the erupting fight before consequences got irreversible. Eden and Maya burst onto the neon-bathed sidewalk outside the club, scanning desperately for Tyler in the jostling crowd. They glimpsed bouncers forcefully removing him toward a side alley where his adversary slumped against the brick wall, blood trickling from his nose.

Just then, raucous laughter swelled as a large group of streakers came barreling down the street, wearing only socks and sneakers.

"Wooooo!! Streaking bar crawl!" they bellowed, waving empty booze bottles overhead as late-night revelers cheered them on.

Before Eden even processed the chaotic scene, Tyler came stumbling from the alley while yelling, "Hey sidewalk, get outta my way! Parking meters! And you're walking around! Hahaha! That's so funny!"

Grinning recklessly, he ripped his shirt over his head, kicked off the remainder of his clothes, and caught up to the nude runners on their way to another bar.

"Tyler! What the hell?" Maya shrieked after him. But he disappeared with the jubilant streakers into the night shadows, leaving her tugging her hair completely at a loss. How could their intended carefree night spiral so far out of control?

Eden rubbed Maya's back consolingly as loud police sirens now pierced the night air, prompting the remaining clubgoers to disperse hastily.

"I need to get you away from this mess, c'mon," Maya finally exhaled, putting an arm around Eden and steering them swiftly down the sidewalk.

As they walked in shaken silence, Maya explained they were

headed to a hidden local gem called the Midnight Bakery. It supplied baked goods wholesale to cafés and bars across the city by day, but between midnight and 3:30 a.m., the public could visit a little window lit up in blue and place orders to the bakers inside.

"It started decades ago for third-shift hospital workers needing a pastry pickup after overtime hours. Now it's an open secret for club kids and restless thinkers wandering the witching hours in search of refuge or inspiration," Maya shared.

As they strode the empty downtown sidewalks past shuttered galleries and trendy lofts now dark, Eden felt Maya's tension slowly unwind with each block between the chaotic club eruption and Tyler's destructive antics. Glancing sideways at her friend's clenched jaw still working itself out, Eden finally broke the fragile silence in soft encouragement.

"This whole disastrous night wasn't your fault, Maya. I just wish I knew the magic words to say that would make Tyler start treating you right." She paused, thinking back on her own recent trials illuminated by city stoplights pulsing overhead.

"I guess with relationships, the healthiest thing we can do is know our self-worth enough to make better decisions... easier said than done, though," Eden remarked as she flipped back a stray hair from her face.

Maya nodded, blinking hard. "I know you're so right. Guess I just hoped Tyler would outgrow the ego if I loved him selflessly enough through these phases..." She trailed off ruefully. Another block passed as both girls sank into contemplative quiet again, until Eden halted abruptly, instantly transported hours prior.

Here was the exact spot where she had passed that soulful stranger. In a few short moments, it dawned on her—the impact of passing this young man on the street.

Eden turned to Maya in disbelief, opening her mouth slowly to recount the tale.

"Once upon a time, in the enchanting embrace of this beautiful April evening, while on my way to your dorm... it was on this hidden little street that my path intersected with his—the cutest guy I've ever seen. He may not have recognized the depths of his impact, but to me, he was the perfect boy for me.

Now, if I were to describe him, it wouldn't be with the usual clichés of physical attractiveness. No, his charm was found in the subtle nuances that transcended traditional beauty standards.

There was a quiet strength in his presence, an authenticity that resonated deeply within me. It wasn't his appearance or his clothes that caught my attention right away, but rather the intricate complexity of his thoughts and emotions that seemed to unfold with every step.

Everyone has their own unique preferences when it comes to an ideal partner. Some are captivated by outward beauty, while others seek a kindred spirit that harmonizes with their own.

For me, I don't think it's about conforming to preconceived notions or ticking off boxes on a checklist. It's about the unspoken connection, the intangible bond that defies definition. He embodied that connection—a reflection of the perfect boy I had always dreamed of.

With each step, our paths converged on this fateful April evening. I walked from west to east, while he ventured from east to west. The air felt humid and heavy, as if the universe itself recognized the gravity of our encounter. It was a joyous set of emotions, a playfulness of possibilities that awaited us.

I expected him to engage me in conversation, to unravel the intricacies of our chance encounter. If only time would grant us a precious half-hour—an exchange of stories, a sharing of vulnerabilities, and an exploration of the complexities that brought us together.

Perhaps we could have arranged for a leisurely lunch or gone to a quiet café, where the aroma of freshly brewed coffee would heighten our connection.

Our day might have continued with a funny movie. And if serendipity smiled upon us, our connection could have blossomed into an intimacy that transcends words—a dance of souls, a harmonious union of stars in the night sky.

But as the distance between us narrowed to a mere twenty or thirty feet, my heart sank, caught in the grip of uncertainty. Did he even notice me? I wondered where he was going, where he was from. Maybe I should have talked to him.

I could have said, 'Good evening, sir! Do you know where the nearest ATM is around here?' No, that wouldn't work. It didn't feel right. It was as if we were both grappling with the weight of societal norms, searching for an authentic connection beyond superficial pleasantries. I began to slow down, my thoughts weighing heavily.

As we passed by a charming flower shop, a soft, warm breeze brushed against my skin, carrying the fragrant whispers of blossoming roses. He walked with a sense of relaxed confidence, wearing a well-fitted dark denim jacket that complemented his rugged charm. The jacket accentuated his strong shoulders.

Underneath, there were hints of a simple yet tasteful solid-colored T-shirt that hinted at his unpretentious nature, as if he were on his way to work. The shirt clung to his frame just enough to showcase his physique without being overly revealing, leaving an intriguing air of mystery. I saw a name neatly stitched on his shirt that read 'Alex.'

His choice of slim-fitting black jeans seemed to flow effortlessly with his movements. As I gazed downward, I noticed his sturdy leather sneakers, showing signs of wear and tear from countless journeys. I couldn't help but find it endearing, imagining the stories behind each scuff and mark on those well-traveled shoes.

With each step, I felt the gap between us widening. And as I turned my head, longing for one final glimpse of his presence, he slipped away into the crowd. The moment dissipated, leaving a bittersweet ache that will forever linger in the depths of my being.

Yet, the world spins on, oblivious to the delicate dance of souls that could have unfolded. And so, I believe it's not to be thought of as one of missed opportunities or sad endings. Instead, it's a tale of possibility."

Sigh.

As the girls rounded the corner, the Midnight Bakery's blue neon sign came into cheerful view. Linking her arm through Eden's, Maya let out a wistful sigh.

"Sweetie... I just got goosebumps! The way you described him—those kind, soulful eyes, yet that air of mystery—Alex sounds utterly dreamy. Your romantic soulmate sent from the stars!"

Eden grinned, her cheeks flushing. "You really think so? I mean, I did feel this intense pull like I already knew his gentle heart somehow. Is his name really Alex?" She peered hopefully up at the glimmering night sky, in sync with Maya, both girls losing themselves in possibilities.

"Clearly the fates crossed your paths for a reason earlier," Maya declared confidently. "When the timing is just right, he'll reappear and finally work up the nerve to ask for your number himself!" Both giggled at the imagined scene as they turned toward the cozy bakery window.

The cheerful bell chimed as Maya gave the service button a quick tap. Footsteps drew near, and a slender elderly gentleman slid the partition window politely open. Emmanuel appeared at the window.

"My friends, what can I prepare for you while my oven finishes this next loaded batch?" His unplaceable dialect mingled fluidly beneath flawless English.

Maya quickly surveyed the posted bakery menu, rattling off a few selections, including Irish teacakes and apple turnovers. Emmanuel smiled in approval, entering notes onto a ticket in flowing script.

"Excellent choices this starry night!" Emmanuel said.

He then glanced inquiringly at Eden, who had been peering intently beyond the partition, trying to unravel more clues about this strangely compelling place.

"Oh! Yes, um... may I have a bear claw and a chocolate cornetto?" she managed in an embarrassed rush.

"Coming right up, ladies!" he said as he bustled away, humming a harmonious foreign melody. Emmanuel returned to the bakery and found Alex preparing to leave.

"Alex," Emmanuel began, his voice a mixture of pride and fondness, "this is it, my friend. I see you are leaving now to embark on new horizons."

Alex, a mix of emotions on his face, nodded in acknowledgment. "It's been an incredible journey, Emmanuel. I can't thank you enough for everything."

Emmanuel placed a hand on Alex's shoulder, his gaze reflecting a profound understanding of the journey ahead. "You've grown into an exceptional baker, but more importantly, into a remarkable individual. May your adventures be as rich as the flavors we've crafted together." Alex nodded in silent agreement.

A brief moment passed before Emmanuel turned toward the counter, and Alex quickly said, "Hey, Emmanuel, one last thing before I go. If you meet a beautiful, seductive woman who's looking for me, tell her 'Hi.' Anyway, I don't think a woman like that would be looking for me." Alex let out a hearty laugh as he finished sorting his belongings.

Emmanuel laughed and shook his head, saying, "Goodbye, Alex. I'll see you soon, my friend." Emmanuel saw part of the order left waiting on the counter, prompting him to reach for the order slip and gather the remaining pastries into a neatly wrapped package.

As Emmanuel returned to the window with their order, Maya turned to Eden and asked, "So, are you planning to find this Alex guy you passed on the street earlier?" Eden stood speechless, with curiosity etched on her face.

"You know, Eden," Maya said merrily, "sometimes you just have to put it out into the universe. If it's meant to happen, serendipity will bring you two together."

Feeling a surge of inspiration, Eden grabbed a pen and wrote something on the money she intended to pay with. Unbeknownst to them, the baker overheard their conversation. Emmanuel realized that the girl in front of him might be the same girl Alex had mentioned earlier. He decided to investigate, telling the girls to wait for a moment while handing them their order.

Hurrying to the back of the bakery, Emmanuel went to call for Alex. However, just as he opened his mouth, the buzzer for the oven went off, drowning out his voice.

Alex, oblivious to the call, walked out the door, unintentionally leaving his cherished book, *Wonders of the World*, resting on a countertop in the heart of the Midnight Bakery.

Maya and Eden waited for a minute, their order in hand. A small line had started behind them. They decided not to wait any longer and left their money and a tip through the window before slowly slipping out of the alley with a final, lingering glance.

The baker stood still for a moment, torn between chasing after Alex or the girls, or attending to the oven. Feeling the pressure of time, he made a swift decision and rushed toward the oven.

As he hurried along, Emmanuel found himself talking to himself, contemplating life's decisions and their consequences.

"Everyone has to make decisions in life and deal with the consequences. Oh well, if you keep talking to yourself like this, people are gonna think you're crazy."

Suddenly, a voice from the window called out, "Hey, thanks! You're right, man."

Emmanuel, scratching his head, responded, "What? I wasn't

talking to you!"

As the night came to an end and the sun began to rise, Emmanuel pondered the role of fate and decision-making, wondering if he had made the right choice in prioritizing the oven over chasing after Alex or finding the girls.

Glancing toward the counter, he found Alex's book, *Wonders of the World*. Reflecting on its importance to Alex, he contemplated the dawn of a new day and the events set in motion, juxtaposed with the closure of his own.

※

<u>**Lesson 3:**</u>
<u>**Setting and Achieving Your Goals**</u>

Setting clear goals empowers you to get what you want out of life. Without them, it's easy to drift aimlessly, hoping dreams will somehow come true if you wish hard enough. But experience shows that dreamers like us are more likely to succeed if we also get tactical. Defining concrete goals translates the change you imagine into achievable stages built step by step toward victory.

Break big challenges into small wins. Outline the milestones. Imagine and believe that you've achieved that "Heck yeah!" rush of checking off objectives, one by one. Momentum multiplies, creating motivation to tackle fiercer challenges.

Goals also help keep your focus when limited on time and resources. You can't do everything at once, though we find ourselves trying to all the time. Outlining the step-by-step battle plan spotlights the high-impact wins that are most urgent right now. If you find yourself lost, define your highest priorities and start with the most important tasks first. You don't need to know what's happening on social media if your house is on fire—this isn't fine.

Lastly, align your goals with your passion. Sync your targets with what makes you feel in harmony with joy, not with what impresses others. Integrate ambition with your values and essence. Living true to yourself, your goals become paths to freedom, not burdens.

Defining Clear Goals

Setting vague or ambiguous goals can hinder progress and leave one feeling lost or overwhelmed. To overcome this challenge, the practice of defining clear and specific goals allows one to navigate life's journey with clarity and purpose. In the pursuit of personal growth and success, setting clear and well-defined goals is paramount.

One effective approach is the SMART goal-setting framework. By applying this framework, you can formulate goals that increase the chances of successfully achieving them. The SMART framework stands for Specific, Measurable, Achievable, Relevant, and Time-Bound.

Goals defined using the SMART criteria tend to be not only inspiring but also practical and attainable. Utilizing this methodology empowers you to craft goals that provide both vision and direction to make consistent progress toward desired outcomes.

1. Specific

Specific goals are clear and focused, leaving no room for ambiguity. To create specific goals, ask yourself the following questions:

- What do you want to accomplish?
- Why is this goal important to you?
- Who else is involved or impacted by this goal?
- Where will you take action to achieve this goal?
- How will you approach and attain this goal?

Example: Instead of setting a vague goal like, "I want to be healthier," a specific goal would be, "I want to run a 10-kilometer race in six months and improve my overall fitness level by attending fitness classes at least three times a week."

2. Measurable

Measurable goals allow for tracking progress and assessing success. To make goals measurable, quantify and establish specific criteria to evaluate your progress.

- How will you measure your progress?
- What are the milestones or markers of success?
- How will you know when you have achieved the goal?

Example: A measurable goal could be "I want to increase my monthly sales revenue by 20% within the next quarter."

3. Achievable

While aiming high is admirable, it is essential to set achievable goals that align with your capabilities and resources. Consider the following questions:

- Is this goal realistic given your current circumstances?
- Do you have the necessary skills and resources to achieve this goal?
- What steps do you need to take to make this goal attainable?

Example: Instead of setting an unattainable goal like, "I want to become a professional tennis player in one year," an achievable goal would be, "I want to improve my tennis skills and participate in a local tennis tournament within six months."

4. Relevant

Relevance ensures that your goals align with your long-term aspirations and values. Reflect on the following:

- Does this goal align with your overall vision for your life or career?
- How does achieving this goal contribute to your personal growth or professional development?

Example: A relevant goal for someone aspiring to be a successful entrepreneur could be, "I want to launch and establish my own online e-commerce business within a year."

5. Time-bound

Setting a deadline for achieving your goals creates a sense of urgency and motivation. Consider the following:

- When do you want to achieve this goal?
- Is the timeframe reasonable and realistic?
- What actions can you take to stay on track and meet the deadline?

Example: A time-bound goal would be, "I want to write a book and have it published within two years."

By applying the SMART framework to your goal-setting process, you can clarify your aspirations and create a pathway for success. These clear and compelling goals will serve as beacons of inspiration, guiding you on your journey of personal growth and achievement.

Breaking Down Big Goals: Embracing Incremental Progress

When it comes to achieving our goals and aspirations, having a clear and effective action plan is like having a well-crafted roadmap that guides us toward success. Creating action plans involves developing a step-by-step strategy that outlines specific tasks, deadlines, and responsibilities needed to reach our desired objectives.

Envision your grand goal as an imposing mountain, seemingly insurmountable from a distance. However, just as climbers conquer peaks step by step, breaking down big goals into smaller, manageable steps empowers you to conquer your dreams.

Here's why it matters:

- Overcoming Overwhelm: The sheer scale of big goals can be overwhelming, leading to procrastination and stagnation. By dividing them into smaller tasks, you create a series of achievable milestones that motivate you to take action.

- Clear Progress Tracking: Smaller steps enable clear and tangible progress tracking. As you achieve each milestone, you gain a sense of accomplishment and momentum, fueling your determination to reach the next phase.

- Flexibility and Adaptability: Life is unpredictable, and circumstances may change. Breaking down goals makes it easier to adapt and adjust your action plan as needed while staying committed to your ultimate vision.

- Facilitating Collaboration: In team settings, breaking down big goals fosters better collaboration. Each team member can contribute to specific tasks, utilizing their expertise to achieve the objective.

Example: "Start Your Own Business"
Big Goal: Launching a successful business venture.
Breakdown into Smaller Steps:

1. Conduct market research and identify a niche or target audience.

2. Develop a comprehensive business plan, including financial projections and marketing strategies.

3. Register the business, secure permits, and set up legal and financial structures.

4. Create a website and develop an online presence.

5. Launch the business and initiate marketing campaigns to attract customers.

6. Regularly evaluate and adapt business strategies based on market feedback and performance.

An action plan is not set in stone; it is a dynamic process that evolves with your growth and experiences. Regularly review and adjust your plan, celebrate successes, and learn from challenges. Embrace the repetitive nature of execution, where each step draws you closer to your vision.

Creating action plans is not merely an exercise in planning but a journey of execution. It is in the decisions we make and the actions we take that dreams come alive and aspirations materialize into tangible realities. The power of execution lies in consistent, intentional effort toward your goals.

Accountability and Review

Having people to keep you on track helps reach goals. Consider an accountability buddy—maybe a friend or relative also working toward self-growth goals.

Agree to check in regularly to update progress and find motivation together. Meet weekly or monthly to celebrate small wins, troubleshoot hurdles, and feel that boost of responsibility.

Reviewing goals quarterly reinforces sticking to your aspirations. Re-evaluate the plans in place. Are they still realistic and aligned with what matters most? Tweak approaches if needed.

Recognize even small progress to feel encouraged. Analyze what obstacles arose to learn for next time. Use reviews to confirm you're living your values while pursuing growth.

No journey forward is linear. Expect changes requiring flexibility in strategies. With a balanced mindset embracing both adaptability and determination, you ready yourself to handle life's uncertainties while still creating the future you desire.

Surround yourself with positive influences. Check assumptions periodically. The path reveals itself step by step. You've got the tools and tenacity to achieve growth goals with guiding wisdom.

<u>Activity: Using SMART Goals</u>

Objective: Set and achieve daily personal goals using the SMART framework. Using a pen, pencil, computer or whatever you feel will be best for you, record the following for one day. If you find yourself needing more of a challenge, go for a week, a month, or even a year. You are in control of your life. Let's make it happen!

1. Identify a Specific Goal:
   - Daily Task: Each morning, choose one specific goal you want to achieve by the end of the day.
   - Example: "I want to write 500 words for my book today."

2. Make the Goal Measurable:
   - Daily Task: Define how you will measure your progress and know when you've achieved your goal.
   - Example: "I will write 500 words and track my word count in my writing software."

3. Ensure the Goal is Achievable:
   - Daily Task: Assess if this goal is realistic given your current schedule and resources.
   - Example: "I have two hours free today, which is enough time to write 500 words."

4. Check for Relevance:
   - Daily Task: Make sure the goal aligns with your larger objectives and passions.
   - Example: "Writing 500 words today helps me stay on track to complete my book by the deadline."

5. Set a Time-bound Deadline:
   - Daily Task: Set a specific time by which you will achieve this goal today.
   - Example: "I will write 500 words between 2 PM and 4 PM today."

Daily Goal-Setting Worksheet:

Morning:

1. Goal:
   - Write down your specific goal for the day.

2. Measurement:
   - Describe how you will measure success.

3. Achievability:
   - Assess if the goal is realistic.

4. Relevance:
   - Ensure the goal aligns with your larger objectives.

5. Time-bound:
   - Set a deadline.

Evening:

1. Review:
   - Did you achieve your goal?
   -

2. Reflection:
   - What worked well?

3. Adjustments:
   - What could be improved for tomorrow?

Accountability and Review:

1. Find an Accountability Partner:
   - Daily Task: Share your daily goal with a friend or family member.

2. Regular Check-Ins:
   - Weekly Task: Meet or call your accountability partner weekly to discuss progress.

3. Quarterly Review:
   - Quarterly Task: Every three months, review your goals and progress.

Final Notes:

- Flexibility: Adjust goals as needed based on daily circumstances.

- Celebrate Success: Reward yourself for achieving your goals to stay motivated.

- Continuous Improvement: Use reflections to improve your goal-setting and achieving process.

By following these detailed steps daily, you can effectively set and achieve your goals, integrating the SMART framework into your everyday life for consistent personal growth and success.

●

In this lesson, we learned about the significance of setting and achieving goals to provide direction and purpose in life. Without clear goals, it's easy to drift aimlessly, hoping dreams will materialize without concrete plans. By defining specific goals, dreams can be broken into actionable steps, creating small wins that build momentum and motivation. This focus is crucial, especially when time and resources are limited, as it helps prioritize high-impact tasks. Goals should resonate with your personal passions and values, ensuring they are fulfilling rather than burdensome.

A vital aspect of goal-setting is clarity. Vague goals can hinder progress, while clear goals offer a sense of purpose and direction. The SMART framework (Specific, Measurable, Achievable, Relevant, Time-bound) is an effective tool for this purpose. Specific goals are clear and focused, leaving no room for ambiguity. Measurable goals allow for tracking progress and assessing success. Achievable goals are realistic, considering current circumstances and resources. Relevant goals align with long-term aspirations and values. Time-bound goals set deadlines, creating a sense of urgency.

To achieve these goals, creating detailed action plans with specific steps and deadlines is essential. Breaking down big goals into manageable steps prevents overwhelm and enables clear progress tracking. Accountability and regular reviews are also crucial in maintaining focus and adaptability. Engaging an accountability partner and conducting regular check-ins help stay on track.

Incorporating the SMART framework into daily routines can be facilitated through practical activities. Setting daily personal goals using the SMART criteria and reviewing them at the end of the day ensures continuous progress. Engaging an accountability partner for support and regular check-ins further reinforces commitment to achieving these goals. By consistently applying these strategies, you can effectively achieve personal growth and success.

<u>Chapter 4: Sunflower Express</u>

As the Sunflower Express began to move once more through the mountain tracks, Harry, a seasoned traveler with a penchant for storytelling, found himself in the company of fellow passengers winding down after an evening of unforgettable entertainment. Harry sat comfortably in his plush armchair, theatrically recalling the tale of Lorelei. His rich baritone voice filled the room, captivating his audience with every word.

"Once upon a time, in the heart of the Rhine Valley, there lived a young woman named Lorelei," Harry began. "She was known for her beauty and enchanting voice that could captivate anyone who heard it."

A guest leaned forward, her eyes filled with curiosity. "Oh, a tale of love and music! How enchanting."

Harry nodded. "Indeed, it is a story of love... and heartbreak. Lorelei fell deeply in love with a young man whom her family disapproved of. They wanted her to marry someone from a wealthy family, but her heart belonged to another. This forbidden love tormented her."

Harry took a heavy breath and continued, "And so, Lorelei found herself torn between her family's expectations and her heart's desires. The weight of the world seemed to bear down on her, and she felt trapped in a loveless life."

"As the pressure mounted, Lorelei's heart broke into a million pieces," Harry added, "and in her despair, she climbed to the highest cliffs overlooking the river."

Another guest leaned in, intrigued by the tragic turn of events. "Oh no, don't tell me..."

"With tears streaming down her face, Lorelei sang a hauntingly beautiful song that echoed through the valley," Harry continued. "Her voice held the pain of a thousand broken hearts, and it reached the ears of sailors passing by on the river."

With each word, Harry painted vivid images of the Rhine Valley. He described the cliffs standing tall and proud, the moon casting a gentle glow upon the waters below. The haunting melodies of Lorelei echoed in the narrative, creating an atmosphere that transcended the confines of the lavish train car.

"Legend has it that her song had a magical allure, captivating sailors and causing them to lose focus on navigating the treacherous waters," Harry explained. "The ships would crash against the rocks, and the sailors would meet their doom."

A young woman gasped. "Oh, how tragic! Her heartbreak became her curse."

Harry nodded. "Indeed, the heartbroken maiden became a mythical figure, forever bound to the cliffs, luring sailors to their fate with her enchanting voice."

As Harry's tale of Lorelei ended, the atmosphere in the train car was filled with a sense of wonder and sadness. The guests sat in silence, each lost in their thoughts, contemplating the tragic beauty of the story.

Meanwhile, in his sleeper cabin, Alex sat alone, shirtless, deeply engrossed in a game of solitaire. The cards were spread out before him, and he methodically flipped and arranged them, his bare chest glistening with a thin layer of sweat.

Lost in thought, Alex didn't notice the passage of time until he heard the sound of heavy footsteps echoing down the hallway outside his door. The footsteps were accompanied by hearty laughter.

Curious, Alex set aside his cards and stood up, moving closer to the door to listen. He could hear snippets of Harry's conversation with someone, though the words were indistinct. Suddenly, the laughter stopped, and there was a brief pause before Harry entered his cabin and fell asleep.

With tired hands, Alex decided to wash up in the small sink provided in his cabin, the warm water offering a brief respite from the day's fantastical journey. He glanced at his wrangled shirt, which he had worn throughout the past day, now a disaster from his adventure, and decided to hang it up to dry overnight after cleaning it thoroughly.

Carefully, Alex draped the shirt over the back of a chair, positioning it near the open window to catch the faint breeze drifting in from outside. He watched for a moment as the fabric swayed gently in the breeze. It reminded him of his birthday celebration in that enchanting city of Venice, where the ancient charm and shimmering waterways made it feel like a scene from a fairy tale. He remembered the breeze coming through the window while bed bugs bit him throughout the night. It was an uncomfortable memory, but the breeze was relaxing nonetheless.

With a yawn, Alex settled back into bed, the exhaustion of the day finally catching up with him. He closed his eyes and drifted off into a deep, peaceful slumber, the distant rumble of the train a comforting lullaby.

As dawn broke, Alex stirred from his sleep. He blinked for a second, and with fluid grace, he rose from the bed and approached his only set of clothes, neatly folded on the seat beside him. His lean, muscular frame moved with natural ease as he reached for the garments one by one, each piece triggering a flood of memories from his adventures across foreign lands.

The worn, leather boots reminded him of his hike through the rugged mountains of Switzerland, where he encountered breathtaking vistas and made lifelong friends while briefly visiting a culinary school. The faded jeans, with their frayed edges and well-worn patches, carried the stories of long walks through the cobblestone streets of Florence and nights spent dancing in the vibrant clubs of Amsterdam.

But as Alex reached for his shirt, his heart sank. The once-crisp white fabric was still damp, clinging to the back of the chair. He realized that it wouldn't be dry in time for breakfast, and a wave of frustration washed over him. Unsure of what to do, Alex stepped out into the hallway, leaving his cabin door open behind him. He leaned against the wall, watching the landscape pass by as the sun peeked over the horizon. The beauty and glory of the day temporarily eased his concerns, and he took a deep breath while staring directly into the rising sun.

Just then, the door to Harry's room opened, and the older gentleman emerged, looking refreshed and ready to face the day. He spotted Alex and approached him with a large smile.

"Good morning, young man," Harry greeted him, his eyes filled with curiosity. "I couldn't help but notice your absence of a shirt. Is everything alright?"

Alex chuckled, lifting off his hat and running a hand through his tousled, chestnut-colored hair. "Last night there was a solitaire tournament, I lost my shirt," he said jokingly, trying to mask his embarrassment as he put his hat back on his head.

Harry raised an eyebrow, amused by Alex's wit. "Ah, the perils of late-night single-player card games," he replied with a grin.

Alex's smile faded slightly as he confessed, "In truth, my shirt is still drying in my room and I have no spare clothes. I'm afraid it's in quite a sorry state from what I went through yesterday."

Harry nodded, his expression softening. "Well, that simply won't do. A young man like yourself can't be wandering around without a proper shirt on this beautiful Sunday morning," he declared. "Come, I have just the solution. Let me fetch you a spare from my own collection."

Before Alex could protest, Harry disappeared back into his cabin, leaving him standing in the hallway, surprised by the older man's kindness. Moments later, Harry returned, holding a brightly colored Hawaiian shirt, complete with a bold floral pattern and a few strategically placed pink flamingos.

"Here you are, my boy," he said gallantly, handing the shirt to Alex. "I picked this up during my travels to the tropics. It's guaranteed to turn heads and put a smile on everyone's face."

Alex took the shirt, a mix of gratitude and amusement on his face. He slipped it on, the vibrant colors a stark contrast to his usual attire.

"Thank you, Harry," he said, chuckling at his own reflection in the window. "I'll be the talk of the dining car."

"That's the spirit!" Harry exclaimed, clapping Alex on the back. "Now, let's head to breakfast, shall we? I have a feeling you have quite the story to tell about how you found yourself with no proper shirt aboard the illustrious Sunflower Express."

This luxury locomotive required reservations far in advance and catered exclusively to discerning guests. This was certainly an elevated experience compared to the budget overnight trains Alex had become accustomed to—worn seats, flickering lights, and the perpetual drafts from cracked windows. But Alex had mastered the art of making any hard surface feel comfortable enough, using his backpack as a pillow and balling up his jacket to block cool air.

With a nod of thanks to Harry, the two men made their way to the dining car, the aroma of freshly brewed coffee and warm pastries filling the air. Upon entering, the other passengers couldn't help but notice Alex's eye-catching shirt, their faces breaking into smiles and laughter. Alex and Harry settled into their seats, the atmosphere light and cheerful.

Harry, his eyes still sparkling with the remnants of sleep, offered Alex a friendly smile. "I must say, I'm quite looking forward to this breakfast. There's something about dining on a train that just feels so... civilized."

Alex nodded, returning the smile with a touch of nervousness. "I know what you mean. It's, uh, something I'm not very used to, that's for sure."

Alex leaned back in his seat and looked at Harry with genuine curiosity. "So, Harry, before I tell my story, what's yours? What brings you aboard the famous Sunflower Express?"

Harry leaned back, a distant stare and a partial smile painting his face. "Ah, my wife has run away from me for a second time... I'm such a lucky man!"

Alex raised an eyebrow, a grin forming on his face. "Lucky?"

Harry laughed deeply, a touch of irony in his voice. "Indeed. There's a peculiar charm in the unpredictability of life—it keeps me on my toes. But, you see, after a lifetime of responsibilities and prestige, my wife decided it was time to rediscover herself, again. So, off she went, to some far-off land."

He chuckled for a second, then continued, "I decided to spend my time seeking meaning as well, and where else to unwind and contemplate than aboard the world-renowned Sunflower Express?"

Alex couldn't help but nod in understanding. "Sounds like quite the time."

Harry waved a hand dismissively. "Oh, nothing too extraordinary. Now your turn. I'm sure your tale has more twists and turns than a mystery novel." Just then, a neatly dressed waiter appeared at their table, his posture impeccable.

"Good morning, gentlemen," he said, his voice smooth and cultured. "May I offer you something to drink to start your day?"

Harry glanced at the menu, his eyebrows raising in appreciation. "Oh, a cup of coffee would be perfect. Black, please."

The waiter nodded, jotting down the order on his notepad. "Excellent choice, sir. And for you, sir?" he asked, turning to Alex.

Alex, still feeling a bit out of his element, cleared his throat. "I'll have the same, please. Black coffee... Oh, you know what? I'll have some orange juice too, please."

The waiter smiled, tucking his notepad into his apron. "Very good, gentlemen. I'll have your two black coffees and orange juice out in just a moment. I've also taken the liberty of bringing you our breakfast menus. Our chef has prepared a delightful selection of dishes for your enjoyment this morning."

The waiter placed a leather-bound menu in front of each of them, the pages crisp and inviting. "Please, take your time perusing the options." With a slight bow, the waiter glided away, leaving Alex and Harry to explore the culinary delights on offer.

Harry opened his menu, his eyes widening in appreciation. "Well, would you look at that? Eggs Benedict, Belgian waffles, a full English breakfast... I must say, I'm impressed by the variety today."

Alex squinted at the menu open in front of him. "It all looks so delicious. I don't even know where to begin."

He scanned the pages, his mouth watering at the descriptions of fluffy omelets, crispy bacon, and fresh fruit. But as he continued reading, his mind couldn't help but wander back to the story he was just beginning to tell.

"You know," he said, looking up at Harry with a slight smile, "as tempting as all of this looks, I have to admit... my appetite has been a bit off since yesterday. With everything that's happened..." He trailed off, his gaze growing distant.

Harry set down his menu, his expression one of genuine concern. "I can only imagine, Alex. From what little I've seen so far, it looks like you've been through quite an ordeal."

Alex hesitated for a moment, unsure of how much to reveal to this relative stranger. But there was something about Harry's warm, inviting demeanor that put him at ease. And after all, he thought to himself, if you can't share your story with someone, is it really a story at all?

"Well," he began, taking a deep breath, "it all started yesterday morning, when I received a phone call that would change my life forever. I had been crashing at my friend's dorm room for a few days. I had plans on going back to this Italian town where everyone lives in caves and makes wine," Alex said, his voice carrying the weight of the early morning. "But instead, I got this phone call from my dad telling me that my last surviving grandparents—my dad's parents—had both passed away suddenly in their sleep, and I need to rush back to Everbrook for the funeral. I'm set to inherit their cottage. I guess life's funny that way."

Harry nodded, his expression sympathetic. "I'm sorry for your loss, Alex. Losing loved ones is never easy."

"Thank you, Harry," Alex said, offering a small smile. "I knew I had to get back home as quickly as possible to sort out the inheritance and attend the funeral. The airport where I'm supposed to depart is like 12 hours away. So, I gathered my clothes into one big sack and rushed to the tiny local train platform. On the way, I downed two espressos, hoping the caffeine would keep me alert and focused."

Alex paused, looking out the train window at endless rows of sunflowers. "When I arrived at the platform, I was buzzing with energy. The caffeine coursed through my veins, making me feel invincible. But that's when I realized I desperately needed to use the bathroom. I ran around the platform to the men's room and knocked on the door, hoping it would be unoccupied. To my surprise, a voice from inside the men's room responded, 'I'm... thinking.'"

Alex scratched his forehead and then his eyebrow, recounting the peculiar encounter. "I couldn't believe it. Who responds with 'I'm thinking' when someone knocks on the bathroom door?"

Harry laughed heartily, shaking his head in amusement. "Perhaps he was pondering the mysteries of life while attending to his business."

Alex chuckled, the tension easing from his shoulders. "Desperate times call for desperate measures, so I decided to try my luck with the women's room. I knocked on the door, hoping for a more accommodating response. To my dismay, a voice from inside the women's room called out, 'Don't try to come in... especially if you don't need to use the bathroom!'"

Harry burst into laughter, his eyes crinkling at the corners. "Oh, my boy, it seems the universe was conspiring against your bladder that day."

Alex grinned, shaking his head at the absurdity of the situation. "It was more than just my bladder, Harry! At that point, I decided my best option was to board the train and hope for an available restroom onboard. This was an emergency! So, I dashed into the nearest car just as the doors were closing."

Harry leaned in, his curiosity piqued. "And did you find relief on the train?"

Alex nodded, a hint of mischief in his eyes. "I did, but that's when things took an unexpected turn. As I exited the bathroom, I noticed a man checking tickets. It suddenly dawned on me that in my haste, I had completely forgotten to purchase a ticket."

Harry's eyes widened, anticipating the next part of the story. "Oh, dear. That must have been quite the predicament."

Alex leaned forward, glancing through the menu. "You know, Harry, the cops are the same everywhere. They don't care; they've got a job to do. What are you gonna do when they come for you?"

Harry closed his menu, understanding the sentiment. "Ah, the eternal struggle between authority and the individual. It's a tale as old as time."

Alex took a deep breath, the memory of the encounter still vivid in his mind. "I tried to avoid the ticket checker by walking toward the back of the train, hoping to find a place to hide. And as luck would have it, I found a nice empty room at the very back. I tried to hide myself as best I could, and I must've napped for about an hour. But I was abruptly woken up from a strange dream—the ticket checker patted me on the shoulder and demanded to see my ticket."

Harry leaned back in his seat, his expression a mix of sympathy and amusement. "I can only imagine the panic you must have felt in that moment. You tried so hard not to get caught!"

Just then, the attentive waiter returned to their table, a silver tray balanced expertly on his hand. With an elaborate style, he set down two steaming cups of coffee, the rich aroma wafting up to greet them.

"Gentlemen," the waiter said, his voice smooth and professional, "I trust you've had a moment to look over our breakfast menu. May I take your order?"

Harry looked at Alex, who was still looking through the menu before looking back at the waiter. "You know, everything looks so tempting. But I think I'll go with the classic Eggs Benedict. There's just something about that combination of poached eggs, Canadian bacon, and hollandaise sauce that never fails to hit the spot."

The waiter stood in agreement, jotting down the order on his notepad. "An excellent choice, sir. And for you, sir?" he asked, turning to Alex.

Alex, still a bit lost in thought from the story he was recounting, took one more moment to focus on the menu. "I'll have the Belgian waffles, please. With a side of fresh fruit and a dollop of whipped cream."

"Very good, sir," the waiter said, his pen flying across the page. "I'll put those orders in right away. Is there anything else I can get for you in the meantime?"

Harry and Alex exchanged a glance, each shaking their head. "No, I think we're all set for now," Harry said, offering the waiter a grateful smile. "Thank you."

With a slight bow, the waiter tucked his notepad into his apron and walked to the table next to them, leaving the two men to their conversation.

●

Harry took a sip of his coffee, savoring the bold, slightly bitter flavor. "I have to say, Alex, you've got me hooked with this story of yours. I can't even imagine what it must have been like, getting caught by the ticket checker."

Alex wrapped his hands around his coffee cup. "Yeah, it was not pleasant. I tried to explain my situation, but the ticket man was having none of it. He gave me an ultimatum: either pay a hefty fine on the spot or be kicked off the train at the next stop. And to make matters worse, he confiscated my clothes as collateral and said I could come back in one week to get them."

Harry shook his head, marveling at the absurdity of the situation. "The audacity of that ticket man! Demanding your clothes as collateral?"

Alex shrugged. "I didn't have the money for the fine, and I couldn't afford to waste any more time. So, with a heavy heart, I surrendered my clothes and was forced off the train. I then found myself standing on the tiny train platform of a cozy little mountain town, wearing nothing but the clothes on my back and a bruised ego."

Harry reached across the table, grabbing a pack of sugar. "Ah yes, one thing I have learned through all these years is that the plight of man is his ignorance of his own self-destruction."

Alex nodded a few times, closing his eyes briefly and raising his hands slightly. "You're right, Harry. Little did I know, my journey was about to take an even stranger turn. With no money and no clothes, I spotted an ATM nearby and decided to withdraw some cash to buy a spare outfit and a train ticket."

Harry smiled, his eyes wide with anticipation. "And did the ATM cooperate?"

Alex laughed, shaking his head in disgust. "Quite the opposite, Harry. As soon as I inserted my card, the machine made a strange whirring noise and promptly swallowed it whole. I stared at the ATM for a good bit, then smacked all the buttons. I thought it would help, but it didn't. The machine kept making an awful mechanical noise. So, there I was, stranded in a foreign mountain town, with no money, no clothes, and now, no access to my funds. I had nothing!"

Harry couldn't help but chuckle at the absurdity of Alex's misfortune. "My boy, between the bathroom, the ticket checker, and now this, it seems the universe was determined to test you that day."

Alex took a sip of his coffee, a strange grin growing on his face. "Just when I thought all hope was lost, I heard the distant sounds of a circus coming from somewhere in the town. The laughter, the music, the sheer joy—it was like a beacon calling out to me."

Harry raised an eyebrow, intrigued by this new development. "A circus, you say? How delightfully unexpected!"

"I know, right?" Alex said, leaning forward. "I saw this man in a feathered hat quickly walking down the alley just next to me. I followed him as fast as I could, and soon enough I could hear the music getting louder—the calliope, the drums, the laughter. And the smells, Harry, you wouldn't believe it. Cotton candy, caramel apples, popcorn—it was like a feast for the senses."

Harry took another sip of his coffee, a smile playing at the corners of his mouth. "It sounds enchanting," he said. "Like something out of a dream."

"That's just it," Alex said, his eyes growing distant. "It was like a dream, but not entirely a good one. There was something about the circus that felt... off, somehow. Like it was calling to me, but not in a way that I could trust."

Harry frowned, setting his cup down on the table. "What do you mean?" he asked. "Did you have a bad feeling about it?"

Alex shook his head. "No, not exactly," he said. "It was more like... a sense of déjà vu, almost. Like, I had been there before, but I couldn't quite remember when or how. It was unsettling, but at the same time, I felt drawn to it. I couldn't resist its pull."

Alex paused for a moment, a nostalgic look in his eyes. "You know, when I was a kid, I always had this fascination with the circus. The allure of the unknown, the fantastical—it was like a siren call to my imagination. But at the same time, I had this preconception about carnival people."

Harry tilted his head, curious. "What do you mean?" he asked.

"Well," Alex said, with a slight frown. "Growing up, I wasn't normally allowed to play out past 9:00 PM. But when the circus came to town, I couldn't play out past 6:00 PM. My parents always said that carnival people were a different breed. They smoked, they drank—it was a whole different atmosphere than what I was used to. So, even though I was drawn to the circus, I also had this sense of... fear, I suppose."

Harry scooted his chair forward, an understanding dawning in his eyes. "So, when you heard the sounds of the circus that night..."

"...I was torn," Alex said, finishing Harry's sentence. "Part of me wanted to run towards it, to lose myself in the wonder and the magic. But another part of me held back, remembering all those warnings from my childhood."

Alex looked out the window at the sunflowers once more, his eyes sparkling with excitement as he turned to Harry to continue his tale. "So I thought to myself, this isn't an alien world, it's a world I've alienated myself from. I made a decision right there to keep going. I followed the sights and sounds of the circus, my heart pounding with anticipation. As I approached the entrance, I was greeted by the most peculiar pair of characters I'd ever laid eyes on."

Intrigued, Harry placed his hand on his chin. "Oh? Who were they?"

"Mimes," Alex said. "But not just any mimes. These two were dressed to the nines in crisp black and white suits, complete with little white napkins tucked neatly into every pocket imaginable. Atop their heads sat the most adorable little round hats, and in their hands, they each carried a smooth black cane with a white tip at the bottom."

Harry chuckled, shaking his head in amusement. "Mimes in suits overflowing with handkerchiefs? Now that's a sight I'd pay to see."

Alex laughed, his grin widening. "Trust me, it was quite the spectacle. But what really caught my attention was the way they moved. It was like they were gliding across the ground, their feet barely touching the earth. And their expressions—oh, Harry, you should have seen their faces!"

"What do you mean?" Harry asked, leaning in closer.

"Well, you know how mimes are supposed to be all serious and stoic?" Alex said, his eyes twinkling with glee. "Not these two. They were wide-eyed with exaggerated frowns, like they were constantly surprised by the world around them and sad at the same time. And the way they interacted with each other—it was like watching a silent comedy routine."

Harry scratched his neck. "They sound like quite the pair," he said. "Did you talk to them?"

Alex laughed, shaking his head. "Talk to them? Harry, they're mimes! They don't talk. But that didn't stop them from trying to communicate with me. As soon as they spotted me trying to leave, they started waving their arms around like windmills, pointing at the circus entrance and then back at me."

"What did you do?" Harry asked, glancing out the window at the river flowing through the rolling hills.

"Well, I tried to walk past them at first," Alex said, a meek look on his face. "I mean, I was there for the circus, not to play charades with a couple of mimes. But they were persistent. They kept stepping in front of me, blocking my path, their faces contorted into these exaggerated expressions of concern. I was just about to push past them and head into the circus when I heard a voice behind me."

Harry grabbed his coffee, his curiosity piqued. "A voice? Whose voice?"

"It was Jaffa," Alex said, adjusting himself in his seat. "Of course, I didn't know his name at the time. All I saw was this tall, slender man. He was the same man I chased down the alley. He wore a green hat with a feather in it, and his clothes had a whimsical, almost fairy-tale quality to them."

"He sounds like quite the character. So, what did he do?" Harry asked, taking a sip of his coffee.

"Well, he walked right up to those mimes and tapped them on the shoulder," Alex said, his eyes sparkling with amusement. "And let me tell you, Harry, the look on their faces—it was like they'd seen a ghost. They just froze, their mouths hanging open, their gloved hands hovering in mid-air."

Harry chuckled, shaking his head. "I can only imagine."

"But Jaffa, he just smiled at them and tipped his feathered hat," Alex continued. "And then he turned to me and said, 'My apologies for the interruption, sir. I am in a bit of a hurry, but I couldn't help but notice that you seem a bit lost. I'm Jaffa, the owner of this magnificent Traveling Circus, how might I be of assistance?'"

Harry set his cup down and wiped the sweat from his forehead with a napkin. "Lost? Did you tell him about your situation?"

Alex nodded. "

I did. I don't know why, but there was something about Jaffa that made me feel like... like I could trust him. So I told him everything —about losing my money and my clothes, about needing to get to Everbrook for my grandparents' funeral. We started walking away from those mimes and through the gates of the circus. And let me tell you, Harry, it was like stepping into another world entirely."

Alex grabbed his coffee and took a sip, letting the warmth spread through his body. "Jaffa led me through the entrance, his feet tapping out a rhythmic beat on the ground as we walked. He started to tell me about the circus, about the wonders and the dangers that lay ahead."

Harry's eyes grew wide, hanging on Alex's every word. "And what sort of wonders and dangers were those?"

Alex chuckled, a hint of mischief in his voice. "Well, that's when things started to get really interesting, Harry. Because as we were walking, Jaffa pointed to this big, colorful sign. And on that sign, in big, bold letters, were two words that would change my life forever... Circus Trials."

Harry's mouth dropped open, a shiver running down his spine. "Circus Trials? What on earth does that mean?"

Alex leaned forward, his hands waving in the air. "That's exactly what I asked Jaffa. And he just looked at me with this twinkling madness in his eyes."

Alex's voice dropped to a conspiratorial whisper. "He explained that the trials were four tasks, each varying in difficulty. Jaffa said that no ordinary person, in the history of the circus, had ever made it past the third trial. But then he looked me right in the eye and said, 'But you, my boy... I believe you have what it takes.'"

Alex bumped his coffee, spilling it over the edges. "And here's the kicker, Harry. Jaffa told me that if I could make it through all four trials, the reward would be more than enough to get me back home to Everbrook."

Alex shook his head, a delighted look on his face. "I couldn't believe it. Here I was, again, stranded in the middle of nowhere, with no money and no idea how I was going to get back home. And then, like some kind of twisted miracle, Jaffa appeared with an offer I couldn't refuse. I didn't hesitate. I shook Jaffa's hand, looked him right in the eye, and told him I was in. And just like that, my fate was sealed."

●

The train took a steep curve around the tracks, and the attentive waiter returned to their table, skillfully balancing a large tray holding their breakfast orders. The aroma of freshly prepared food filled the air, making both Alex and Harry's stomachs grumble in anticipation.

With an elegant motion around the bend, the waiter gently set down a plate in front of Harry. "For you, sir, our classic Eggs Benedict. Two perfectly poached eggs atop a bed of Canadian bacon and a toasted English muffin, drizzled with our signature hollandaise sauce."

Harry licked his lips in appreciation, taking in the sight of the beautifully presented dish. "This looks absolutely delightful, thank you.."

The waiter, with a graceful twist, turned to Alex. "And for you, sir, our Belgian waffles. Crisp, golden, and dusted with powdered sugar, served with a side of fresh, seasonal fruit, and a generous dollop of whipped cream."

Alex grinned, his mouth watering at the sight of the fluffy waffles and colorful fruit. "It's almost too pretty to eat. Almost."

The waiter chuckled, placing the plate in front of Alex with a flourish. "I assure you, sir, it tastes even better than it looks. Now, is there anything else I can get for you gentlemen at the moment? More coffee, perhaps?"

Harry and Alex exchanged a glance, each shaking their head. "Yes, sir, we'll take more coffee," Harry said, picking up his fork and knife. "This food should keep us fueled for quite some time."

With a slight bow, the waiter stepped back. "Very well, gentlemen. Please, enjoy your breakfast, and I'll be back shortly with more coffee for you two."

Harry took a bite of his Eggs Benedict, closing his eyes in bliss as the rich, creamy hollandaise mingled with the perfectly runny yolk of the poached egg.

"My goodness, Alex," he said, his voice muffled by the mouthful of food. "If the rest of our journey today is half as good as this breakfast, we're in for quite the treat."

Alex laughed, cutting into his waffles and spearing a piece with his fork. "I couldn't agree more, Harry. There's just something about dining on this train that makes it feel like we're part of some grand adventure."

Alex leaned back in his seat, his gaze growing distant as he vigorously chewed his waffles. "So, Jaffa led me deeper into the circus, through crowds of people, past the swirling lights and colors, until we came to a stop in front of a small red booth. Inside was a small line of people and a whole slew of barrels, each filled to the brim with water, and bobbing on the surface... dozens of shiny, red apples."

Harry continued eating, pausing briefly to say, "Wait, don't tell me..."

Alex frowned at the memory. "Yeah, you know it, bobbing for

apples. That was the first trial, the first step on the path back home. At the time, I thought it was just a silly game."

Harry's eyes widened, a flicker of understanding crossing his face. "But that's not all, is it? There was more to it than just that."

Alex shuddered, a piercing jab running through his body. "The water... it wasn't just water. When I got closer to it, I noticed it was murky and kind of dark, filled with swirling shadows that seemed to reach out and grab at me. And the apples... they weren't just apples. Some of them were gnarled and twisted, their skin sickly shades of red."

He closed his eyes, his voice dropping to a whisper. "But the worst part... the worst part were the faces I could see in my mind. The faces of everyone who had ever bobbed for those apples before me. I could see them in the water, their mouths open in silent screams, their eyes deep with terror."

Harry reached across the table, his hand coming to rest on Alex's arm. "My God," he breathed, his voice filled with horror. "That's... that's unspeakable."

Alex agreed, his eyes still closed. "I wanted to run, Harry. I wanted to turn and flee, to put as much distance between myself and that cursed tub of water as possible. But Jaffa... Jaffa just smiled. I closed my eyes, took a deep breath, and plunged my face into the water. The cold was a shock, but it was nothing compared to the feeling of those apples, those twisted, unnatural things, brushing against my skin."

"I grabbed an apple," Alex said, his voice shaking slightly. "I felt my teeth sink into its skin, felt the sickly sweet juice flood my mouth. And then... then I was pulled under. The water closed over my head as I tried to keep the grip of the apple in my mouth, and suddenly I was in another place, another time. It all happened so incredibly fast. I saw flashes of my life, moments I had forgotten, or tried to forget. I saw my parents, their faces twisted with disappointment. I saw my childhood home, empty and abandoned. I saw all the mistakes I had made, all the opportunities I had squandered."

He took a deep breath, his gaze focusing on the untouched orange juice in front of him. "Just when I thought I couldn't take it anymore, just when I thought I would drown in that darkness, I felt a hand on my shoulder. It was Jaffa, pulling me out of the water, with that same smile on his face."

Harry's forehead creased. "He was smiling? After what you had just been through?"

Alex looked straight at Harry, a humorless laugh escaping his lips. "Oh yes, he was smiling. 'Congratulations,' Jaffa said, 'You've completed the first trial. You've got a good apple, and now you're one step closer to your prize. But I'm afraid I must take my leave. I have some urgent business to attend to. But fear not, my boy. I am leaving you in good hands.'"

Harry raised an eyebrow, curious. "He just left you there? In the middle of the circus?"

"Not exactly," Alex said. "He said something that made me feel a little better. He said that he had arranged for his three best circus helpers to guide me the rest of the way. Three kids, each with their own unique talents and personalities, who would be my guides through the remainder of the Circus Trials."

Alex chuckled, remembering the moment. "I have to admit, I was a little skeptical at first. I mean, kids? How much help could they really be? But Jaffa assured me that these were no ordinary kids. They were the cream of the crop, the best of the best, and they would stop at nothing to help me succeed. And then Jaffa did something unexpected. He reached up, took off his feathered hat, and placed it on my head."

Harry's mouth dropped. "His hat? Why on earth would he do that?"

Alex shrugged, a bemused expression on his face. "I asked him the same thing, Harry. And he just looked at me with that twinkle in his eye and said, 'Every great adventurer needs a signature look, my boy. And I have a feeling you're going to be a legend in the making.' I have to admit, Harry... in that moment, wearing Jaffa's hat... I felt different. Like I was stepping into a role, becoming someone new."

Alex took a deep breath, his expression growing serious. "Just as I was settling into my new role as the adventurer with the feathered hat... Jaffa disappeared."

Harry blinked, surprised. "Disappeared? Just like that?"

"Just like that," Alex said. "One moment he was there, grinning at me like a Cheshire Cat... and the next, he was gone. He vanished into thin air, like a magic trick. And just as soon as Jaffa left, Harry, the kids showed up. I knew I was in for the adventure of a lifetime as soon as I saw them."

Harry shoveled food into his mouth before saying, "Well, now I must know more about these kids!"

Alex took a bite of his waffles and continued, "They were like nothing I had ever seen before. Each one was a different age, with their own quirky style and energy. The oldest was a lanky teenager with a mop of curly hair and a serious look in his eye. The middle one was a spunky girl with pigtails and a smile that could light up the whole circus. And the youngest was a little boy with wide, curious eyes and a skip in his step that made me feel like anything was possible."

Harry shook his head in amusement. "They sound like quite the trio."

"Oh, they were," Alex agreed, grinning. "And the way they moved, it was like they were filled with this crazy, infectious energy. They were bouncing, skipping, and twirling, and came running up to me, their faces split wide with smiles and their eyes shining with excitement. It was like they had been waiting their whole lives to show me around the circus, like they couldn't contain their excitement."

He cleared his throat and pitched his voice higher, imitating the children's excited chatter. "'Oh, you must be Alex!' they all said, bouncing up and down like they were on springs. 'You're going to love the circus, there's so much to see and do! Come, come with us!'"

Harry laughed hard, his voice bellowing through the dining car. "They sound absolutely delightful, and your impression is fantastic!"

"They were," Alex said, taking another big bite of his waffle, barely chewing it before swallowing. "The oldest kid, the one with the curly hair, had these lights attached to his shoes. Every time he took a step, they would flash and change color, leaving this trail of rainbow footprints behind him. The middle kid, the girl with the pigtails, had them woven into her hair like some kind of crazy, futuristic crown. And the youngest, the little boy with the wide eyes, had them sewn onto his jacket, turning him into a walking, talking kaleidoscope. They grabbed my hands and pulled me deeper into the circus, their laughter and chatter filling the air."

Harry's face lightened, trying to picture the spectacle. "That must have been quite the sight."

Alex took a sip of his coffee and said, "I was so caught up in the lights and the colors and the sheer, unbridled excitement of those kids, I barely even noticed where we were going. It was like I was in some kind of trance, letting them lead me wherever they wanted to go. And before I knew it, we were standing next to a large stage. The kids were bouncing on the balls of their feet, their lights flashing faster and faster with anticipation. 'This is it,' they told me, their voices hushed with excitement. 'The magic show. You won't believe your eyes.'"

Just as Alex was about to delve deeper into his story, the attentive waiter suddenly appeared at their table, a steaming pot of coffee in hand.

"Pardon the interruption, gentlemen," the waiter said, a polite smile on his face. "Would you still like a refill of coffee?"

Alex, momentarily caught off guard, glanced down at his nearly empty cup. "Oh, yes, please," he said, nodding appreciatively as the waiter filled his cup.

Harry, equally engrossed in Alex's tale, held out his own cup for a refill. "Thank you," he said, offering the waiter a grateful smile.

With a final nod, the waiter took a step back, the coffee pot still in hand. "If you gentlemen need anything else, please don't hesitate to let me know. I'll be just a signal away."

Alex and Harry both said their thanks, and the waiter glided away, leaving them to the story that hung in the air between them.

●

Alex took a sip of his freshly poured coffee, savoring the rich, invigorating flavor. "Now, where was I?" he mused, setting his cup back down on the saucer.

Harry looked intently at Alex, eager to hear more. "You were just about to tell me about the magic show the kids led you to."

"Ah, yes," Alex said, reaching into his memory. "What I saw on that stage... it defied all explanation. It was like the laws of physics had been thrown out the window, replaced with something altogether more wild and unpredictable."

Harry twirled his fork on his plate and said, "What happened on the stage, Alex? What did you see?"

Alex shoved a few more bites of his food into his mouth with excitement as he recalled the magic show. "The kids led me to a front-row seat, their faces split wide with anticipation. 'Watch closely,' they whispered to me, their voices hushed with excitement. 'You don't want to miss a single trick.'"

Harry barely blinked, his own curiosity piqued. "I can only imagine what kind of tricks a circus magician might have up his sleeve."

"Oh, you have no idea," Alex said with a grin on his face. "The magician, he was like no one I had ever seen before. He had this presence about him, this air of mystery and power that made the whole crowd go silent the moment he stepped on stage. He was dressed in all black, from his top hat to his polished shoes, and his eyes... they seemed to shimmer with some kind of otherworldly light."

He took another sip of his coffee to help swallow the barely chewed waffles in his mouth. "The show started off simple enough. He did a few card tricks, pulled a rabbit out of his hat, that sort of thing. But then... then things started to get weird."

Harry raised an eyebrow, intrigued. "Weird how?"

"Well, for starters, he made his assistant levitate," Alex said, his voice filled with wonder. "Not just a few inches off the ground, either. She was floating a good three feet in the air, her body rigid and her eyes closed like she was in some kind of trance. The magician, he walked around her, waving his hands like he was controlling her with some kind of invisible strings."

Harry's eyes widened, trying to picture the scene. "That's incredible. How do you think he did it?"

"I have no idea," Alex admitted, shaking his head. "But that was just the beginning. Next, he made a flock of doves appear out of nowhere, their wings flashing silver in the light of the stage. They flew above us in perfect formation, creating these intricate patterns in the air like they were dancing to some unheard music."

Alex leaned back in his seat, a faraway look in his eyes. "But the real showstopper... that was the finale. The magician, he brought out this huge, ornate mirror, its obsidian frame covered in strange, arcane symbols. He told the audience that it was a portal to another dimension, a gateway to a place where the impossible became possible."

Harry looked deeply at Alex, his voice hushed with anticipation.

"And then what happened?"

"He stepped through it," Alex said simply, his voice filled with awe. "One moment he was there, the next... he was gone. The mirror rippled like water, and then... nothing. Just an empty stage and a stunned audience. The kids, they were beside themselves with excitement. They kept tugging on my sleeve, whispering in my ear about how I had just witnessed the greatest magic trick of all time. But me... I couldn't shake this feeling that what I had seen was more than just a trick. It was like... like I had glimpsed something real, something that defied all explanation."

Harry's head moved slowly up and down, a look of understanding on his face. "I can see why that would stick with you. It's not every day you see a man walk into a mirror and disappear."

"No, it's not," Alex agreed, a humorous smile spreading from ear to ear. "After the magic show, the kids led me out and around the circus, chattering excitedly about the trial that awaited me. 'The Juggling Jester,' they said, 'It's the second trial, but it's the third hardest in the whole circus!'"

Harry crossed his arms in curiosity. "The Juggling Jester? That sounds... intriguing."

Alex laughed, shaking his head. "Oh, it was more than intriguing, Harry. It was downright bizarre. When we got there, the tent was decked out in this crazy orange color, so bright it almost hurt your eyes to look at it. And in the center of the room... there was this huge, grinning jester, its face painted half black and half white. The kids, they were circling around me, each one holding a jack-in-the-box with a look on their face that made me more than a little nervous."

Harry waved his right hand in the air, imagining the scene. "I can picture it now. Those little rascals, always up to something."

Alex took another bite of his waffles, lost in the memory for a moment. "The jack-in-the-boxes in their hands were each painted with beautiful multi-colored patterns. They told me that to win the trial, I had to juggle all three boxes at once until the song was over, and I wasn't allowed to drop any of them. They started winding up the boxes, cranking the handles faster and faster until the whole tent was filled with this crazy, discordant music."

Alex took some whipped cream and lathered up one of the last remaining pieces of his waffle, savoring the recollection. "And then... they threw them at me. All at once, like some kind of coordinated attack. I barely had time to react before the boxes were flying through the air, straight towards my head."

Harry's arms uncrossed and he said, "They threw them at you? That sounds dangerous!"

"It was," Alex said, "But I didn't have time to think. I just reacted on instinct, my hands reached out to grab the boxes before they could clock me in the face. And then... I started juggling."

Alex leaned back in his seat, his voice growing animated. "It was like my body was moving on its own, my hands tossing and catching the boxes in this crazy, frenzied rhythm. The music was getting louder and louder, and I could feel the vibrations running up my arms with every catch."

Harry shook his head, impressed. "That's some quick reflexes you've got there, Alex."

"I surprised myself, honestly. I didn't think I could do it," Alex said, a note of pride in his voice. "As I juggled, the kids started to circle around me. They were chanting and laughing under their breath, like they were talking in some kind of strange, otherworldly language that I couldn't understand. But then... something strange happened. As I juggled, I started to feel this weird sensation in my gut, like a kind of... I don't know, like a kind of energy building up inside me. It was like the boxes were feeding off my own strength, getting lighter and easier to handle with every toss."

Harry took a sip of his coffee, a look of understanding on his face. "It sounds like you found your groove, you were in the zone, right?"

"I did, I was in the zone, man," Alex agreed. "And that's when things really got crazy. The music... it shifted and became something darker and more intense, like the soundtrack to a fever dream."

Alex took another deep breath, his voice growing more excited. "And all of a sudden... boing! The jack-in-the-boxes went off. All at once, like some kind of crazy, synchronized explosion. The lids flew open, and out popped these... these faces. Jester faces, half smiling, half frowning, like they couldn't decide whether to laugh or cry as they swayed around."

Alex glanced out the train car window, a satisfied smile on his face. "The kids... they were beside themselves with joy. They kept hugging me and patting me on the back, telling me I had passed the trial with... 'flying colors.'"

Harry laughed out loud. "That's incredible, Alex. I can't even imagine what that must have felt like."

"It was... it was indescribable," Alex said softly, his eyes distant. "But it was more than just the thrill of winning. It was like... like I had tapped into something deep inside myself, some kind of primal energy that I never even knew I had. I actually thought when I started juggling that I would never be able to do it, but..."

As Alex continued to weave his tale, the train suddenly plunged into darkness. The soft, ambient light of the dining car was swiftly replaced by the inky black of a tunnel, the only illumination coming from a few small, strategically placed lamps along the walls.

The sudden change in atmosphere caused Alex to pause mid-sentence, his words trailing off as he looked up, momentarily disoriented. Harry, too, glanced around, his eyes adjusting to the dim lighting.

●

"Well, that was unexpected," Harry remarked, a slight chuckle in his voice. "It seems even the train itself wants to add a bit of drama to your story."

Alex continued, "So, that was weird. Anyways, after the Juggling Jester trial, the kids led me out of the orange tent and into the main thoroughfare of the circus. The air was thick with the scent of popcorn and cotton candy, and the sounds of laughter and music filled my ears. But the kids, they were absolutely bursting with energy. They practically dragged me through the circus, pointing out all the different attractions and booths. But the one that really caught my eye was the Hall of Oddities."

Harry leaned forward, his interest piqued. "The Hall of Oddities? That sounds intriguing."

Alex rubbed his palms together and said, "The kids were practically vibrating with anticipation as they pushed open the door and ushered me inside. The first thing that hit me was the smell. It was like burnt rubber, this thick, syrupy scent of dust and decay, mixed with something else... something sharper, like formaldehyde or chemicals. The room was dimly lit, with only a few flickering lights casting strange shadows on the walls."

Harry sipped his coffee. "What kind of oddities were in there?"

"Oh, where do I even begin?" Alex said, a hint of wonder in his voice. "The exhibits were strange, unlike anything I'd ever seen before. There was a two-headed calf floating in a jar, a collection of shrunken heads, even a mummified merman that looked like it had been pulled straight from a nightmare."

Alex paused, placing his hands to his forehead. "But the kids, they were loving it. They were running from exhibit to exhibit, pointing and laughing at the oddities on display. And at first, I have to admit... I was right there with them. They were cracking jokes and making these awful puns the whole time we were in there. Pointing at the specimens and saying things like, 'I bet he's got a bone to pick with us!' or 'Looks like she's in a pickle!' And finally, 'Is that a human or a chicken dumpling?'"

Harry couldn't help but chuckle, shaking his head in disbelief. "A chicken dumpling? Oh, that's brilliant. Kids, huh? Always finding the humor in things. Sometimes, laughter is the best way to cope with the things that scare us."

Alex agreed. "But something changed. We came to this exhibit— a display of vintage circus posters featuring sideshow performers. The Bearded Lady, the Human Skeleton, the Conjoined Twins... they were all there, staring out at us from the faded pages of history. And that's when it hit me, Harry. These weren't just oddities or freaks to be gawked at. They were people—human beings with hopes and dreams and fears, just like the rest of us."

Harry adjusted his chair and looked off to the side. "It's easy to forget that. To get caught up in the spectacle and the strangeness, and lose sight of the humanity behind it all. We are all the same, everyone's always searching for something."

"Exactly," Alex agreed. He looked down at his hands, his voice heavy with regret. "And in that moment, standing there in front of those posters, I felt ashamed. Ashamed of my own ignorance and insensitivity."

The train emerged from the tunnel just as suddenly as it had entered, the bright light of day flooding the dining car once more. Alex and Harry blinked, their eyes adjusting to the change in light, a moment of introspection passing as quickly as it had arrived.

Alex continued, "After the Hall of Oddities, the kids kept going on about the next trial, how it would be the ultimate test of my strength and determination. Nobody has passed the third trial—a feat of strength."

He grabbed his glass of orange juice, untouched until now, his face growing serious. "The kids led me to another large tent, its canvas a bright and bold yellow. Inside, there was this huge arena, with a giant circular platform in the center."

"What kind of feat of strength was it?" Harry asked.

"It was a classic strongman challenge," Alex explained, his voice filled with emotion. "On the platform, there were these enormous, old-fashioned barbells. The kind you see in black-and-white photos of circus performers from a hundred years ago. The air was thick with the scent of sweat and shame."

He took another sip of orange juice. "And then, out of nowhere, the strongman himself appeared. He was eyeing me up and down, this cocky grin on his face. 'Well, well, well,' he says, 'looks like we have a challenger.'"

Harry grabbed his coffee and took a gulp. "He challenged you? Just like that?"

"Just like that," Alex confirmed. "He starts going on about how he's undefeated, how no one's ever been able to match him. I could see he was trying to get under my skin, to psych me out before we even started."

"But you didn't let him, did you?" Harry asked, a knowing smile on his face.

"I did, honestly, but just a little bit at first..." Alex grinned. "I just smiled right back at him and said, 'I accept your challenge. Let's see what you've got there, big guy.'"

Alex stopped for a second to eat the last of the whipped cream on his plate. "So the strongman lays out the rules. We're going to take turns lifting progressively heavier weights for five rounds. First one to fail loses."

"Sounds simple enough. You look like a pretty strong guy," Harry remarked.

Alex took a deep breath, his gaze turning to the winding river outside the train window. "I won't lie to you, Harry. Those weights, they were intimidating. My muscles were screaming, my whole body shaking with the effort. The kids were jumping up and down, cheering me on, their voices echoing through the tent. But I kept pace with the strongman, matched him weight for weight. My form was clean."

Harry looked at Alex with admiration on his face. "So, what happened? Did you beat him?"

Alex paused for effect, letting the suspense build, distracted once again by the scene outside his train window: seemingly endless fields of sunflowers. "So, in the final round, he lifts this enormous weight, and he makes it look really easy. Everyone's sure I'm done for. The crowd is gasping, gawking, and one guy was even laughing at me hysterically. But something about the strongman didn't sit right with me, Harry. Maybe it was the way he talked, all bluster and no substance. Or maybe it was the way the weights seemed to shift and wobble, like they were off-balance somehow."

"Off-balance? What do you mean?" Harry asked, curiosity written all over his face.

"I mean that as I watched him, as I studied the way he moved and the way the weights behaved... I started to suspect that something was amiss. That the strongman wasn't quite as strong as he appeared to be." Alex said, sipping his cup of coffee. "So, I decided to put my theory to the test. I don't even try to lift my weight."

Harry's face crumpled with confusion. "You didn't? Then how...?"

"I walked right over to the strongman's barbell," Alex said, a note of triumph in his voice. "I flexed my arms, made a little show for the audience, then bent over and lifted it with ease. Turns out, his weights were lighter than they looked. He'd been cheating the whole time—a phony who relied on deception and illusion to maintain his reputation and intimidate his challengers. I stood there with it well above my head and tossed it aside like a rag doll."

Harry's jaw dropped, his eyes wide with shock. "You exposed him? In front of everyone?"

"I did," Alex continued. "I guess I just trusted my instincts, Harry. I listened to that little voice inside me that said something wasn't right, and I followed it to the truth. The crowd cheered me on, clapping and waving. But the kids, they didn't let me bask in the glory for too long. Before I knew it, they were leading me away from the arena. They said they had a little surprise in store for me—a bit of a break between the challenges, to help me catch my breath and clear my head."

"Oh? Do tell," Harry said, picking at the last remnants of food on his plate.

Alex shook his hands and said, "Well, picture this, Harry. We quickly walk to a small, dark purple structure, neatly tucked away in a quiet corner of the circus. And inside, a woman sitting at a table, her face obscured by a veil and her hands hovering over a crystal ball."

Alex paused, his voice dropping to a lower tone. "The fortune teller, they called her. A mystic who could peer into the depths of your soul and see the secrets of your past, present, and future."

Harry's face lit up, a shiver running down his spine. "That sounds... mystifying," he said, chuckling briefly afterward.

"Oh, it was," Alex confirmed, leaning back in his seat. "But I was curious, Harry. After everything I had experienced in the circus, all the lessons I had learned... I wanted to see what the fortune teller had to say. So, I sat down at the table, and I looked into the crystal ball. And as I did, the fortune teller began to speak, her voice low and haunting."

Alex closed his eyes, remembering. "She told me that I was on a journey, Harry. A journey of self-discovery and transformation, one that would take me to the very depths of my being."

He opened his eyes, a look of wonder on his face. "She said that I had already faced many challenges, many trials that had tested my strength and resolve. But that the greatest challenge was yet to come —a final test that would determine the course of my entire life."

Harry's brow furrowed, trying to make sense of the cryptic message. "A final test? What kind of test?"

Alex shook his head, a remorseful smile on his face. "She didn't say, exactly. But she did give me a clue—a hint of what was to come. She said that I would have to confront my deepest fears, my darkest doubts. That I would have to look within myself and find the courage to let go, to surrender to the unknown and trust in the journey."

Harry nodded slowly, a look of understanding dawning on his face. "That's heavy stuff, Alex. I can't even imagine what that must have felt like, hearing those words."

Alex took a deep breath, his expression growing thoughtful. "It was overwhelming, Harry. But it was also... illuminating, in a way. Like the fortune teller had tapped into some deep, hidden part of myself that I had never fully acknowledged before. She finished by saying that my fortune, my true destiny... it wouldn't come to fruition today. That the path I was on, the journey I had started... it was just the beginning. She said that later in my life, when the time was right... I would see a star dancing in the sky above. And that would be the sign—the signal that I was ready for the next step, the next great adventure."

Harry's expression began to glow. "A dancing star? That's... that's quite the image. Did she say anything else, anything about what this adventure might entail?"

Alex shook his head again. "No, that was all she would say... After the fortune teller's reading, I was feeling a bit off-balance, like I was standing on the edge of something big, but I couldn't quite see the shape of it yet."

"That kind of insight can be unsettling, for sure. Things like that come and go throughout your life," said Harry.

"Definitely," Alex agreed. "But the kids, they had a way of keeping things light. They led me to the final trial at this massive white tent, and inside was the most incredible sight: acrobats flying through the air, spinning and twirling while circus animals performed tricks below."

Alex picked a piece of fruit with his fork before saying, "And that's when I saw it, Harry. The high wire, stretched out across the length of the tent, so high up it made my stomach drop just to look at it."

Harry raised an eyebrow. "Don't tell me you..."

"Oh, I did," Alex grinned. "The kids, they were all excited, telling me that this was the final trial—the ultimate test of my courage and trust. I had to cross the high wire and then let the acrobats throw me from one end to the other. And maybe it was the adrenaline, or maybe it was just the magic of the circus, but I found myself climbing up that ladder, my heart pounding in my chest."

Harry leaned forward, engrossed. "So, what happened? Did you make it across?"

Alex's smile quickly turned upside down. "Not exactly. I stepped out onto the wire, and for a moment, it was like the whole world fell away. I could hear the music, the laughter, the roar of the crowd, but it all seemed distant from so far up."

Alex took a deep breath, his voice growing softer. "And then, about halfway across, I lost my balance. It was like the wire just disappeared from under my feet, and suddenly I was falling, tumbling through the air like dust in the wind."

Harry gasped. "That must have been terrifying!"

"It was," Alex admitted. "But it was also... freeing, in a strange way. As I fell, I felt this incredible sense of surrender, like I was letting go of everything that had been holding me back—all the fears and doubts and limitations. It all slipped away. Of course, that feeling didn't last long. Because as I landed in the safety net, my feathered hat went flying off my head, and wouldn't you know it, it landed right on the back of a tied-down baby elephant!"

Harry's hands went up in the air. "Oh no..."

"Oh yes," Alex confirmed. "That baby elephant let out a mighty trumpet of surprise, and started thrashing around, pulling free from its chains. The kids were yelling, the crowd was gasping, and I was just lying there in the net, watching the baby elephant rampage through the tent, my feathered hat still perched comically on its head."

Harry laughed at the picture forming in his mind. "It must have been chaos. What happened next?"

Alex continued, "The circus was falling apart around me, quite literally. The tent was collapsing, people were running and screaming, and the younger animals... well, they were making a break for freedom. It was like something out of a movie, Harry. Clowns all crammed into a car started tripping over each other while running out and around to stop the mayhem. The older, more experienced animals stayed put, watching the chaos unfold with a kind of detached amusement. But the younger ones, the ones who hadn't yet been fully trained... they saw their chance and took it."

Alex took the last gulp from his cup of orange juice. "As I stumbled through the wreckage, trying to find a way out, one of the circus kids pressed something into my hand. It was a deck of cards, worn and faded from years of use. 'For good luck,' they whispered before disappearing into the disturbance."

He looked up, meeting Harry's gaze. "I tucked the cards into my pocket, feeling like I needed all the luck I could get."

Alex took a deep breath. "As I made my way to the edge of the circus grounds, I couldn't help but think about the animals. How the older ones stayed put, while the younger ones ran wild. It made me think about the power of learned behavior and how hard it can be to break free of the patterns that have been ingrained in us."

"That's a deep insight, Alex," Harry said, a look of understanding on his face.

"It was," Alex said, "and it gave me a new perspective on my own life and the choices I had made up until that point. But I didn't have long to dwell on it, because I soon found myself face to face with an even bigger problem. The young animals, Harry. They'd made their way to the train tracks, and were gathered there like some kind of bizarre welcoming committee. And in the distance, I could see the lights of an approaching train—the Sunflower Express."

Harry gasped. "Oh no, so that's why we stopped..."

"Yep," Alex confirmed, a note of tension creeping into his voice. "I watched in horror as the train drew closer, its whistle blowing frantically. The animals seemed oblivious, milling about on the tracks like they owned the place. And then, with a screech of metal on metal, the train ground to a halt, just inches from the gathered herd. And that's when things got really weird, Harry. The conductor came rushing out of the train, his face pale and his eyes wild. He looked at the animals, then at me, and do you know what he said?"

Harry leaned forward, caught up in the story. "What?"

"He said, 'Thank goodness this train stopped. The bathroom was full on the train, and I've been holding it for miles. Young man, can you tell me where the nearest restroom is?'" Alex said, throwing his head back, laughing. "I couldn't believe it, Harry. Here we were, in the middle of this life-or-death situation, and the conductor, not worried about the animals or anything like that, had to go to the bathroom!"

He wiped a tear of merriment from his eye, his shoulders still shaking with laughter. "But I pulled myself together and led him to a nearby cluster of port-a-potties. And while he was taking care of business, I turned my attention to the animals."

Alex's voice grew soft, almost reverent. "I approached them slowly, speaking in a low, but audible tone. I coaxed them, gently but firmly, to move away from the tracks. It was like a delicate dance, a negotiation between man and beast. And slowly, one by one, they began to drift back towards the safety of the circus grounds."

Alex smiled, a note of pride in his voice. "It took some doing, Harry, but eventually, I managed to clear the tracks. And as the last of the animals wandered back to their pens, I felt this incredible sense of accomplishment wash over me, like I had passed some final, crucial test. Of course, it wasn't all smooth sailing. Somewhere in the midst of all the chaos, my shirt got defiled by the animals. But oddly enough, I didn't mind. It felt like a badge of honor, a reminder of all the crap I had been through."

Alex continued, a note of gratitude creeping into his voice. "And then, as if by magic, the conductor reappeared. He clapped me on the shoulder, his eyes shining with admiration. 'Young man,' he said, 'I don't know how you did it, but you saved the day. The Sunflower Express is in your debt.'"

Alex chuckled, shaking his head. "I explained to him my situation, and he told me to wait. After a few short moments, he returned with a first-class ticket to board the Sunflower Express, all the way to the airport. It was like a dream come true, a way out of the crazy, wonderful nightmare that had been my life for the past 24 hours."

Alex took a deep breath as he recalled the final moments of his circus adventure. "And so, I took one final look at the circus and smiled as I boarded the Sunflower Express. The first thing I noticed was the plush carpets, then the gleaming brass fixtures, and finally the soft clatter of the wheels against the tracks as we started moving... it all seemed so surreal after the chaos and the madness of the circus. I found my way to my room, a cozy little cabin with a window that looked out over the passing moonlit countryside. And as I sat down on the bed, I felt this incredible sense of exhaustion wash over me, like all the adrenaline and excitement had finally caught up with me."

Alex chuckled, shaking his head. "But I wasn't ready to sleep, not yet. I reached into my pocket and pulled out the deck of cards the circus kid had given me. And before I knew it, I was playing solitaire, and that's when I heard it, Harry, your laughter echoing through the halls of the train. It was a warm, jovial sound, like the laughter of an old friend. And I remember thinking to myself, 'I wonder what's so funny?'"

A look of realization dawned on Harry's face. "The story of Lorelei," he murmured while staring out the window excitedly, "I had just finished telling the story before I retired for the night. And look, out of the train window right now, here we are, passing the very spot where that story takes place. The Rhine River, with its towering cliffs and its legendary siren."

"I have to admit, Harry, I've never heard the story of Lorelei. Would you... would you mind telling it to me?" Alex asked.

Harry propped himself up in his chair, getting ready to tell the story. His rich, baritone voice filled the room, captivating Alex with every word. "I'd be delighted, Alex. It's a tale as old as time—a story of love and loss, of beauty and betrayal.

Once upon a time, in the heart of the Rhine Valley, there lived a young woman named Lorelei," Harry began. "She was known for her beauty and enchanting voice that could captivate anyone who heard it..."

Alex closed his eyes, picturing the story in his mind as Harry detailed the scene. Harry continued telling the story, and at the end, Alex opened his eyes again. He became overcome with the feeling that he had just dreamed a strange tale. A ticket checker patted him on the shoulder, demanding to see his ticket. Alex let out a deep, foreboding sigh.

※

<u>**Lesson 4:**</u>
<u>**Personal Growth and Success**</u>

Limiting beliefs shape our thoughts, emotions, and actions, creating self-imposed limitations that prevent us from taking risks, pursuing our dreams, and embracing opportunities for growth. These beliefs often originate from past experiences, societal conditioning, or internalized criticism, creating a barrier between us and our aspirations. By recognizing and challenging these beliefs, we open ourselves to new possibilities, uncover hidden potentials, and unlock doors to personal fulfillment.

Transforming limiting beliefs is a journey of self-discovery and growth that involves several interconnected steps. This process isn't linear but rather a fluid experience, where each aspect supports and reinforces the others, ultimately leading to personal empowerment and a stronger sense of self.

For instance, imagine someone who has always been told they are not good at math. This person may develop a belief that they are inherently incapable of understanding mathematical concepts. As a result, they might avoid careers or hobbies that involve math, thereby limiting their opportunities for growth and success. However, if they were to challenge this belief and take steps to improve their math skills, they could potentially discover a newfound ability and interest in a field they once avoided.

Self-Awareness and Reflection

Transforming limiting beliefs starts with building a strong foundation of self-awareness. This process begins by taking a closer, honest look at your thoughts, emotions, and behaviors. It requires a commitment to regularly observe and reflect on your inner experiences. One effective way to do this is by setting aside time each day for self-reflection. Journaling is especially powerful in this practice because it allows you to document your thoughts and feelings as they happen, creating a tangible record that you can review and analyze over time.

As you journal, pay attention to recurring themes—especially those related to self-doubt, fear, or negativity. These patterns are often clues pointing to deeper, underlying limiting beliefs. For example, you might notice a habit of thinking, "I'm not good enough" when faced with a challenge, or feel anxious about trying something new. By identifying these recurring thoughts, you begin to uncover the specific beliefs that are holding you back.

Through consistent journaling and reflection, you not only become more aware of these limiting beliefs but also start to see how they influence your actions and decisions. This awareness is the first crucial step in transforming them. Once you've identified a limiting belief, you can challenge its validity and replace it with a more empowering perspective. Over time, this practice helps shift your mindset, enabling you to break free from self-imposed limitations and embrace a more confident, positive approach to life.

Challenging and Reframing Beliefs

Once you've pinpointed your limiting beliefs, the next crucial step is to challenge their validity. This involves critically examining the evidence that upholds these beliefs. Ask yourself: Are these beliefs truly based on facts, or are they rooted in assumptions, past experiences, or outdated perceptions that no longer align with who you are today?

For instance, if you believe you're not qualified for a particular career path, take a moment to list your skills, achievements, and experiences that directly contradict this belief. By doing so, you confront the belief with hard evidence, which helps to weaken its hold over you. This exercise not only highlights your capabilities but also starts the process of dismantling the power these limiting beliefs have over your decisions and self-perception.

As you challenge these beliefs, it's equally important to reframe any negative thoughts that surface. These thoughts often slip by unnoticed, subtly reinforcing limiting beliefs. However, with increased self-awareness, you can catch these thoughts as they arise. When you notice a negative thought, pause and ask yourself if it's truly useful or reflective of reality.

For example, if you catch yourself thinking, "I always fail," take a moment to reframe it into something more constructive, like "I am constantly learning and improving." This simple shift can transform your outlook, creating a more positive and supportive internal dialogue. Reframing negative thoughts isn't about ignoring challenges or sugarcoating reality; it's about consciously choosing perspectives that empower rather than limit you.

By systematically challenging and reframing limiting beliefs, you replace them with more empowering, realistic perspectives. Over time, this practice not only shifts your mindset but also builds a stronger, more resilient foundation for pursuing your goals and embracing new opportunities.

Building Self-Confidence Through Positive Practices

Once your beliefs and thoughts are aligned with a more positive perspective, the next step is to actively cultivate self-confidence. This involves embracing self-acceptance, setting realistic goals, and celebrating your achievements—no matter how small. Self-confidence isn't just about feeling good in the moment; it's about building a sustainable foundation of trust in your own abilities.

Start with Self-Acceptance: The journey to confidence begins with accepting yourself as you are, including your strengths and areas for growth. Self-acceptance means recognizing that you are worthy, not despite your imperfections, but because of them. When you accept yourself fully, you create a solid foundation from which genuine confidence can grow.

Set Realistic Goals: Break down your larger aspirations into smaller, manageable goals. Setting realistic, achievable goals gives you clear, attainable targets to work toward. Each time you reach a goal, no matter how minor it may seem, take the time to acknowledge and celebrate your progress. These small victories accumulate, gradually reinforcing your sense of capability and boosting your self-confidence.

Celebrate Achievements: Recognize that every milestone, big or small, is a testament to your hard work and determination. Celebrating these achievements isn't just about marking a moment; it's about reinforcing your belief in your abilities. These celebrations act as positive reinforcement, encouraging you to continue pushing forward.

Incorporate Positive Affirmations: Positive affirmations are powerful tools for reshaping your self-perception. These are statements that emphasize your worth, potential, and capabilities. By regularly repeating affirmations like "I am capable," "I am deserving of success," or "I am growing every day," you begin to rewire your brain. Over time, these affirmations help shift your focus away from perceived weaknesses and toward your strengths, fostering a more confident mindset.

Practice Visualization: Visualization involves creating vivid mental images of yourself achieving your goals. This technique doesn't just boost motivation; it also conditions your mind to expect success. When you regularly visualize your achievements, you mentally prepare yourself to recognize and seize opportunities as they arise. Visualization builds confidence by making your goals feel tangible and within reach.

By combining self-acceptance, realistic goal-setting, the celebration of achievements, positive affirmations, and visualization, you create a comprehensive approach to building lasting self-confidence. This process not only empowers you to pursue your goals with greater determination but also equips you with the resilience needed to overcome challenges along the way.

Creating a Supportive Environment

Surrounding yourself with positivity extends beyond your internal mindset—it also involves the external environment and the people you interact with. Seek out individuals who uplift and inspire you, and minimize exposure to negativity, whether it comes from people, media, or your own inner critic. Building a network of supportive, encouraging individuals can provide the necessary reinforcement to stay on track with your goals and beliefs.

In tandem with cultivating positive relationships, practicing gratitude can further enhance your mindset. By focusing on the positive aspects of your life, you naturally shift away from negative thinking. Starting a daily gratitude practice, such as listing three things you're thankful for each day, can reinforce this positive shift.

Finally, self-care plays a crucial role in maintaining the momentum of this transformational journey. Prioritizing activities that nurture your physical and mental well-being—such as exercise, meditation, or hobbies—ensures that you have the energy and resilience to continue growing. This also includes taking care of your basic needs, like getting enough sleep and eating well, which are foundational to your overall well-being.

Equally important is the act of celebrating your achievements. No matter the size, each success should be acknowledged and celebrated. This not only boosts your self-esteem but also serves as a reminder of how far you've come. Celebrating your progress reinforces the belief that you are capable of achieving your goals, further dismantling any lingering limiting beliefs.

Overcoming self-limitations is not a one-time event but a continuous journey that requires dedication, self-compassion, and persistence. By integrating self-awareness, challenging and reframing beliefs, building self-confidence, creating a supportive environment, and prioritizing self-care, you can transform limiting beliefs and unlock your true potential. Embrace this process with an open heart and mind, knowing that each step forward brings you closer to a more fulfilled and empowered self.

Activity: The Empowerment Journey - Uncover Limiting Beliefs, Cultivate Positivity, and Celebrate Your Success

In this activity you will embark on an empowerment journey to uncover limiting beliefs, cultivate a positive mindset, and celebrate your personal achievements. This comprehensive approach will help you gain clarity, build self-confidence, and propel you towards your full potential. Let's get started:

Step 1: Conduct a Belief Inventory

Begin by contemplating different areas of your life, such as relationships, career, self-worth, health, or personal growth. Ask yourself: "What beliefs do I hold about this area of my life?"

Write down any beliefs that come to mind without judgment or analysis. It's important to capture your initial thoughts and reactions. Be honest and open with yourself during this process.

Step 2: Reflect and Transform

Once you have identified a belief, ask yourself: "Is this belief empowering or limiting?" Consider how this belief affects your thoughts, emotions, and actions in the specific area of your life you are exploring.

Reflect on the origin of each belief. Ask yourself: "Where did this belief come from? Did someone else instill this belief in me? Did past experiences shape this belief?"

Evaluate the validity of each belief. Challenge its accuracy and examine whether it aligns with your current reality and goals. Ask yourself: "Is this belief based on facts or assumptions? Does it support my growth and well-being? Is it serving me positively or holding me back?"

Choose one or two limiting beliefs that you are ready to challenge and transform. Write them down on a separate piece of paper or in a digital document.

Make a commitment to replace these limiting beliefs with empowering ones. Affirm to yourself that you have the power to reshape your beliefs and create a more positive and empowering mindset.

Step 3: Positive Affirmations and Visualization Exercises

Prepare a list of positive affirmations that reflect your desired beliefs and goals. These affirmations should be present tense, personal, and uplifting. For example, "I am confident in my abilities," "I embrace challenges as opportunities for growth," or "I am deserving of success."

Find a quiet and comfortable space where you can relax and focus your attention. This could be a quiet room, a serene outdoor setting, or any place where you feel calm and undisturbed.

Begin with deep breathing to enter a state of calmness. Take a few moments to take deep, slow breaths, inhaling through your nose and exhaling through your mouth.

Repeat your chosen affirmations slowly and intentionally. Visualize the words as you say them, allowing their meaning and positive energy to sink into your consciousness. Engage all your senses to make the visualization as real and immersive as possible.

Embrace positive emotions as you practice positive affirmations and visualization. Feel the joy, confidence, and fulfillment that come with accomplishing your goals. Let these emotions nourish your belief in your abilities and your vision of success.

Step 4: Celebrate Your Personal Achievements

Reflect on your past accomplishments, both big and small. Consider personal milestones, academic or professional achievements, acts of kindness, or personal growth experiences. Write them down in a journal or create a list on your computer or phone.

Identify your unique strengths and qualities. Reflect on personal traits like kindness, resilience, creativity, or skills and talents you possess. Write down at least three strengths that you recognize in yourself.

Craft positive affirmations using your achievements and strengths. For example, "I am proud of my accomplishments and eager to achieve more," or "I embrace my strengths and use them to overcome challenges."

Take time to celebrate your achievements, no matter how small they may seem. Acknowledge the effort, dedication, and progress you have made. Treat yourself to something special or engage in an activity that brings you joy. Celebrating achievements reinforces positive self-beliefs and encourages further growth and success.

Create a visual reminder of your affirmations and achievements. You can make a vision board or display your affirmations in a prominent place where you will see them daily. This serves as a constant reminder of your worth, strengths, and the progress you have made.

Regularly review and update your affirmations and achievements. Set aside dedicated time to reflect on any changes or new accomplishments that have occurred since you started. Update your affirmations as needed to align with your current aspirations and goals.

By engaging in this comprehensive empowerment journey, you will uncover limiting beliefs, cultivate positivity, and celebrate your personal achievements. Embrace this process with self-compassion, curiosity, and a genuine desire to transform your thoughts and beliefs. With dedication and perseverance, you will empower yourself to embrace your full potential and journey towards personal growth and success.

●

The *Sunflower Express* has taken us on a journey, exploring the profound impact of empowering beliefs in shaping our mindset and unlocking our true potential. Throughout this chapter, we have witnessed Alex confront his limiting beliefs and embark on a path of personal growth and self-discovery.

Empowering beliefs have the remarkable ability to shape our thoughts, attitudes, and actions. They create a foundation of self-belief, resilience, and determination that propels us forward in our pursuit of success and fulfillment. By embracing empowering beliefs, we tap into our innate strength and capabilities, allowing us to overcome obstacles, navigate challenges, and achieve remarkable feats.

It is crucial to recognize that our beliefs are not fixed or predetermined. We have the power to choose and cultivate empowering beliefs that serve our highest good. By replacing self-limiting thoughts with positive, affirming beliefs, we rewire our mindset and open ourselves to a world of possibilities.

As we conclude this chapter, I encourage you to embrace the power of empowering beliefs. Challenge the narratives that hold you back, and replace them with empowering truths that resonate with your aspirations and values. Believe in your inherent worth, abilities, and potential.

The journey of transforming our beliefs requires patience, self-compassion, and consistent effort. Celebrate your progress, no matter how small, and be gentle with yourself along the way. Remember, it is through the accumulation of small, positive shifts in our beliefs that we experience profound personal transformation.

"All truly wise thoughts have been thoughts already thousands of times; but to make them truly ours, we must think them over again honestly, til they take root in our personal experience."

-Johann Wolfgang von Goethe

<u>Chapter 5: An Unexpected Twist of Fate</u>

The lecture hall was abuzz with the sound of furiously scribbling pens and the occasional cough or rustling of papers. Eden's hand flew across her notebook, trying to capture every prominent point as the professor delved into the nuances of integrating traditional herbal remedies with modern medical practices. This was the culmination of the semester's work—tying together the various strands they had studied into a cohesive, holistic approach to healthcare.

As she flipped through the textbook, her mind replayed the professor's words—a blend of ancient healing wisdom and cutting-edge medical science. It was this synthesis of old and new that had drawn Eden to Everbrook in the first place. Here, at one of the few medical schools that embraced alternative medicine alongside conventional methods, she believed she could find the tools to make a real difference... especially for people like her grandmother, Beatrice, who suffered from chronic ailments often dismissed by mainstream doctors.

For Eden, it wasn't just about acing the exams, though her relentless work ethic showed in her consistently stellar grades. She had a deeper drive, an innate need to truly understand how to heal people on all levels—body, mind, and spirit. Her grandmother's deteriorating health was a constant motivator for her to master both the scientific rigors of medicine and the ancient wisdom of natural remedies.

As she sat in the lecture hall listening to the professor, she pushed aside thoughts of the cozy home she shared with her grandmother, the soothing clink of teacups, and the comforting smell of her grandmother's lavender perfume. There would be time for that later. For now, there was only her commitment to learn, to grow, and to forge a path that could one day meld the wisdom of the past with the innovations of the future.

Once the lecture concluded, Eden didn't head back to her house to relax, as many of her peers did. Instead, she ventured further into the community, her steps leading her to the Everbrook Free Clinic, where she volunteered several evenings a week. The clinic served the town's less fortunate, providing care that was otherwise inaccessible to many of its residents. It was here that Eden felt her efforts had the most impact, where her studies in traditional and modern medicine could come to life and address real-world problems.

At the clinic, Eden slipped into a different role. Under the supervision of an elite team of doctors, she assisted with patient consultations, her knowledge of both herbal remedies and pharmaceutical treatments proving invaluable. One particular doctor, who had taken a keen interest in Eden's education, often allowed her to suggest alternative treatments for patients with chronic diseases— treatments that were less invasive and more cost-effective than conventional medicine.

Eden's dedication to the clinic was not just professional, but deeply personal. Each patient reminded her of her grandmother, who had often been dismissed by traditional doctors unwilling to look beyond their standard protocols. Eden listened to their stories with genuine empathy, advising them on dietary changes, stress management, and the appropriate use of herbal supplements alongside their prescribed medications.

The evening stretched on, and with each patient Eden saw, her resolve to bridge the gap between old and new grew stronger. She knew that rural communities like Everbrook needed practitioners who were not only skilled in modern medical techniques but who also respected the traditional wisdom that had sustained these communities for generations.

Finally, as the clinic's lights dimmed and the last patient left with a word of thanks, Eden packed up her notes and prepared to head home. It was getting late into the evening, and the streets were quiet as she made her way back, the cool night air a remedy after the intensity of the day. Her thoughts drifted to her grandmother waiting at home, likely asleep but sure to have left a plate of food in the fridge for her.

The short walk from the clinic to the cozy house she shared with her ailing grandmother allowed Eden's mind to rest for a few moments. She loved this tree-lined street in Everbrook—the peaceful surroundings of the countryside juxtaposed with the cutting-edge medical resources of the university. It was the perfect place to immerse herself in her studies while still being able to care for her grandma.

Arriving home, Eden unlocked the door to find the house silent except for the soft ticking of the living room cuckoo clock. She hung her coat and walked into the kitchen, where her grandmother's plate of dinner awaited her, as anticipated. The warmth of the house, so different from the clinical sterility of the lab and the clinic, wrapped around her like a comforting embrace.

Before sitting down to eat, Eden made her way to her grandmother's room to check on her. She found her asleep, a book resting open on her chest, and the soft glow of the bedside lamp casting gentle shadows across the room. Eden adjusted the blanket around her grandmother, noticing with a frown the pack of cigarettes on the nightstand—a stark reminder of the bad habit her grandmother couldn't seem to kick.

Beatrice's persistent cough, a raspy sound that often echoed through the house, was worse at night. It was a cough that had started years ago, mild and seemingly harmless, but had grown more troubling over time, exacerbated by decades of smoking. Despite numerous doctors' visits and many attempts to quit, her grandmother's addiction to nicotine held firm, a testament to the powerful grip of long-established habits.

Eden sighed softly, her heart heavy with concern. She knew that the smoking not only compromised her grandmother's lung function but also increased her risk of other severe conditions—a reality Eden faced daily in her medical studies and volunteer work. The knowledge made her feel powerless, a rare and uncomfortable sensation for someone who spent so much time learning how to heal others.

Turning off the lamp, Eden quietly exited the room, her mind racing with thoughts of treatments and interventions. She grabbed her dinner and sat at the kitchen table, but her appetite was lessened by worry. She thought about the herbal remedies and breathing exercises she had introduced to her grandmother, which provided temporary relief but weren't enough to reverse the years of damage.

As she ate, Eden pondered deeper on how she could help her grandmother combat this stubborn habit. It wasn't just about prescribing the right medication or suggesting another alternative treatment; it was about understanding the psychological ties that bound her grandmother to smoking and finding a way to address them effectively. Her thoughts drifted to a community support group held at the library for smokers that she had read about at the clinic, wondering if a social approach might complement the medical strategies she had already tried.

Determined to explore every possible avenue, Eden decided to talk to her grandmother about the support group the next morning, hoping that perhaps sharing experiences with others could inspire her to take the final step toward quitting. Her resolve strengthened by this new plan, Eden finished her dinner, the weight of her grandmother's health ever-present in her mind but tempered by a renewed sense of purpose and a plan of action.

After cleaning the dishes and tidying up, Eden returned to her grandmother's room, carrying a fresh pot of herbal tea. She found her grandmother now awake, sitting up against her pillows, the book still on her lap.

"Couldn't sleep after all, Grandma?" Eden asked gently, setting the tea tray on the nightstand.

Beatrice chuckled softly, her voice raspy. "That cough wouldn't let me rest. But it's always a bit better with you around, dear."

Eden poured the tea, the soothing aroma of chamomile and mint filling the room, and sat beside her on the bed. "I thought we might read a bit together," she suggested, nodding towards the book.

"Oh, I'd like that," her grandmother replied, her eyes lighting up with a mixture of fondness and anticipation. She handed Eden the book, an old collection of world folktales they had often read together when Eden was a child.

As Eden opened to a bookmarked story, her grandmother sipped her tea and gazed at her with a reflective expression. "You know, Eden, every time we open this book, it reminds me of all those years I spent with a cigarette between my fingers instead of enjoying more moments like these with you."

Eden paused, looking into her grandmother's eyes, seeing the depth of her regret. "It's never too late to create new memories, Grandma. We're doing that right now."

Beatrice nodded, a tear escaping her eye. "I know, darling. But if I had known then what I know now about what those cigarettes would do to me, how they would steal my breath... I would have dropped them long ago. It's just so hard to let go of something that's been a part of you for so long."

Eden reached out and squeezed her grandmother's hand reassuringly. "We can't change the past, but we're working on making the future better," she said softly. "And I'm here with you, every step of the way."

Encouraged by Eden's words, her grandmother smiled and urged her to continue with the story. As Eden read aloud, their shared space filled with tales of distant lands and courageous characters. Her grandmother's intermittent coughing spells seemed a little less harsh in the comfort of their bond.

The story ended, and they spent a few minutes discussing the morals and the cultures that shaped such narratives. It was during these discussions that her grandmother often imparted wisdom about life's lessons, sometimes circling back to her own experiences and choices.

"Books have a way of making us reflect, don't they?" Beatrice mused. "They make you think about life, about mistakes, about chances for redemption."

"Yes, they do," Eden agreed, feeling the weight and warmth of the shared moment. "And sometimes, they show us that change is possible, no matter where we start." She hesitated for a moment before continuing, "Grandma, I was thinking... maybe tomorrow we could go to the library together. There's a support group

for smokers. I thought it might help."

Beatrice looked at her, eyes softening with both surprise and understanding. "You know, I think that's a good idea," she said, a small smile playing on her lips. "Let's go together."

As they settled down for the night, Eden's mind was filled with a mixture of emotions: sadness for her grandmother's struggles, hope for her healing, and a strengthened resolve to help her overcome her battle with smoking. This night, like many others, reinforced their bond—a foundation built on stories, shared regrets, and mutual support, guiding them toward a future where old habits could be confronted and new chapters written together.

●

A few miles away, at the top of Old Dirt Hill Road, Alex dragged his well-worn suitcase up the overgrown stone steps to the sagging porch of a quaint cottage that stood quietly against the backdrop of rolling hills and sprawling fields. This old house, with its peeling paint and overgrown garden, was a relic from his grandparents' days, filled with memories and echoes of laughter.

Alex paused at the top of the steps, taking a moment to breathe in the fresh, earthy air of the countryside. It had been a few weeks since he had returned from his travels across Europe, and he had just gotten around to moving his belongings from his parents' house in the city to the country cottage. As enriching as his travels were, they had also left him feeling lost, adrift between the old-world charms of cobblestone streets and the relentless pace of modern life.

Looking around, Alex felt a surge of nostalgia mixed with relief. Here, in this old cottage that he had inherited after his grandparents passed away, he hoped to reconnect with his roots and the simpler, steadier rhythms of country living. It was a stark contrast to the bustling cities of Europe, where the constant noise had made it hard for him to think, to create, to be himself.

With a determined sigh, he heaved his suitcase over the threshold and stepped into the dimly lit hallway. The air inside smelled of must and mold. Cobwebs clung to the corners of the high ceilings, and tumbleweeds of dust floated through the living room as shafts of evening light spilled through the dirty windows. Alex set his suitcase down and walked through the house, each room whispering stories of his childhood summers spent running through the halls and playing hide-and-seek with his sister among the old furniture.

In the living room, he ran his fingers over the back of the timeworn sofa, a smile tugging at his lips as he remembered his grandmother scolding him for putting his dirty shoes up on the cushions. His grandfather's old record player still stood in the corner, alongside stacks of vinyl that hadn't been played in years. Alex felt a wave of inspiration as he imagined reviving the old player, filling the house with music once again.

He made his way to the kitchen, where jars of preserved fruits, honey, and vegetables lined the dusty shelves, remnants of his grandmother's once-bustling culinary efforts. Alex opened the refrigerator, which was empty except for a bottle of wine left over from his last visit a week earlier. He took it out and poured himself a glass, leaning against the counter as he contemplated the work that lay ahead.

Restoring the cottage would be a challenge, but Alex was ready to embrace it. He envisioned modernizing the place without stripping it of its character, making it a sanctuary for his own creative pursuits and a haven from the world outside. More importantly, he hoped that reconnecting with his grandparents' way of life—simple, grounded, connected to nature—would help him rediscover the purpose and peace he had been searching for.

As the sun set, casting long shadows across the wooden floors, Alex stepped out onto the back porch, his eyes scanning the horizon where the countryside stretched out like a patchwork quilt. The peace he felt in that moment confirmed his decision. This was where he needed to be, where he could build a new life on the foundations of the old and, perhaps, find himself in the process.

He had almost forgotten the particular scents of rural life after spending the last year wandering around Europe's storied cities. The aroma was a heady mix of tilled soil, newly blossomed wildflowers, and the musky hint of livestock and manure in the distance. It felt... comforting, honest in a way the air in Paris or Rome could never be.

Alex returned inside as the twilight deepened into night, his silhouette framed by the doorway of the cottage. The house, with its creaking floors and the echo of his own footsteps, seemed to welcome him back into its arms. He began searching around the house, unfolding memories, and revealing pieces of the past.

In the attic, he found three boxes marked "Grandpa's Tools," covered in a thick layer of dust. Inside, the tools of his grandfather's beekeeping trade lay meticulously arranged: a beekeeper's suit, still fully functional and fitting him just right; a smoker, used to calm the bees; various hive tools, slightly rusted but still solid; and a stack of old beekeeping journals, their pages yellowed with age. Alex lifted the smoker, turning it over in his hands, imagining his grandfather moving around the hives in the golden light of dawn. It was these mornings, watching the hives and tasting fresh honey, that had sweetened his childhood summers.

He carried the box down to the kitchen, setting it on the table with reverence. As he flipped through the journals, Alex felt a profound connection to his grandfather, a man who had found peace and purpose in the rhythms of nature. Each entry was a testament to a life lived with patience and persistence, qualities Alex hoped to embody as he took up the mantle of caretaker for the bees.

His exploration continued, leading him to a hallway closet where an array of family heirlooms had been stored. He discovered an old leather-bound photo album, the cover embossed with intricate designs. Inside, photographs of his grandparents in their youth, their smiles timeless and full of life, greeted him. There were pictures of them at the cottage, surrounded by friends and family, and snapshots of his grandfather standing proudly by his beehives. Alex traced his fingers over these images, feeling a surge of inspiration and nostalgia.

Among the heirlooms, he also found his grandmother's old gardening hat and gloves. The fabric was faded and stained, but the scent of lavender and soil still clung to them. It was as if pieces of his grandparents' essence remained, woven into the very fabric of these objects. Alex placed the hat and gloves on a shelf in the sunroom, intending to use them when he revived the cottage's long-neglected garden.

He ended the night in the living room, surrounded by unpacked boxes and heirlooms, a small fire crackling in the fireplace. The flickering light cast dancing shadows across the walls, and as Alex sipped his wine, he felt a peace settle over him. He was no longer just passing through; he was home. Here, among the memories and dreams of his grandparents, Alex was ready to weave his own story into the fabric of this place, finding his way back to a life grounded in the beauty and simplicity of nature.

●

The following morning, downtown Everbrook was alive with activity. The square, framed by its array of quaint shops and the stately library, hummed with the steady rhythm of daily commerce and leisure. Alex, having just made his final selections at the hardware store nestled among the charming row of storefronts, maneuvered his way to the checkout with an armful of tools and supplies.

With a fresh coat of paint, a new set of hinges, and various other essentials piled in his cart, he was ready to tackle the restoration of his cottage. After paying, he pushed his cart outside, the bright sun becoming overcast with heavier, darkening clouds. His truck was parked right in front of the store, conveniently placed for loading his supplies.

Meanwhile, just as Alex was organizing his purchases in the bed of his truck, Eden arrived at the square. She parked her car just a few spots away from Alex's truck.

"Are you sure you don't want me to drop you at the door, Gram?" Eden asked, cutting the engine to her blue sedan. "It's not too late for me to find a spot closer."

Beatrice gave a dismissive wave from the passenger seat. "Don't fuss over me, my dear. The fresh air will do me good, and I need to stretch out these old legs."

Eden watched as her grandmother slowly unbuckled and eased herself out onto the sun-warmed curb. She quickly circled around to offer her arm as a steadying brace.

"I've got you," Eden soothed, draping her grandmother's hand over her elbow as they proceeded at a measured pace up the tree-lined pavement. "Just take your time. We're in no hurry."

Her grandmother responded with a grateful pat. "You know, this street hasn't changed a lick since your granddad and I were walking these very bricks sixty years ago. Why, that bakery there on the corner is where he first..."

Eden hid a small grin as her grandmother trailed off in wistful reminiscence, her pace automatically slowing as she soaked in the sights and scents of her youth. Perfectly content to linger in the moment together, Eden allowed her eyes to roam their rustic surroundings.

It was then, over the sounds of traffic and pedestrians, that a familiar, comforting aroma wafted from somewhere nearby, immediately transporting Eden's soul to a place of cherished memories and mysteries yet to be unraveled. Fresh coffee and sweet pastries perfumed the air in an inviting summons she almost couldn't resist...

Alex turned in the opposite direction from the intoxicating bakery perfume, whistling a snappy tune between his grinning lips. But the universe's choreography for their destined convergence remained exquisitely, painstakingly unhurried. Alex, focused on securing his materials, didn't notice Eden and her grandmother walk by as he shut the tailgate of his truck with a satisfying click. He climbed into the driver's seat, his mind already on the projects awaiting him at home.

Starting the engine, he pulled out of the parking space just as Eden, her head turned away, admiring the arrangement of baked goods, made her way toward the library's grand entrance. With a subtle tug, Eden's awareness was drawn back to the present by her grandmother's guiding hand squeezing her arm as they entered the cool, quiet sanctuary of the library. The opportunity for their paths to cross slipped away silently, unseen and unrealized by either of them.

Inside the library, Eden and her grandmother arrived with some time to spare before the start of the support group. They began walking through the aisles in search of books on ancient medicine. The library was quiet, a stark contrast to the bustling activity outside.

As Eden reached up to a high shelf, her movements were careful yet clumsy, her mind preoccupied with thoughts of her grandmother's health. Behind her, a librarian was restocking a cart with recently donated books. Lost in thought, Eden stepped back without looking, bumping into the librarian and sending a stack of books crashing to the floor.

Flustered, Eden quickly dropped to her knees to help gather the scattered books. As she picked them up, one book in particular caught her eye: a worn copy of *Wonders of the World*. Curious, she flipped through its pages, and a photograph slipped out.

It was an image of a young man, casually posed in the cozy interior of a bakery, the name "Midnight Bakery" clearly visible in the background. His smile was genuine, and there was something familiar about his eyes. Eden's heart raced as she recognized him... it was the same perfect boy she'd briefly passed on the street almost a year ago, whose image had lingered in her mind ever since.

Her grandmother, watching Eden's expression change from frustration to intrigue, asked about the photograph. Eden showed it to her, explaining her sudden recollection of the man she had once seen. Intrigued and always a believer in fate, her grandmother encouraged Eden to find out more about him.

"Maybe it's a sign, dear," Beatrice suggested with a mysterious smile. "Perhaps this is the universe guiding you. Why don't you try to find this bakery? Maybe you'll find him again."

Inspired by her grandmother's words and driven by a mix of curiosity and destiny, Eden decided to embark on a quest to return to the Midnight Bakery and find the mysterious man from the photograph. Eden securely tucked the photo into her bag, and they made their way back to the support group meeting.

Before leaving her house later that day, Eden attempted to dispatch a spider with a magazine, and her hand collided sharply with the whirling ceiling fan. The sharp pain caused her to wince and curse under her breath, but with a quick shake of her hand, she dismissed the discomfort, chuckling at her own clumsiness. Yet, the incident left her with a throbbing pain in her finger, prompting a nervous habit of nail-biting as she left her house.

Eden's heart was filled with a mix of determination and anticipation, ready to unravel the threads of this unexpected mystery. The photograph of the man from the Midnight Bakery beckoned to her, a silent puzzle waiting to be solved. The more she thought about it, the more she felt a pull toward this mystery, as if solving it would unravel something significant, not just about the man in the image but perhaps about herself as well.

She drove for an hour before parking on a side street in the heart of the big city where she and Maya had spent their evening the day she found out Nate had been cheating on her with Monica. By the time the chipped red door of the Midnight Bakery finally came into view, Eden's lips were pushed in a tense line, her meticulous manicure in tatters.

Her excitement quickly deflated like a punctured balloon when she found the bakery closed, a sign hanging in the window reading "Temporarily Closed – On Vacation." Disappointment gnawed at her as she peered through the glass, the empty interior echoing her frustration.

As she turned from the bakery's door, a hurrying businessman collided with her, his hot coffee splashing across her jacket and blouse.

"Oh! Shoot, I'm so sorry!" the businessman stammered, his pinched voice already receding in a rapidly diminishing blur as he forged onward without breaking stride. "Oh man, I'm late...!"

His hurried apology, tossed over his shoulder as he continued on his way, did little to soothe her irritation. She closed her eyes, pinched the bridge of her nose, and willed herself to remain centered despite this accumulation of exasperating setbacks. Wiping at the stains proved futile. Eden sighed, the day's frustrations mounting.

"It's okay, Eden... just breathe. Don't let these silly little mishaps throw you off course," she murmured aloud to herself. With a few fortifying inhales, she squared her shoulders and strode purposefully back toward her trusty blue sedan, parked awkwardly along the curb.

She hoped to salvage some part of her day by perhaps finding another clue or even just clearing her head with the drive home. Yet, fate seemed to have other plans. About ten miles from her home, her car began to sputter and jerk alarmingly, finally rolling to a stop on a dirt road. Heavy, ominous clouds gathered overhead as the car sat in silence.

"Are you kidding me?" she exclaimed to the empty car, her voice filled with exasperation as she slammed her hands against the steering wheel. The first heavy drops of rain began to fall, drumming loudly on the roof of the car.

As if in fervent reply, a window-rattling concussive roll of thunder boomed overhead. Chest heaving from pent-up aggravation, Eden sat in a daze, hands trembling as she fumbled to start the car's ignition once more, but to no avail.

She reached for her cellphone, her only lifeline, only to fumble and drop it in her flustered state. As she scooped up the device, Eden felt a nauseating pit form in her stomach – the screen remained stubbornly, tauntingly dark no matter how frequently she jabbed at the home button.

"No... no, no, no!" she pleaded desperately under her breath, frantically stabbing away in denial as the harsh truth gradually sank its insidious hooks. Hours ago, when leaping out of bed that morning, Eden had careened straight out into the day without taking the split second to ensure her phone was properly charged.

As she sat in the dimming light, the rain enveloping her car in a curtain of water, Eden felt a profound sense of isolation. The countryside, usually so serene and inviting, now felt like an alien landscape, cold and indifferent to her plight.

In that moment, trapped by the storm and her own series of unfortunate events, Eden could only laugh... a short, humorless sound, more of a release of frustration than anything else. Here she was, driven by a sudden impulse to unravel a mystery, only to be thwarted at every turn by the most mundane obstacles. As the storm raged with unrelenting fury all around her, Eden sat motionless behind the wheel, staring despondently at her useless phone's blank screen. The windshield wipers sat motionless, the heavy rain blurring her view of the countryside that mere hours ago had felt so welcoming and inviting.

All of her hopes, her burning yearnings to glean some pivotal insight from the photograph's clues, had been washed away in the deluge – displaced by a yawning emptiness that swelled together with the rhythmic hammering of raindrops pelting her car's surface. Eden slumped back against the headrest, bone-weary exhaustion replacing her previous frantic energies.

As she released a soul-scouring sigh, her body untensed, succumbing at last to the acknowledgment that some pursuits, no matter how cosmically preordained they appear to be, simply aren't meant to unfold in seamless, providential accordance. No matter how fervently we invoke the universe's unseen forces to align in divine favoritism, chaos will always demand its entropic due.

●

Alex's quaint cottage, nestled among the lush rolling hills, seemed to embody an idyllic retreat, a picturesque scene straight out of a pastoral painting. However, the serene exterior negated the chaos that unfolded within as the cottage unwittingly became a battleground in an insect invasion of epic proportions.

Shortly after returning from the hardware store that morning, Alex watched with a mix of fascination and dismay as an industrious army of ants marched tirelessly across his countertops. Their tiny legs carried morsels of food with calculated precision, forming a relentless conga line from a tiny crack near the window straight to the sugar bowl he'd left unguarded. His tranquil home in the countryside was morphing into a war zone with every passing hour.

As if to add insult to injury, Alex soon discovered an even more dreaded invader: cockroaches had taken up residence in his pantry. He tried a variety of natural remedies, from sprinkling diatomaceous earth to setting up boric acid traps. Yet, the roaches seemed to mock his efforts, skittering away into the shadows, ever elusive.

The outside proved no refuge either. Aggressive yellow jackets relentlessly dive-bombed him every time he ventured onto his front porch. After the third painful sting, which left his arm throbbing and swollen, Alex decided that after lunch, he would put on his beekeeper's suit and dispose of the nest once and for all.

The ceaseless activity of his insect adversaries wore on Alex's nerves and routines. Stress from the unending battle with the insects while he worked on fixing the house pushed Alex toward comfort eating. The disciplined eating habits he had envisioned, meals composed of fresh, local produce lovingly prepared in his own kitchen, were now replaced by indulgent treats – chocolate, soda, chips, anything that offered a momentary respite from the frustration.

As he questioned his decision to move to the countryside, seeking a quiet, purposeful life away from the urban sprawl, the infestation tested his resolve. But Alex was not one to give in. Suddenly, dark clouds quickly rolled overhead, heralding a thunderous rainstorm. Alex was reminded of nature's might and unpredictability.

He rushed from room to room, closing windows against the incoming torrent, occasionally stumbling over a rug or a chair in his haste. The rain began to fall in sheets, drumming loudly on the metal roof, a natural symphony that drowned out the hum of insects.

Standing at his living room window, watching the storm blanket the countryside, Alex felt a strange peace. The rain was washing away the old, both literally and metaphorically, offering a fresh start. Alex decided now was the time to take care of those yellow jackets. He pulled out the familiar suit, a thick, protective ensemble that included a full-body white coverall, gloves, and a veiled hat. The suit was a bit stiff from disuse but still in good condition, a testament to the quality materials used.

He carefully donned the suit, zipping it up to ensure no gaps were left for the bees to find their way in. The veil came down over his face last, the mesh fine enough to keep the bees at bay while allowing him a clear view of his buzzing charges. Pulling on the gloves, he felt a connection to the generations of beekeepers in his family who had worn similar garb, a lineage of caretakers of nature's tiny workers.

Fully suited, Alex took a deep breath, enjoying the filtered scent of wax and honey that the suit couldn't quite keep out. With a sense of purpose and a bit of excitement, he stepped toward the front door before noticing another battalion of ants heading straight for the honey he had left out on his coffee table in the living room.

●

Panicking but trying to keep a clear head, Eden turned the key in the ignition several more times, hoping for a miracle. The car responded with nothing but a few ineffective clicks… she was going nowhere. With the rain obscuring her vision and the nearest help likely miles away, Eden felt a knot of anxiety tighten in her stomach. She knew staying in the car during such a storm could be dangerous, especially if the weather worsened or if she needed to escape quickly.

Wiping the steam from the window to peer outside, she spotted a faint light in the distance... a house, perhaps, that could offer her refuge and a phone to call for help. With no other options, she grabbed her purse, secured her coat as best as she could, and opened the door to the storm.

The cold rain hit her like a wall, drenching her instantly. She locked her car, pocketing the keys, and began the precarious trek toward the light. Each step was a battle against the wind and water, and she stumbled several times on the uneven ground, her shoes sinking into the mud.

After what felt like an eternity, Eden reached the porch of the house, shivering and soaked through to her bones. She knocked desperately, water dripping from her hair and running in streams down her face. Moments later, the door flew open to reveal a frazzled man wearing a beekeeping outfit, waving his arms frantically, trying to corral an ant infestation overtaking his living room. Before Eden could explain her dripping presence, a lone bee zoomed through the open doorway, expertly eluding the man's swatting attempts.

In a panic, Eden dashed inside, the door left gaping open behind her. As she twisted and turned to evade the angry bee's erratic flight path, she lost her footing on the ant-covered floor and careened directly into the flustered man. They both flung their arms out wildly to brace against the collision, inadvertently knocking over a nearby jar of honey in the process. The glass vessel shattered on impact, splattering the hardwood with sticky golden sweetness. The rogue bee seized the opportunity to zip back out the open door as quickly as it had invaded.

"Shut the door!" the man shouted over the buzzing chaos.

Eden scrambled upright, her shoes slipping in the pooling honey as she rushed to obey.

"I'm so sorry!" she cried, profusely apologizing to the bewildered, frantic stranger. As she spun back around to help him to his feet, she felt the worn photograph of Alex slip free from her purse, fluttering slowly toward the sticky floor.

She made a desperate grab for the precious memento mid-air, but only succeeded in clipping the poor man's head with her wildly flailing elbow. He stumbled backward from the glancing blow, finally collapsing onto a nearby sofa with a dazed, heavy thud.

Eden cringed in mortification at the chaotic whirlwind of mishaps she'd caused within mere seconds of her arrival. The stunned man took off his veiled hat and shook his head groggily, blinking away his disorientation before his gaze landed on the fallen photograph at his feet. As he reached down to retrieve it, Eden turned to face him once more, a fervent apology already forming on her lips.

But the words never came, catching in her constricting throat as she focused on the man's familiar features. The chiseled jawline, the sparkling hazel eyes she knew so well from her arduous study... it was him. Alex, flesh and blood, staring back at her with equally widening disbelief.

In that endless, suspended moment, the obstacles of searching melted away into insignificance. Despite the sticky situation surrounding them, their two paths had finally, inevitably converged once more—fated travelers reuniting against all odds.

They both stood frozen, drinking in the sight of the other, lost in a whirlwind of thoughts and reawakening feelings. Then, almost in slow motion, Alex rose from the sofa and quickly took off his beekeeping outfit, the photograph still clutched in his hand. Eden's heart raced as she realized this was the pivotal moment she had pursued with such unrelenting determination.

"I've been looking for you," she breathed, taking an unconscious step forward as if pulled by gravitational forces.

"I know," Alex replied, his voice low and husky with reverence. "Nice to meet you, my name is Alex."

Eden swallowed hard, pacing herself closer until they were only inches apart, close enough to feel the magnetic charge crackling between their bodies.

"I'm Eden," she murmured, soaking in his masculine scent, comfortingly familiar yet utterly new.

Without warning, Alex reached out to caress her rain-chilled cheek, pulling Eden into a searing embrace as their lips nearly came together in a soul-searing inferno of longing and passion. They clung to each other desperately, gasping for air in deep, shuddering gulps as wave after wave of euphoria washed over them. When they finally broke apart, Eden felt her knees buckle, her senses utterly overwhelmed.

"I can't believe it's really you," Alex rasped in wonderment, cradling her face in his calloused palms.

"I know," Eden replied, leaning into his touch, anchoring herself against the ferocious tide of emotions threatening to sweep her away completely. "It's like fate itself brought us back together."

Alex nodded dazedly, seemingly just as adrift in the intoxicating moment. His eyes then looked toward the photograph still clutched in his hand, and a slow, dashing grin tugged at the corners of his mouth.

"I remember this," he chuckled, carefully fanning his flushed face with the glossy print. "Emmanuel took it at the Midnight Bakery that same night we passed each other on the street."

Eden smiled, recollections of that spellbinding, ephemeral encounter flooding back with visceral clarity.

"You were wearing the most gorgeous sundress," Alex murmured wistfully, trailing a finger down the delicate curve of her jawline. "I remember thinking you were the most stunningly perfect girl I'd ever seen."

"And I thought the exact same thing about you," Eden confessed, nestling deeper into his embrace as the savage lightning storm outside began giving way to radiant sunbeams spilling through the broken clouds.

Alex's brilliant smile was brighter than any sun, setting Eden's heart pounding with unbridled joy and possibilities. With utmost tenderness, he clasped her hand and led Eden outside to the back porch, leaving behind the wreckage of honey and wayward insects in favor of this new, infinitely sweeter reality.

In hushed tones, they began recounting the twisting journeys that had ultimately led them back into each other's lives. Slowly at first, then cascading downstream in a torrential downpour of stories, dreams, and unapologetic yearnings to reignite the spark of connection that had been smoldering on a slow burn since that fateful night on the street.

●

Alex pulled into the café's small parking lot, his heart hammering with nervous anticipation. It was hard to believe just a couple of days had passed since his and Eden's fateful reunion amid the chaos of the storm-tossed cottage. So much had happened in that compressed span of time, their lives becoming irreversibly entangled like the vines of an ancient, unstoppable root.

Alex made his way to the small, artisan café, known among locals for its inviting ambiance and excellent coffee. He chose a table in a cozy corner with a good view of the entrance and settled in, his eyes occasionally drifting to the door in anticipation.

Moments later, Eden walked in, her presence lighting up the room. He allowed himself a lingering moment to simply admire her unguarded state from a distance—the delicate swatch of freckles dusting her long nose, the subtle rise and fall of her chest underneath the powder-blue blouse, the hypnotic way she anxiously gnawed gently at her plump lower lip. Even at rest, Eden radiated vibrancy and grace far surpassing anything Alex had encountered during his year of compulsive roaming.

Spotting Alex, her face broke into a wide, genuine smile, marked with a hint of nervous excitement that mirrored his own feelings. As they greeted each other with a warm, somewhat lingering hug, the initial awkwardness quickly dissolved, replaced by a comforting familiarity.

"Great choice for the café," Eden commented as she took her seat, her eyes taking in the rustic décor and the soft music playing in the background.

Alex laughed, handing her the menu. "I thought you might like the vibe here. Plus, the coffee's really something."

They ordered their drinks—French vanilla cappuccino for Alex, and a crème brulée cappuccino for Eden. As they waited for their order, they dove into conversation, catching up on recent events in their lives. Alex shared stories of his ongoing efforts to restore his grandparents' cottage, describing his battles with the local wildlife and the quirks of rural living.

Eden listened intently, her laughter ringing out as Alex described a particularly feisty encounter with a pile of pincher bugs. In turn, she talked about her medical studies and the challenges and rewards of caring for her ailing grandmother. The conversation flowed easily, with neither of them noticing the passage of time as their drinks arrived.

Their talk gradually shifted to memories of how they first met, the unexpected twists of fate that had brought them back together, and their mutual acquaintances in Everbrook. This trip down memory lane brought them closer, bridging the gap of time apart with fond recollections and shared smiles.

As they sipped their coffee, the air between them filled with playful banter and an undercurrent of flirtation. Eden teased Alex about his newfound life as a beekeeper, suggesting he might need to start making honey-themed puns.

"Oh, bee-lieve me, I have a hive full of them," Alex quipped, earning an eye roll and a laugh from Eden. Their eyes met often, lingering a little longer each time, and their smiles grew more intimate.

Feeling a connection rekindling, Alex leaned forward, resting his arm on the table. "How about we take a walk around the square?" he suggested. "It's a beautiful day this May, and the market should be in full swing. We could check out some of the local crafts."

Eden's eyes lit up at the idea. "I'd love that," she said, her tone enthusiastic. They left their empty coffee cups behind, stepping out into the sunlit streets of Everbrook, ready to explore the town square together. As they walked side by side, their shoulders brushed occasionally, a tangible sign of their growing closeness.

The quaint storefronts lining Everbrook's main road bustled with vigor. Elderly couples strolled the sun-warmed sidewalks hand-in-hand, pausing intermittently to exchange greetings with the shopkeepers sweeping their sidewalks. Lively chatter and musical refrains drifted through propped-open windows, mingling with the sound of songbirds and the drone of lawnmowers tending to the manicured town square.

Alex let the atmosphere soak into his pores as he and Eden meandered in an unhurried flow, his palm tingling with the whisper of her slender fingers entwined through his. He was acutely, almost painfully aware of the denim brush of her hip occasionally grazing his with each turn of their aimless ambling.

"You're unusually quiet over there," Eden's velvet voice rippled through his reverie. Alex blinked, giving himself a slight mental shake to resettle into the present moment.

"Wait, what? I was just... soaking it all in, I guess. This place really is like something out of a storybook," he said.

Eden seemed to radiate an easy joy, alive with the excitement of the day ahead and the presence of Alex beside her. She pointed out various shops and boutiques as they strolled past.

"I recently visited the record store on the corner over there with my grandma. She said that it's the oldest record store in existence," Eden remarked with an affectionate smile. "Mr. Eugene, the owner, is like the unofficial mayor of this stretch. Claims he can tell you the entire discography of every piece in his shop."

Alex laughed loudly, charmed by her lively commentary and appreciation. He gave her hand a gentle squeeze, relishing how perfectly her fingers seemed to interlock with his own.

They wandered further, the bustling energy of the street giving way to the tranquil setting of the town square. Flower gardens in full bloom surrounded a sprawling lawn area where children chased each other, filling the air with sounds of laughter. An old man strummed a guitar nearby, singing a familiar folk tune.

"The farmers' market is usually happening by now," Eden remarked wistfully. "You can smell the fresh bread and produce from blocks away. My favorite time of year, hands down."

"Oh yeah?" Alex met her eyes with a playful grin. "I would have figured summer was more your thing—the season for sundresses and lounging in the park."

A faint blush tinted Eden's cheeks at his words, but she didn't look away. "Maybe so, but there's just something about spring that feels... resonant, you know? Like the world holding its breath for a beat before everything comes back to life again."

He nodded slowly, admiring the wistful, dreamy quality that had seeped into her expression. The words seemed to hang between them, laden with meaning that stretched beyond the superficial. For a moment, Alex felt like he could see the entire lifespan of Everbrook's sprawling elm trees reflected in the golden speckle of Eden's eyes—wisdom and grace earned over decades, anchored into the earth yet swaying with the seasons.

They wandered through the market, stopping occasionally to admire handcrafted jewelry and homemade preserves. Each stall offered something unique, and Alex watched Eden as she interacted with the vendors, her curiosity and enthusiasm drawing smiles from the locals.

"Look at these," Eden said, holding up a pair of delicately painted ceramic earrings. "They're so beautiful, aren't they?"

"They are," Alex agreed, enjoying the sparkle in her eyes. "They'd look great on you."

Blushing slightly, Eden set the earrings back down. Alex made a mental note of the vendor. As they moved on, their conversation turned to their childhoods, sharing stories of family holidays and school antics. Eden laughed at Alex's recount of an ill-fated camping trip, while her tale of a surprise birthday party gone awry had him grinning broadly.

Eventually, their leisurely pace brought them to the center of the square where a large park spread before them. They walked for several minutes, the trees and shrubbery thickening until Everbrook's modest municipal buildings faded from view entirely. Just when Alex wondered if they had become thoroughly turned around, the foliage opened up to reveal a stunning discovery.

In a small clearing among the lush ferns and wildflowers stood an ornate, slightly weathered gazebo encircled by meandering footpaths. Yellow jasmine and crimson honeysuckle blossoms wound their way up the iron trellises.

"Shall we?" Alex gestured toward the gazebo, and Eden nodded.

They stepped into the shelter of the structure, and Alex was suddenly aware of how close they were. The gazebo provided a private little bubble away from the noise of the town square, and the intimacy of it made his heart beat a little faster.

Sitting side by side on a wooden bench, their conversation deepened. Eden spoke of her dreams to integrate traditional medicine into modern healthcare practices, her passion evident in her expressive gestures and earnest tone. Alex listened intently, impressed by her dedication and sharing his own aspirations of turning the cottage into a sustainable homestead.

As the conversation flowed, the atmosphere grew charged with emotion, and the air between them thickened with unspoken words. When Eden looked up at Alex, her eyes reflecting the soft light that filtered through the gazebo's latticework, he knew this was the perfect moment.

Leaning in, Alex paused inches from her face, searching her eyes for any hesitation. Seeing none, he closed the distance, and their lips met in a gentle, exploratory kiss that quickly deepened with shared desire.

It started soft and tentative, an exploratory brush like the wings of a butterfly stirring up an ancient cosmic dust. But then Eden's hand cradled the back of his neck, fingernails scratching through the hairs at his neck, and everything detonated into a whirlwind of passion.

Their mouths slanted and slid with heated desperation, tongues tangling in searing exploration as their bodies curved inward to close any residual distance.

Certainly! Here is the continuation of your text with proofreading for grammatical coherence, punctuation, and flow, while maintaining the original sentence structure and dialogues:

A low groan of sheer relief rumbled from deep in Alex's chest, echoed by Eden's breathless whimper. It felt like reuniting after a thousand-year vigil, every suppressed moment of longing and need boiling over at once into a single, molten inferno of blissful completion.

When oxygen starvation eventually forced them apart, their gasps mingled with heated pants between them, foreheads still pressed tenderly together. The afternoon birdsong and buzzing of the park beyond seemed deafeningly distant compared to their rapid heartbeats thundering in tandem.

"That was..." Eden started, her voice a whisper.

"Something special," Alex finished for her, his hand finding hers.

They sat for a long while, talking softly and laughing together, the initial awkwardness of their first kiss giving way to a comfortable companionship. As the sun began to set, casting a golden light over the square, Alex suggested dinner.

"I know a great Italian place not far from here," he said, standing and offering her his hand.

"I'd love that," Eden replied, her smile bright.

Hand in hand, they left the gazebo, their hearts light and filled with anticipation for the evening ahead. The day was shaping up to be more wonderful than either of them could have imagined, each moment together deepening their bond and hinting at the promise of many more to come.

Leaving the serene bubble of the gazebo behind, Alex and Eden walked through the vibrant evening ambiance of downtown Everbrook, heading toward Cosimo's Italian restaurant. The streets were softly lit with the golden hues of streetlamps and strung lights, casting a romantic glow over the town as day turned into night.

The restaurant, nestled between the quaint record store and a flower shop, welcomed them with the rich aromas of garlic, herbs, and freshly baked bread. The hostess greeted them warmly and led them to a cozy corner table, tucked away under a canopy of ivy and fairy lights, perfect for continuing their intimate conversation.

As they settled into their seats, a waiter promptly arrived to take their order. They chose a bottle of wine to share, and after some deliberation over the enticing menu, they decided on a classic spaghetti carbonara for Alex and a risotto al funghi for Eden. As they waited for their food, they toasted to their day, clinking glasses with a smile.

"The best first date?" Alex asked, his tone playful yet sincere.

"Absolutely, to the best first date," Eden responded, her eyes sparkling. "You've set the bar pretty high, you know."

Their dinner arrived, and they enjoyed their meal immensely, the flavors as delightful as the company. Between bites, their conversation ventured into deeper territories—discussing not just personal histories and future aspirations but also their thoughts on relationships, love, and what each sought in a partner. The more they shared, the more apparent their compatibility became, and the connection deepened.

After their delightful dinner, Alex and Eden lingered over cups of rich espresso and a shared dessert of tiramisu, its sweetness a perfect pick-me-up to end the meal. The restaurant, dimly lit and intimate, had slowly emptied, leaving them in a quiet bubble of warmth and soft music. Outside, the patio doors stood open to the garden, where strands of fairy lights twinkled in the trees, casting a magical glow over the outdoor seating area.

As they were savoring the last bites of their dessert, the soft sound of an old wind-up record player filled the air. The music, gentle and evocative, seemed to speak directly to them, weaving into the fabric of their evening and adding another layer of romance.

Noticing the perfect setting and feeling the moment was just right, Alex stood and extended his hand toward Eden.

"Would you like to dance?" he asked, his voice soft yet laden with emotion.

Eden smiled, her eyes lighting up with delight. "I'd love to," she responded, placing her hand in his.

They stepped out onto the patio, moving between the tables and under the canopy of lights. The air was cool, with a gentle breeze that made the lights sway slightly, enhancing the dreamlike quality of the night. As they reached an open space under the stars, Alex pulled Eden close, and they began to sway to the music. The world seemed to fall away as they moved in sync, her head resting lightly against his shoulder, his arms securely around her. The melody enveloped them, soft and sweet, a perfect echo of the emotions that had deepened throughout their evening together.

The dance was slow and intimate, a silent conversation between them that needed no words. Each step, each turn, felt like a natural expression of their growing feelings. Eden's heart beat faster, her senses heightened by the closeness of Alex, the scent of his cologne mixing with the fresh night air. Alex felt a profound sense of connection, the kind that he had only read about in novels or seen in films, now more real than ever and within his grasp.

As the song ended, they gradually stopped moving, yet remained in each other's arms, reluctant to break the contact. The record player played the final note, which hung in the air between them like a soft sigh. Alex leaned back slightly, looking into Eden's eyes, which reflected the twinkling lights above.

"Thank you for this beautiful evening," Eden whispered, her voice filled with genuine emotion.

"Thank you for being here, with me," Alex replied, his voice equally soft. He leaned in, and they shared a passionate, lingering kiss under the starlit sky, a kiss that seemed to seal the promises and possibilities of future meetings.

Reluctantly, they parted, and as they walked back through the restaurant and out into the night, their hands found each other's again, fingers intertwining naturally.

The evening had ended, but it was clear to both that this was just the beginning. With hearts full and spirits high, they looked forward to their next encounter, each moment until then undoubtedly filled with anticipation and the sweet echo of their night under the stars.

※

Habits quietly shape our lives in profound ways. Often operating beneath our conscious awareness, they guide our actions, influence our decisions, and ultimately set the course for our future. Some habits act as powerful forces that propel us toward our goals, while others subtly sabotage our efforts, holding us back from reaching our true potential. To fully unlock that potential, it's crucial to recognize the immense power of habits and learn how to master them for personal growth and success.

In this lesson, we dive deep into the transformative power of habits, uncovering how they can be both a source of strength and a hidden barrier. We'll explore the process of cultivating positive habits that align with your aspirations, offering practical strategies to reinforce behaviors that support your goals. Simultaneously, we'll examine the steps needed to identify and break free from habits that hinder your progress, clearing the path for meaningful change.

This journey is one of self-discovery, where you become more aware of the patterns that shape your life. It's about understanding that every small action, repeated consistently, has the potential to bring you closer to the life you envision. As you learn to harness the power of habits, you'll find that each step forward not only builds momentum but also strengthens your resolve, guiding you toward a more intentional and fulfilling future.

Ultimately, mastering your habits is about taking control of your destiny. It's a lifelong commitment to growth and improvement, where every positive habit you cultivate serves as a building block for the life you aspire to live. This lesson is your road map, offering the tools and insights needed to transform your daily routines into a powerful engine for lasting change.

The Power of Positive Habits

Habits are the foundation of our daily lives, subtly guiding our thoughts, emotions, and actions. When we intentionally cultivate positive habits, they have the potential to transform our character, mindset, and overall well-being. These habits don't just influence isolated behaviors—they create a ripple effect that shapes how we approach life as a whole.

When practiced consistently, positive habits become second nature, freeing up mental energy and willpower for other important tasks. This efficiency boosts productivity and allows you to focus on growth and meaningful pursuits. Over time, these habits reshape your mindset, rewiring your neural pathways to support your goals and aspirations. They reinforce a mental framework that aligns with your values and drives success.

Beyond enhancing productivity, positive habits provide effective coping strategies. Establishing routines like regular exercise, meditation, or journaling offers healthy outlets for managing stress and maintaining emotional balance. By building these habits, you take control of your life, steering it toward fulfillment and purpose. This journey of self-improvement is ongoing, requiring continuous reflection, adaptation, and growth.

Overcoming Bad Habits

While positive habits propel us forward, bad habits can keep us stuck. These negative patterns can seep into various aspects of life, impacting relationships, work, health, and overall happiness. Breaking free from bad habits is essential for personal growth and well-being.

The first step in overcoming a bad habit is cultivating self-awareness. This involves recognizing the behaviors that no longer serve you and acknowledging their impact without judgment. Self-reflection is key here—by observing your actions and emotions, you can identify the triggers that prompt these habits. Understanding these triggers enables you to interrupt the cycle and consciously choose a different, more constructive response.

One effective strategy for breaking bad habits is to replace them with positive alternatives. Instead of just trying to eliminate a negative behavior, redirect your energy toward a healthier option. For example, if you're trying to quit smoking, you might substitute the urge with deep breathing exercises or physical activity. This approach not only disrupts the old pattern but also builds new neural pathways that reinforce better habits.

Approach this process with patience and a gradual mindset. Attempting to quit a habit abruptly can lead to frustration and setbacks. Focus on making small, consistent changes over time, and celebrate each step forward. Understand that setbacks may occur, but with persistence and commitment, you can gradually overcome bad habits and create space for positive growth.

Cultivating Positive Habits

Positive habits are the cornerstone of personal growth and achievement. By deliberately cultivating habits that align with your goals, you build a strong foundation for lasting success. These habits not only shape your actions but also influence your character, mindset, and overall well-being, becoming an integral part of who you are.

When you consciously choose to engage in behaviors that contribute to your well-being, success, and happiness, you empower yourself to create meaningful change. Whether it's establishing a regular exercise routine, practicing mindfulness, or dedicating time to personal development, these positive habits reinforce your commitment to self-improvement.

Consistency and commitment are essential in building positive habits. Start small, focusing on manageable actions that you can repeat daily. As you build momentum, your confidence grows, and the habit becomes ingrained. Clear intentions behind your habits help maintain focus and motivation. Setting specific, measurable goals allows you to track your progress, making it easier to adjust and refine your approach as needed.

Positive habits also nurture a growth mindset. By engaging in behaviors that align with your personal development goals, you reinforce the belief that you can improve and evolve. This mindset fosters optimism and empowerment, creating a positive feedback loop that drives continuous self-improvement.

Building Routines and Rituals

Routines and rituals provide the structure needed to maintain positive habits over the long term. They create stability and consistency, making it easier to reinforce desired behaviors.

Routines help reduce decision fatigue by establishing a predictable schedule and sequence of activities. This structure increases the likelihood of effortlessly engaging in positive habits.

For instance, a morning routine that includes a healthy breakfast, exercise, and meditation creates a cohesive pattern where each activity supports the others, reinforcing the overall positive behavior.

Rituals add intention and mindfulness to your habits. By consciously designing and practicing specific rituals, you become more present and aware of your actions, amplifying the positive impact on your well-being.

Creating meaningful transitions between different parts of your day can enhance your routines. For example, an evening ritual of journaling can help you unwind, providing closure and setting the stage for relaxation and reflection. These transitions help anchor your habits, making them more sustainable and rewarding.

<h1 style="text-align:center"><u>Activity: Cultivate Your Best Self</u></h1>

This activity will guide you through the process of identifying harmful habits, designing new positive routines, and tracking your progress as you cultivate your best self.

1. Habit Assessment:

Make a list of your current daily and weekly habits. Assess how each one serves you and impacts your goals and well-being. Identify 1-2 habits you'd like to change.

2. New Habit Goals:

Choose 1 new positive habit you'd like to cultivate that better aligns with your values and aspirations. Define your motivation and commitment. Break it into small, achievable steps using the SMART goal system.

3. Implementation Plan:

Design a specific plan for practicing your new chosen habit. Decide when and where you'll integrate it into your routine. Use habit stacking if helpful.

4. Tracking System:

Create a tracking system to monitor your progress with your new habit. This can be a simple checklist or app. Review regularly.

5. Lifestyle Routine:

Outline your ideal daily or weekly routine that aligns with your goals and incorporates self-care, relationships, hobbies. Schedule in your new habit.

6. Start Small:

Begin implementing your routine by taking small steps. Focus on just 1-2 habit changes for now. Be patient and celebrate all progress.

7. Adjust & Evolve:

Monitor how your new routine and habits make you feel. Make adjustments as needed. Allow your practices to organically evolve.

8. Share & Inspire:

Share your experiences with others who are looking to cultivate their best selves. Offer mutual support and inspiration. Remember that personal growth is a gradual, lifelong process. Focus on progress over perfection as you discover your best self through positive habits and intentional living.

•

Throughout our exploration, we have witnessed the power of habits in shaping our daily lives and influencing our behavior and mindset. Building positive habits is not merely about making small changes; it is about creating a solid foundation for personal growth and success. By consciously cultivating empowering habits, we lay the groundwork for a fulfilling and purposeful life.

The significance of building positive habits lies in their ability to provide structure, discipline, and focus. They serve as the building blocks of our routines and rituals, guiding us toward our goals and aspirations. Positive habits fuel our motivation, increase our productivity, and enable us to overcome obstacles along the way.

Throughout this lesson, we have discovered practical strategies for breaking bad habits and overcoming obstacles that hinder personal growth. We have explored the importance of self-awareness and self-reflection in identifying negative patterns and replacing them with positive alternatives. By recognizing the impact of our habits, we empower ourselves to make conscious choices that align with our values and aspirations.

In addition, we have delved into the process of designing and implementing effective routines and rituals. By integrating self-care activities, goal-focused actions, and positive habits into our daily lives, we create an environment that supports our personal growth journey. These routines and rituals serve as anchors, providing stability and consistency within the ever-changing nature of life.

Cultivating empowering habits is not a one-time event but rather a lifelong journey. It requires commitment, dedication, and a willingness to embrace change. As we conclude this chapter, I encourage you to make a solemn commitment to the process of habit building.

I invite you to embrace the process of habit building as an integral part of your personal development journey. Apply the insights from this chapter and those before it to your life with purpose and mindful intention. As you commit to building positive habits, remember to celebrate your successes, learn from your setbacks, and always stay focused on the power of habit building.

<u>Chapter 6: Funny Farm</u>

Eden stood in her bridal suite, looking out the window at the beautiful rolling hills while adjusting the delicate lace veil cascading down her shoulders. Her mother, Maria, and grandmother, Beatrice, bustled around her, their excitement evident.

"Just look at you, darling," Maria said, her voice trembling with emotion as she straightened the hem of Eden's dress. "You're absolutely radiant."

Eden smiled, her eyes shimmering with a mixture of joy and nerves. "I can't believe this day is finally here. It feels like a dream."

Beatrice, with her snow-white hair pinned up in an elegant hairstyle, adjusted her glasses and gazed fondly at her granddaughter. "It's not just a dream, my dear. It's the beginning of a beautiful new chapter. Your love story with Alex is like a novel unfolding, each page more captivating than the last."

The room was filled with the soft light of the morning sun, streaming through the lace curtains and casting a warm glow on the floral arrangements that decorated the suite. The scent of roses and lilies lingered in the air, adding to the airy ambiance. Maria took Eden's hands in hers, their matching sapphire rings glinting in the light.

"Remember, no matter what happens today, it's about you and Alex. The vows you're about to exchange are the promises that will carry you through the highs and lows of life," Maria said.

Eden nodded, feeling the weight of her mother's words. "I know, Mom. It's just… I want everything to be perfect."

Beatrice chuckled softly, her laughter like a gentle breeze. "Perfection is an illusion, my dear. What matters is the love you share and the memories you create. And trust me, those memories are rarely perfect, but they are always beautiful."

Eden's heart swelled with gratitude and love for these two women who had shaped her life. She turned back to the mirror, taking a deep breath to steady her racing heart.

"Thank you both for being here with me. I couldn't have made it this far without you," she said.

Maria dabbed at the corner of her eye with a handkerchief. "Oh, Eden, we're so proud of you. You've grown into such a strong, compassionate woman. Alex is a lucky man."

Beatrice stepped forward, placing a gentle hand on Eden's shoulder. "And you, my dear, are a lucky woman to have found someone who cherishes you as much as Alex does. Now, let's get you ready to walk down that aisle."

The conversation flowed naturally, filled with laughter, shared memories, and words of wisdom. Maria recounted the story of her own wedding day, how she had tripped on her gown and how her husband had caught her just in time. Beatrice shared tales of her youth, painting vivid pictures of love and courtship from a bygone era.

Eden absorbed every word, feeling her nervousness give way to a sense of calm and anticipation. The love and support of her family wrapped around her like a comforting embrace, fortifying her for the moments ahead.

As they made the final adjustments to her dress and veil, a strong gust of wind rattled the windows, drawing their attention outside.

The sky, which had been a clear blue just moments ago, was now dotted with dark clouds rolling in.

Beatrice peered out the window, a mischievous glint in her eye. "Looks like we might have a bit of drama to add to the day. But remember, my dear, a little rain never hurt anyone. In fact, it's considered good luck!"

Eden laughed, feeling a newfound lightness in her heart. "Then we'll take it as a blessing."

With everything in place, Maria and Beatrice stepped back, admiring their work. Eden looked like a vision from a fairy tale, her gown shimmering like spun sugar, her eyes bright with hope and love.

"It's time," Maria said softly, her voice filled with emotion. "Let's go make some beautiful memories."

Hand in hand, the three women left the bridal suite and walked into the lush, sprawling grounds of the estate. The outdoor pavilion where the ceremony would take place stood proudly around the greenery, its wooden columns and flowing drapery giving it an almost dreamlike quality. The pavilion was decorated with delicate flowers—roses, lilies, and peonies—that seemed to bloom with a vibrancy that echoed the joy of the occasion.

Rolling hills stretched out in every direction, their emerald expanse broken only by the occasional cluster of wildflowers. Birds flew from tree to tree, their cheerful songs adding a lively backdrop to the serene setting.

Near the pavilion, a large barn waited, its weathered wooden exterior a charming contrast to the pavilion's pristine elegance. The barn, restored with a touch of rustic chic, would host the reception later in the day. Ivy vines crept up its sides, and lanterns hung from its eaves.

As Eden, Maria, and Beatrice walked towards the pavilion, another strong gust of wind swept across the landscape, rustling the leaves of the nearby oak trees and sending a ripple through the draped fabric. The sudden breeze brought with it a hint of rain, a reminder of the unpredictable nature of spring weather. Eden's veil fluttered gently, and she instinctively reached up to hold it in place.

The sky, which had been a perfect bright blue, was now marked by dark clouds gathering on the horizon. They moved swiftly, propelled by the strengthening wind, casting shifting shadows over the countryside.

Guests began to arrive, making their way to the rows of white chairs arranged in neat lines before the pavilion. Laughter and chatter filled the air as friends and family greeted one another, their conversations a blend of excitement and anticipation. The organist, a distinguished man with a gold tooth that flashed when he smiled and thick eyebrows that met in the middle, began to play a soft, melodious tune. The music drifted on the breeze, creating an atmosphere of elegance and romance.

As more guests arrived, they were guided to their seats by ushers. Among them were Sarah and Tom, whose strained relationship was evident in their body language. Sarah, Alex's sister, wore a nervous smile, while Tom, always busy with his city job, seemed distracted, checking his phone frequently. Their twin ten-year-old boys, Claus and Lucas, ran ahead, their laughter echoing across the open space.

Leo, Eden's brother, arrived and found his seat, exchanging warm greetings with Alex's parents and other guests. The wind continued to blow, and the clouds moved steadily closer, but the impending storm only added to the drama and excitement of the day. It felt as if nature itself was joining in the celebration, its unpredictability mirroring the surprises and adventures that lay ahead for Eden and Alex.

As the final guests took their seats, the organist's music slowly fell silent, signaling that the ceremony was about to begin. Eden took a deep breath, savoring the moment and the beauty of the venue. She was ready to step into the pavilion and begin the next chapter of her life, surrounded by the love and support of her family and friends, and blessed by the ever-changing, ever-beautiful countryside.

Alex stood at the altar, flanked by his best man, Gabriel, and the groomsmen, Maya's husband, Tyler, and Sarah's husband, Tom. Despite the stormy clouds gathering overhead, Alex's face radiated joy and anticipation. His eyes searched the path from the bridal suite, eagerly awaiting the sight of his bride.

Gabriel, noticing Alex's nervous energy, clapped a reassuring hand on his shoulder. "You look like you're about to explode," he teased gently. "Just breathe. She's going to take your breath away."

Maya, the maid of honor, and the bridesmaids, Monica and Sarah, lined up at the entrance to the pavilion. They held their bouquets tightly, their dresses fluttering slightly in the increasing wind.

Maya glanced at Eden, offering her a warm smile. "You okay?" she asked softly.

Eden nodded, though her eyes betrayed her lingering tension. "Yeah, just a bit nervous."

Maya gave her hand a quick squeeze. "It'll be fine. Focus on the happiness today brings."

The organist began to play the processional music, and one by one, the bridesmaids walked down the aisle, their steps measured and graceful. As they reached the altar, they took their places opposite the groomsmen, forming a semicircle around Alex.

Finally, it was Eden's turn. She took a deep breath, feeling her mother's arm loop through hers. Maria smiled at her daughter, her eyes brimming with pride and love.

"Ready, sweetheart?" she said.

Eden nodded, her heart pounding with a mix of excitement and nervousness. "Ready."

As they stepped out into the aisle, a collective sound of admiration swept through the guests. Eden looked stunning, her dress shimmering softly, her veil cascading elegantly over her shoulders. The organist's music filled the air with a melody that was both timeless and touching.

As Eden and her mother began their walk down the aisle, a sudden bolt of lightning split the sky, followed by a rumble of thunder. The storm was no longer just a distant threat—it was here, adding a dramatic backdrop to the moment. Eden tightened her grip on her mother's arm, her eyes locked on Alex's as they drew closer.

Despite the storm, or perhaps because of it, the moment felt intensely magical. The guests watched in awe, the dramatic weather only amplifying the emotion of the scene. As Eden reached the altar, her mother placed her hand in Alex's, giving it a gentle squeeze before stepping back.

Alex gazed at Eden, his eyes reflecting the love and devotion he felt. "You look breathtaking," he whispered.

Eden smiled, her heart swelling with joy. "So do you."

The priest, a kindly older man with a warm smile, began the ceremony, his voice strong and reassuring despite the storm's rumbling presence. "Dearly beloved, we are gathered here today to witness the union of Alex and Eden in holy matrimony. Despite the storm that surrounds us, it is love that brings us together, shining brightly even in the darkest of times." As he spoke, the wind picked up, rustling the fabric of the pavilion and causing the flowers to sway.

Alex took a deep breath, steadying himself as he began his vows. "Eden, from the moment I met you, my life changed forever. Your beauty, both inside and out, has captivated me. You inspire me to be the best version of myself. Today, I vow to love you fiercely and loyally, to stand by your side through every storm, and to cherish each moment we share. Together, we will write our story, one filled with love, laughter, and endless adventures."

A single tear rolled down Eden's cheek as she listened to Alex's heartfelt words. She took his hands in hers, her voice steady and filled with emotion.

"Alex," she said, "You are my keystone and my greatest adventure. With you, I have found my home. I vow to support you, to laugh with you, and to be your steadfast partner in all that life brings our way. Our journey together is just beginning, and I am so excited to walk this path with you, hand in hand."

As she finished her vows, a final, resounding clap of thunder echoed across the countryside. Then, as if on cue, the storm began to subside. The wind calmed, and the dark clouds started to disperse, revealing patches of blue sky. A warm, humid air settled over the gathering, carrying with it the fresh scent of rain.

The priest smiled, his voice resonant with warmth. "By the power vested in me, I now pronounce you husband and wife. You may kiss the bride."

Alex and Eden leaned into each other, their lips meeting in a tender kiss that sealed their vows. The guests erupted into applause, their cheers mingling with the soft patter of the last raindrops. As Alex and Eden turned to face their loved ones, hand in hand, they were greeted by a scene of pure joy and celebration. As they walked down the aisle together, Eden felt a profound sense of peace and happiness. She glanced up at Alex, who squeezed her hand gently.

"We did it," he whispered, his eyes shining with love.

"We did," Eden replied, her heart full.

But amidst the joy, Eden felt a familiar ache in her chest. Her father had passed away when she was young, never getting the

chance to see her grow into the woman she had become. She wished
he could be there today, to witness this moment, to walk her down
the aisle. As if sensing her thoughts, the breeze seemed to carry a
warmth around her, and for a brief moment, she imagined him
smiling down, proud and content.

With Alex by her side and the love of those around her, Eden
knew that, in some way, her father was here with her, watching over
this new chapter of her life.

●

The guests began to disperse across the scenic venue grounds,
mingling and enjoying the beautiful surroundings. The air was thick
with humidity, but it did little to dampen the joyous atmosphere.
Eden and Alex, surrounded by their bridal party, made their way to a
picturesque spot near the barn for photos.

The photographer, a cheerful woman with an eye for detail,
directed everyone into position. "Alright, everyone, gather around
the happy couple! Let's capture these beautiful moments."

Eden and Alex stood at the center, their hands entwined and
smiles radiant. Maya, the maid of honor, stood to Eden's left, while
Gabriel, the best man, took his place next to Alex. The bridesmaids,
Monica and Sarah, and the groomsmen, Tyler and Tom, filled in the
spaces, creating a semi-circle around the newlyweds.

Monica glanced at Gabriel, who was standing a few feet away,
adjusting his suit. Her heart gave a familiar flutter. She had harbored
feelings for him since they first met just a few months prior, but she
had always kept them hidden, unsure if he felt the same. Gabriel,
with his easy smile and warm personality, had always been a bit of a
mystery to her. She wondered if he had noticed her admiration or if
he was entirely oblivious.

"Everyone look here and smile! Say, 'Fuzzy Pickles!'" the
photographer instructed, breaking Monica's thoughts.

As the group smiled for the camera, Monica's mind wandered
back to college days, to the time she had betrayed Eden by getting
involved with her then-boyfriend, Nate. It had been a painful chapter
for both of them. Eden had been hurt deeply, but over time, she had
chosen to forgive rather than hold onto the anger. It was a testament
to Eden's kind and understanding nature that their friendship had not
only survived but thrived.

"Okay, now just the bride and groom, please," the photographer instructed. The bridal party stepped back, giving Eden and Alex the spotlight.

Monica watched as Eden and Alex shared a tender moment, their love evident in every glance and touch. Monica sighed, feeling a mixture of happiness for her friend, and longing for something similar in her own life after remembering the heartbreak of Nate's betrayal of her during their final year of college. Monica's eyes drifted back to Gabriel, who was now talking with Sarah.

Gabriel had always been driven and ambitious, recently gaining recognition for his musical talent. He had formed a band that was starting to make waves, and his future seemed bright. But despite his success, Gabriel often felt a sense of incompleteness. His eyes frequently found their way to Sarah during the ceremony, and now as they talked, he found himself drawn to her warmth and genuine kindness.

Sarah, on the other hand, was struggling with her own issues. Her relationship with Tom had become strained due to his demanding city job and frequent absences. She felt isolated and lonely, raising their twins, Claus and Lucas, largely on her own. Gabriel's attention made her feel seen and appreciated in a way she hadn't felt in a long time.

Meanwhile, Tyler and Maya stood a short distance away, watching the photo session with their hands clasped. Their relationship had faced numerous challenges in its early days, but they had weathered each storm together, emerging stronger and more committed. Tyler glanced at Maya, his eyes filled with love and gratitude.

"We've come a long way, haven't we?" he said softly, kissing her forehead.

Maya nodded, a smile playing on her lips. "Yes, we have. And I wouldn't change a thing."

As the photo shoot continued, the photographer captured candid moments... Alex whispering something that made Eden laugh, Monica exchanging a playful glance with Gabriel, and Tyler and Maya sharing a quiet, affectionate moment. The photographer lowered her camera, smiling warmly.

"I think we got some fantastic shots. You all look wonderful," she said.

Eden and Alex thanked her, their happiness infectious. As the group began to make their way back to the barn for the reception, there was a sense of anticipation in the air. Despite the rain, the day had been perfect so far, and it promised to get even better as the celebrations continued.

The barn was a sight to behold. Lanterns hung from the rafters, casting a warm, golden glow over the space. The tables were elegantly set with vintage china, polished silverware, and centerpieces of antique books and wildflowers. The scent of freshly baked bread and blooming flowers filled the air, mingling with the lively chatter of the guests.

Sarah stood near the entrance, watching as her twins, Claus and Lucas, darted around, their laughter ringing out. She sighed, glancing over at Tom, who was standing a few feet away, his phone glued to his ear. His brow was furrowed in concentration as he discussed some urgent matter from work.

"Tom," Sarah called softly, hoping to catch his attention. "Can you please help with the boys?"

Tom held up a finger, signaling her to wait. "Just a minute, Sarah. This is important."

Sarah's shoulders sagged slightly. It was always the same... Tom's job came first, and she often felt like she was raising the children on her own. She turned her attention back to Claus and Lucas, who were now being corralled by Leo.

Leo, with his infectious enthusiasm and childlike spirit, had taken charge of the children's table. He had a group of kids around him, all of them listening intently as he animatedly described how to defeat the boss on level six of some popular video game.

"Alright, kiddos, gather around," Leo said, tying his tie around his head like a bandana. "This is how you conquer the dragon! First, you need the magic sword, which you can find in the enchanted forest. Then you need to hide behind the boulder and when the dragon comes out of the cave, shoot him three times with your magic arrows. The dragon's head will start to spin, and that's when you need to get on top of the boulder and jump off doing a downward thrust with the magic sword and boom, level six is done."

The children clapped, their eyes wide with excitement. Leo's antics brought a smile to Sarah's face. She was grateful for his presence, knowing the boys adored him.

As more guests settled into their seats, the buzz of conversation grew. Emmanuel, a close family friend known for his culinary talents, found himself in a lively conversation with a group of guests at one of the tables. Emmanuel was a humble man, his passion for food evident in every word he spoke.

"I must say, the bread tonight is absolutely divine," one of the guests remarked, taking another bite of the freshly baked roll.

Emmanuel beamed with pride. "Thank you, I actually had the pleasure of baking it myself," he replied. "I've been baking bread for years, and when Alex and Eden asked me to contribute to their wedding, I knew I wanted to do something special."

He gestured towards the table, where intricately woven baskets held artisan bread rolls, and delicate porcelain dishes showcased charming butter sculptures shaped like lambs. The guests leaned in to admire the detail.

"And these butter lambs," Emmanuel continued, his eyes twinkling, "are my little contribution to the festivities. I sculpted each one by hand. It's an old tradition in my family to create butter sculptures for special occasions, and I thought it would add a whimsical touch to the tables."

The guests admired the delicate details of the butter lambs, each one meticulously crafted with care and skill. The lambs rested atop their dishes, their serene expressions almost too perfect to disturb with a knife.

"Your work is incredible," another guest commented. "It must have taken you hours to create these."

Emmanuel nodded, a modest smile on his face. "It did take some time, but it was worth it. I wanted to give Alex and Eden something unique and memorable. Plus, I believe that the little details are what make an event truly special."

The guests nodded in agreement, appreciating the effort and love that went into each creation. The butter lambs not only added a whimsical charm to the tables but also sparked conversations and brought smiles to everyone who noticed them. The music shifted, and the DJ, a lively man who looked like he never left the 1980s, took to the microphone.

"Ladies and gentlemen, may I have your attention, please?" he called out, his voice booming over the speakers. "It is my great pleasure to introduce, for the very first time, the newlyweds... Mr.

and Mrs. Alex Freeman!"

The barn doors swung open, and Alex and Eden stepped inside, hand in hand. The guests erupted into applause and cheers, the sound echoing off the barn's wooden walls. Eden's face lit up with joy, and Alex couldn't take his eyes off her.

They made their way to the dance floor, their steps synchronized as if they had been together their whole lives. The music grew louder, and the couple began their first dance as husband and wife. The room fell silent, all eyes on them as they moved gracefully to the rhythm of their song. As they danced, Alex leaned in close, whispering something in Eden's ear.

"I can't believe we're finally here. You look absolutely stunning, and I love you more than anything," Alex said, his voice filled with emotion.

Eden's heart swelled with love. "Our love is so right, I was empty until the day we met," she whispered back, resting her head on his shoulder.

The guests watched with smiles, many of them moved by the obvious love and connection between Alex and Eden. Emmanuel and his wife, Catherine, exchanged loving glances. Emmanuel leaned over to Catherine, his eyes twinkling.

"They remind me of us on our wedding day," he said, squeezing her hand.

Catherine nodded, her smile warm. "Yes, they do. Young love is such a beautiful thing."

As the dance continued, the guests couldn't help but be drawn into the magic of the moment. For those few minutes, it was as if the world outside didn't exist... there was only the music, the dance, and the love radiating from the newlyweds.

When the song ended, the room erupted into applause once more. Alex and Eden took a bow, their faces glowing with happiness. They made their way to their table, ready to join their guests and continue the celebration.

●

The DJ's voice came over the speakers again, energetic and engaging. "Alright, folks, let's keep this party going! Please take your seats as we get ready to serve the first course."

The waitstaff moved gracefully between the tables, delivering plates of the first course: a delicate salad composed of fresh greens, heirloom tomatoes, and edible flowers. The colors of the dish mirrored the vibrant decorations around the barn, creating a feast for both the eyes and the palate.

As the guests began to enjoy their salads, the DJ took to the microphone again. "Ladies and gentlemen, please direct your attention to the maid of honor, Maya, who has a few words she'd like to share."

Maya stood up, her face radiant with excitement and emotion. She held a champagne flute in one hand and a small stack of notes in the other. The room quieted as all eyes turned towards her.

"Hello, everyone," Maya began, her voice steady but filled with emotion. "For those of you who don't know me, I'm Maya, and I've had the privilege of being Eden's best friend since we were just kids."

She glanced over at Eden, who was sitting beside Alex, her face glowing with happiness. "Eden and I have been through so much together, from our awkward teenage years to our college adventures, and now, to this incredible moment. I've always admired her strength, her kindness, and her ability to forgive, even when it wasn't easy."

Maya took a deep breath, her eyes shining as she continued. "But tonight, I want to tell you all about one of the most beautiful moments I've ever witnessed: Alex's proposal to Eden."

The guests leaned in, intrigued, as Maya began her story.

"It was a little over a year ago, on a crisp autumn evening. Alex had been planning the proposal for months, and let me tell you, it was nothing short of magical. He wanted to make it perfect, to show Eden just how much she means to him."

Maya's voice softened, her words weaving a vivid picture. "Alex transformed their cottage into a fairy tale. When Eden walked in, she found the rooms aglow with candlelight and trails of rose petals leading her out to the back patio. There, she found Alex standing with a book in his hands."

Eden blushed, her eyes misting with happy tears as she relived the memory.

"Now, this wasn't just any book," Maya continued, her voice tinged with emotion. "It was a custom-made book, titled '*Our Love Story.*' Inside, Alex had written the story of their journey together, filled with memories, love notes, and little illustrations of their adventures."

The guests listened intently, some dabbing at their eyes with napkins.

"On the last page," Maya said, her voice breaking slightly, "Alex had cut out a hollow space, and nestled inside was the most beautiful engagement ring. As Eden turned to that page, Alex got down on one knee and asked her to marry him."

A collective sigh swept through the room, and a few audible "awws" could be heard.

"Eden, of course, said yes," Maya added with a smile. "And here we are today, celebrating their love and the beginning of their next chapter together."

She raised her glass, her eyes meeting those of the newlyweds. "Eden, Alex, may your life together be filled with endless love, joy, and countless more magical moments. To the bride and groom!"

The guests raised their glasses in unison, toasting to the happy couple. "To the bride and groom!"

Eden and Alex clinked their glasses together, their eyes locked in a moment of shared love and happiness. The room erupted in applause, and Maya, wiping away a tear, returned to her seat, her heart full.

As the waitstaff cleared away the remnants of the first course, they seamlessly brought out the second: a rich and creamy butternut squash soup, served in elegant, porcelain bowls. The fragrant aroma of the soup filled the barn, mingling with the warm laughter and chatter of the guests.

The DJ returned to the microphone, his voice lively and engaging. "Ladies and gentlemen, I hope you're enjoying this delicious meal. Now, it's time to hear from our best man, Gabriel. Let's give him a warm round of applause!"

Gabriel stood up, a confident smile on his face as he took the microphone. The guests clapped enthusiastically, eager to hear what he had to say.

"Good evening, everyone," Gabriel began, his voice steady and clear. "For those of you who don't know me, I'm Gabriel, Alex's best friend and neighbor. We've known each other ever since we were little kids, and I've had the honor of watching Alex grow into the incredible person he is today."

He paused, glancing over at Alex and Eden, who were both smiling warmly at him. "When Alex asked me to be his best man, I was thrilled. But then I realized I had to write a speech, and I started to panic a little. What could I possibly say to capture how amazing these two are together?"

Gabriel's eyes twinkled with humor as he continued. "Then I remembered a story that I think sums up their relationship perfectly. It was a night when Alex decided to impress Eden with his culinary skills. For those who don't know, Alex is an amazing cook. He can whip up a gourmet meal from scratch, no problem."

The guests murmured in appreciation, and Eden nodded with a knowing smile.

Gabriel grinned. "So, one evening, Alex decided to prepare this elaborate five-course dinner for Eden. He spends the entire day cooking, meticulously planning each dish. When Eden arrives home later in the evening, she's blown away by the setup. There are candles, music, and the most delicious aroma wafting through the apartment."

Eden blushed slightly, remembering that magical evening.

"But here's the funny part," Gabriel continued, his tone playful. "In the middle of serving the main course, Alex realized he'd forgotten the dessert in the oven. He dashed into the kitchen, only to find it filled with smoke, alarms going off throughout the house. He looks at Eden, expecting her to be disappointed, but instead, she bursts out laughing. They end up eating ice cream straight from the tub, sitting on the kitchen floor, laughing about the whole thing."

The guests laughed, the image of Alex and Eden enjoying a spontaneous, imperfect moment together bringing a smile to everyone's faces.

Gabriel's expression softened, his voice growing more heartfelt. "That's what their relationship is about... finding joy in the little moments, supporting each other, and always making the best of any situation. They turn every challenge into a shared adventure, and that's what makes them so special."

Gabriel continued, "So, here's to Alex and Eden, to love, laughter, and many more unforgettable moments. Cheers!"

The guests raised their glasses, toasting to the happy couple once more. Gabriel returned to his seat, his speech having left a warm and lasting impression on everyone.

At the children's table, Leo was in the middle of a comedic scene with Claus, Lucas, and a group of their friends. Wearing a funny pair of sunglasses, Leo was passionately explaining the intricacies of pencils and erasers.

"Alright, kids," Leo said with a theatrical flourish, "let me tell you about an invention I've been working on, the greatest invention of all time... the pencil eraser! It's an eraser that erases pencils!"

The kids giggled, their eyes wide with amusement.

"But Uncle Leo," Claus interrupted, "what about the eraser eraser? You know, an eraser that erases other erasers?"

Leo gasped dramatically, playing along. "An eraser eraser? Now that's revolutionary! We need to patent that idea ASAP, that means right now!"

Nearby, Grandma Beatrice approached the children's table, intrigued by the children's laughter. Leo, always the prankster, scribbled a note and handed it to Claus.

"Take this to that pretty girl at the table over there," he said, pointing discreetly. Claus ran off to deliver the note, giggling.

Beatrice, noticing the scene, smiled and shook her head. "What are you up to, Leo?"

"Oh, just spreading a little mischief," Leo replied with a wink. "But you know what, Grandma? You should go up there and give a speech. I think everyone would love to hear from you."

Beatrice's eyes sparkled with mischief. "Well, if you insist."

Beatrice made her way to the front of the room. Without missing a beat, she gently took the microphone from the head table.

In a state of dementia, Beatrice began to toast, "Welcome, fellow armadillos! We're here to toast my son-in-law Alistair and his new hamster, Eden, on their wedding day," she began, eliciting confused chuckles.

"Riverrun, past Eden and Alex, from swerve of shore to bend of bay, since she was just a little chickadee, though sometimes I confuse her for my late Aunt Bonna," Beatrice continued endearingly. She then veered into a winding tangent about ballroom dancing in the 1960s, demonstrating a clumsy waltz move.

"Of course, back then we danced the foxtrot to that hip cat Frank Kerouac, not like you butter lambs with your algorithms and whatnot!" she exclaimed, leaving the guests tickled but bewildered.

Chuckles rippled through the room as Beatrice wandered through tangents. Guests' foreheads furrowed questioningly, exchanging glances with each other as they tried to follow her disjointed train of thought.

Just as it seemed her toast was about to run away, she added, "Eden, I'm so proud of you and wish you and Alex a wonderful dance through life together!"

Beatrice then waved her hands about and tried to cue the DJ to play a tango as she attempted to find her way off the stage. Alex gently guided her back to her seat as the guests erupted into sympathetic applause after her dementia-tinged toast.

As the waitstaff brought out the third course, the barn filled with the mouthwatering aroma of tender roast beef accompanied by garlic mashed potatoes and a medley of seasonal vegetables. The guests eagerly began to enjoy their meals, the flavors rich and satisfying.

At the head table, Marco, the head chef, approached with an air of focused determination. Balancing several plates on his arms, he moved gracefully despite the weight of the dishes. As he reached the table, he started placing the plates in front of Alex, Eden, and the bridal party.

In his effort to ensure everyone was served promptly, Marco leaned over a bit too far, and his elbow accidentally knocked over the microphone stand. The microphone hit the floor with a loud clang, causing the room to fall silent and all eyes to turn toward the source of the commotion. Marco's face turned a deep shade of red as he quickly picked up the microphone and set it back in place. Nervous chuckles rippled through the crowd.

Embarrassed, he began to retreat back to the kitchen, but the guests, sensing an opportunity for some lighthearted fun, started to chant, "Speech! Speech! Speech!"

Marco turned back, holding up his hands in a gesture of polite refusal. "Oh no, I'm just the cook," he said, his voice a bit shaky.

But the crowd's encouragement grew louder and more insistent. Marco glanced at Alex and Eden, who smiled and nodded at him encouragingly. Realizing there was no easy way to escape this situation, he took a deep breath and stepped back up to the microphone.

"Uh, good evening, everyone," Marco began, his voice trembling slightly. "I'm Marco, the head cook here tonight. I'm much more comfortable behind a stove than a microphone, but I appreciate the warm welcome."

The guests quieted down, eager to hear what he had to say.

"I've had the pleasure of preparing tonight's meal for you all. I hope it was delicious for everyone!" Marco continued, gaining confidence. "But enough about the food," Marco said with a grin. "I want to talk about something even more important. Love is like cooking. It requires the right ingredients... trust, respect, and a lot of patience. You need to nurture it, let it simmer, and sometimes add a little spice to keep things interesting."

The guests chuckled, nodding in agreement.

"And just like in cooking," Marco continued, "there will be times when things don't go as planned. Maybe you forget the dessert in the oven, or you forget to buy butter for the bread. But those moments, those little mishaps, are what make the journey worthwhile. They teach us to laugh, to adapt, and to appreciate the imperfect beauty of life.

Love, my friends, is the secret ingredient that brings it all together. Just as spices add depth to a dish, love adds depth to our lives. It's the subtle notes of care, the bold flavors of compassion, and the lingering aroma of understanding that make life's experiences truly memorable.

In cooking, we share our creations with others, inviting them to partake in the feast we've prepared. Similarly, in life, we share our journeys with those around us. We open our hearts, not just in the moments of celebration, but also in times of vulnerability and sorrow, creating connections that nourish our souls.

And so, as we gather here tonight to celebrate love and unity, let's remember that we are all part of a larger recipe: a recipe that combines the ingredients of friendship, family, and community. Just as in the kitchen, where every ingredient plays a vital role, each one of us contributes to the beauty of this gathering.

As we savor this delicious meal tonight, let's also savor the moments we share with one another. Let's remember that life, like cooking, is a blend of flavors and experiences that come together to create something remarkable. And let's continue to infuse our lives with the most essential ingredient of all... love."

As he reached the conclusion of his unexpected soliloquy, a

round of applause erupted. Eden dabbed her eyes with a napkin, a single tear slipping down her cheek. The cook's accidental encounter with the microphone had transformed into an unexpected moment of joy.

He raised his glass, his eyes shining with emotion. "So, here's to Alex and Eden. May your life together be as rich and flavorful as the meal we've shared tonight. May you always find joy in the little moments, and may your love continue to grow and nourish your souls. Cheers!"

The guests raised their glasses, toasting to the newlyweds once more. "Cheers!"

The DJ smiled from across the room. "Thank you, Marco, for that beautiful speech. Now, let's enjoy the rest of this amazing meal and get ready for some more fun and dancing!"

●

Alex, ever the gracious host, began to walk around the room, greeting guests and catching up with old friends. He stopped at each table, sharing stories and laughter, his warmth and charm making everyone feel included in the celebration.

As Alex made his rounds, Eden found herself on the dance floor, twirling and laughing with her bridesmaids and friends. Her joy was contagious, and soon a lively dance circle formed around her. Nearby, Leo, always the prankster, spotted an unattended butter lamb on one of the tables. With a mischievous grin, he picked it up and hid it on an empty seat. He then called over Claus and Lucas, who had been watching him with keen interest.

"Hey, you two," Leo said, his eyes twinkling with mischief. "Want to help me out a little bit? I've got an idea. We're going to have a good time at this party and make this a funny farm, whaddya say, kiddos?"

The boys nodded eagerly, their eyes wide with excitement. Leo handed them a couple more butter lambs, whispering instructions as they giggled and ran off to find hiding spots. Soon, the other children joined in, and the game of hiding butter lambs began in earnest. The kids scurried around the barn, tucking the buttery sculptures into the most unexpected places: on windowsills, under napkins, and even atop the decorative shelves.

After making his way through the crowd, Alex returned to the head table, where he found Eden waiting for him, her eyes sparkling with happiness.

"Are you ready for the cake cutting?" he asked, offering her his hand.

Eden nodded, taking his hand with a smile. Together, they walked to the beautifully decorated cake table. The cake itself was a masterpiece—a four-tier confection adorned with cascading flowers and intricate designs. The top tier featured a charming cake topper that depicted Alex and Eden holding hands, gazing lovingly at each other.

The DJ's voice boomed over the speakers, drawing everyone's attention. "Ladies and gentlemen, it's time for the cake cutting! Let's gather around and watch Alex and Eden share this special moment."

The guests stood and moved toward the cake table, eager to witness the ceremony. Alex and Eden picked up the silver cake knife together, their fingers interlacing around the handle. With smiles of pure joy, they carefully sliced into the cake, the crowd erupting into applause and cheers.

As Alex delicately fed Eden the first bite of cake, Eden had a mischievous look in her eyes. She giggled and smashed a piece all over Alex's face. The guests laughed and clapped, enjoying the sweet moment between the newlyweds.

Meanwhile, Claus, Lucas, and their circle of young friends continued their mission of sneaking around and finding new spots to hide the remaining butter lambs. Their laughter and whispers added a charming backdrop to the festivities.

The DJ's voice came over the speakers again, lively and engaging. "Alright, folks, let's get this party started! The dance floor is open, so let's see those moves!"

The music shifted to an upbeat tune, and the guests eagerly flooded the dance floor. Couples twirled, friends laughed, and the joyous energy of the evening continued to build.

As the dancing and celebration continued, the guests began to discover the hidden butter lambs. Laughter erupted at each new find —a butter lamb perched on a chair, another nestled among the photo booth props, and one daringly placed on the DJ's turntable.

Grandma Beatrice, ever the sharp-eyed observer, spotted a butter lamb sitting on the cake topper, delicately balanced between the statues of Alex and Eden.

"Well, now, isn't that a sight!" she exclaimed, pointing it out to the nearest guest. "Those kids sure know how to have fun."

As the music continued to play and the guests enjoyed the festive atmosphere, Sarah and Tom made their way through the crowd to find Eden. They had been trying to catch up with her since the reception started and finally saw an opportunity as she stepped off the dance floor.

"Eden!" Sarah called, waving her hand.

Eden turned and smiled brightly when she saw them approaching. "Sarah! Tom! I'm so glad to see you again!"

Sarah gave Eden a warm hug, while Tom offered a polite smile.

"It's been an amazing evening," Sarah said, stepping back to look at Eden. "You look absolutely stunning. The whole day has been magical."

Eden beamed. "Thank you so much. It means a lot to have you both here."

Tom glanced around the bustling barn, trying to maintain his composure despite the strain between him and Sarah. "It's a beautiful reception," he said, his voice a bit strained. "Everything's perfect."

Just then, one of the waitstaff called out with a grin, holding up a butter lamb they had found inside an empty punch bowl. The guests nearby erupted in laughter, and even Tom couldn't help but smile at the sheer creativity of the children's mischief.

"At least they're keeping everyone entertained," Tom said, his tone cheering up.

Eden nodded, her eyes sparkling with amusement. "It's wonderful. It adds such a playful touch to the evening. I think everyone will remember this."

As they continued talking, another butter lamb was found, this time inside a decorative birdcage that was part of the barn's decor. The guests gathered around, snapping pictures and sharing the joy of the whimsical finds.

The playful atmosphere and shared laughter seemed to bridge the gap between Sarah and Tom, if only for a moment. They exchanged a glance, both appreciating the lightheartedness of their children.

Eden noticed the brief connection and felt a glimmer of hope for her friends. She squeezed Sarah's hand.

"Thank you for being here, both of you. It means so much to

Alex and me," she said.

Sarah returned the squeeze, her eyes softening. "We're happy to be here, Eden. Truly."

Tom nodded in agreement, his expression sincere. "Congratulations again, Eden. You and Alex deserve all the happiness in the world."

Eden smiled warmly. "Thank you, Tom."

As the guests continued to dance and celebrate, the barn was alive with joy and laughter. In one corner, a long table was loaded with an impressive array of cookies, each variety more tempting than the last. Chocolate chip, sugar cookies, biscotti, and elaborately decorated wedding-themed treats were arranged in neat rows, enticing everyone who passed by.

Children and adults alike made frequent trips to the cookie table, their faces lighting up with delight as they selected their favorites. The sweet treats added an extra layer of enjoyment to the festivities, with guests chatting and sharing bites as they mingled.

Meanwhile, the DJ's voice cut through the music, drawing everyone's attention once more.

"Alright, ladies and gentlemen, it's time for the bouquet toss! All the single ladies, please make your way to the dance floor!"

A cheer went up from the crowd as the single women gathered in the center of the room, positioning themselves eagerly for the toss. Eden, holding her beautiful bouquet of white roses and lavender, stood with her back to the group, a playful smile on her face.

She glanced over her shoulder, giving a teasing wink to the crowd before turning back around. With a quick countdown from the DJ, Eden tossed the bouquet high into the air. The bouquet soared above the guests, spinning slightly as it descended.

The women reached up, their hands outstretched, and in a flurry of excitement, Monica leapt forward and caught the bouquet. A cheer erupted from the guests as Monica held the bouquet aloft, her face beaming with a mix of surprise and happiness.

As the applause died down, Monica's eyes drifted to Gabriel, who was standing nearby, talking with Leo and the kids. Gabriel, noticing her gaze, offered a polite smile but couldn't help the slight unease that settled in his stomach.

Leo, ever observant, noticed Gabriel's reaction. "What's up, Gabe? You look like you've seen a ghost."

Gabriel chuckled nervously, scratching the back of his neck. "It's just Monica. She caught the bouquet."

Leo raised an eyebrow. "Yeah, I noticed. Something bothering you?"

Gabriel responded, "Remember the rehearsal dinner last night?"

Leo nodded. "Yeah, how could I forget? You seemed to be having an interesting time."

Gabriel sighed, leaning against the table. "Monica was... intense. She was making me feel a bit awkward, but in a funny way, I kind of enjoyed it."

Leo raised an eyebrow. "Awkward and enjoyable, huh? That's a new one."

Gabriel chuckled, shaking his head. "I know it sounds strange. She was flirting with me all night, playing footsies, winking at me occasionally, and I wasn't sure how to react. Part of me felt uncomfortable, but another part of me was... intrigued."

Leo nodded, understanding. "So, what's the verdict? Do you like her or not?"

Gabriel sighed again, looking around the room. "I'm not sure. Monica's always been a bit of a mystery to me. I mean, she's beautiful and smart, but she's also got this... clingy feeling that I'm not sure I can handle."

Leo laughed. "Sounds like you're torn. Maybe you should give it a shot and see where it goes. Worst case, you figure out it's not for you."

Gabriel nodded thoughtfully. "Yeah, maybe you're right. She did catch the bouquet, after all. Maybe it's a sign."

Leo grinned, giving Gabriel a friendly nudge. "There you go. At least you'll know for sure. Plus, it could be fun. Who knows where it might lead?"

Gabriel smiled, feeling a bit more at ease. "Thanks, Leo. You always know how to put things in perspective."

Leo grinned. "No problem, buddy."

The DJ's voice boomed over the speakers once more. "Alright, ladies and gentlemen, now it's time for the garter toss! Alex, get ready to do the honors!"

The guests gathered around, forming a semicircle near the dance floor. Alex led Eden to a chair placed in the center, and she sat down with a playful smile. Alex knelt before her, lifting the hem of her dress just enough to reveal the garter. With a teasing wink, he slipped his fingers under the garter, causing the crowd to cheer and clap.

Unbeknownst to the crowd, Claus, Lucas, and their friends had crawled underneath the head table with a microphone. Their mischievous minds quickly hatched a plan. Giggling and whispering, they switched on the microphone just as Alex started to remove the garter.

As Alex's fingers gently slipped under the garter, a loud, exaggerated fart noise echoed through the speakers. The room fell silent for a moment before erupting into laughter. Alex paused, momentarily confused, but then grinned and continued. The kids, encouraged by the crowd's reaction, escalated their antics. They made exaggerated kissing noises, followed by more fart sounds and moans, creating a hilariously raunchy soundscape.

As Alex's hand inched up Eden's leg, a chorus of wolf whistles and even one of the kids saying, "Oh yeah, baby!" blared through the speakers.

The crowd was in stitches, laughing so hard that some had tears in their eyes. Even Eden couldn't help but laugh, her face turning red with amusement.

The DJ, trying to keep a straight face, commented, "Well, it seems we have some unexpected sound effects tonight!"

The children's giggles could be heard faintly through the microphone, adding to the hilarity. Finally, after a few more moments of laughter, the DJ managed to regain control of the situation.

As he turned off their microphone, the DJ said, "Alright, kids, you've had your fun! Let's give a round of applause for our impromptu comedians!"

The guests clapped and cheered, and the children, still giggling, emerged from under the table, looking pleased with their successful prank.

As the laughter died down, Leo approached Eden, who was still smiling from the children's antics. "Care for a dance?" he asked, extending his hand.

Eden nodded, taking his hand. "I'd love to."

Leo led her to the dance floor as a slow, sad tune began to play. They moved together gracefully, and for a moment, the lively energy of the room softened. As they danced, Eden's thoughts drifted to their father, who had passed away when they were young. The absence of his presence on this important day weighed heavily on her heart.

Leo, sensing her change in mood, spoke softly. "I know you miss him, Eden. He'd be so proud of you."

Eden's eyes filled with tears, but she smiled. "Thank you, Leo. It's hard not having him here, especially today. But I feel his spirit with me."

Leo nodded, holding her a little closer. "He's definitely here in spirit, and he's watching over you. You're surrounded by so much love."

As they continued to dance, the guests observed the tender moment, their own reflections and emotions mingling with the poignant scene before them. The camera captured the tears in Eden's eyes, the gentle way Leo held her, and the deep connection shared in that quiet dance.

Around the room, couples shared their own moments. Tyler and Maya danced together, their hands clasped and their movements in sync, a testament to their enduring love. Monica and Gabriel exchanged a glance, the bouquet catch still fresh in their minds, and Gabriel, deciding to take Leo's advice, gave Monica a reassuring smile.

Emmanuel and Maria swayed together, their love and companionship evident in their synchronized steps. Tom and Sarah, though still navigating their own complexities, found themselves momentarily united by the evening's joy.

As the song ended, Eden hugged Leo tightly. "Thank you, Leo. You're a wonderful brother."

Leo smiled, patting her back gently. "Anytime, Eden. You deserve all the happiness in the world."

●

The DJ's voice returned, this time inviting everyone back to the dance floor for a friendly game of musical chairs. The guests eagerly assembled in a large circle around a cluster of chairs arranged in the center of the dance floor. The children, still buzzing with energy, joined in, along with many of the adults, ready to relive some childhood fun.

The music started, and a lively tune had everyone moving and laughing. As the participants began to circle the chairs, the atmosphere was filled with anticipation and joy. The first round saw a few playful shoves and lots of laughter as people scrambled for seats when the music abruptly stopped.

Among the players were Sarah and Gabriel, both caught up in the spirited competition. As the rounds progressed and chairs were removed, the tension and excitement grew. Gabriel, ever the gentleman, found himself constantly ensuring the kids got seats, which earned him a few playful boos and cheers from the crowd.

In one of the final rounds, only a handful of players remained, including Sarah and Gabriel. The music played, and they circled the remaining chairs, eyes locked on their targets. As the music suddenly stopped, Sarah and Gabriel lunged for the same chair. Gabriel, with a quick move, slid into the chair first, leaving Sarah standing.

But instead of stepping away, Sarah, with a mischievous smile, plopped down onto Gabriel's lap. The crowd erupted into cheers and laughter at the sight. Gabriel, caught off guard but laughing, wrapped an arm around Sarah to keep her from falling.

Sarah remained seated on Gabriel's lap, the two of them sharing a moment of unexpected closeness. They exchanged glances, a hint of something more than just friendly competition in their eyes.

While this was happening, Tom stood on the sidelines, his phone glued to his ear as usual. He glanced up briefly, noticing Sarah and Gabriel's playful interaction, but quickly returned to his conversation. His expression was indifferent, as if he were more preoccupied with his call than with what was happening on the dance floor.

As the game continued, Tom finally ended his call and looked around the room. He saw Sarah laughing and enjoying herself with Gabriel, but instead of approaching, he simply shrugged and went to the bar to get a drink. His detachment was apparent, leaving Sarah free to enjoy the moment without his interference. When the game finally ended, and the last chair was claimed, the crowd cheered and clapped for the participants.

Sarah stood up, offering Gabriel a hand. "Good game," she said with a grin.

Gabriel took her hand and stood, smiling back. "You too. I didn't know musical chairs could be this much fun."

As they rejoined the rest of the guests, the DJ's voice called out once more, inviting everyone back to the dance floor. The music shifted to a slower, more romantic tune, and couples began to pair off, swaying gently to the rhythm.

Sarah and Gabriel found themselves standing together, the memory of their shared chair moment lingering between them.

Gabriel offered his hand again, a silent invitation. "Shall we?"

Sarah smiled, taking his hand. "Why not?"

As they danced, the laughter and excitement of the musical chairs game seemed to melt away, leaving a softer, more intimate atmosphere. Around them, other couples swayed to the music, sharing quiet moments and whispered words.

As the evening ended, the barn remained alive with the soft hum of conversation and the gentle strains of music. Alex and Eden, their faces glowing with happiness, began making their rounds to bid farewell to their guests. They moved through the crowd, stopping to chat and share a few final moments with friends and family.

"Thank you so much for coming," Eden said, hugging her grandmother tightly. "It means the world to us."

Beatrice smiled, her eyes twinkling with affection. "You looked beautiful, darling. I'm so happy for you both."

Alex shook hands with old friends, sharing laughs and reminiscing about past adventures. "We really appreciate you being here," he said to Gabriel, who had just finished his dance with Sarah.

Gabriel grinned. "Wouldn't have missed it for the world. Congratulations, you two."

Nearby, Leo was entertaining the group of children with his usual antics, keeping them laughing and engaged. As Alex and Eden approached, he gave them a theatrical bow.

"Your majesties, may your reign be long and prosperous," he said.

Eden laughed, giving him a hug. "Thanks, Leo. You've been amazing tonight. Thank you so much for taking care of the kids."

As they continued to move through the room, they found Tom standing near the bar. He gave them a brief nod, still seeming somewhat detached.

"Congratulations," he said simply, raising his glass.

"Thanks, Tom," Alex replied, offering a friendly smile. "Glad you could make it."

Sarah, standing nearby, gave them a warm hug. "It's been a wonderful night. I'm so happy for you both."

"Thanks, Sarah," Eden said, squeezing her hand. "It means a lot to have you here."

While this was happening, Monica stood off to the side, watching Gabriel and Sarah with a mixture of emotions. She had caught the bouquet earlier, and though she had smiled, there was a lingering sadness in her eyes as she observed Gabriel's interactions with Sarah.

Monica took a deep breath and approached Gabriel as he stood alone for a moment. "Hey, Gabriel," she said, trying to keep her tone light.

Gabriel turned and smiled at her. "Hey, Monica. You caught the bouquet. Maybe you're next?"

Monica laughed softly, though her eyes were serious. "Yeah, maybe. It's been a beautiful night, hasn't it?"

Gabriel nodded. "It really has. I'm glad we could all be here to celebrate with Alex and Eden."

Monica hesitated for a moment before speaking. "I hope you're happy, Gabriel. You deserve it."

Gabriel looked at her, sensing the deeper meaning behind her words. "Thanks, Monica. I hope you find happiness too. Maybe we could go out sometime?"

Monica responded excitedly, "I'd love to, let's go out tonight!" Gabriel nodded his head in agreement, and the two of them found themselves on the dance floor in each other's embrace.

Meanwhile, Maya and Tyler were dancing together, swaying gently to the music. Despite their rocky start, they had found a way to make their relationship work, and tonight they seemed more in sync than ever.

Maya rested her head on Tyler's shoulder, smiling contentedly. "I think this is the most fun we've had in a long time."

Tyler chuckled, squeezing her hand. "It's been a great night. I'm glad we came."

As the music played, they shared a quiet moment together, their love evident in their easy, comfortable closeness. As the final notes of the song played, Alex and Eden made their way to the door, showered with well-wishes and confetti. Outside, a car waited to take them to their next adventure.

"Ready for our honeymoon?" Alex asked, helping Eden into the car.

"Absolutely," she replied, her eyes sparkling with excitement. "Egypt, here we come!"

The guests gathered outside, waving and cheering as the car pulled away. Alex and Eden leaned out the window, waving back until they were out of sight.

As the car drove off into the night, Eden rested her head on Alex's shoulder, sighing contentedly. "Today was perfect," she said softly.

Alex kissed her forehead, smiling. "It really was. And now, we've got the rest of our lives to make memories together."

The car drove slowly down the quiet country road, the moon shining brightly above, illuminating the path ahead. Alex and Eden, hand in hand, looked forward to their future together, filled with love, adventure, and endless possibilities.

※

<u>**Lesson 6:**</u>
<u>**The Transformational Power of Language**</u>

In the heart of human experience lies a force that wields immense power, a force that transcends the boundaries of mere communication and touches the very core of who we are. This force is language... a symphony of words that weaves the tapestry of our identity, orchestrates the melody of our emotions, and dances through the intricate steps of our interactions. In this lesson, we venture into the profound realm where language, like an artist's brush, shapes the canvas of our lives in ways we may never fully grasp.

Imagine a world where words are not just carriers of meaning but also architects of destiny. A world where the choices we make, the freedoms we enjoy, and the beliefs that guide us all bear the mark of language's touch. Think of the momentous shifts in history, where the pages of time are illuminated by the speeches of visionaries who wielded words as their greatest arsenal. From the rallying cries of leaders to the whispered promises of lovers, words possess a mesmerizing ability to stir emotions, incite actions, and change the course of generations.

As we journey through life, we often find ourselves at the crossroads of expression, where the words we choose become not only our voice but also our essence. Pause for a moment and recall a time when someone's words deeply touched you. How did it shape your perception of yourself or the situation? The beauty and complexity of language lie not only in its power to communicate but also in its power to shape how we perceive the world. Have you ever pondered how the words you habitually choose subtly influence your perspective, coloring your experiences with shades of emotion you may not even be aware of?

Consider the labyrinth of human emotion, where words serve as guides through its intricate passages. It's here that we discover the magic of vocabulary's impact on our inner landscapes. Just as a skilled conductor molds a symphony's emotions through the choice of tempo and tone, our vocabulary plays a similar role in the symphony of our feelings. The words we select can either elevate our spirits or cast shadows upon our souls, ultimately determining the color and depth of our emotional palette.

But the tale doesn't end with the intimate connection between words and emotions. Our linguistic choices extend their influence to the world around us, shaping the very fabric of our interactions. Think of a conversation where words seem to dance effortlessly between participants, each syllable carrying nuances of meaning that transcend their dictionary definitions. It's in these moments that we witness language as a living entity, an egregore sculpting connections, fostering understanding, and sometimes even sparking conflicts.

The Influence of Words on Emotions and Actions

In the intricate tapestry of human experience, there exists a thread of incalculable influence: the thread of words. These seemingly simple units of communication hold within them a power that transcends their conventional meanings. As we embark on a journey into the heart of language's impact, we find ourselves at the threshold of a revelation: the words we choose possess an astonishing ability to shape not only our emotions but also our actions and the very trajectory of our lives.

Consider the last time you were engrossed in a book or captivated by a speech. What held you spellbound was not just the arrangement of letters and sounds, but the emotions that those words stirred within you. This is the essence of the capacity of language... the ability to kindle emotions that can alter the very course of our lives. Quickly jot down the first three words that come to your mind when you think of "home." How do these words influence your feelings about this place?

Yet, the influence of words doesn't end with emotions alone. It extends its grip onto the realm of actions, serving as both a catalyst and a conductor. Think of those moments when a powerful statement spurred you into action, when the right words were all you needed to take that leap of faith, to overcome a daunting challenge, or to chase a seemingly impossible dream.

The connection between words and actions is not coincidental; it's a symbiotic relationship. Our emotions, nurtured by language, guide our intentions, and intentions, in turn, shape our actions. This intricate dance forms the very crux of our personal development, our relationships, and our contributions to the world.

The Power of Vocabulary in Shaping Experiences

Words possess the remarkable ability to unconsciously mold our perception of experiences. Imagine encountering a vibrant sunrise... the words you use to describe it can significantly color your memory. Describing it as a "breathtaking display of colors" evokes a sense of wonder, while labeling it as "just a sunrise" diminishes its magic. This unconscious effect reveals the power words hold in shaping our outlook on life.

The vocabulary we habitually choose can either enrich or belittle the tapestry of our life experiences. When we use vibrant words to depict our encounters, we amplify their significance. Conversely, mundane language flattens the richness of experiences. For instance, transforming "meeting an old friend" to "rekindling a cherished connection" transforms an ordinary event into a heartwarming memory.

Often, words serve as unconscious shortcuts to express our feelings. We may use common phrases like "I'm fine" to hide deeper emotions. Are you really fine? Or are you hiding something? This leads to an incomplete expression of our experiences and feelings, underscoring the importance of choosing words that truly resonate with our internal world.

Understanding the power of vocabulary serves as a catalyst for change. By mindfully selecting words that encapsulate the essence of our experiences, we honor the depth of our emotions and encounters. This conscious choice elevates the quality of our interactions with both ourselves and the world around us. Find a mundane sentence from a recent conversation or text you've had. Now, rephrase it using more vibrant and descriptive language. How does the new sentence alter your perception of the experience?

When we consciously alter our habitual vocabulary, we create a shift in how we think, feel, and behave. Elevating our language elevates our experiences. Embracing this understanding empowers us to enhance the vividness of our journey.

As we navigate this intricate relationship between words and experiences, we unearth the art of consciously selecting words that enhance the hues of our memories, elevate our emotions, and enrich the tapestry of our existence.

The Impact of Language on Others

The reach of language extends far beyond our individual experiences, reaching out to touch the lives of those around us. In this exploration, we'll uncover the intricate ways in which our words shape not only our own reality but also the perceptions and reactions of others. As we navigate this terrain, we'll discover the profound responsibility that accompanies our choices of words when engaging with the world. Imagine telling a colleague, "Your work was okay" versus "Your work was insightful." Reflect on the different impressions these two statements might create.

Words are more than mere carriers of information... they are architects of perception. Dive into the realm of how the words we choose can paint vivid pictures in the minds of others. Consider how a single word can shape an entire narrative, evoking emotions and conjuring images that color the listener's understanding. In literature, journalism, and even everyday interactions, a single word can redefine the reader's or listener's understanding of a situation.

For instance:

A political leader might be described as "assertive" by supporters but "aggressive" by detractors. The former word connotes confidence without undue aggression, while the latter implies potential belligerence. This subtle change can sway public opinion about the leader's actions.

The way an event is described can drastically change the narrative. Consider a protest:

1.   "Thousands gathered today in a passionate display of unity, advocating for their rights and voicing their concerns."

2.   "Crowds swarmed the streets today, causing disruptions and airing grievances."

While both descriptions may be technically accurate, the former highlights the purpose and unity of the protesters, whereas the latter emphasizes inconvenience and unrest. Readers might sympathize with the cause in the first case and be annoyed by the disturbance in the second.

<u>Language has a dual capacity</u>: it can be a profound tool for understanding or a source of profound confusion.

<u>Bridging Understanding:</u> Active listening, clear articulation, and choosing words that resonate with the listener's emotions or experiences can foster mutual respect and empathy. For example, diplomatic language is often meticulously crafted to bridge cultural and political divides.

<u>Creating Confusion:</u> On the flip side, jargon, ambiguous phrases, or culturally specific idioms can lead to misunderstandings. If a non-native English speaker is told they've "hit it out of the park," they might be perplexed unless they're familiar with baseball idioms. Moreover, even subtle changes in tone, context, or word choice can lead to misconceptions. A casual remark can be misconstrued as sarcasm, or genuine praise might be misinterpreted as flattery.

In essence, language is both an art and a science, a tool and a weapon. Its nuances, when harnessed correctly, can enlighten, empower, and connect. But without care, it can also mislead, divide, and estrange. This delicate balance underscores the importance of mindful communication in all areas of life.

Words are catalysts for action. A well-placed word can inspire, motivate, or ignite change. Conversely, words have the potential to harm—thoughtless language can inflict wounds, altering moods, relationships, and even destinies.

Consider the following scenarios:

<u>The Turning Point at College</u>:

Nina had always been an above-average student but never the top of her class. One day, after giving a class presentation, her professor pulled her aside and said, "You have an innate ability to engage and teach others. Ever considered becoming an educator?" This single statement from a respected figure shifted Nina's entire career trajectory. Instead of pursuing finance, she became a beloved college professor. Those words of encouragement tapped into a potential she hadn't recognized within herself.

The Casual Comment with Lasting Impact:

James and Keith were good friends since high school. One day, while trying on clothes in a store, James made an offhand remark about Keith's recent weight gain. Although said jokingly, it deeply affected Keith. For years afterward, he felt self-conscious about his body and struggled with self-esteem issues. Words, even when said without malicious intent, can sometimes leave lasting scars.

Unity Through Shared Phrases:

During a difficult period in a small town, the local community leader began ending each meeting with the phrase, "Together, we grow." This mantra started appearing in local stores, on car bumpers, and even in the speeches of school children. It became a rallying cry for the community, reminding them that despite challenges, their unity was their strength. Words can foster a collective identity, giving groups a shared purpose.

Misunderstandings and Discord:

In a multinational company, a newly transferred manager from France used the phrase "That's not possible" frequently in meetings. In his previous workplace, this was a common way of expressing a need for further discussion. However, his American colleagues interpreted this as dismissive and rigid. Tensions escalated until an HR mediator stepped in to clarify the cultural misunderstanding. Language nuances, when misunderstood, can unintentionally sow discord.

The profound impact of words on individuals and communities cannot be overstated. Whether it's a timely compliment that launches someone into a new career or a misunderstood phrase that creates friction, language shapes our experiences and narratives in powerful ways. With the power of words comes great responsibility. Delve into the ethical considerations that arise when choosing words for communication. As we influence others through our language, we must recognize the moral imperative to use this influence judiciously.

Language is an influential tool. While it has the power to uplift and inspire, it equally possesses the capacity to tear down and wound deeply. Careless words, even if unintentional, can reinforce stereotypes, perpetuate harmful biases, and undermine an individual's self-worth.

For many, careless remarks about their appearance, intelligence, or capabilities can leave lasting scars. Over time, repeated exposure to such language can contribute to chronic feelings of inadequacy, impostor syndrome, or even lead to mental health issues like anxiety, depression, and social withdrawal. In extreme cases, relentless negative language and bullying can contribute to suicidal ideation.

Ethical Language Use: The Power of Conscious Communication

Using language ethically goes beyond merely selecting the right words; it involves fostering understanding, building connections, and navigating conflicts with empathy and respect.

The foundation of ethical language use begins with empathy. Before speaking or writing, it's essential to consider the emotions and perspectives of others. This simple practice can profoundly influence the words you choose and the tone you adopt, leading to more compassionate and effective communication.

Avoiding stereotypes and generalizations is another critical aspect of ethical communication. Language that categorizes or pigeonholes groups of people can be harmful, even when unintentional. Striving to avoid such broad generalizations ensures that your communication remains respectful and inclusive.

Active listening plays a significant role in ethical language use. Often, the most ethical way to communicate is to listen more than you speak. By genuinely hearing others, you demonstrate respect and position yourself to respond more thoughtfully and constructively.

When it comes to offering constructive feedback, focusing on actions or situations rather than personal characteristics is key. For instance, using "I" statements—such as "I felt worried when the report was late" instead of "You are always late"—can help keep the conversation productive and centered on resolving the issue at hand.

Conscious word choices are particularly important in conflict resolution. The words you use can either escalate or de-escalate a situation. Opting for neutral, non-emotional language helps prevent further conflict; for example, saying "I'm having trouble understanding your perspective" instead of "You're being irrational" can keep the dialogue open and respectful. If you're unsure about what someone means, asking for clarification rather than making assumptions can also prevent misunderstandings. Additionally, acknowledging and validating the other person's feelings or viewpoint, even if you disagree, can lay the groundwork for a more productive conversation.

Building deeper relationships through language involves being present, engaged, and appreciative. Expressing genuine interest in conversations, such as saying, "Tell me more about that," can lead to more meaningful interactions. Asking open-ended questions encourages richer discussions and helps avoid superficial exchanges. Simple expressions of gratitude, like "I value our conversations" or "Thank you for sharing that with me," can significantly strengthen connections and foster a sense of mutual respect.

Activity: Emotional Language Odyssey

In this activity, you will explore the profound connection between language and emotion, learning how the words you choose can shape your experiences and influence others. By engaging in this reflective and practical exercise, you will deepen your understanding of how language impacts your emotional state and interactions with others. The goal is to become more intentional with your communication, recognizing the power your words have to uplift, inspire, and create positive change in your life and the lives of those around you.

Step 1: Embracing the Spectrum of Emotion

Begin by selecting three emotionally charged words from the list below that resonate with you the most. These words will serve as the foundation for your reflection and exploration:

- Joy
- Melancholy
- Serenity
- Passion
- Gratitude
- Longing
- Triumph
- Desolation
- Euphoria
- Resilience

Step 2: Word-to-Emotion Reflection

For each word you've chosen, recall a personal experience where that emotion played a significant role. Reflect deeply on the memories, feelings, and actions associated with each word, allowing yourself to fully immerse in the emotions that these memories evoke.

Step 3: Crafting Your Narrative

Now, take your reflections and weave them into a personal

narrative. Describe the details of each experience, the emotions you felt, and the lessons you learned. This exercise will help you connect the dots between words, emotions, and actions, highlighting the powerful influence language has on your emotional state and decision-making process.

Step 4: The Challenge of Positive Intent

For the next 24 hours, commit to using language that is intentional, uplifting, and positive. This challenge extends beyond just the words you speak—it includes what you write, text, and even think. Your mission is to communicate in a way that inspires and resonates with positivity, consciously choosing words that build up rather than tear down.

Step 5: Observing the Ripples

As you go through this 24-hour period, pay close attention to the responses your intentional language elicits. Observe the shifts in conversation dynamics, the nuances in reactions, and the overall atmosphere you create with your words. Notice how your choice of language impacts not just others, but your own emotional state as well.

Step 6: The Grand Reflection

After completing the 24-hour challenge, take some time to reflect on your experience. Analyze the changes in your interactions, the effects your words had on others, and the internal shift you may have experienced. Consider how intentional communication influenced the overall quality of your day.

Step 7: Sharing the Journey

Finally, crystallize the lessons you've learned throughout this activity. Recognize the power you hold to uplift others through positive communication, understanding that just a few well-chosen words can make a significant difference in someone's day, motivate change, or strengthen relationships. Remember, the influence of language works both ways—others' words affect you just as much. By being mindful of this, you can better mitigate negativity and embrace your role as a creator of positive realities through language.

Let this experience be a catalyst for growth, both for yourself and those around you. Speak your truth with courage, listen with empathy, and use the poetry of your words to change the world for the better.

●

The power of language is a remarkable force that shapes every facet of human existence, from the individual to the collective, from emotions to actions, and from personal relationships to societal interactions. We have delved into the potential of language, exploring its influence on perception, emotion, action, and connection. It paints a vivid picture of language as an artist's brush, capable of crafting the intricate canvas of our lives.

At its core, language is more than a mere tool for communication; it's a vehicle for expressing our thoughts, emotions, and values. It's through language that we share our experiences, hopes, and dreams. It's through language that we construct our understanding of the world, and, in turn, it shapes the world around us. We have learned how words have the power to ignite revolutions, mend relationships, inspire growth, and foster unity.

We have also examined the ethical considerations surrounding language use, acknowledging that while words can empower, they can also inflict deep wounds. The importance of conscious word choices in fostering empathy, understanding, and positive connections is highlighted. Through empathetic communication, we can break down barriers, bridge gaps, and contribute to the well-being of individuals and society as a whole.

Understanding the relationship between language and human experience showcases the dynamic interplay between words and their profound impact. It serves as a reminder that each word we utter carries weight and that the choices we make in our language can have far-reaching consequences. As we navigate the complexities of human interaction, understanding the power of language equips us to communicate with intention, empathy, and the potential to create positive change in ourselves and the world around us.

Chapter 7: The Nile's Redemption

The plane touched down at Cairo International Airport just as the sun began its descent, casting a spectacular tapestry of orange, pink, and purple across the sky. The golden light bathed the city, creating a romantic and mysterious atmosphere that seemed to welcome Alex and Eden into its embrace.

As they disembarked, the warm, dry air of Cairo greeted them, carrying a blend of exotic scents and the distant hum of the bustling city. Alex and Eden exchanged excited glances, their hearts pounding with anticipation for the adventure ahead.

Waiting for them at the exit was a neatly dressed chauffeur, holding a sign that read "Alex and Eden." He greeted them warmly, his smile as bright as the setting sun, and quickly took charge of their luggage.

"Welcome to Cairo!" he said, his voice carrying a hint of the city's rich history. "I hope you had a pleasant flight."

The drive through Cairo was a sensory overload. The streets were alive with the energy of vendors peddling their wares, colorful lights twinkling in the twilight, and the musical call to prayer echoing from minarets. Alex and Eden pressed their faces to the windows, taking in the vibrant life of the city.

"Huge...!" Eden pointed excitedly as they caught their first glimpse of the pyramids.

"Why, thank you!" Alex chuckled, his eyes wide with amazement.

"No, not you! I was talking about the pyramids!" Eden exclaimed, trying to contain her laughter.

Silhouetted against the setting sun, the ancient structures rose majestically from the desert sands, their forms inspiring awe and wonder.

The car pulled up to the grand entrance of the Pyramids Hotel, a luxurious establishment that offered an unobstructed view of the Pyramid of Khafre. The hotel itself was a blend of luxury and history, with intricate designs and an air of timeless elegance.

Checking in was smooth and efficient. The staff were both welcoming and professional, swiftly guiding Alex and Eden to their room. Their suite was spacious and well-appointed, but it was the balcony that took their breath away. Stepping outside, they were met with a stunning view of the Pyramid of Khafre, its massive structure bathed in the majestic light of the crescent moon.

"This is perfect," Eden said, her voice filled with awe. She leaned into Alex, wrapping her arm around his waist.

"Our adventure starts now." Alex smiled, pulling her closer. "To new adventures, Mrs. Newlywed," he whispered, pressing a kiss to her forehead.

As they stood there, watching the sun set behind the pyramids, they felt a deep sense of connection... to each other, to the past, and to the incredible journey that lay ahead. The country of Egypt, with its rich tapestry of history and culture, awaited them, promising a honeymoon filled with wonder and discovery.

After settling into their room, Alex and Eden freshened up and made their way to the hotel's rooftop restaurant, where they were scheduled to meet their guide, Hazem. The evening air was cool and pleasant, carrying the faint scent of jasmine from the hotel's lush gardens below.

The rooftop offered a panoramic view of Cairo, with the pyramids standing tall and majestic in the distance. The tables were elegantly set, each with a flickering candle casting a warm glow.

As they approached their table, a tall man with deep-set eyes and a salt-and-pepper beard rose to greet them. He had an air of authority, but his eyes sparkled with mischief and warmth.

"Alex, Eden, welcome to your Egyptian adventure! I'm Hazem, your guide," he said, extending a hand.

"Thank you, Hazem," Alex said, shaking his hand firmly. "We're excited to be here."

"Please, have a seat," Hazem said, gesturing to the table. "I've taken the liberty of ordering some traditional Egyptian dishes for you to try. I spared no expense."

As they settled in, the waiter brought out an array of dishes: hummus, baba ghanoush, falafel, and a fragrant lamb tagine. Hazem poured them each a glass of hibiscus tea, a refreshing drink with a deep red hue.

"So, tell me," Hazem began, leaning back in his chair, "what brings you both to Egypt, besides your romantic getaway?"

Alex glanced at Eden, who smiled encouragingly. "I'm working on becoming an author, and I'm looking for inspiration for my first book," he said. "I've always been fascinated by ancient Egypt, and I hope to find some ideas here."

"And I'm a medical professional," Eden added. "I'm particularly interested in ancient Egyptian medicine and healing practices. I hope to learn more about them to someday open my own private practice."

Hazem nodded thoughtfully. "Egypt has a rich history in both fields. I'm sure you'll find plenty of inspiration here."

As they ate, Hazem shared stories about his childhood, growing up in the shadows of the pyramids, and his deep passion for Egyptian history.

"Did you know," Hazem said, his eyes twinkling, "that ancient Egyptians were among the first to practice beekeeping? They believed honey had magical and medicinal properties."

Alex's eyes lit up. "Really? You know, I'm something of a beekeeper myself. I never knew it was magical, you'll have to tell me more."

"Yes, it is indeed very magical," Hazem replied. "They used honey in everything from food to medicine, and even in the mummification process. It's a testament to their ingenuity and understanding of nature."

As the night progressed, the candles flickered in the gentle breeze, and the sounds of Cairo below created a soothing backdrop. Hazem laid out their plan for the next few days, explaining that they would need to be up early the next morning to depart for their boat ride on the Nile River, which would take them to some of the most well-preserved ancient sites Egypt has to offer.

After dinner, they stood by the railing, gazing out at the pyramids illuminated against the night sky. Hazem bid them goodnight, and Alex and Eden lingered a moment longer, soaking in the magic of the evening.

"It's only our first night and already it feels magical," Alex said softly, his arm around Eden's shoulders.

"I can't wait to see what tomorrow brings," Eden replied, her eyes shining with excitement.

After a delightful evening on the rooftop, Alex and Eden returned to their room, still buzzing from their conversation with Hazem. The moonlight filtered softly through the curtains, casting a serene glow over their suite.

They changed into their nightclothes and climbed into the plush bed, snuggling under the soft quilt. As they settled in, they talked about the dinner.

"I can't believe how much we learned just over dinner," Eden said, her eyes still wide with excitement. "Hazem is amazing. I'm so glad we booked him to be our guide."

"Yeah, he really knows his stuff," Alex agreed, yawning. "I can't wait to see what he has in store for us tomorrow." They kissed each other goodnight and crawled between the silky sheets, anticipating the adventures that awaited them.

●

During the night, in a deep and lucid dream, Eden found herself standing alone in the cool sands of the Giza Plateau. The pyramids rose ominously before her, their shadows stretching out like ancient guardians. The sky was an eerie, unnatural shade of red, casting everything in an unsettling light.

She walked towards the pyramids, the sands shifting under her feet with each step. As she got closer, she heard faint, echoing footsteps behind her—irregular and heavy, like the thunderous strides of some enormous, extinct dinosaur.

Her heart pounded in her chest as she turned, but there was nothing there... just the endless expanse of desert. Strange voices whispered her name, carried on the wind.

Suddenly, the ground beneath her began to tremble. The sand shifted and swirled, forming cymatic shapes and patterns that seemed to tell ancient stories. She felt a presence behind her, something ancient and powerful. She turned again, but all she could see were the looming pyramids, their stone faces inscrutable and silent.

In the blink of an eye, she found herself inside the heart of the Great Pyramid. The confined space amplified every sound, her footsteps echoing in the silence. Ancient chants began to resonate around her, synchronizing with her heartbeat. It felt as if the pyramid itself was alive, pulsating with energy. The vibrations under her feet grew stronger, and she felt a connection to something far greater than herself.

Suddenly, a beam of radiant light descended from the top of the pyramid, surrounding her. The chants grew even louder, and she felt an overwhelming rush of emotions and memories, as if centuries of knowledge and secrets were being unlocked within her.

The light became blinding, and just as it seemed to engulf her completely, Eden woke in a panic, her heart racing. The room was dark and quiet; the only sound she could hear was Alex, slightly snoring next to her. She glanced at the clock... it was just past four a.m.

Alex woke and stirred beside her. "Eden? What's wrong?"

"I had a nightmare," she whispered. "It was... unsettling. I need some fresh air."

Alex nodded, still half-asleep. "Let's go outside for a bit, maybe see if we can watch the sunrise."

They quietly slipped out of bed and put on their robes. They

made their way to the fire escape, stepping out into the cool early
morning air. The city was still, the only sound the distant hum of
traffic.

They stood there, side by side, looking out at the pyramids. The
sky was beginning to lighten, the first hints of dawn creeping over
the horizon.

"Do you think we'll be able to see the sunrise with all this
smog?" Eden asked, her voice still shaky.

"Maybe," Alex said, wrapping his arm around her shoulders.
"Even if we can't, it's still beautiful."

They waited in silence, watching as the sky gradually brightened.
However, the smog was too heavy that morning, obscuring their
view of the sun. The pyramids were mere silhouettes, shrouded in a
mysterious haze.

Eden sighed, disappointed. "I was hoping for a clear view."

Alex massaged her shoulders. "Don't worry, we'll have plenty of
opportunities when we come back here next week. Besides, there's
something magical about the way the pyramids look right now, don't
you think?"

Eden nodded, leaning her head against his shoulder. "Yeah,
you're right. It's still beautiful in its own way."

"Let's head downstairs and grab a quick breakfast, then get our
luggage," Alex said as they made their way back to their room.

"Sounds like a plan, my stomach is grumbling!" Eden agreed,
feeling a bit more settled. She couldn't shake the feeling from her
dream, but she was determined not to let it spoil their adventure.

They quickly dressed, packed their bags, and headed down to the
hotel's dining area for a hurried breakfast. The anticipation for their
journey down the Nile and their first stop at the Temple of Isis began
to overshadow the lingering unease from Eden's nightmare.

After a quick breakfast, Alex and Eden checked out of the
Pyramids Hotel and met Hazem in the lobby. The morning was crisp,
with the promise of a sunny day ahead. Hazem greeted them with his
usual warm smile.

"Ready for our adventure?" Hazem asked, raising his eyebrows
up and down with fervor.

"Absolutely," Eden replied, her enthusiasm evident. Alex
nodded, though there was a hint of nervousness in his eyes.

They made their way to the waiting car, which would take them to the dock where their boat awaited. Alex, wearing a wide-brimmed hat reminiscent of a famous archaeologist, looked out at the bustling city, trying to mask his unease.

The drive to the south dock was filled with interesting sights and engaging conversation. Hazem pointed out various landmarks, weaving stories of Cairo's rich history and culture. Eden was captivated, asking questions and soaking in every detail.

Alex, however, was quieter than usual. His mind was preoccupied with the upcoming boat ride. Boats and water had always made him uneasy, a fear he rarely discussed.

The memory that haunted him most was during his trip overseas, during what was supposed to be a simple ferry ride from France to Great Britain. The weather had seemed fine at first, but as soon as the ferry left the safety of the port, the sea turned vicious. Massive waves slammed into the sides of the ferry, throwing it around like a rag doll. Alex had clung to the nearest railing, eyes wide with terror, certain that at any moment they'd all be pitched into the icy waters below.

Amid the chaos, he had noticed a man sitting calmly at the bar, utterly unfazed by the storm and laughing in short spurts. Dressed in a casual sweater and khakis, the man looked completely out of place, like he should be sitting in a library, not on a ferry that was flirting with disaster. Desperate for a distraction from his own mounting panic, Alex had shuffled over, gripping the chair for dear life.

"How can you be so calm?" Alex had shouted over the roar of the wind and waves, his voice trembling.

The man had turned to him with a serene smile. "I used to work on cruise ships," he said, as if that explained everything.

"What did you do?" Alex had asked, hoping for some words of wisdom to cling to as the boat took another stomach-churning dip.

"I was a clown," the man replied, his tone as nonchalant as if he were discussing the weather.

Alex had blinked, sure he'd misheard. "A clown? You mean… with the makeup and balloons?"

The man nodded. "That's right. I spent my twenties and part of my thirties performing nonstop on ships three times the size of this one. Juggling, doing tricks, making people laugh. You wouldn't believe how many times I had to keep my balance while the boat was tossing around like this."

The image of this unassuming man in full clown gear, juggling or pulling rabbits out of hats while the boat pitched and rolled, had awakened an old fear of clowns from within him. The ferry, as if sensing this, lurched violently again, snapping him back and forth in his chair.

"So, you're not scared of the boat sinking?" Alex had asked, barely managing to stay on his feet.

The man had chuckled softly. "Scared? I've had kids' birthday parties in the middle of the Atlantic during a storm. Once, I got hit with a flying cream pie right as the boat took a dive. Went over the edge of the stage and landed face-first in a stack of folding chairs. And I still got back up and finished the show."

As the ferry had continued its chaotic journey, the clown had kept telling stories—tales of seasick passengers laughing so hard they forgot their nausea, of performing tricks while dodging sliding furniture, and of a particularly memorable day when a giant wave had sent an entire buffet table skidding across the deck mid-performance. Before Alex could process that mental image, the boat hit another particularly nasty wave, sending him sprawling.

As he struggled to his feet, the clown just chuckled, completely at ease during the chaos. "Just remember," he said with a wink, "life's a circus, and this boat's just the first act. You've got to roll with the punches—or the waves."

Hazem noticed Alex's deep gaze. "You okay, Alex?" he asked, his tone concerned. Alex chuckled nervously, adjusting his hat.

"Yeah, just... taking it all in," Alex replied, forcing a smile.

Eden couldn't resist a playful jab. "Nice hat, babe. What are you trying to do, look like a secret agent?" she teased, her eyes sparkling with mischief.

Hazem joined in, laughing. "Yes, Alex, are you here to solve mysteries or write about them?"

Alex smiled, feeling a bit more at ease. "A bit of both, maybe."

Eden, sensing his discomfort, reached over and squeezed his hand. "It's going to be great, you'll see."

●

When they arrived at the dock, the sight of the Sunboat took their breath away. It was a magnificent vessel, elegant and grand, with luxurious details that spoke of comfort and adventure.

Hazem led them aboard, his pride evident. "Welcome to the Sunboat! Our company spared no expense when constructing this luxurious boat for our tours," he said, a hint of playfulness in his voice.

Alex hesitated at the gangway, taking a deep breath.

Hazem noticed and gave him a reassuring pat on the back. "Come, no need to worry! It could only cost you your life, and you got that for free!" he joked, trying to lighten the mood.

Alex smiled for a second, then took small, somewhat labored baby steps onto the magnificent Sunboat. Shortly after settling into their luxurious accommodations on the Sunboat, the trio disembarked for their first stop: the Temple of Isis. The temple stood proudly on its island, a testament to the ingenuity and dedication of those who had relocated it to save it from the rising waters of the Nile.

Hazem began the tour with his characteristic enthusiasm. "The Temple of Isis was originally located on Philae Island, but it was moved to its current location on Agilkia Island to protect it from flooding caused by the Aswan High Dam. The cult of Isis was one of the most significant in ancient Egypt, with worshippers coming from all over to pay homage to the goddess of magic and motherhood."

He paused, allowing them to take in the grandeur of the temple. "Isis was the wife of Osiris and the mother of Horus. She was revered as the ideal mother and wife, as well as the patroness of nature and magic. According to mythology, when Osiris was murdered by his brother Set, it was Isis who gathered the pieces of his body and brought him back to life. Her story is one of love, dedication, and incredible power."

As they walked into the temple, Alex remained at the entrance, staring up at the massive structure, lost in a daydream. Hazem, with Eden next to him, pointed out various carvings and inscriptions.

"The ancient Egyptians believed in a holistic approach to healing," Hazem explained. "They understood the connection between the mind and body. For them, spiritual well-being was just as important as physical health."

Eden thought about the modern emphasis on holistic health and how it paralleled ancient practices. "So, they combined mental, emotional, and spiritual health in their treatments?" she asked.

"Exactly," Hazem replied. "They performed rituals and prayers dedicated to Isis, seeking her blessings for healing."

Eden made a mental note to explore how she could integrate more holistic approaches into her own practice, recognizing the importance of addressing all aspects of a patient's well-being.

Hazem led them to a section of the temple adorned with detailed carvings of plants and herbs. "Here, you can see the various herbs they used in their remedies," he said. "Garlic for digestive issues, aloe for skin problems. They had an extensive knowledge of plant-based medicine."

Eden leaned in closer, studying the carvings. "And how did they prepare these remedies?"

"They would dry, grind, and mix the herbs with other substances like honey or wine," Hazem explained.

Her mind raced with possibilities. She had always been interested in herbal medicine but seeing how advanced the ancient Egyptians were inspired her to delve deeper into this area. She could imagine creating a line of natural remedies, using age-old recipes and methods.

Next, Hazem showed her carvings depicting surgical procedures. "The ancient Egyptians performed basic surgeries like suturing wounds, draining abscesses, and setting broken bones. They even had specialized surgical instruments."

Eden marveled at the sophistication of their techniques. "They were far more advanced than I realized," she said, tracing the carved figures with her finger.

"Yes, and their instruments were quite sophisticated for their time," Hazem added. They moved to another part of the temple where Hazem pointed out inscriptions related to diet and nutrition. "Diet was an integral part of maintaining health. They believed in balanced meals that included vegetables, fruits, and fish."

Eden smiled. "So, they understood the importance of nutrition just as we do today."

"Indeed," Hazem replied. "Certain foods were believed to have healing properties and were incorporated into treatments."

Eden thought about incorporating nutritional counseling into her practice, inspired by the ancient Egyptians' understanding of food as medicine. In another chamber, Hazem explained the use of amulets and magic in healing.

"The Egyptians used protective amulets, like the ankh or the eye of Horus, in their healing rituals. They also believed in the power of incantations and spells," he said.

Eden was fascinated by the blend of medicine and magic. "It's incredible how they combined physical treatments with spiritual and magical practices." She pondered the potential benefits of integrating more symbolic and holistic elements into her practice, recognizing the power of belief and ritual in healing.

Hazem led her to a final section where he described the role of healer-priests. "Priests and healers were highly trained, both medically and spiritually. They served as both medical practitioners and spiritual advisors."

Eden was impressed by the depth of their knowledge and the respect given to healers. "It must have been an incredible responsibility," she said.

"It was," Hazem agreed. "Their training was rigorous, but it made them well-rounded healers."

As the tour concluded, Eden felt a deep respect for these ancient practitioners and was inspired to continue her own education, striving to be as well-rounded and knowledgeable as possible. She had learned so much from the temple and was eager to incorporate these insights into her own practice.

"Thank you, Hazem," she said sincerely. "This has been an eye-opening experience."

Hazem smiled. "I'm glad you found it enlightening. The wisdom of the ancients is timeless, and there's always something new to learn from them."

Alex, who had gotten lost in the temple during the tour, took Eden's hand as they left. "You look inspired. I got lost, but I found some pretty cool stuff. I took pictures of a lot of the walls—maybe it will help remind you what you learned today," he said.

"Aww, thanks, babe," she replied, her eyes shining with excitement. "There's so much we can learn from the past. I can't wait to start incorporating these ideas into my work."

Together, they walked back to the Sunboat, feeling more connected to each other and to the ancient wisdom they had discovered. As the Sunboat set sail down the Nile, Alex and Eden marveled at the luxurious accommodations and the stunning views of the river. The boat was designed with elegance and comfort in mind, featuring spacious cabins, a sun deck with plush loungers, and a dining area with large windows offering panoramic views of the Nile's lush banks.

The gentle sway of the boat was soothing, and the sound of the water lapping against the hull added to the tranquil ambiance. Palm trees and small villages dotted the shoreline, and the occasional call of a bird punctuated the calm.

Onboard, Alex and Eden mingled with a diverse group of travelers. There was an elderly couple celebrating their golden anniversary, a family with two curious children, and a group of friends on a cultural exploration. Each group had their own guides and itineraries, adding to the mix of stories and experiences.

Eden found herself chatting with the elderly couple about their travels, while Alex entertained the children with stories of his circus adventures. The boat's communal areas buzzed with conversation and laughter, as everyone shared their reasons for embarking on this Egyptian adventure.

As evening fell, the Captain's cocktail dinner commenced. The dining area was beautifully set with white tablecloths, flickering candles, and an assortment of Egyptian delicacies. The Captain, a jovial man with a twinkle in his eye, welcomed everyone with a hearty toast.

"To new friends and unforgettable journeys!" he declared, raising his glass.

Alex and Eden, seated at a table with Hazem and a few other travelers, listened as the Captain continued. "I'm delighted to have you all aboard the Sunboat. We spared no expense with the food and amenities to ensure your comfort and enjoyment. From the finest Egyptian cuisine to the most luxurious accommodations, we want this to be an experience you'll never forget."

Alex and Eden smiled at each other, appreciating the Captain's efforts to make their journey special. The table was filled with an array of delicious dishes, and the service was impeccable. During a heating conversation Alex and Eden couldn't help but share a funny story from their wedding.

"We had these butter lamb sculptures as part of the dinner spread," Alex began, grinning. "The kids at the wedding decided it would be hilarious to take them and place them around the venue."

"And my poor Grandma Beatrice ended up sitting on one of the lambs," Eden added, laughing. "She didn't realize it until she stood up and had butter all over her dress!"

The table erupted in laughter, and Hazem followed with a humorous anecdote of his own. "Once, while guiding a particularly energetic group, we lost a member during a visit to Karnak Temple. Turns out, he had wandered off to find a perfect photo spot and got stuck trying to climb a palm tree!"

After dinner, Alex and Eden retreated to the top deck, where the night sky was a canvas of twinkling stars. The Nile stretched out before them, a ribbon of silver under the moonlight.

They found a quiet spot and lay back, gazing up at the stars. The gentle sound of the river and the soft breeze made the moment feel magical.

"Look at that," Alex said softly, pointing out a particularly bright constellation. "Imagine if it's our destiny to live among the stars, just like the Egyptians believed."

Eden nestled closer to him, her hand finding his. "Why dream of just being a star when we could be our own constellation?"

Alex smiled, her words filling him with a sense of wonder. "You always know how to make everything sound magical."

She turned to look at him, her eyes reflecting the starlight. "It's because I have you by my side. You make everything better."

Alex felt a rush of emotion. "Eden, you're my universe. Every moment with you is an adventure, and I can't wait to see where this journey takes us."

They leaned in, their lips meeting in a tender kiss. The stars above seemed to shine brighter, as if blessing their love. They lay there in each other's arms, dreaming about their future and the adventures they would have together.

"I think this trip is going to change us," Eden said, her voice barely above a whisper. "We're going to learn so much, not just about Egypt, but about ourselves."

Alex nodded, feeling a deep connection to her and to the journey they were on. "Whatever happens, I'm glad we're doing this together."

•

The next morning, Alex and Eden awoke early, excited for the day ahead. After a hearty breakfast, they disembarked from the

Sunboat and made their way to the Temple of Kom Ombo. The temple stood proudly on a natural elevation overlooking the Nile, its imposing columns and intricate carvings bathed in the morning light.

As they approached, Alex couldn't help but marvel at the sheer scale of the structure.

"Huge..." he said, his voice filled with awe.

"How rude!" Eden exclaimed, looking back at him with a sinister smile.

"No, not you!" Alex pleaded as Eden laughed, clutching his arm and kissing him on the cheek.

Hazem led them through the grand entrance, his enthusiasm evident. "Kom Ombo is unique because it's dedicated to two gods: Sobek, the crocodile god, and Horus, the falcon god. The temple is perfectly symmetrical, with twin entrances, halls, and sanctuaries."

Inside, Hazem guided them through the temple, pointing out various carvings and hieroglyphs. "The dual dedication reflects the balance between the forces of nature and the protection of the people," he explained. "Sobek was associated with the Nile and its fertility, while Horus represented kingship and protection."

Alex's mind raced with ideas. "The balance between chaos and order... I can use this in my book," he murmured to himself. "Characters or forces representing these opposing traits, struggling to find equilibrium."

Eden nodded, understanding his line of thought. "It's a powerful theme, one that's as relevant today as it was back then."

They paused in front of a series of intricate carvings depicting medical instruments and surgical procedures. "This temple is also famous for its depictions of ancient Egyptian medical practices," Hazem said. "The carvings show the tools used by physicians and the treatments they administered. It's a fascinating glimpse into the advanced state of Egyptian medicine."

As Eden examined the carvings closely, Alex imagined himself as a pharaoh, overseeing the construction of such a magnificent temple.

"I can see why this place inspires so many stories," Alex said, a thoughtful look on his face.

Hazem stopped before a relief depicting a battle between Sobek and Horus. "These myths often depict conflicts between the gods, which ultimately lead to balance and harmony."

Alex stared at the relief, inspiration flooding his thoughts. "Conflict leading to resolution… I can create a dramatic arc where the characters' struggles mirror these ancient battles, showing growth and transformation."

As they left Kom Ombo, Alex felt a renewed sense of purpose. The ancient wisdom and stories had provided him with a wealth of material to enrich his book. He turned to Hazem, gratitude shining in his eyes.

"Thank you, Hazem. This visit has given me so much inspiration. The themes of duality, conflict, and healing… they're exactly what I needed."

Hazem smiled. "The ancient Egyptians had a profound understanding of life and the universe. There's always something new to learn from them."

Eden held Alex's hand. "I can't wait to see how you incorporate all of this into your book."

After the temple tour, Hazem led them to a nearby cooking school where they would participate in a traditional Egyptian culinary class. The aroma of spices and fresh ingredients filled the air as they entered the bright, bustling kitchen.

The instructor welcomed them warmly and began by explaining the dishes they would be preparing: kofta, dolmas, and a refreshing cucumber salad. Alex's eyes lit up at the prospect of cooking, while Eden watched with amusement.

"Alright, everyone, let's get started," the instructor said, handing out aprons and guiding them to their stations. Alex quickly got to work; his years of culinary experience evident in the way he handled the ingredients. Eden watched him with admiration, her heart swelling with pride.

"You're really in your element, aren't you?" she teased, nudging him playfully.

Alex grinned. "You know I love this stuff. And it's always more fun with you by my side."

Hazem, meanwhile, was attempting to shape his kofta with less success. "I think mine are going to look more like meatballs," he joked, eliciting laughter from everyone.

As they cooked, the room filled with laughter and the occasional playful jab. Alex's kofta turned out perfectly shaped, while Hazem's creations were a bit more haphazard, but he took it all in stride.

When the dishes were finished, they sat down to enjoy the fruits of their labor. The food was delicious, and the sense of camaraderie made the meal even more enjoyable.

After lunch, the Sunboat docked at Edfu, and they visited the Temple of Horus, one of the best-preserved ancient monuments in Egypt. Upon docking, a quaint horse-drawn carriage awaited them. The journey to the temple was nostalgic, the rhythmic clopping of hooves grounding them in the ancient city's atmosphere.

The carriage ride was a charming experience, with Alex and Eden enjoying the slow, rhythmic pace. The streets of Edfu were bustling with life, but the ride allowed them to take in the sights and sounds at a leisurely pace. The clip-clop of the horse's hooves on the cobblestones and the gentle sway of the carriage transported them back in time.

Arriving at the Temple of Horus, they were immediately struck by its grandeur. The massive pylons at the entrance, adorned with reliefs of Horus and Pharaoh Ptolemy VIII smiting their enemies, were awe-inspiring.

Hazem led them inside, his voice filled with reverence. "The Temple of Horus at Edfu is dedicated to the falcon god Horus and is one of the best-preserved temples in Egypt. It was built during the Ptolemaic period and completed in 57 BC."

Inside the temple, the tale of Horus's battle against Seth unfolded in stunning carvings and hieroglyphs. Hazem's voice, narrating tales of Horus, echoed softly in the dimly lit hallways.

"Horus, the son of Isis and Osiris, avenged his father's death by defeating his uncle Seth in a fierce battle. This temple commemorates that victory and Horus's role as the protector of the pharaoh," Hazem said.

The walls were covered in elaborate reliefs depicting scenes of offerings, rituals, and the epic battles between Horus and Seth. Alex and Eden marveled at the artistry and the stories embedded in the stone.

"This place is incredible," Alex said, his voice filled with wonder. "The detail in these carvings is just astounding."

Eden nodded, equally captivated. "It's like stepping into a storybook. You can almost feel the history here."

They wandered through the temple, taking in the sanctuaries, halls, and courtyards. Hazem's narration brought the ancient tales to life, making the experience even more immersive.

They returned to the horse-drawn carriage for the ride back to the Sunboat, feeling enriched by the day's experiences. Back on the Sunboat, they reflected on the day's adventures. The combination of history, culture, and hands-on activities had made for an unforgettable experience.

"That was so much fun," Eden said, leaning against Alex as they walked back to their cabin. "I love seeing you in your element."

Alex smiled, feeling content. "And I love sharing these moments with you."

As the sun set over the Nile, the Sunboat came alive with the anticipation of the evening's entertainment. The dining area was transformed into a vibrant stage, adorned with colorful lights and rich fabrics that swayed gently in the breeze.

The night began with the rhythmic beat of traditional Egyptian music, setting the tone for the performances to come. As they ate dinner, the first act was a belly dancer, her costume glittering with every move as she gracefully swayed and twirled. Her movements were mesmerizing, each step and gesture telling a story of ancient traditions and celebrations.

Alex and Eden watched in awe, captivated by the dancer's skill and the energy of the performance. The crowd clapped and cheered, their enthusiasm adding to the electric atmosphere.

Next came the whirling dervish. Dressed in flowing robes and a tall conical hat, the dervish began his performance with slow, deliberate spinning movements, gradually increasing his speed. As he spun faster and faster, his robes billowed out, creating a mesmerizing display of colors and patterns.

Hazem leaned over to Alex and Eden, his voice reverent as he began to explain. "The whirling dervish dance, known as the Sama, is a deeply spiritual practice. It originates from the Sufi tradition, where the aim is to achieve a state of spiritual ecstasy and closeness to God."

As the dervish spun, Hazem continued, "Each element of the dance holds profound meaning. The dervish's white robe represents the shroud of ego, symbolizing the renunciation of worldly attachments. The tall conical hat he wears is a symbol of the tombstone, indicating the death of his ego." Alex and Eden listened intently, their eyes following the dervish's fluid movements.

"The dance itself," Hazem went on, "is a form of active meditation. By spinning in repetitive circles, the dervish attempts to emulate the planets orbiting the sun, drawing closer to the divine source of life. His right hand is raised towards the heavens to receive God's blessings, while his left hand is turned downwards to distribute these blessings to the earth."

As the dervish spun faster, his movements became a blur, yet there was a serene, almost otherworldly quality to his dance. The music intensified, and the energy in the room grew electric.

"The Sama is not just a performance," Hazem said softly, his eyes reflecting the dervish's motion. "It is a spiritual journey. The spinning symbolizes the journey of the soul as it ascends to divine love, transcending the material world. The repetition of the dance mirrors the cyclical nature of life and the eternal search for enlightenment."

Eden whispered, "It's like he's reaching for something beyond our understanding."

Hazem nodded. "Exactly. The dervish seeks to lose himself in the divine, to become one with the cosmos. Each turn brings him closer to the heart of existence, where time and self dissolve into the infinite."

Alex watched, entranced by the dervish's movements. "It's incredible. I can't imagine spinning like that without getting dizzy."

Eden chuckled, nudging him playfully. "You'd probably fall over after a few spins."

Hazem joined in the teasing. "Yes, Alex, perhaps you should stick to writing and cooking. Leave the spinning to the professionals."

Alex laughed, holding his head as if already feeling dizzy. "I think you're right. I'll admire from a distance."

The dervish's dance reached its climax, his movements a blur of grace and spirituality. As he slowed to a stop, ending with his hands over his heart and head bowed in silent reverence, the crowd erupted into applause. The performance had been a moving, almost hypnotic experience.

Afterwards, Alex, Eden, and Hazem lingered on the deck, discussing the symbolism and beauty of the dances. The stars twinkled above them, and the gentle lapping of the Nile created a serene backdrop.

"That was an amazing show," Eden said, her eyes still sparkling from the evening's excitement. "I love how much meaning is embedded in their movements."

Hazem nodded. "Egyptian culture is rich with symbolism and tradition. There's always something deeper to discover. As you can see, we spared no expense in hiring the best performers Egypt has to offer."

Alex took Eden's hand, feeling a profound sense of connection to her and to the journey they were on.

"I can't wait to see what tomorrow brings," she said. "The Valley of the Kings and Queens, the Temple of Hatshepsut... it's all so fascinating."

Hazem smiled. "You're in for a treat. The Valley of the Kings and Queens is a testament to the grandeur of ancient Egypt, and the Temple of Hatshepsut is one of the most impressive architectural achievements of its time."

With their spirits lifted and their curiosity piqued, Alex and Eden bid Hazem goodnight and retired to their cabin.

●

The next morning, the Sunboat docked early, and Alex, Eden, and Hazem set off for the Valley of the Kings and Queens. The journey took them through the rugged, sun-drenched landscape of the West Bank, with the majestic Theban mountains rising in the distance.

As they approached the site, the sheer scale and historical significance of the valley struck them. The air was dry and filled with a sense of ancient mystery.

Hazem pointed ahead. "The Valley of the Kings and Queens is one of the most important archaeological sites in Egypt. It served as the burial ground for pharaohs, queens, and nobles during the New Kingdom period."

Their first stop was the tomb of Tutankhamun. Hazem led them through the narrow corridors, the air cool and still. The walls were adorned with vivid hieroglyphs and scenes depicting the young pharaoh's journey to the afterlife.

"This tomb was discovered in 1922 by Howard Carter," Hazem explained. "Its discovery was one of the greatest archaeological finds of the 20th century, providing invaluable insights into ancient Egyptian burial practices and beliefs."

Eden ran her fingers lightly over the carvings, marveling at their detail. "It's incredible to think these were created thousands of years ago and are still so well-preserved."

Alex took Eden's hand, squeezing it gently. "It's moments like this that make me grateful we chose Egypt for our honeymoon. It feels like we're stepping into another world."

Next, they visited the tomb of Ramses VI. The tomb's grandeur and the intricacy of the decorations left them in awe. Hazem narrated the stories depicted on the walls, bringing the ancient history to life.

"This tomb is a prime example of the artistry and craftsmanship of ancient Egyptian workers," Hazem said. "The scenes here depict the pharaoh's journey through the underworld, guided by the gods."

Alex was particularly struck by the deep blues and golds used in the tomb's decorations. "The colors are so vibrant."

Eden looked at Alex, her eyes shining with love and excitement. "I can see why you wanted to come here. I never imagined something like this could exist. How did they do it?"

After exploring several tombs, they made their way to the Temple of Hatshepsut. The temple, nestled against the towering cliffs of Deir el-Bahari, was a stunning example of ancient architecture.

As they approached the temple, Hazem shared its history. "This temple was built by Hatshepsut, one of the few female pharaohs of Egypt. She ruled with wisdom and strength, leaving behind a legacy of peace and monumental architecture."

The grandeur of the temple was awe-inspiring. Alex and Eden walked through the columned terraces, marveling at the intricate carvings and statues depicting Hatshepsut's reign and her divine birth.

Eden, deeply moved by the temple's beauty and significance, turned to Alex. "You know, Alex, I've been thinking. Your main character should be a female pharaoh. Hatshepsut's story is so inspiring. Imagine the impact of a strong female lead in your book."

Alex looked around, absorbing the suggestion. "A female pharaoh... that's a powerful idea. I've been focusing so much on the themes of conflict and balance, but a female protagonist could bring a unique perspective."

As they continued exploring, Alex's mind began to weave a new story. He paused before a relief depicting Hatshepsut's achievements and turned to Eden, excitement in his eyes.

"What if the story is about the first female pharaoh?" Alex proposed. "But her brother, jealous and power-hungry, murders her to become pharaoh. Except, she doesn't die. She survives and must reclaim her throne and her country."

Eden's eyes lit up. "That's brilliant, Alex! It adds layers of intrigue, resilience, and empowerment. It's the perfect blend of myth and drama."

Alex nodded, his mind racing with ideas. "She could embody the wisdom of Hatshepsut and the strength of Isis. Her journey to reclaim her throne could parallel the struggles of Sobek and Horus, representing the balance between chaos and order."

Hazem, overhearing their conversation, smiled. "It sounds like you've found a story worth telling, Alex. The struggles of ancient Egypt are timeless, and a female pharaoh's journey will resonate deeply."

As they walked through the temple's sanctuaries, Alex and Eden discussed potential titles for the book.

"We need a title that captures the essence of an epic journey," Alex said. "Something that reflects resilience, struggle, and ultimately, redemption."

Eden thought for a moment. "How about *The Nile's Redemption*? It ties in with the historical setting and symbolizes both the protagonist's journey and her rise back to power."

Alex's eyes lit up. "That's perfect, Eden. *The Nile's Redemption* captures everything I want to convey. The protagonist's journey is like a phoenix rising from the ashes, reclaiming her place, and transforming her world."

Eden smiled and gave Alex a kiss. "It's a powerful title. I'm sure it will resonate with readers and draw them into the story."

With the title decided, Alex felt a renewed sense of purpose. He was ready to pour his heart and soul into *The Nile's Redemption*, bringing the powerful story of the first female pharaoh to life.

Upon returning to the Sunboat late that afternoon, Hazem began outlining the itinerary for the next few days. "We'll be leaving the Sunboat and heading to Luxor this evening. You'll be staying at a five-star hotel where we've booked a penthouse room for the night.

We spared no expense to ensure your comfort and relaxation."

Eden's eyes lit up at the thought of a luxurious night. "That sounds wonderful."

Alex smiled, feeling a sense of relief and anticipation. "I think a night in a nice hotel will be perfect after all the exploring we've done."

Hazem nodded. "Indeed. Tomorrow, we'll visit the Temple of Hathor at Dendera and then travel to Abydos. These sites are rich in history and should provide more inspiration for both of you."

Arriving in Luxor, Hazem arranged for transportation to their hotel. As they approached, the grandeur of the five-star establishment came into view. The hotel, an architectural blend of modern luxury and traditional Egyptian design, promised a night of comfort and elegance.

The lobby was adorned with intricate decor, and the staff greeted them warmly, quickly facilitating their check-in. Their suite was spacious and opulently furnished, offering stunning views of the Nile.

Alex and Eden felt their exhaustion melt away as they settled into their room. They decided to take advantage of the amenities, enjoying a relaxing evening by their in-room Jacuzzi and a sumptuous dinner at the hotel's Michelin-star restaurant.

●

Overnight, Alex was overcome by a peculiar dream. He found himself standing in a dimly lit chamber, the air thick with an ancient, earthy scent. The walls around him were covered in hieroglyphs that seemed to move and shift in the flickering light. He realized he was inside the Great Pyramid.

A soft, creeping shadow began to take form, and Alex watched as Anubis, the god of mummification and the afterlife, emerged from the darkness. The jackal-headed deity moved with a graceful, otherworldly presence, his eyes glowing with an eerie light.

Anubis approached Alex and extended a hand, holding an Ankh, the symbol of life. The metallic Ankh touched Alex's lips, and he felt it enter and open his mouth. It was as if centuries of wisdom and secrets were being unlocked within him, flooding his mind with images and emotions.

The chamber around him began to vibrate, and the hieroglyphs on the walls started to glow. Alex felt a connection to something much greater than himself... a profound understanding of life, death, and the mysteries of existence.

Suddenly, a beam of radiant light descended from the top of the chamber, enveloping Alex in its warmth. The light grew brighter and brighter until it was blinding, and just as it seemed to consume him entirely, Alex woke up, drenched in sweat.

He lay in bed, his heart pounding, the vividness of the dream lingering in his mind. He looked over at Eden, who was peacefully asleep beside him. The dream had felt so real, so powerful, that it left him both exhilarated and confused. Alex shared his dream with Eden over breakfast. She listened intently, her eyes widening with each detail.

"That's incredible, babe," Eden said with a smile. "I had a similar dream the first night we spent in Cairo. Maybe Egypt is trying to tell us something."

"Yeah, you're right. I feel like there's a message in it," Alex replied, still trying to piece together the meaning. "Something about life and the knowledge we can uncover."

After breakfast, Hazem met them in the lobby, outlining the plan for the day. "Today, we'll visit the Temple of Hathor at Dendera first, followed by a trip to Abydos. These sites are crucial in understanding the spiritual and cultural depths of ancient Egypt."

Eden looked excited. "I'm particularly interested in Hathor and the healing practices associated with her temple."

Hazem nodded. "You'll find the Temple of Hathor fascinating. It's dedicated to the goddess of love, beauty, music, and healing. You'll learn a lot about the holistic healing practices of the time."

Alex added, "And I'm looking forward to Abydos. The Osirion is incredibly interesting. I read about it in a book called *Wonders of the World*, and I think there's more there that will help shape my story."

Hazem continued, "After we've explored Dendera and Abydos, we'll head back to Aswan and take a plane to Cairo for the final leg of your honeymoon. In Cairo, I've arranged for private time with the Sphinx and the Great Pyramid. Then we will visit other iconic locations."

Eden looked at Alex. "This has been such an incredible journey so far. I can't wait to see what Cairo has in store for us."

Alex nodded. "It's been an unforgettable experience, and I'm sure the final days will be just as amazing."

Hazem smiled warmly. "I'm glad to hear that. Now, let's get started on our day. We have a lot to see and learn."

With that, they set off for another day of exploration. Hazem arranged for transportation to the Temple of Hathor at Dendera. As they approached the temple, the impressive structure loomed ahead, its columns adorned with intricate carvings and its façade radiating the timeless beauty of ancient Egyptian architecture.

Hazem led them through the entrance, his voice filled with reverence. "Welcome to the Temple of Hathor. This temple is dedicated to Hathor, the goddess of love, beauty, music, and healing. It's one of the best-preserved temples in Egypt and holds significant insights into the holistic healing practices of the time."

As they walked through the temple, Hazem pointed out various carvings and inscriptions. "Hathor was not only the goddess of love and beauty but also a healer. The ancient Egyptians believed in the power of music and dance as part of the healing process."

Eden's eyes sparkled with curiosity. "Music and dance as healing practices? That's fascinating."

Hazem nodded. "Yes, they believed that certain melodies and rhythms could restore balance and harmony to the body and mind. They also used various herbs and plants in their remedies, many of which are depicted in the carvings here."

Eden leaned in closer to study the detailed inscriptions. "The holistic approach to healing is so advanced. They understood the connection between the mind, body, and spirit."

Hazem guided them to a chamber filled with depictions of Hathor's rituals. "This is where the priests and priestesses would perform their ceremonies. They believed that invoking Hathor's blessings could heal the sick and bring comfort to the distressed."

Eden made a mental note to integrate these practices into her own approach to medicine. "The idea of combining spiritual and physical healing is something I can definitely incorporate into my practice. It's about treating the whole person, not just the symptoms."

Alex watched Eden with admiration. "You're really inspired by this, aren't you?"

Eden smiled. "Absolutely. There's so much we can learn from

ancient practices. It's incredible how they understood the importance of balance and harmony. I just don't understand why we don't do this now."

After exploring the Temple of Hathor, the group took a short break before setting off for Abydos, enjoying a nice lunch at the Palm Club. Hazem then arranged for a comfortable ride, ensuring they had everything they needed for the journey. They arrived at Abydos, the sacred site known for its deep connection to Osiris, the god of the afterlife.

Hazem led them towards the main temple complex where he began explaining the significance of Abydos. "This is one of the oldest and most significant religious sites in Egypt. It's believed to be the burial place of Osiris and a center for pilgrimage and worship."

Hazem led them through the grand entrance, his voice filled with reverence. "This temple was built by Seti I and was completed by his son, Ramesses II. It's one of the most significant religious structures in Egypt, known for its exquisite art and connection to the Osiris myth."

The Osirion, partially submerged in water, stood as a testament to the enduring legacy of ancient Egyptian spirituality. The massive granite blocks and the intricate carvings created an awe-inspiring sight.

Hazem led them inside, the air thick with history. "The Osirion symbolizes death and resurrection. It's a place of great spiritual significance, representing the eternal cycle of life."

As they walked through the Osirion, Hazem continued his narration. "According to the myth, Osiris was the first king of Egypt who brought civilization to the land. He was murdered by his brother Set, who dismembered his body and scattered the pieces across Egypt. Isis, Osiris's wife, gathered the pieces and resurrected him long enough to conceive their son, Horus. Osiris then became the lord of the underworld, overseeing the judgment of souls and the cycle of life and death."

As they walked deeper into the Osirion, Alex's mind began to race with ideas. He could see the protagonist of his book, the first female pharaoh, navigating her own journey of death and resurrection, reclaiming her throne, and restoring balance to her kingdom.

"What if after she's betrayed by her brother and left for dead," Alex mused aloud, "she harnesses the wisdom and strength of the gods to reclaim her throne?"

Eden nodded, excited by the idea. "She could undergo a transformation, symbolizing her rebirth and the renewal of her kingdom. It's a powerful metaphor."

Hazem smiled, sensing Alex's excitement. "The ancient stories of Osiris have inspired many. It sounds like you've found the perfect way to incorporate these themes into your book."

As they continued exploring the Osirion, Alex's vision for his book became clearer. He saw the protagonist's journey as a reflection of the eternal struggle between chaos and order, life and death.

"She'll have to navigate political intrigue, face betrayal, and forge new alliances," Alex said, his voice filled with determination. "Her resilience and wisdom will be her greatest strengths."

Eden added, "And her journey can be paralleled with the rituals and practices we've learned about. It's not just about reclaiming her throne; it's about restoring balance and harmony to her kingdom."

As they left Abydos, Alex felt a renewed sense of purpose. The insights from the Temple of Hathor and the Osirion had provided him with the inspiration and direction he needed for his book, now titled *The Nile's Redemption*.

He turned to Eden, gratitude in his eyes. "Thank you, Eden. Your idea has transformed my story. It's going to be powerful and meaningful."

Eden smiled, then kissed him gently. "I'm glad I could help. I can't wait to see it come to life."

After their transformative experiences in Dendera and Abydos, Alex, Eden, and Hazem made their way to Aswan Airport. The airport buzzed with activity, a stark contrast to the ancient serenity they had just left behind. Travelers hurried to their gates, announcements echoed through the halls, and the scent of various foods wafted through the air.

As they navigated through the bustling crowd, Alex and Eden took in the sights around them. The mix of tourists and locals created a dynamic, almost chaotic atmosphere. The couple moved through security and made their way to the departure lounge, where they found a quiet corner to sit and wait for their flight.

While they were sitting, an older, well-dressed man wearing a sweater and khakis approached them. He had a charming smile and his eyes held a depth that seemed out of place in the busy airport.

"Excuse me," the man said, his voice melodious and calming. "But I felt an overwhelming urge to advise you both to leave Egypt now." His words, though spoken kindly, sent a shiver down Eden's spine. Alex and Eden exchanged glances, uncertainty flickering in their eyes. The man's presence felt almost otherworldly, as if he knew something they didn't.

"Why should we leave?" Alex asked, trying to keep his voice steady.

The man's smile faded slightly, replaced by a look of concern.

"There are events unfolding that you do not want to be a part of. Trust me, it's best for you to leave as soon as possible," he said. Without waiting for a response, the man tipped his hat and continued on his way, disappearing into the crowd.

Eden turned to Alex, worry etched on her face. "What do you think he meant by that?"

Alex shook his head. "I don't know, but we should be cautious. Let's keep an eye out and be prepared for anything."

They recounted the encounter to Hazem, who tilted his head thoughtfully. "Egypt is a land of mysteries, and its people are no different," he mused. "But we must keep moving. We have a flight to catch."

The flight back to Cairo was filled with a growing sense of unease. The words of the mysterious stranger lingered in their minds, casting a shadow over their thoughts. Alex and Eden couldn't shake the feeling that they were heading into something unknown and potentially dangerous. As the plane touched down and they disembarked, the familiar sights and sounds of Cairo did little to ease their tension. The bustling city, usually so vibrant and full of life, now felt heavy with an undercurrent of tension.

The concierge greeted them warmly as they checked in to the familiar Pyramids Hotel. Their room, with its luxurious furnishings and stunning view of the pyramids, felt like a sanctuary after the day's travels. They unpacked quickly, eager to see the Sphinx's laser show they had heard so much about.

"Let's not waste any time," Alex said, excitement in his voice. "I've been looking forward to this."

Eden nodded in agreement. "Me too. Let's go."

They made their way to the Giza Plateau, where the Sphinx and the pyramids stood silhouetted against the night sky. The air was cool, and a gentle breeze carried the scent of the desert. A sense of awe and anticipation filled the air as other visitors gathered for the show.

As the laser show began, vibrant beams of light illuminated the ancient monuments, bringing them to life with color and movement. The history of Egypt was narrated, accompanied by a mesmerizing display of lights and music. The Sphinx, bathed in hues of blue, green, and red, seemed almost unreal.

Alex and Eden stood hand in hand, completely captivated by the spectacle. The laser show wove stories of pharaohs, gods, and the mysteries of the pyramids, creating a magical atmosphere.

"This is incredible," Eden whispered. "It's like the past and present are merging before our eyes."

Alex nodded, his eyes fixed on the illuminated Sphinx. "It's moments like these that make our journey so unforgettable."

After the show, they returned to their hotel room, still buzzing with excitement. Alex stepped out onto the balcony to smoke a hookah filled with shisha, enjoying the view of the pyramids lit up against the night sky. As he gazed at the constellation of Orion, a sudden, inexplicable event caught his eye.

One of the stars in Orion's belt blinked and vanished. Suddenly, a radiant orb of light descended onto the top of the Great Pyramid. The light pulsed for a moment before shooting upwards into the night sky. The star began dancing in strange patterns while fading in and out, leaving Alex in a state of shock.

"Eden!" he called out, his voice filled with urgency. "Come here, you need to see this!"

Eden joined him on the balcony, her eyes widening in disbelief as she witnessed the celestial phenomenon. "What in the world is that?"

As they stood in stunned silence, a memory from Alex's past surfaced. He remembered being at the circus, captivated by the sights and sounds. One particular memory stood out... the fortune teller.

She was an enigmatic woman, her tent filled with the scent of incense and decorated with colorful tapestries. Alex had been fascinated by her mystical aura and the crystal ball she gazed into.

"You have a destiny intertwined with the stars," she had told him, her voice hauntingly prophetic. "One day, a star will disappear and dance in the sky above, and you will find yourself at a crossroads."

At the time, he had dismissed her words as part of the circus act. But now, standing on the balcony in Cairo, her prophecy echoed in his mind with startling clarity. Was this the event she had predicted?

As they stood there, trying to make sense of what they had just seen, a thunderous roar echoed through the city. Tanks began to flood the streets, and the hotel's loudspeakers crackled to life with an urgent announcement.

"Attention, all residents and visitors. Martial law has been declared. Please stay indoors and remain calm."

Hazem, who had been with them for the evening, rushed through the hotel and into their room. "I need to get to my family. It's not safe here anymore. I have to protect them, it is my duty."

Hazem explained briefly, "The social stratification has reached a breaking point. The wealthy have become too rich while the poor struggle to survive. The people are lashing out, trying to overthrow the government. It's dangerous out there." With that, Hazem left, leaving Alex and Eden to process the gravity of the situation.

Eden panicked, her voice trembling. "He left us! He left us!"

Alex took her by the shoulders, trying to calm her. "Well, it is his duty, you know. When you gotta go, you gotta go," he said, trying to inject a bit of humor into the dire situation, though his own heart pounded with fear.

Realizing they had to act quickly, Alex and Eden began gathering their essentials. The sounds of unrest outside grew louder, with gunfire and cries echoing through the streets.

"We need to get out of here, Alex," Eden said, her voice steady despite the fear in her eyes. "We need to find a way to the airport and leave Cairo."

"We need to leave at first light," Alex suggested. "The streets might be quieter, and we'll have a better chance of getting to the airport."

Eden nodded, her determination solidifying. "Let's pack only what we need and get ready to move."

They quickly assessed their belongings, prioritizing passports, money, essential documents, and a few changes of clothes. Eden packed a small first aid kit, while Alex ensured they had enough water and snacks to sustain them for the journey ahead.

"We're leaving behind a lot," Eden said, looking at the items they couldn't take with them.

"We'll make do with what we have," Alex replied, trying to sound reassuring. "The most important thing is that we stay safe."

●

The first light of dawn shone bleakly through the thin curtains of their hotel room. Alex and Eden knew they had to leave early to avoid the worst of the chaos. They had barely slept, the night filled with the sounds of gunfire and distant explosions.

As they stepped out of the hotel, the force of the situation hit them. The streets were filled with protesters, military vehicles, and soldiers clashing with civilian militias. The air was thick with tension and smoke from burning barricades. They knew they had to stay vigilant and move quickly.

Alex took Eden's hand, giving it a reassuring squeeze. "We'll get through this together," he said firmly.

With a shared look of determination, they hailed a taxi and set off into the early morning light, ready to face whatever challenges awaited them in the chaos of Cairo.

The journey to the airport was fraught with danger. They encountered numerous military checkpoints, each one more intimidating than the last. Soldiers demanded identification and searched their bags, adding to their anxiety.

At one checkpoint, a soldier eyed them suspiciously. "Why are you out during martial law?" he asked, his tone stern.

"We need to get to the airport," Alex explained, trying to keep his voice calm. "We have a flight to catch."

The soldier studied them for a moment before waving them through. "Be careful. The city is not safe."

The streets were far from empty. Protesters filled the roads, waving signs and chanting slogans. The tension was high as they passed groups of civilians armed with makeshift weapons, ready to defend their neighborhoods. Military vehicles rumbled by, adding to the volatile mix.

At one point, they were forced to take a detour to avoid a clash between soldiers and protesters. The air was heavy with tear gas, and the sounds of gunfire echoed through the streets. Their taxi hurried through alleyways, trying to avoid the worst of the conflict.

When they finally reached the airport, it was a scene of utter chaos. Protesters, worried travelers, and stone-faced military personnel collided in a maelstrom of fear and uncertainty. Eden clutched Alex's hand tightly, relying on his strength. Inside, pandemonium reigned. The crush of bodies, the stifling heat combined with the anxiety of missing flights, and the desperation to leave was overwhelming.

The air was foul, both from the lack of ventilation and the intense sense of fear. Long queues twisted in every direction, while hapless officials bore the brunt of everyone's frustration. Trying to stay optimistic, both Alex and Eden thought, *Surely, we'll be able to find a flight somewhere.* But when confronted with the news of cancellations, their spirits plummeted.

To add insult to injury, they embarked on a wild goose chase from one counter to another, each time with the hope that maybe, just maybe, they could find another way out of this nightmare.

The scenes surrounding Alex and Eden were heart-wrenching. Exhausted children lay sprawled, dehydration evident in their features. A sudden jostling from the crowd brought them back to the present.

Eden clutched Alex's arm. "We can't stay here," she whispered, her voice choked with emotion.

The impending curfew, the claustrophobia of the terminal, and the escalating tension forced a decision. They would attempt to return to their hotel. They approached the line of taxis outside the airport, the drivers wary and demanding exorbitant fares. The few drivers willing to risk the streets were visibly on edge. Alex and Eden had already spent most of their cash and knew that the ATMs were empty. Desperation clawed at them as they realized they couldn't afford the fare.

Alex took a deep breath and approached one of the drivers, a wild-eyed man with a weathered face. "We need to get back to the Pyramids Hotel," Alex said, trying to keep his voice steady.

"We'll pay you when we get to our hotel safely," Eden pleaded.

The driver eyed them suspiciously, then looked around at the chaotic scene. "Get in and hold on to your butts!" he said sharply.

Alex and Eden exchanged a tense glance but had no choice. They climbed into the backseat, and the driver started the engine with a roar and pulled away. The streets of Cairo had transformed into a war zone. Protesters clashed with soldiers, and civilian militias fought to protect their neighborhoods. Fires burned in the distance, and the air was thick with smoke and the acrid smell of tear gas.

As the taxi sped through the streets, the driver began to rant, his voice filled with manic energy. "You should have seen it last night," he said, his eyes darting around. "People running, screaming. The army's cracking down hard. It's chaos out here."

As they drove, Alex and Eden were confronted with scenes of unimaginable horror. Bodies lay in the streets, some hogtied and others mutilated as grim warnings. The sheer brutality of it left them speechless, their minds struggling to process the violence.

The driver laughed, a high-pitched, almost hysterical sound. "Look at them!" he shouted. "Animals! This is what happens when the world falls apart."

Eden clung to Alex, her face pale and eyes wide with terror. "This is a nightmare," she whispered, her voice trembling.

Alex held her close, his own fear barely contained. "We'll get through this," he said, more to reassure himself than her.

The taxi driver weaved through the chaos with reckless abandon, narrowly avoiding collisions with other vehicles and debris. His laughter and erratic driving only added to the terror of the journey. At one point, he swerved to avoid a burning barricade, sending the car skidding dangerously close to a group of armed protesters.

"You see this?" he yelled, gesturing wildly. "This is what our world has come to! No order, no peace!"

Alex tried to keep his voice calm. "Just get us to the hotel safely, please."

The driver shot him a wild look through the rearview mirror. "I'll get you there, but it might cost you more than money."

As they approached the Pyramids Hotel, the scenes of horror became less frequent, but the tension remained. The streets around the hotel were heavily guarded by military personnel, their expressions grim as they monitored the area.

When they finally reached the hotel, the driver pulled up to the entrance and turned to face them. "Where's my money?" he demanded.

Alex handed over the last of their cash, a pitiful amount compared to the fare.

The driver's face twisted with anger. "This isn't enough! You think you can just stiff me?"

Before Alex could respond, the hotel's security guards intervened, pulling the driver away and allowing Alex and Eden to dash inside. The relative safety of the hotel was a stark contrast to the chaos they had just escaped.

They collapsed in the lobby, their exhaustion and relief causing tears to rush down their weary faces. The weight of their ordeal settled heavily upon them, but they knew they had to stay vigilant. The situation in Cairo was deteriorating rapidly, and they needed to find a way out.

With the hotel's resources dwindling and the uncertainty of the situation growing, Alex and Eden joined forces with other stranded travelers, pooling their resources and strategizing their next move.

As they sat in a quiet corner of the lobby, discussing potential escape routes and methods, Eden took charge, her natural leadership skills coming to the fore. She rallied the group, keeping their spirits up and organizing their efforts.

"We need to stick together and stay strong," Eden said, her voice steady and confident. "We cannot be contained—life will find a way —but we have to work as a team."

Her voice was steady despite the fear in her eyes. "We need to find a way out of here," she said. "The airport is chaotic, but we have to try again. We need a solid plan, and we'll need to stick together. In three days, we should try again. I'm sure that planes will start leaving by then. In the meantime, we need to gather up as many supplies as possible."

The group was diverse, consisting of tourists from various countries, all desperate to escape Cairo. There was a couple from Germany, an older man from Canada, a young backpacker from Alaska, and several others. They shared their resources, pooling what little they had left in terms of food, water, and money.

One of the group members, a middle-aged man named George, shook his head in frustration. "I tried calling the embassy, but they didn't do a dang thing. We're on our own. I can't believe it's come to this. We're stuck in a foreign country, and our own government can't help us."

One of the travelers, a middle-aged woman with a calm demeanor, spoke up. "I'm a pilot. I've flown commercial and private planes. If we can get to a plane, I can fly us out of here. But we need to reach the airport safely first."

Her words sparked a flicker of hope in the group. Eden turned to her, her eyes widening. "You can fly? That's incredible. What's your name?"

"Susan," she replied, offering a reassuring smile.

"We'll form a human chain," George suggested. "That way, we can stay together and move as one. We can't afford to get separated."

Eden added, "We need to gather everything we have and be ready to leave at a moment's notice. Let's make sure everyone knows what to do and where to go."

The group spent the next few days preparing, hoping that the protests would ease up, but they didn't. The tension in the air was thick, but a sense of solidarity began to form. People who had been strangers just days before were now relying on each other for survival.

As they packed their bags, Alex and Eden had a quiet moment together. Alex looked at Eden, seeing the determination in her eyes.

"I'm proud of you," he said softly. "You're handling this so well."

Eden smiled, though her eyes were tired. "We've been through so much already, Alex. I just want us to be safe. I want us to make it through this together."

He nodded, taking her hand. "We will. We'll get through this, and we'll come out stronger."

The third night passed slowly, filled with anxious whispers and quiet preparations. Alex and Eden lay in bed, holding each other tightly, drawing strength from their shared resolve.

"We're going to be okay," Alex whispered, more to reassure himself than Eden. "We're going to make it out of here."

Eden nodded, her head resting on his chest. "Yes, we will. Together."

As dawn approached, the group gathered in the lobby, their faces set with determination. The plan was simple but fraught with risk. They had chartered a bus and would move as one, sticking close and supporting each other, with Eden leading the way.

"We're ready," Susan said, her voice calm and steady. "Let's get out of here."

With a shared look of determination, they set off into the early
morning light, ready to face whatever challenges awaited them in the
chaos of Cairo. The group, led by Eden and Alex, had pooled their
remaining resources to charter a small bus. The tension was high as
they gathered in the lobby, their faces set with determination. Susan,
the pilot, coordinated the final details with the driver, ensuring they
had the best possible route to the airport.

"We need to move quickly and stay together," Eden instructed.
"Once we get to the airport, form a human chain and don't let go. It's
our best chance to stay safe."

With the plan in place, they boarded the bus just as the first light
of dawn broke over Cairo. The streets were filled with protesters and
military personnel clashing violently, the air still thick with smoke
and the acrid smell of tear gas. The bus driver, a young man with a
determined look, navigated the chaos with skill and caution.

The drive to the airport was nail-biting. Alex and Eden sat close
together, holding hands tightly. Eden's heart raced as she glanced out
the window, taking in the scenes of destruction and chaos.

"We're almost there," Alex whispered, squeezing her hand. "Just
a little longer."

When they finally reached the airport, the scene was no less
chaotic. The sound of gunfire echoed in the distance, and the cries of
those caught in the crossfire added to the clamor. The group quickly
disembarked from the bus, forming a human chain as they had
planned.

Hand in hand, they made their way through the throngs of
people, their hearts pounding with fear and determination. Gunshots
rang out behind them, and they knew that if they had arrived just
minutes later, they might have been caught in the deadly violence
around them.

"We have to keep moving!" Eden urged, her voice steady despite
the chaos around them.

Inside the terminal, the group barreled through every checkpoint
without care. The security personnel, overwhelmed by the sheer
number of people, barely glanced at their documents. The group's
unity and determination propelled them forward, their only goal to
reach a flight out of the country.

They managed to secure boarding passes to any available

destination, not caring where they ended up as long as it was away from the chaos of Cairo. Alex and Eden, along with a few other members of their group, rushed through the terminal, dodging obstacles, and trying to ignore the chaos around them. They reached their gate just as the final boarding call was announced, barely making it onto the plane.

As they found their seats and the plane began to taxi down the runway, the emotional weight of their ordeal began to lift. Tears of relief streamed down their faces as they realized they were finally safe.

As the plane took off and climbed into the sky, Alex and Eden looked down at the city below, the scenes of insanity growing smaller. A sense of peace and safety began to wash over them. They were leaving the chaos behind, heading toward an uncertain but hopeful future.

Eden leaned her head on Alex's shoulder, her eyes closing in exhaustion. "I can't wait to get home," she murmured. "Back to our life, our safety."

Alex kissed her forehead, his heart swelling with love. "And when we get back, I'll start writing *The Nile's Redemption*. It will be our story, a testament to everything we've experienced."

Eden smiled, her eyes closing as she drifted off to sleep. "I can't wait to read it," she whispered.

※

<u>**Lesson 7:**</u>
<u>**Building Resilience**</u>

In life, we often face unexpected challenges and obstacles that test our strength and determination. It is during these moments of adversity that resilience becomes our greatest ally. Resilience is the ability to bounce back from setbacks, adapt to change, and persevere in the face of adversity. It is a quality that not only helps us overcome obstacles but also fuels our personal growth and propels us toward success.

In this lesson, we will gain a deeper understanding of the different aspects of resilience and the strategies we can employ to overcome the challenges we face. We will explore the qualities and mindset of resilient individuals, discover the power of problem-solving and resourcefulness, and learn to embrace failure as a catalyst for growth.

Resilience is a fundamental aspect of personal growth and success. It is the capacity to navigate through life's challenges, setbacks, and uncertainties with strength and determination. Building resilience is a lifelong process that involves developing certain skills, cultivating a positive mindset, and adopting effective strategies to overcome obstacles.

One key aspect of building resilience is cultivating emotional intelligence. Emotional intelligence, as you may recall from Chapter Two, allows us to recognize and understand our emotions, as well as manage and express them effectively. By honing emotional intelligence, we can navigate through difficult situations with greater self-awareness, empathy, and self-control.

Another crucial factor in building resilience is developing a growth mindset, something we will cover in greater depth in a later chapter. A growth mindset is the belief that our abilities, intelligence, and talents can be developed through dedication, effort, and learning from experiences. It enables us to view setbacks and failures as opportunities for growth and learning, rather than as permanent barriers.

Building resilience also involves fostering a strong support system. Having a network of supportive relationships can provide emotional support, guidance, and encouragement during difficult times. It enables us to lean on others for assistance and helps us maintain a sense of belonging.

Developing resilience requires the cultivation of effective coping strategies and stress management techniques. These strategies can vary from person to person, but they often involve practices such as mindfulness, self-care, problem-solving, and seeking social support.

Lastly, building resilience necessitates embracing change and adaptability. Life is constantly evolving, and the ability to adapt to new situations, challenges, and environments is paramount. Building resilience is a lifelong endeavor that requires conscious effort, self-reflection, and a commitment to personal growth. By incorporating these elements into our lives, we can develop resilience that empowers us to face adversity head-on, grow from challenges, and ultimately thrive in the face of uncertainty.

Understanding Resilience

To truly understand the importance of resilience in overcoming obstacles, it's essential to explore its key traits and mindset. Being resilient means being adaptable, showing flexibility in your thoughts and approaches to challenges. This means you can embrace change, adjust your strategies, and find new paths when faced with obstacles. Even in difficult situations, you can maintain a positive outlook, focusing on possibilities and staying optimistic about the future. You'll believe in your ability to overcome difficulties.

Resilience also involves effective emotional regulation. Those who are resilient acknowledge their emotions but do not let them dictate their actions. They develop healthy coping mechanisms to handle stress and maintain emotional balance.

Problem-solving is another hallmark of resilience. Resilient people see obstacles as opportunities for growth. They approach situations with objectivity, actively seek solutions, and are resourceful, creative, and persistent in finding ways to overcome challenges.

The strength of resilience is often reinforced by social support. Resilient individuals cultivate and maintain healthy relationships. They seek help when needed and offer support to others. This network provides emotional comfort, practical assistance, and fresh perspectives during difficult times.

Resilience plays a crucial role in helping you bounce back from setbacks and persevere through challenges. It enables you to manage stress effectively, recover from traumatic events, and minimize the negative impact of stress on mental health. Through resilience, you'll enhance your problem-solving skills, approaching obstacles with a focus on finding solutions. Moreover, resilience fosters personal growth, allowing you to learn from experiences, gain new perspectives, and develop skills that contribute to your overall development and future resilience.

Developing Problem-Solving Skills

Problem-solving is a vital skill that plays a key role in effectively overcoming obstacles. By honing problem-solving abilities, you can tackle challenges with a clear and systematic mindset, allowing you to find solutions and move forward. Several strategies and techniques can help you navigate obstacles more efficiently.

Brainstorming is a powerful technique that encourages generating a wide range of ideas without judgment. This approach allows you to explore multiple perspectives and potential solutions to a problem. The aim is to produce as many ideas as possible, fostering creativity and opening up new possibilities. Brainstorming helps break free from conventional thinking and encourages innovative solutions.

Seeking alternative perspectives is another important strategy. Often, our own limited viewpoint can hinder effective problem-solving. By actively seeking different perspectives, you can gain new insights and ideas you might have missed. This can be done by engaging in discussions with others, seeking advice from mentors or experts, or imagining yourself in someone else's shoes. Considering different viewpoints broadens your understanding of the problem and helps identify unique solutions.

Breaking problems into manageable parts is a practical approach when faced with overwhelming challenges. Complex problems can feel daunting, but by dividing them into smaller, more manageable tasks, you can tackle each component one at a time. This method not only reduces the sense of helplessness but also provides a sense of accomplishment with each step.

Resourcefulness is the ability to effectively utilize available resources, including knowledge, skills, networks, and external assets.

Resourceful individuals are creative and flexible in finding solutions, even when resources are limited or unexpected challenges arise. They approach problems with the mindset of making the most of what they have and exploring alternative ways to overcome obstacles. This involves thinking outside the box, exploring different avenues, and adapting to new circumstances.

Creative thinking plays a crucial role in problem-solving by encouraging you to approach problems from unconventional angles. It involves challenging assumptions, thinking critically, and generating innovative ideas. Creative problem-solving often requires combining different concepts, making connections between unrelated ideas, and considering non-traditional approaches. It encourages embracing ambiguity, taking risks, and exploring new possibilities.

By integrating these problem-solving strategies into your approach, you can significantly enhance your ability to overcome obstacles. These skills promote adaptability, resilience, and a proactive mindset, enabling you to tackle challenges with confidence and discover practical solutions.

Embracing Failure and Learning

Failure is often viewed as something to be avoided or feared, but in reality, it plays a crucial role in personal growth and resilience. When we experience setbacks or failures, it presents an opportunity for us to learn, adapt, and develop the strength to overcome future challenges.

Failure is not a reflection of our worth or abilities; rather, it is a natural part of the journey toward success. It is through our failures that we gain valuable insights and lessons that propel us forward. Thomas Edison, the brilliant inventor behind the light bulb, famously said, "I have not failed. I've just found 10,000 ways that won't work." This mindset demonstrates his resilience and determination to learn from each setback, eventually leading him to groundbreaking success. Many famous authors and entrepreneurs faced numerous rejections before finding a publisher or angel investor who believed in their work. Their persistence and refusal to give up transformed their failures into successful ventures that have touched the lives of millions and sometimes changed the world as we know it.

At the core of embracing failure is the concept of a growth mindset. A growth mindset is the belief that our abilities and intelligence can be developed through effort, learning, and perseverance. It enables us to view failures not as endpoints, but as stepping stones toward improvement. By cultivating a growth mindset, we shift our focus from seeking validation to seeking growth and continuous learning.

To embrace failure and use it as a stepping stone for success, there are several strategies we can employ. First, we can think about failure differently by changing our perspective. Instead of seeing it as a negative outcome, we can view it as a valuable learning experience. Each failure brings us closer to finding the right path, providing us with insights and lessons that shape our future actions.

Seeking feedback and support is another important aspect of embracing failure. By seeking input from trusted mentors, friends, or colleagues, we gain different perspectives and insights that can guide us on our journey. Their constructive feedback helps us identify areas for improvement and discover new approaches.

It is essential to set realistic expectations and avoid striving for perfection. Perfectionism often hinders progress and amplifies the fear of failure. By setting realistic goals and acknowledging that setbacks are part of the process, we can navigate challenges with resilience and a growth-oriented mindset.

Practicing self-compassion is also crucial in embracing failure. It is important to treat ourselves with kindness and understanding when we face setbacks. Self-reflection allows us to learn from failures without harsh self-criticism, fostering a supportive and nurturing environment for personal growth.

Remember, failure is not a permanent state but a stepping stone on the path to success. Embracing failure and adopting a growth mindset empower us to learn, adapt, and persevere in the face of challenges. By changing how we think about failure, seeking support, setting realistic expectations, and practicing self-compassion, we can harness the power of failure to propel us toward personal and professional growth.

Activity: Building Resilience: A Comprehensive Workshop

This activity is designed to help you reflect on your personal strengths and resilience, apply problem-solving techniques to current challenges, and extract valuable lessons from past failures.

Part 1: Reflect on Personal Strengths and Resilience

Objective: Recognize and appreciate your personal qualities that have contributed to your resilience in the face of challenges.

Self-Assessment: Sit in a quiet and comfortable space without distractions. Reflect on your personal strengths and past experiences of resilience by considering the following questions:

- What are some personal strengths or qualities that helped you overcome difficult situations in the past?

- Think about a specific challenging experience or setback. How did you navigate through it? What inner resources or strengths did you rely on?

- Are there any particular skills or abilities that have proven valuable in building resilience?

- Reflect on moments when you demonstrated adaptability, perseverance, or problem-solving skills. What traits or characteristics allowed you to overcome those obstacles?

Journaling Prompts: Use the following prompts to deepen your understanding of your own resilience. Write your thoughts and reflections in a journal or a notebook:

- Describe a specific situation where you demonstrated resilience. What was the challenge and how did you respond?
- How did your strengths come into play?
- Reflect on the qualities or strengths you identified earlier. How have these strengths contributed to your ability to bounce back from adversity?

- Think about a time when you faced a setback or failure. How did you recover from it? What lessons did you learn from that experience?
- Consider any areas where you would like to further develop your resilience. What steps can you take to strengthen those areas?

Part 2: Apply Problem-Solving Techniques

<u>Objective</u>: Develop practical solutions to address a current challenge or obstacle.

<u>Choose a Current Challenge or Obstacle</u>: Identify a specific challenge or obstacle that you're currently facing. It could be a work-related issue, a personal struggle, a relationship problem, or any other area of your life where you feel stuck or in need of a solution

<u>Define the Problem</u>: Clearly define and describe the problem. Jot down the details of the situation, its impact on your life, any constraints or limitations to consider, and any specific aspects that make it challenging.

<u>Generate Possible Solutions</u>: Brainstorm as many potential solutions as you can think of. Focus on generating a wide range of ideas without judging their feasibility or practicality at this stage.

<u>Evaluate and Select a Solution</u>: Evaluate each potential solution considering its feasibility, potential outcomes, alignment with your goals and values, required resources, potential risks, and likelihood of success. Choose the most suitable option.

<u>Implement the Chosen Solution</u>: Create an action plan that breaks down the solution into smaller, manageable steps. Define clear timelines for each step and consider any additional resources or support needed. Commit to following through with your plan.

<u>Reflect on the Outcomes and Lessons Learned</u>: After implementing the solution, reflect on the outcomes and lessons learned. Evaluate the effectiveness of your chosen approach, note

what worked well and what could be improved, and consider the insights and skills gained throughout the process.

Part 3: Reflect on Past Failures and Extract Lessons

<u>Objective</u>: Extract valuable lessons from past failures or setbacks that have shaped your personal growth and resilience.

<u>Recall Past Failures or Setbacks</u>: In a quiet and comfortable space, recall a specific failure or setback from your past. Approach it with self-compassion and a growth-oriented mindset. Reflect on the lessons learned from that experience by considering the following questions:

- What were the circumstances surrounding the failure or setback?
- What were your initial reactions or emotions?
- What specific lessons did you learn from the experience?
- How did the failure or setback contribute to your personal growth and resilience?
- Did it change your perspective, values, or priorities?
- Did it teach you about your strengths, weaknesses, or areas for improvement?
- How did you overcome the challenges associated with that failure?

<u>Journal Your Reflections</u>: Journal your reflections, writing freely and honestly about the failure or setback, the lessons learned, and its impact on your personal growth and resilience. Include any insights or realizations that arise during this process.

<u>Identify Patterns or Recurring Themes</u>: Reflect on multiple past failures or setbacks and try to identify any patterns or recurring themes. Recognizing these patterns can provide deeper insights into your own resilience and personal development.

<u>Express Gratitude for the Lessons</u>: Express gratitude for the lessons learned from your past failures or setbacks. Acknowledge the strength and resilience that have grown within you as a result of

these experiences.

Acknowledge and celebrate the insights and growth you have gained through this workshop. Embrace the knowledge that failure is not a measure of your worth but a stepping stone on the path to growth and success.

By recognizing your strengths, applying problem-solving techniques, and extracting lessons from past failures, you empower yourself to navigate future challenges with confidence and resilience.

•

In this lesson, we have explored the theme of building resilience and overcoming obstacles. We have discovered that resilience is not about avoiding or eliminating obstacles, but rather about developing the inner strength and mindset to navigate through them with determination and adaptability.

Resilient individuals possess certain characteristics such as perseverance, optimism, and a growth mindset, which enable them to bounce back from setbacks and continue moving forward.

We have emphasized the significance of understanding resilience, acknowledging our personal strengths, and reflecting on past experiences of resilience. By recognizing our own resilience factors, we can harness them during challenging times and draw inspiration from our previous triumphs over adversity.

Moreover, we have explored problem-solving techniques that can assist us in effectively overcoming obstacles. Techniques like brainstorming, seeking alternative perspectives, and breaking problems into manageable parts h us to find innovative solutions and navigate through complex situations.

Finally, we have provided strategies for changing our perspective on failure, embracing it as a learning experience, and using it as a stepping stone to success. By adopting a positive and growth-oriented perspective, we can extract valuable lessons from our failures, develop resilience, and use these lessons to fuel our personal growth and future achievements.

As we end this lesson, it is essential to remember that building resilience is an ongoing journey. By cultivating resilience, we empower ourselves to overcome obstacles, embrace challenges as opportunities for growth, and lead more fulfilling lives.

<u>Chapter 8: Bad Beef</u>

A few days after their Egyptian honeymoon, Alex and Eden had settled back into their cozy home. Bees buzzed lazily around the hives Alex tended in their backyard, a serene backdrop to their newlywed bliss. He looked up to see Eden walking toward him, her smile radiant as she approached.

"Hey, honey," she called, her voice carrying a melody that always lifted his spirits. "Gabriel and Monica are coming over for dinner tonight. Did you forget?"

Alex looked up, brushing a hand through his hair and trying to recall the conversation. "Of course not," he said, grinning. "How could I forget? I've been looking forward to it."

While Alex and Eden were on their honeymoon, Gabriel and Monica had started dating. The news had come as a delightful surprise to Alex and Eden, who had known the two separately for years.

As the evening breeze picked up, Alex and Eden busied themselves in the kitchen, preparing for dinner. The smell of roasted chicken and fresh herbs filled the air, mingling with the earthy scent of the garden just outside. Eden, a dedicated doctor balancing her career with her pursuit of a master's degree, moved efficiently, her hands deftly arranging the final touches on the meal. Alex, meanwhile, was putting the finishing touches on a salad, a contribution from their garden.

The doorbell rang, pulling them both from their thoughts. "That must be them," Alex said, wiping his hands on a towel. "I'll get the drinks."

Eden nodded, smoothing her apron as she moved to the door. When she opened it, she was greeted by the sight of Gabriel and Monica, both beaming with excitement. Gabriel, tall and chubby with an easy smile, carried his guitar case over one shoulder, while Monica, with her warm, expressive eyes and a laugh that could light up a room, seemed to glow with happiness.

"Dinner smells amazing!" Gabriel exclaimed as they stepped inside, the aroma of the meal wrapping around them like a warm hug.

Eden beamed, ushering them in. "I hope you're hungry. Alex helped with the salad... his contribution from our garden."

Gabriel laughed, clapping Alex on the back as he entered the kitchen. "Good to see you, man. I've missed these dinners."

"Same here. I remember doing this a lot when Eden and I were dating," Alex replied, handing them drinks. "Make yourselves at home."

As they settled around the table, the conversation flowed easily, filled with laughter and shared memories. Gabriel strummed his guitar lightly, playing soft melodies as they reminisced about old times. Monica and Eden exchanged stories from their school days, their friendship rekindled after years of busy lives pulling them in different directions.

"So," Monica said, leaning forward with a curious smile, "how was the honeymoon? Egypt sounds incredible."

Eden's eyes sparkled as she began to recount their adventures. "It was magical. We saw the pyramids, sailed on the Nile, and explored ancient temples. The belly dancer and whirling dervish on our cruise down the Nile took our breath away."

Alex, always the storyteller, added with a grin, "That cruise was something else. The way the belly dancer moved, and the dervish spun... it was mesmerizing. But things took a dark turn toward the end."

Gabriel's smile faded slightly, his brow furrowing with concern. "Yeah, we heard about the trouble. We were worried sick."

Eden nodded, her expression darkening. "It was terrifying. One moment we were watching a laser show at the Sphinx, and the next, the country was under martial law. We had to navigate military checkpoints, curfews... there was this constant tension in the air."

Monica reached across the table, squeezing Eden's hand. "I can't imagine how scary that must have been."

Alex sighed, his gaze distant for a moment. "It was a nightmare, but we got through it together. I think it showed us how much we could rely on each other."

The room fell silent for a moment, the gravity of their story sinking in. Gabriel, sensing the need to lighten the mood, raised his glass. "To surviving, and to new beginnings."

They all clinked their glasses together, the tension easing as they shifted the conversation to dreams and future plans. Gabriel's eyes sparkled as he spoke about his latest music project, while Monica shared her excitement about a new job opportunity as a wedding planner in Everbrook.

"And what about you two?" Monica asked, turning to Alex and Eden. "How's life treating you?"

Alex glanced at Eden, their fingers intertwining under the table. "Life's good," he said, his voice filled with contentment. "The bees are thriving, the book's coming along, and we're just... happy."

Eden nodded, her smile serene. "We've been talking about the future, about starting a family someday, and I've been thinking of starting my own business here in Everbrook."

Gabriel raised his glass again. "Monica and I are just happy to see you both alive and well! To Alex and Eden," he toasted, and they all clinked their glasses together.

As the evening ended, Alex and Eden walked their friends to the door, the night air cool and crisp. "Thanks for coming, guys," Alex said, shaking Gabriel's hand. "We should do this more often."

"Absolutely," Gabriel agreed, his arm around Monica's

shoulders. "It's good to be with friends, and we're right down the road, so it's not far," he said with a chuckle.

Monica hugged Eden tightly. "Take care, and let's catch up again soon."

With farewells exchanged, Alex and Eden stood together on the porch, the stars twinkling above them, a silent promise of the future they envisioned.

Alex wrapped his arms around Eden, pulling her close. "I love you," he whispered, pressing a kiss to her forehead.

"I love you too," Eden replied, resting her head against his chest. "We've got a good life, Alex. Let's keep it that way."

In the weeks following that dinner with Gabriel and Monica, life at the country cottage settled into a steady rhythm for Alex and Eden. The days were long, filled with the tasks that came with managing their home, careers, and ambitions. But beneath the surface, the cracks in their perfect life began to widen, fed by the pressures of work, the strain of balancing responsibilities, and the inevitable end of the honeymoon phase.

Alex spent most mornings in his writing nook, a small room with a large window overlooking the garden. The view of the rolling hills and the gentle hum of the bees provided the perfect backdrop for his creativity. His novel, *The Nile's Redemption*, was taking shape, but the demands of writing, combined with the realities of their financial situation, weighed on him. To make ends meet, Alex started selling honey and homemade beeswax products at the local market. His beekeeping, once a hobby, was now an essential part of their income.

Every Saturday, Alex would load up the truck with jars of honey, beeswax candles, and bottles of mead, then head to the market. The market was a lively place, filled with the scent of fresh produce, baked goods, and flowers. He enjoyed the camaraderie with the other vendors, but the long hours on his feet were exhausting. By the time he returned home in the afternoon, he was often too tired to focus on his writing, which only added to his frustration.

Eden, meanwhile, was juggling her job at the hospital with her master's degree classes. Her days were packed with patient consultations, lab work, and late-night study sessions. She was determined to excel in both her career and her studies, but the workload was relentless. The time she used to spend with Alex became increasingly scarce as her responsibilities grew. She found herself coming home later and later, her mind too preoccupied with medical cases and academic deadlines to fully engage in their conversations.

Their evenings together, once filled with laughter and shared stories, began to change. Dinner became more about refueling than reconnecting. The small talk that once flowed easily now felt strained, punctuated by long silences as they both grappled with their own stressors. They tried to maintain their tradition of dancing in the living room to their favorite songs, but even that began to feel forced, a hollow echo of what it once was.

One evening, after a particularly grueling day at work, Eden came home to find Alex in the kitchen, trying to unclog the sink. The mess of tools and wet towels only added to her exhaustion.

"Hey," she greeted him, dropping her bag on the counter. "How's it going?"

Alex looked up, wiping sweat from his brow. "Just trying to fix this daggum sink. It's been backed up all day."

Eden sighed, feeling the weight of her day settle on her shoulders. "I can call a plumber tomorrow. You don't have to do everything yourself, you know."

Alex shook his head, his frustration bubbling over. "We're already stretched thin, Eden. We can't afford a plumber right now."

Eden bit her lip, the tension between them thickening. "I know, but you're exhausted. You've been working all day at the market, and now you're spending your evening fixing this. It's too much."

Alex dropped the wrench with a clatter, leaning against the counter. "I'm just trying to keep us afloat. Between the writing, the beekeeping, and the market, I feel like I'm constantly juggling."

"And I feel like I'm constantly falling behind," Eden replied, her voice tinged with frustration. "I'm barely keeping up with work and school, and when I finally get home, I just... I don't know how to switch off."

They stood there in silence, the air between them heavy with unspoken fears and frustrations. The honeymoon phase had well and truly ended, replaced by the harsh realities of married life. They both knew it, but neither wanted to admit it.

Finally, Alex spoke, his voice soft. "We need to figure this out, Eden. We're barely seeing each other, and when we do, we're too tired to even talk."

Eden nodded, tears welling up in her eyes. "I miss you, Alex. I miss us."

Alex stepped forward, pulling her into a tight embrace. "I miss us too. We'll get through this, okay? We just need to find a way to balance everything."

But even as they stood there, holding each other, they both knew that finding balance would be easier said than done.

•

Six months had passed since Alex and Eden returned from Egypt, and life had settled into a predictable, if slightly strained, routine. Gabriel and Monica's invitation to a small celebration for Gabriel's latest musical release at their home was a welcome break, offering a chance to relax with friends and momentarily escape the pressures of daily life.

Gabriel's home, a charming ranch nestled among towering oak trees down the road from Alex, was alive with the sounds of laughter and clinking glasses. Fairy lights draped across the backyard twinkled against the early evening sky, casting a warm glow over the gathering. The scent of grilled vegetables and freshly baked bread mingled with the crisp autumn air, making the atmosphere feel both festive and cozy.

As Alex and Eden arrived, they were greeted by the familiar sight of Gabriel strumming his guitar on the patio. He was surrounded by a small group of personal friends and some musicians, all captivated by the easy rhythm of his music. Monica, ever the gracious hostess, was circulating among the guests, her laughter rising above the hum of conversation.

"There you two are!" Gabriel called out, pausing mid-strum to wave them over. He set his guitar aside and greeted them with a broad grin. "Just in time for the good part."

"Wouldn't miss it," Alex replied with a smile, hugging Gabriel briefly. "How've you been?"

"Busy," Gabriel said, with a glance at Monica, who was beaming as she approached. "But in a good way."

Monica joined them, her eyes sparkling with excitement. "We're so glad you could make it. We were just saying how it feels like we see you guys all the time, but never enough."

"Right? We might be neighbors, but we aren't strangers," Eden said, hugging Monica warmly. "Life gets so hectic, but it's nice to have these moments."

As they settled into the backyard, the atmosphere was one of easy familiarity, the kind that comes from long-standing friendships. The conversation flowed naturally, with Gabriel and Monica sharing stories about their latest adventures. Gabriel spoke animatedly about his recent trip to a music festival where he performed with a few old friends. His eyes lit up as he recounted the thrill of playing for a crowd again.

"You should have seen the energy; it was pure chaos," Gabriel said, his hands moving expressively as he spoke. "The crowd was alive, and I felt like I was feeding off their vibe. It reminded me why I started doing this in the first place. I think we might get together as a group—we really hit it out of the park. We've been thinking about some band names; any ideas?"

Alex nodded, a smile playing on his lips. "Sounds like it was incredible. I've missed that feeling too—when you're so deep into your work that everything else fades away. How about the Runaway Brothers?"

"Not bad," said Gabriel. "It's a start. There are six of us, maybe the Runaway Six?"

Eden, who had been quietly sipping her drink, chimed in. "I think that's a great name! You should go with it," she said. "It's been a while since you played live, Gabriel. How's that balancing with everything else?"

Gabriel's smile faltered slightly. "It's tough, honestly. I've been thinking about taking a step back from performing for a while. Monica and I have been talking about... well, focusing on some other things."

Before Alex could ask what he meant, Monica stepped forward, her expression a mix of excitement and nervousness. She cleared her throat, drawing everyone's attention. "Actually, we've got some news that we wanted to share with all of you."

The conversations around them hushed as the guests turned to listen. Gabriel took Monica's hand, his earlier tension melting into a broad smile. "We're having a baby," he announced, his voice brimming with pride and joy.

For a moment, there was stunned silence, then the backyard

erupted into cheers and applause. Eden gasped, her eyes widening in surprise and delight. She rushed forward, pulling Monica into a tight embrace. "Oh my God, Monica! That's amazing! Congratulations!"

"You really pulled a fast one on us, Gabriel," Alex said with a grin. "You sandbaggin', motorboatin', deep-sea divin' son of a gun! You guys aren't even married yet!"

Gabriel laughed, shaking his head. "Yeah, I know. We've talked about it, and we decided to get married after the baby is born. Right now, we're just focused on the baby."

Alex gave Gabriel a friendly push. "Well, congratulations, man. I'm really happy for you. You're going to be a great dad."

Gabriel smiled, the relief evident on his face. "Thanks, Alex. That means a lot."

As the initial excitement settled, the conversations turned to the future. Gabriel and Monica were peppered with questions about names, due dates, and nursery plans. The atmosphere was filled with a mixture of joy, anticipation, and a touch of nostalgia, as the friends realized how much their lives were evolving.

Later in the evening, after the dinner plates had been cleared, the group gathered around the bonfire. Gabriel, ever the entertainer, picked up his guitar again and began strumming a gentle tune. The soft crackling of the fire and the distant chirping of crickets created a backdrop of serene calm.

"So," Monica began, looking at Eden with a playful smile, "when are you and Alex going to join the parents' club?"

Eden laughed lightly, though there was a hint of wistfulness in her eyes. "Oh, I don't know... maybe sooner than you think."

Alex, sensing the shift in her tone, glanced at her with a mixture of curiosity and understanding. He knew they had been avoiding the conversation, dancing around the topic of starting a family, unsure of when the right time would be. But Gabriel and Monica's news had sparked something in both of them—an unspoken realization that life was moving forward, whether they were ready or not.

As the night wore on, the group shared stories of their childhoods, their dreams, and the unexpected twists life had taken. Gabriel told a particularly amusing tale of how he once tried to impress a girl in high school by writing her a song—only to accidentally sing the wrong name during his performance.

"And that," Gabriel concluded, grinning sheepishly, "is why I don't do love songs anymore."

The group burst into laughter, the easy camaraderie lifting everyone's spirits. But even as they laughed, Alex couldn't shake the feeling that they were all standing on the cusp of something new, something that would change the dynamics of their friendships and their lives.

By the time the fire had burned down to glowing embers and the guests began to trickle out, the sense of impending change lingered in the cool night air. Alex and Eden said their goodbyes to Gabriel and Monica, promising to meet up again soon. As they walked to their car, hand in hand, they were both quiet, lost in their own thoughts.

Finally, as they walked home under a blanket of stars, Eden broke the silence. "Gabriel and Monica seem so ready, don't they? Like they've got everything figured out."

Alex nodded, his gaze focused on the road ahead. "Yeah, they do. But it's not about having it all figured out. It's about taking the leap, trusting that you'll land on your feet."

Eden smiled softly, reaching over to squeeze his hand. "Maybe it's time we took that leap too."

Alex looked at her, his eyes filled with love and understanding. "I think we should, honey. Let's start trying."

Eden smiled, her heart swelling with hope and anticipation. "Thank you, Alex. I know it won't be easy, but I'm ready."

Alex massaged her shoulders. "We'll do this together, Eden. Whatever it takes."

●

A few weeks after Gabriel and Monica's joyous announcement, life at the cottage took an unexpected turn. It was a chilly morning, and the first hints of winter were in the air. The sky was overcast, and the soft light filtering through the windows gave everything a muted, cozy feel. Eden stood in the bathroom, her heart racing as she stared at the pregnancy test in her hand. Two pink lines slowly appeared, clear and undeniable.

"Alex!" she called out, her voice trembling with a mixture of excitement and disbelief. "Come here!"

Alex rushed in, concern flashing across his face as he tried to read Eden's expression. "What's wrong?"

Eden turned to him, her eyes wide with joy as she held up the test. "We're pregnant."

For a moment, Alex was silent, his mind racing to process the words. Then a broad smile broke across his face, and he let out a joyful laugh, sweeping Eden into his arms. "We're going to have a baby," he whispered, his voice choked with emotion. "We're really going to have a baby."

The days that followed were filled with a whirlwind of emotions, phone calls, and plans. They shared the news with their families, who responded with an outpouring of love and support. Eden's mother, Maria, cried tears of joy when she heard, and Alex's parents, George and Cindy, immediately began making plans to visit more often.

As the pregnancy progressed, they learned they were expecting twins—a boy and a girl. The news left them both elated and slightly overwhelmed. The nursery, which they had only just begun to think about, was quickly transformed into a cozy haven, filled with soft colors and matching cribs. Weekends were spent painting walls, assembling furniture, and sorting through tiny clothes. Each task brought them closer together, reinforcing their shared excitement and anticipation.

Despite the joy, the months weren't without their challenges. Eden's work at the hospital became more taxing as her pregnancy advanced. Balancing her job with her studies was already difficult, and now with the added strain of pregnancy, there were days when she felt completely drained. Alex, too, found himself stretched thin. Between his writing, the beekeeping, and his market stall, he was constantly on the move. But even in the busiest moments, they found time to check in with each other, to share their hopes and fears for the future.

One evening, as they sat on the couch, Eden resting her head on Alex's shoulder, she felt the baby's kick. She grabbed his hand, placing it on her belly so he could feel the movement too. "They're so active," she said with a tired but happy smile.

Alex's eyes lit up as he felt the tiny kicks. "They're getting ready to take on the world," he said softly. "Just like their mom."

Eden laughed quietly, though there was a hint of nervousness in her voice. "I hope we're ready for this. Two babies at once... it's going to be a lot."

Alex kissed her forehead, pulling her closer. "We'll figure it out. We always do. And we've got our families, our friends... we're not in this alone."

As the due date approached, their excitement was tempered by a growing sense of responsibility. The reality of becoming parents to twins began to sink in, and with it came a flurry of final preparations. They attended childbirth classes, practiced breathing techniques, and mapped out routes to the hospital. Their evenings were filled with discussions about parenting philosophies, baby names, and how they would manage sleepless nights and endless diaper changes.

There were moments of doubt, of course—moments when Eden wondered how she would balance motherhood with her career, or when Alex worried about providing for their growing family. But those worries were always met with reassurances, with reminders of the strength of their partnership and the love that had carried them through so much already.

●

The call came late one night. Alex and Eden were in bed, drifting off to sleep, when the phone rang. Alex answered, his voice groggy. "Hello?"

Gabriel's voice on the other end was filled with panic and grief. "Alex, it's Monica. She... she didn't make it. There were complications during the birth."

Alex sat up, his heart racing. "Oh my God, Gabriel. What do you mean she didn't make it? What happened?"

Gabriel's voice broke. "It was sudden. They couldn't save her. Our baby boy is in the intensive care unit. I don't know what to do, Alex."

Alex felt a wave of shock and sorrow wash over him. "We're coming over. We'll be there soon."

He hung up and turned to Eden, his face pale. "Monica didn't make it. We need to go to the hospital."

Eden's eyes filled with tears as she shook her head in disbelief. "No... no, this can't be happening," she whispered, her voice breaking. "Monica..."

Alex embraced her, feeling her body shake with sobs. "I know, I know. Let's go."

They dressed quickly and drove to the hospital, the night air heavy with grief. When they arrived, they found Gabriel waiting for them, his face etched with pain and exhaustion. Eden rushed to his side, her tears flowing freely.

"I'm so sorry, Gabriel," she whispered, her voice choked with sorrow. "I just don't understand."

Gabriel clung to her, his sobs wracking his body. "I don't know how to do this, Eden. I don't know how to be a father without her."

Eden held him tighter, her own grief overwhelming. "You're not alone, Gabriel. We're here for you. We'll get through this together."

The days leading up to the funeral were a blur of grief and support. Alex and Eden did their best to help Gabriel, making arrangements and providing a shoulder to lean on. The house was filled with visitors offering condolences and sharing memories of Monica. The air was heavy with sorrow but also with the faint undercurrent of hope as Eden's pregnancy progressed.

On the morning of the funeral, the sky was overcast, matching the somber mood. The small chapel was filled with friends and family, all gathered to pay their respects. The sound of quiet sobs and murmured prayers filled the air as Gabriel stood by the casket, his face a mask of pain.

Eden felt a mix of emotions as she watched Gabriel. Her heart ached for her friend, but there was also a nervous excitement she couldn't ignore. She was due any day now, and the anticipation was always in the back of her mind. She clutched Alex's hand, drawing strength from his presence.

The service began with a heartfelt eulogy from Gabriel. His voice cracked with emotion, and there wasn't a dry eye in the room. He spoke of Monica's kindness, strength, and the unwavering love she had shown her family and friends.

"Monica taught me that life is not about the moments that take your breath away, but about those small moments that give you breath. She always believed in cherishing each day, no matter how mundane it might seem. As we say goodbye to her today, I remember her words and find comfort in knowing that she lived her life fully and loved us deeply."

As Gabriel spoke, Eden felt a sharp pain in her abdomen. She tried to dismiss it as nerves, but the pain returned, more intense this time. She glanced at Alex, her eyes wide with concern, but she forced herself to focus on the ceremony, wanting to be there for Gabriel.

After the service, the congregation made their way to the cemetery. The procession was solemn, the sky threatening to break open with rain at any moment. They gathered around the grave site, the casket ready to be lowered into the ground. The minister said a few final words, and the tension in the air was noticeable.

As the casket began its descent, Eden felt another sharp pain, followed by a sudden rush of warmth. She gasped, clutching Alex's arm.

"Alex, it's happening. My water just broke," she said.

Alex's heart raced as he looked at her, concern etched on his face. "Are you sure?"

Eden nodded, her eyes wide with fear and excitement. "Of course I'm sure! My legs are wet, and I'm standing in a puddle of water. We need to get to the hospital now!"

They quickly informed Gabriel, who, despite his grief, managed to muster a reassuring smile. "Take care of Eden. I'll be okay," he said, his voice thick with emotion.

Amid the chaos and urgency, Alex and Eden made their way to their car. The drive to the hospital felt like an eternity, with Alex's mind a whirlwind of fear and anticipation. The rain began to fall, creating a rhythmic pattern on the windshield that somehow calmed his nerves a bit. When they arrived at the hospital, Eden was immediately taken to the maternity ward. The staff quickly assessed her condition and prepared for the delivery.

Meanwhile, back at the cemetery, Gabriel and the others completed the final rites. As the casket settled in its final resting place, Gabriel whispered a silent prayer for Monica, finding a strange mixture of sorrow and hope in the midst of the day's events.

Eden's labor was intense and fast-paced, the emotional toll of the day adding to the stress. Alex stayed by Eden's side, holding her hand and offering words of encouragement.

"Just a little more, Eden. You're doing great," Alex whispered, his voice shaking. The sound of her cries and the beeping of monitors filled the room.

Finally, the cries of their newborn twins filled the room. A baby boy and a baby girl, both healthy and strong. The nurses placed them in Eden's arms, her face radiant with relief and joy.

"We did it, Alex," she whispered, tears streaming down her face. "We really did it."

Alex leaned down, kissing her forehead and gazing at their children with awe. "Welcome to the world, Isaac and Abigail," he said softly. "You've already brought us so much joy."

As they held their newborns, the grief of the past days mingled with the profound joy of new life. It was a bittersweet moment, a reminder of the cycle of life and death and the strength of their love.

●

The first few weeks at home with Isaac and Abigail were a whirlwind of sleepless nights and constant demands. The once serene atmosphere of Alex and Eden's country cottage was now filled with the cries of their newborns and the perpetual hum of a baby monitor. The joy of bringing their twins home was quickly tempered by the realities of caring for two infants.

Days blurred into nights, and the rhythms of their lives shifted to the needs of their babies. Feeding, changing diapers, and soothing their cries became an endless cycle that left little room for anything else. Alex, who had once prided himself on balancing his writing with his beekeeping, found it nearly impossible to focus. The lack of sleep weighed heavily on his mind, turning his creative spark into a distant memory. Eden, still grappling with the grief of Monica's death, struggled to cope with the relentless demands of new motherhood. Her energy, once boundless, seemed to drain away with each passing day.

One night, as Eden rocked a crying Isaac in the nursery, she glanced at Alex, who was pacing the room with Abigail in his arms. Dark circles under his eyes mirrored her own. "I don't remember the last time we slept," she said wearily, her voice barely above a whisper.

Alex managed a tired smile. "Me neither. It feels like one long, endless day."

As the weeks dragged on, the exhaustion began to take its toll. What started as small disagreements over household chores quickly escalated into full-blown arguments. The strain of trying to maintain a semblance of normalcy left them both feeling frustrated and disconnected, unable to find the time or energy to bridge the growing gap between them.

One afternoon, as the twins napped, Eden found herself snapping at Alex over the dishes left undone in the sink. "You promised you'd do the dishes," she said, her patience wearing thin.

"I'm sorry, I forgot," Alex replied, rubbing his temples. "I was trying to get some writing done while the babies were napping."

Eden's eyes flashed with anger. "You're always forgetting! I'm doing everything around here while you're off in your own world."

Alex threw his hands up in exasperation. "I'm doing the best I can, Eden! We're both exhausted. Can't we cut each other some slack?"

Eden shook her head, tears welling up in her eyes. "I just feel so alone, Alex. Like I'm the only one carrying this weight."

The tension hung heavy between them, but there were still moments that reminded them of the love they shared. One evening, after a particularly rough day, Alex found Eden in the nursery, softly singing to the twins. He stood in the doorway, watching her with a mixture of awe and gratitude. The soft melody she hummed seemed to soothe not only the babies but also the frayed edges of his heart.

"You're amazing, you know that?" Alex said quietly, stepping into the room.

Eden looked up, her eyes filled with exhaustion and love. "I don't feel amazing. I feel like I'm barely holding it together."

Alex wrapped his arms around her, pressing a kiss to the top of her head. "We're in this together, remember? We'll get through it."

They held each other close, finding comfort in their shared resolve. The twins gurgled softly in their cribs, a reminder of the joy that had brought them to this point. Despite the exhaustion and the frayed tempers, moments like this gave them hope that they could navigate the challenges ahead.

As the weeks turned into months, the routine settled into something that felt more manageable, though the strain still lingered. Then, one weekend, Alex's parents, George and Cindy, invited them over for dinner. The aroma of Cindy's famous pot roast filled the air, creating a warm and comforting atmosphere as they gathered around the dining table. Isaac and Abigail, nestled in their grandparents' arms, were blissfully content, giving Alex and Eden a rare moment to relax.

"You two look exhausted," George remarked, his voice gentle

with concern. "How are you holding up?"

Eden sighed, giving a tired smile. "It's been tough, but we're managing. The twins are a handful."

Cindy exchanged a look with George before turning to Alex and Eden. "You know, your father and I have been talking. We'd love to help out more. Maybe you two could use a break... a little time away to recharge."

Alex raised an eyebrow. "Are you sure? The twins can be a lot to handle."

George nodded firmly. "We're sure. We raised you, didn't we? We can handle our grandkids for a few days."

Eden's eyes filled with gratitude. "That sounds... amazing. We haven't had a moment to ourselves since the twins were born."

Cindy smiled warmly. "It's settled then. You two plan a little getaway, and we'll take care of everything here."

On the drive back home, Alex and Eden talked about their parents' generous offer. The idea of a break felt like a lifeline amidst the chaos. "I think this could be really good for us," Alex said, glancing at Eden. "We need to remember why we fell in love and find some time to reconnect."

Eden nodded, her eyes bright with hope. "You're right. Let's do it."

They made plans for a short weekend vacation to a seaside house, hoping the change of scenery would help them find some peace and rediscover the connection that had been buried under the weight of parenthood. As they prepared for the trip, there was a renewed sense of hope and determination. The road ahead wouldn't be easy, but for the first time in a long while, they felt like they were facing it together.

●

The morning was a blur of activity as Alex and Eden packed for their short vacation. The twins, Isaac and Abigail, were staying with Alex's parents, giving them a much-needed break. As they moved through the house, tension simmered just beneath the surface.

Eden paced the living room, casting worried glances at the twins' cribs. "Are you sure they'll be okay with your parents?"

Alex, trying to keep his patience, replied, "My parents have raised children before, Eden. They'll be fine."

Eden sighed, her anxiety clear. "I know, but I just feel so guilty leaving them."

Alex walked over and put his hands on her shoulders. "We need this break, Eden. For us. We'll be better parents if we're not completely burnt out."

Eden nodded, her eyes still lingering on the cribs. "You're right. It's just hard."

In the midst of their hurried packing, Alex reached for the fridge to grab a drink, but in his frustration, he slammed the door shut, unknowingly leaving the freezer slightly ajar.

Eden looked at him, exasperation evident in her eyes. "You don't have to be so rough with everything. This trip is supposed to help us relax."

Alex rubbed his temples, trying to calm down. "I'm sorry, I'm in a hurry. Let's get going."

A few hours later, they were on the road, the twins safely with their grandparents. The tension inside the car was still noticeable, but both of them were attempting to concentrate on the idea of a peaceful vacation. As Alex drove down the highway, he noticed the speedometer creeping up.

"We're making good time," he said, trying to lighten the mood.

Eden glanced at him, worry etched on her face. "Just slow down a bit, okay? I don't want to get pulled over."

Alex nodded. "You're right. Sorry, I'm just eager to get there."

Suddenly, flashing lights appeared in the rearview mirror. "Oh, great! You said it, now it happened!" Alex muttered, pulling over to the side of the road.

The midday sun beat down on the car as it sat idling on the shoulder of the turnpike. The steady hum of traffic filled the air, punctuated by the occasional blare of a horn. Alex's hands were clenched tightly around the steering wheel, his knuckles white. Eden sat beside him shaking her head, her face a mask of concern.

The crunch of gravel under heavy boots signaled the approach of the police officer. Alex could see him in the side mirror, a stocky, broad-shouldered figure with a funny mustache and wire-rimmed glasses, moving with deliberate authority. The officer's stern expression only added to the air of intimidation.

The officer reached the driver's side window and rapped on it with his knuckles. Alex rolled down the window, the smell of hot asphalt mixing with the cool breeze from the air conditioning.

"I'm Officer Zuchalota with the police. License and registration, please," he said, his voice gruff and devoid of warmth.

Alex handed over the documents with a shaky hand, trying to maintain an air of calmness. "What's the problem, officer?"

"You were going twelve miles per hour over the speed limit," the officer replied coldly, his eyes piercing through Alex even from behind the reflective lenses.

Alex's heart pounded even harder, a wave of panic washing over him. He glanced at Eden, who was sitting in the passenger seat, her face pale and eyes wide. Desperate, he blurted out, "I'm sorry, officer. My wife is in labor."

Eden, catching on quickly, clutched her stomach and let out a soft groan, playing along with the ruse. The officer's expression softened slightly, but only for a moment.

"Is that so? In that case, I'll escort you to the hospital," he said with a strict smile.

Alex's heart sank. The last thing they needed was this overbearing officer following them.

"Uh, no, it's really not necessary..." Alex muttered.

"Nonsense," Officer Zuchalota interrupted, his tone allowing no room for an argument. "Let's get going."

"No, no! We can't!" Alex stammered, his mind racing for an excuse. "This baby is a demon child!"

The officer's face twisted from concern to irritation. "A demon child? Really?" He leaned in closer, his eyes narrowing to slits. "You think this is some kind of joke?"

Alex felt a surge of frustration. "Look, officer, we've been through a lot. We're exhausted and just trying to get to our vacation house by the sea for the weekend."

The officer's irritation morphed into anger, his face contorting with contempt. "You think your sob story matters to me?"

Alex sighed, pleading with the officer. "We're just trying to get away for the weekend. Can't you cut us some slack? I feel like if you could be a bit more understanding, this situation could be different."

Officer Zuchalota's eyes flashed dangerously. He slammed his fist twice on the car's roof, causing the loose change in the cup holder to jingle and flip around.

"Nobody gives a crap about your feelings, buddy," he said

loudly, making Alex twitch. "You're getting a ticket."

Alex, unable to contain himself any longer, snapped back. "I'm getting a ticket? You're being outrageous! I wasn't even going 20 over the limit! You must've gotten the wrong guy, Officer Suckalotta."

The officer's face reddened further, veins bulging in his neck. "It's pronounced Zoo-ka-lotta!" he barked, spittle flying from his mouth. "And you'd better watch your mouth."

"Oh, I'm sorry, Suckalotta. Did I hurt your feelings? Well, last I heard, nobody gives a crap about feelings!"

The officer's hand shook with barely restrained fury as he wrote out the ticket, his eyes never leaving Alex's face. "Here's your fine. Drive safely and learn some respect."

Alex snatched the ticket from the officer's hand, crumpling it in his fist. "Respect? You don't know the meaning of the word. You're the one pounding on my car like it's your little punching bag! What makes it right for you to do that, huh? You're nothing more than a bully with a badge."

The officer's eyes narrowed, his face turning a deeper shade of red. "Watch it, pal. I was going to let the whole pregnant lie slide, but now I'm taking you to court for lying to a police officer. You can explain your rudeness to the judge."

Eden, sensing the escalating tension, placed a hand on Alex's arm, trying to calm him. "Alex, please, let's just go."

Officer Zuchalota stepped back, his lips curled into a sinister sneer. "Yeah, listen to your pesky little wife. But don't think this is over. You'll be hearing more about this in court."

Alex's jaw clenched, but he knew Eden was right. As the officer walked away, Eden turned to Alex, her eyes blazing. "Why did you have to make things worse?"

Alex sighed, starting the car again. "I'm sorry. I just lost my cool."

Eden crossed her arms, staring out the window. "Great start to our vacation."

Alex put the car in gear and pulled away, the officer's glare burning into the back of his head. As they drove in tense silence, Alex's hands gripped the steering wheel tightly.

"Can you believe that guy? The nerve of him pounding on my car!" Alex fumed.

Eden watched him, her eyes filled with concern. "I understand, Alex. But you getting angry won't change anything. We need to find a way to address this constructively."

Alex took a deep breath, trying to let go of the anger that still simmered inside him. "Okay. We'll take it one step at a time. But I'm not letting this go that easy."

Eden sighed, rubbing her temples. "I know, Alex, that's your problem—you don't ever let things go. But we need to pick our battles. You aren't going to win against him, and you know it. Let's just focus on getting to the seaside house and try to enjoy our weekend."

The tension from the police incident lingered in the car as Alex and Eden continued their drive. The silence between them was heavy, broken only by the hum of the engine and the occasional sigh.

Alex tried to make small talk. "So, what do you think the beach will be like this time of year?"

Eden shrugged, staring out the window. "Probably nice. It's always nice by the ocean."

Alex nodded, drumming his fingers on the steering wheel. "Yeah, I'm looking forward to it."

The conversation died down again, both of them lost in their thoughts. The road stretched out before them, winding towards the promise of a peaceful getaway that seemed increasingly unlikely.

●

When they finally pulled up to the seaside house, a wave of relief washed over them. The exterior looked charming enough, with weathered wood and a wraparound porch that faced the ocean. But as they got out of the car and took a closer look, their relief quickly turned to disappointment.

"What the heck?" Alex muttered, noticing the peeling paint and broken shutters. He glanced at Eden, who was already looking defeated.

They walked up the steps, which creaked ominously under their weight, and unlocked the door. The inside was worse. Large portions of the back wall were missing, offering an unobstructed view of the ocean, and there were holes in the floor, though not large enough to see the ground beneath.

Alex tried to stay positive. "Well, at least we have an ocean view," he said with forced cheerfulness.

Eden shot him a look, her frustration boiling over. "An ocean view? Alex, this place is falling apart! How are we supposed to relax here?"

Alex's shoulders slumped. "I know it's not what we expected, but maybe we can make the best of it. We needed to get away, remember?"

Eden gestured around the room, her voice rising. "Make the best of it? Alex, look at this place! I can't believe you thought this would be a good idea. How much did you even pay for this?"

Alex sighed, trying to keep his cool. "I got it for a good deal, okay? I thought it would be fine. We needed a break, and this was what I could afford."

Eden crossed her arms, her eyes filling with tears of frustration. "Well, now I see why it was a good deal. This place is a disaster."

They continued to explore the house, finding more issues at every turn. The kitchen sink leaked, the bathroom tiles were cracked, and the furniture was covered in a fine layer of dust.

Eden's composure finally snapped when she tripped over a loose floorboard, nearly falling. She caught herself on the counter, but tears of frustration and exhaustion welled up in her eyes. "This is just too much," she cried. "I wanted this to be a break, a chance to reconnect, and now it feels like everything is falling apart."

Alex hurried to her side, trying to comfort her. "I'm sorry, Eden. I really thought this would be a good idea. Maybe we can still salvage it. We can clean up a bit, make it comfortable."

Eden shook her head, wiping her tears. "I just don't know if I have the energy for this, Alex. I'm so tired of everything being so hard."

Despite the poor condition of the house, they attempted to spend quality time together. Alex set up his laptop on the rickety kitchen table, trying to lose himself in his writing. Eden wandered down to the beach, hoping the sound of the waves would soothe her frayed nerves. They shared a quiet meal on the porch, watching the sun set over the ocean. But the underlying tension and disappointment were hard to shake.

Later that evening, as they sat together, Alex took Eden's hand and said, "I know this isn't what we planned, but I'm glad we're here together. I know we'll get through this."

Eden turned to Alex, a small smile playing on her lips. "I know. I just need to let go of my expectations and try to enjoy the moment."

As they sat in the dimming light, Eden took a deep breath and looked at Alex. "Maybe you should write about what happened with the police officer. Turn a negative into a positive, you know?"

Alex raised an eyebrow. "You think so? It was pretty stressful."

Eden nodded. "Exactly. Maybe writing about it will help you process it. Plus, you always manage to find humor in the worst situations. It might actually be a good story."

Alex considered this, then smiled. "You're right. I'll give it a shot."

The next morning, Alex set up his laptop on the kitchen table and started typing. He decided to transform the police incident into a humorous short story, reimagining his characters as living dual lives—one as an ordinary family and the other as undercover spies. In this fictional world, the encounter with Officer Zuchalota was just one of many close calls they had while trying to keep their true identities hidden.

He wrote with fervor, the words flowing easily as he transformed their stressful experience into an entertaining narrative. The story, titled "My Secret Life Vol. 1," was a blend of humor, tension, and absurdity, capturing the ridiculousness of the situation they had found themselves in. As he wrote, he felt a sense of release. The act of turning a negative experience into a creative outlet helped him process his frustration and find a bit of humor in the chaos. When he finished, he took his scribbled notes and stored them safely in one of the drawers in the living room.

Over the weekend, Alex and Eden began to reconnect, sharing moments of laughter and closeness. They spent the rest of the day walking along the beach, collecting shells, and talking about their hopes and dreams. At night, they sat on the porch, wrapped in blankets, listening to the sound of the waves and the distant call of seagulls. Despite the underlying stress, they made the best of their situation, focusing on each other and their time together.

"This isn't so bad, is it?" Alex said, smiling at Eden as they set the table on the porch.

Eden smiled back. "No, it's not. I'm actually starting to enjoy myself."

As they ate dinner on their final night, they talked about their lives, their children, and the challenges they faced. The stress of the past couple of days slowly faded away, replaced by a renewed sense of connection and understanding. By the end of the weekend, Alex and Eden felt more connected and ready to face their challenges together. They packed their bags, leaving the seaside house with a mix of relief and gratitude. The weekend had been far from perfect, but it had given them the chance to reconnect and find strength in each other.

The drive back to their cottage was quieter than either Alex or Eden had anticipated. The initial relief of their weekend getaway was overshadowed by an underlying tension, knowing they had to return to the routine of parenthood and the demands of their kids. They stopped at Alex's parents' house to pick up Isaac and Abigail. The twins were restless and fussy, adding to the growing stress.

As they approached their home, Alex tried to muster some sense of optimism. "Let's make the best of it," he said, forcing a smile as they pulled into the driveway. "We've had a good break, and we can carry that feeling forward."

Eden nodded, but her smile didn't reach her eyes. "Yeah, let's try."

As they opened the door to their cottage, they were immediately hit by a nauseating stench. The sweet, sickening smell of spoiled meat assaulted their senses, forcing them to recoil.

"Oh my God, what is that smell?" Eden exclaimed, covering her nose with her hand.

They inched further inside, and the source of the odor materialized before them. Thawed packs of beef lay in bloody puddles on the floor. Stagnant fluids from the thawed meat formed viscous pools of red, spreading across the floorboards in branching streams like the fractured capillaries of a damaged heart.

Alex's eyes widened in horror as he realized what had happened. The freezer door had been left ajar, but that wasn't the worst of it. The slow thawing had caused the meat to soften and shift, until, piece by piece, it began to slide out onto the floor. Gravity did the rest. The packages, once neatly stacked, had spilled over, tearing open as they hit the hard ground, releasing their contents in a gruesome, blood-soaked cascade.

The weight of the top shelves had eventually caused the entire tray to collapse, flinging half-thawed meat across the room like a grotesque rainstorm. It splattered onto the counters, dripped down the walls, and pooled in the exact spot where he and Eden had first met years ago, bonding over a spilled jar of honey.

Now that sweet memory was fouled by the reeking chaos before them, the sight of blood and spoiled meat creating a sickening contrast to the warmth of their past. It felt like some cruel trick of the universe, turning a place of joy into a scene of decay.

Jets of scarlet spray painted the walls in abstract anguish. The freezer resembled an open chest cavity, with various organs leaking out. It was a slaughterhouse vision out of a horror scene. At the epicenter of the carnage lay the prize cut of ribeye they had earmarked for their anniversary dinner, now just a mushy, liquefying lump, left only for the maggots to eat.

Alex and Eden stared in horror at the gore before them. It mirrored the current state of their relationship... once so full of life and nourishment, now savagely torn apart at the seams, innards exposed, and their hearts rotting from within.

The oozing bodily remains choked their hopes and stained the foundation of their home. This stinking mess would require deep cleansing and purging before they could restore the warmth and sustenance their relationship once held.

Eden's eyes filled with fury and tears. "How could you be so careless, Alex? Look at this mess! It's disgusting!"

Alex tried to apologize, but the words got caught in his throat. "I'm sorry, Eden. I didn't realize..."

"Of course you didn't!" Eden cut him off, her voice trembling with anger. "You never realize! You're always so wrapped up in your own world that you don't see what's happening around you!"

Isaac and Abigail, sensing the tension, began to cry. Their wails added to the dissonance of the moment, amplifying the chaos and stress.

Alex's own frustration bubbled to the surface. "I'm trying, Eden! I really am. But it feels like nothing I do is ever good enough for you!"

Eden shook her head, tears streaming down her face. "I'm exhausted, Alex. I'm tired of feeling like I'm the only one holding everything together."

Alex threw his hands up in exasperation. "I just told you! I'm doing the best I can! Maybe if you weren't so demanding…"

"Demanding?" Eden interjected accusingly. "I'm just trying to keep our family afloat!"

"By nitpicking every little thing I do?" Alex shot back. "I can't live like this, always feeling inadequate."

He turned to storm off, but Eden grabbed his arm. "Don't you walk out that door until we resolve this." Their raised voices drowned out Isaac and Abigail's cries, though their wailing echoed into the fight.

Alex tore his arm away. "I need some space to think. This is going nowhere."

As he turned to leave again, Eden called out, "You're gonna carry that weight! This mess, our relationship... it's on you too!"

Alex paused at the door, his face twisted with frustration. "I can't deal with this right now," he snapped.

He slammed the door forcefully behind him, sending a plume of dust swirling. The force of the slam caused pictures on the wall to fall, the frames cracking upon impact. In particular, a hand-drawn calligraphy haiku from Eden's mother fell to the floor, the glass shattering.

The haiku read:

"When on your way out,
Be sure that you say goodbye,
Then lock the door tight."

The weight of those words settled over Eden, mingling with the heavy silence of the house. As the dust settled, the gravity of the situation sank in. Eden stood motionless, stunned by the heated exchange. Their angry words echoed in her mind. She sank to the floor as sobs wracked her body. The wails of the twins mingled with her own cries. She had never felt so alone.

Wiping her eyes, Eden slowly began gathering paper towels and cleaning supplies. She started soaking up the blood and gore, working methodically through her tears. With each stain she scrubbed, her despair grew.

What if Alex didn't come back? What if this was the final straw? The more Eden cleaned, the more anxiously she glanced at the door, praying to see Alex walk through it. But the door remained shut, the house empty except for her quiet sobs.

Blood slowly dissolved into pink sudsy puddles as Eden scoured the floor. But inside, she felt a stain taking hold, a sinking fear that her family was coming undone at the seams. Her heart couldn't take another loss.

Lesson 8:
Relationships

Our personal growth and resilience are deeply influenced by the quality of our relationships and how well we communicate. The connections we form shape our experiences, affect our emotions, and have a profound impact on our overall well-being. Similarly, effective communication strengthens these bonds and deepens our connections.

In this lesson, we'll explore strategies to improve both relationships and communication, focusing on active listening, empathy, conflict resolution, and nurturing meaningful connections. Building positive relationships and mastering communication isn't always easy, but the rewards—support, understanding, and love—are invaluable. Effective communication helps bridge differences, resolve conflicts, and fosters deeper connections.

Research consistently shows that strong relationships enhance well-being by providing emotional support, especially during difficult times. Having people who care about us helps process emotions, reduce stress, and offer new perspectives, which bolsters our resilience.

Moreover, positive relationships create a sense of understanding and acceptance. When empathy and open communication are present, we feel seen and heard, creating safe spaces to express our true selves. This leads to deeper connections and a greater sense of belonging.

Engaging in meaningful relationships also positively impacts mental health. Studies suggest that supportive connections reduce the risk of depression, anxiety, and loneliness, promoting overall well-being. These relationships also provide stability, reassurance, and a shared belief in our ability to overcome challenges.

Strong relationships bring joy and fulfillment to our lives. Sharing experiences, creating memories, and celebrating achievements with loved ones enriches our lives and fosters a resilient, optimistic outlook.

To nurture these relationships, it's crucial to invest time and effort. Open communication, quality time, appreciation, empathy, and constructive conflict resolution are key strategies for building strong connections.

While it requires effort and vulnerability, the benefits of strong relationships—support, understanding, and enhanced well-being—are immeasurable. These connections equip us with the resilience needed to navigate life's challenges.

Effective Communication Skills

Effective communication is key to maintaining healthy and fulfilling relationships. It enables us to express ourselves, understand others, and build strong connections. By honing our communication skills, we can strengthen relationships, resolve conflicts, and foster deeper understanding and empathy.

A cornerstone of effective communication is active listening. This means fully engaging with the speaker, focusing on their words, nonverbal cues, and emotions. It involves setting aside distractions, maintaining eye contact, and providing feedback to show genuine interest. Active listening creates a safe space for open dialogue, encouraging the speaker to express themselves freely and promoting mutual understanding.

Empathy is another critical component. It involves putting ourselves in others' shoes to understand their perspectives and emotions. Practicing empathy requires genuine care, attentiveness, and the ability to suspend judgment. By showing empathy, we validate others' feelings and demonstrate that we value their experiences, which strengthens our relationships.

Nonverbal communication is equally important. Cues like facial expressions, body language, and tone of voice often convey more than words alone. Being aware of our own nonverbal signals and attentive to others' can greatly enhance communication. For example, maintaining an open posture, nodding in agreement, and using appropriate facial expressions contribute to meaningful interactions.

Consider a scenario: Alex and Eden are discussing a recent disagreement. Instead of interrupting or becoming defensive, they practice active listening, taking turns to express their viewpoints while the other listens with the intent to understand. This approach shows respect and creates a space where both feel heard and validated.

They also use empathy, acknowledging and validating each

other's emotions, even when their perspectives differ. This deepens their emotional connection and fosters understanding and support.

Moreover, they pay attention to nonverbal cues—maintaining open body language, making eye contact, and speaking calmly. These signals convey their willingness to listen and understand, creating an atmosphere of trust and openness.

By practicing active listening, empathy, and being mindful of nonverbal communication, we can enhance our communication skills and build healthier, more meaningful relationships.

Conflict Resolution

Conflicts are a natural part of any relationship, and how we handle them can shape the strength and resilience of our connections. Dealing with disagreements constructively is crucial for maintaining healthy, supportive relationships.

When conflicts linger unresolved, they can harm our emotional well-being and strain our relationships. The stress and anxiety that come from unresolved issues can even affect our physical health. But by addressing conflicts head-on, we can strengthen our relationships and improve our overall sense of well-being.

To manage conflicts effectively, it's important to focus on strategies that encourage open communication, empathy, and collaboration. Here are some key approaches:

– <u>Open and Honest Communication</u>: Being upfront about our thoughts and feelings helps build trust. When we express ourselves openly, we can address the real issues behind conflicts and work toward solutions that meet everyone's needs.

– <u>Active Listening</u>: Truly hearing the other person's perspective is vital. This means paying attention, asking questions, and showing that we understand their feelings and needs. Active listening fosters empathy and opens the door to meaningful dialogue.

– <u>Empathy and Understanding</u>: Putting ourselves in the other person's shoes helps us see their side of the story. By recognizing their emotions and underlying needs, we create a sense of connection that makes it easier to resolve conflicts with care and compassion.

–   <u>Finding Common Ground</u>: In any disagreement, it's helpful to focus on what we agree on. Identifying shared goals or interests allows us to build on common ground, encouraging cooperation and compromise that leads to a win-win outcome.

–   <u>Problem-Solving Mindset</u>: Shifting from a desire to "win" to a focus on finding solutions changes the way we approach conflicts. By breaking down the problem, brainstorming ideas, and considering what works best for everyone, we can collaboratively address the issue and move forward together.

–   <u>Calm and Respectful Communication</u>: Keeping our tone calm and respectful is key to productive conversations. Avoiding personal attacks or defensiveness helps keep the discussion focused on finding a solution, allowing both sides to feel heard and respected.

By practicing these strategies, we can handle conflicts in a way that not only resolves the issue at hand but also strengthens our relationships, creating a foundation for deeper understanding and mutual respect.

Case Studies and Examples

<u>Case Study: Sarah and Emily</u>

Sarah and Emily have been friends since high school. They share everything with each other, and their friendship means a lot to both of them. However, a conflict arose when Emily borrowed Sarah's favorite dress and returned it with a stain. Sarah was upset and accused Emily of being careless. Emily, on the other hand, felt that Sarah was overreacting.

Resolution: The key to resolving this conflict was active listening and empathy. Sarah had to express her feelings without attacking Emily, and Emily had to listen without becoming defensive. They both took turns speaking and listened to each other's perspectives. Sarah explained that the dress had sentimental value, and Emily expressed her regret and explained that it was an accident. Understanding each other's feelings and perspectives helped them come to a resolution. Emily offered to pay for the dress to be cleaned, and Sarah accepted her apology.

Guidance: When faced with a conflict, it is essential to express your feelings and perspectives without attacking the other person. Use "I" statements to express your feelings, for example, "I felt hurt when…" Listen to the other person's perspective without interrupting and try to understand their feelings and point of view. Expressing empathy and understanding can go a long way in resolving conflicts.

<u>Case Study: Jeremy and Todd</u>

Jeremy and Todd are a father and son who have been having conflicts regarding Todd's career choices after college. Jeremy wants Todd to pursue a traditional career path like law or medicine. However, Todd is passionate about becoming an artist and struggling to get his father's support. Their different perspectives have led to arguments, with neither feeling understood by the other. There is tension in their relationship and a lack of productive communication.

Strategy Employed: To help improve their communication, Jeremy and Todd scheduled a time to sit down together without distractions. They set ground rules ahead of time, agreeing to listen openly without judgment. During the discussion, Todd explained his lifelong passion for art and desire to pursue it as a career. Jeremy was able to express his concerns about stability and income. But he also heard the sincerity of Todd's calling. Todd listened to Jeremy's guidance as a father who wants the best for his son. He gained empathy for his dad's perspective.

Outcome: This open and honest dialogue allowed them to gain clarity. Jeremy realized Todd needed to follow his dreams, even if the path looked different than he imagined. Todd understood his father's care and support, even if it came from a place of worry. They didn't agree 100%, but found common ground. This case highlights how setting expectations, actively listening, and compromising can greatly improve family communication during points of conflict.

Nurturing Positive Connections

Building strong relationships is not only about effective communication and conflict resolution; it also involves cultivating trust, intimacy, and meaningful connections. In this section, we will delve into the importance of these aspects and explore activities and strategies to foster positive connections in our relationships.

– Trust: Trust forms the foundation of any healthy relationship. It is the belief that we can rely on and have confidence in the other person's reliability, honesty, and support. Trust creates a sense of safety and security, allowing individuals to open up and be vulnerable with each other.

– Intimacy: Intimacy goes beyond physical affection; it encompasses emotional closeness, vulnerability, and a deep sense of connection. It involves sharing thoughts, feelings, and experiences in a safe and non-judgmental space. Intimacy allows individuals to feel seen, heard, and understood by their partners or loved ones.

– Meaningful Connections: Meaningful connections are built on shared values, interests, and a genuine sense of care and appreciation for one another. These connections provide a sense of belonging, support, and a shared sense of purpose, contributing to overall life satisfaction and well-being.

Strategies to Cultivate Positive Connections

– Quality Time: Carve out dedicated time to spend with your loved ones without distractions. Engage in activities that promote connection and create shared memories, such as going for walks, cooking together, or having meaningful conversations.

– Open and Honest Communication: Foster an environment of open and honest communication where all parties feel comfortable expressing their thoughts, feelings, and needs. Practice active listening, empathy, and non-judgmental responses to foster understanding and deeper connection.

– <u>Express Appreciation and Gratitude</u>: Regularly express appreciation and gratitude for the presence and support of your loved ones. Acknowledge their efforts, strengths, and qualities that you value. Small gestures, like leaving a heartfelt note or expressing verbal appreciation, can go a long way in nurturing positive connections.

– <u>Support and Empathy</u>: Show support and empathy when your loved ones are going through challenging times. Offer a listening ear, provide encouragement, and validate their emotions. Be present and available for them, offering a safe space for them to express themselves.

– <u>Engage in Shared Activities</u>: Engaging in shared activities and hobbies strengthens bonds and creates opportunities for connection. Find activities that both you and your loved ones enjoy and make time to participate in them together. It could be anything from playing sports, taking art classes, or exploring nature.

– <u>Cultivate Trust</u>: Build trust through honesty, reliability, and consistency in your actions. Be true to your word, follow through on commitments, and maintain confidentiality. Trust takes time to develop, so it's essential to prioritize honesty and integrity in your relationships.

Activity: Strengthening Connections: A Holistic Approach

In this integrated activity, you will practice active listening, engage in conflict resolution through role-playing, and partake in activities that foster connection and strengthen relationships. This holistic exercise is designed to enhance communication, address and resolve conflicts, and deepen bonds, ultimately contributing to more meaningful and effective interactions in your relationships.

Instructions:

1. Active Listening and Reflection:
Start by practicing active listening with a partner or on your own by reflecting on a personal experience or topic. Take turns being the speaker and the listener, focusing on maintaining eye contact, using nonverbal cues, paraphrasing, and summarizing. After the exercise, reflect on the experience and share any insights gained.

2. Role-Play and Conflict Resolution:
Next, engage in a role-play exercise where you and your partner (or you alone, taking on both roles) act out a common conflict scenario. Assign roles and immerse yourselves in the characters' thoughts, emotions, and communication styles. Apply active listening, empathy, open communication, finding common ground, and a problem-solving approach to address the conflict. Reflect on the strategies that were effective and any challenges encountered.

3. Fostering Connection:
Select two activities from the following list that you and your partner would enjoy doing together:

    - Exploring nature
    - Cooking or baking
    - Watching a movie
    - Taking up a new hobby
    - Volunteering
    - Planning a day trip or weekend getaway
    - Playing games
    - Exercising or practicing mindfulness

- Sharing personal stories and memories
- Collaborating on a project
- Engage in the chosen activities, focusing on fostering connection, teamwork, and enjoying each other's company.

4. Comprehensive Reflection:

After completing all the exercises and activities, sit down together and reflect on the entire experience. Discuss how practicing active listening and engaging in conflict resolution impacted your communication and connection. Reflect on how the chosen activities contributed to strengthening your bond and what you learned about each other and your relationship throughout the process.

5.   Goal Setting and Commitment:

Together, set specific goals for actively listening to each other, constructively resolving conflicts, and regularly engaging in activities that foster connection. Make a commitment to each other to implement these practices in your daily interactions and long-term relationship goals.

Building and maintaining a strong and healthy relationship requires ongoing effort and commitment from all parties involved. By actively listening, constructively resolving conflicts, and regularly engaging in activities that foster connection, you can create a resilient and fulfilling relationship.

The key to reaping the benefits of these activities is regular engagement. Make a commitment to incorporate them into your routine and prioritize quality time with your loved ones. By actively participating in activities that foster connection and strengthen relationships, you create a foundation of shared experiences and mutual growth, fostering long-lasting bonds.

●

Throughout this lesson, we have explored the importance of building strong relationships and enhancing communication, delving into the strategies and activities that foster positive connections. In a world where relationships are the bedrock of our lives, investing time and effort into nurturing them becomes paramount. We have witnessed the power of effective communication, where active listening, empathy, and understanding lay the foundation for meaningful connections. By honing these skills, we open the doors to deeper understanding and a greater sense of unity.

We have also delved into the realm of conflict resolution, recognizing that conflicts are an inevitable part of any relationship. Armed with strategies to navigate these conflicts constructively, we have discovered the power of open communication, empathy, and compromise. Through case studies and practice scenarios, we have seen firsthand how conflicts can be transformed into opportunities for growth and strengthened bonds.

Furthermore, we have recognized the significance of trust, intimacy, and meaningful connections. Engaging in activities that foster connection not only creates memorable experiences but also deepens our emotional well-being and support system. By dedicating time to shared hobbies, adventures, and moments of vulnerability, we cultivate the fertile soil in which relationships can thrive.

As we conclude this lesson, let us carry the wisdom gained and continue to apply it in our own lives. Let us be mindful of the importance of effective communication, conflict resolution, and nurturing positive connections. By doing so, we build bridges that withstand the test of time and challenges, empowering us to face life's trials with resilience and a strong network of support.

Remember, the power to shape and nurture our relationships lies within us. Together, let us embrace the beauty of connection, communication, and love as we navigate the intricate tapestry of our lives.

Chapter 9: Pain In The Neck

The February morning was crisp and cold as Alex, Eden, and their six-year-old twins, Isaac and Abigail, prepared for their trip to the Big City. Snow blanketed their country cottage in Everbrook, creating a beautiful winter scene. The children were bundled up in bright, puffy coats, their excitement almost uncontrollable as they hopped into the car.

"Is it going to snow in the city too, Mommy?" Abigail asked, her cheeks rosy from the cold.

Eden smiled as she helped buckle Abigail into her car seat. "It might, sweetheart. But we'll see lots of big buildings and busy streets. It's going to be an adventure."

Alex loaded the last of their bags into the trunk and started the

282

engine, the car heater working overtime to warm up the interior.

"Alright, everyone ready for a two-day road trip to the Big City?" he asked, turning to look at his family.

"Ready!" Abigail and Isaac said in tandem, their faces pressed against the windows as they watched the snow-covered fields and forests slowly pass by.

The drive to the Big City was about two hours, giving Alex and Eden time to chat about the upcoming book signing event and the chance to reconnect with Grandma Maria. The children, captivated by the snowy landscape, kept a running commentary on everything they saw.

"Look, Isaac! A deer!" Abigail exclaimed, pointing to a small herd grazing near the edge of the woods.

Isaac nodded enthusiastically. "And there's a big red barn! I wonder if they have animals inside."

Eden chuckled, her heart warmed by their innocent curiosity. "We'll have to ask Grandma Maria if she knows."

As they approached the city, the scenery began to change. Towering buildings and bustling streets came into view, covered in a thin layer of snow. The children's amazement was clear as they stared at the urban landscape.

"Wow! The buildings are so tall!" Isaac exclaimed, his eyes wide with wonder.

"And so many cars and people!" Abigail added, her breath fogging up the window.

Alex navigated through the busy streets, finally pulling up to Maria's apartment building. The cozy atmosphere of her apartment was a refreshing change from the cold city air. Maria greeted them at the door, her arms wide open.

"Welcome, welcome!" Maria said, hugging each of them in turn. "It's so good to see you all!"

Alex sat with Maria and the kids, recounting the trip and discussing the upcoming book signing event, while Eden started unpacking their bags. The children immediately launched into tales of their journey, describing the snowy sights and asking about the city. Maria listened patiently, her eyes twinkling with affection.

As Eden unpacked the last of their bags, she noticed a photo on the wall... a picture from their wedding day. She paused, the image drawing her in. Next to it were photos of their early years of marriage, filled with smiles and happy moments. She couldn't help but be swept away by the memories.

Her mind drifted back to the time after their honeymoon in Egypt, vividly recalling one particularly tense evening. They had just returned from a weekend getaway, hoping for a break from their troubles, only to discover viscous pools of rotting, bloody meat on the floor of their cottage.

"What the heck is this?" Alex shouted, his voice echoing through her memory. Eden covered her nose with her hand, trying to suppress her gag reflex.

"How could you be so careless, Alex? Look at this mess! It's disgusting!" The argument escalated quickly, the stress and fear of the past months oozing to the surface.

"I'm sorry, Eden. I didn't realize the freezer door was left open." Alex's frustration was clearly bothering him as he slammed the door, leaving the cottage in a rage. Eden stood there, stunned and hurt, tears welling up in her eyes as she stared at the broken pictures that fell from the wall.

The memory of that night was a turning point in their relationship. It was after this fight that they decided to seek help. They knew they couldn't go on like this, and therapy became a lifeline. The memories then shifted to happier times. Alex, Eden, and the kids were at a park at the Everbrook square, playing and laughing.

The sense of relief and joy was clearly visible as they chased each other, the children's laughter echoing in the open space. These moments emphasized the progress they had made as a family, highlighting the importance of communication and support.

"Eden, come here, dinner's ready!" Alex called from the kitchen, breaking her daydream. She shook off the memories for the moment and joined her family, leaving the past behind but carrying its lessons with her. They gathered around the kitchen table, enjoying the dinner Maria prepared for them while looking forward to the book signing event.

•

The next morning, the family headed to a large, bustling bookstore for Alex's book signing event. As they approached the store, snowflakes danced in the air, adding a touch of magic to the day. The bookstore was alive with activity, with fans gathered eagerly to meet the author of the best-selling book, *The Nile's Redemption*. The sight of the crowd filled Alex with a mixture of excitement and nerves.

Eden nestled close to him, whispering in his ear, "You've got this, Alex. We're all so proud of you."

Abigail and Isaac, holding hands with Grandma Maria, looked around in awe. "Look at all the books, Mommy!" Abigail exclaimed, her eyes wide with wonder.

"Yes, sweetheart. Daddy's book is here too," Eden replied, smiling.

As they walked through the store, the manager greeted them warmly and led Alex to a table set up with stacks of his books. A large poster with the book's cover art stood behind him, drawing the attention of everyone in the store.

"Welcome, everyone!" the manager announced. "We are thrilled to have Alex Freeman here with us today. Let's give him a big round of applause!"

The room filled with applause, and Alex took his seat, feeling a surge of gratitude. The line snaked around the store, starting from the signing table at the front and weaving through the aisles of neatly arranged bookshelves. Readers of all ages held copies of the book close to their chests, eager to get them signed. Some clutched additional memorabilia, like bookmarks or posters, while others held their phones, ready to snap a picture with the author.

One young woman approached the table, holding a well-worn copy of his book. "This story meant so much to me. It helped me through a really tough time. Thank you," she said, her voice trembling with emotion.

Alex looked up, moved by her words. "Thank you for sharing that. It means the world to me to know my work has made a difference."

Meanwhile, Eden, Maria, and the children mingled with the crowd, listening to snippets of conversations, and feeling the excitement in the air. Abigail and Isaac, curious and eager, asked questions about the books and the people around them. As the event continued, Alex took a moment to glance over at his family. Seeing them smiling and enjoying themselves filled him with a deep sense of fulfillment. This journey, with all its ups and downs, had brought them to this moment.

After the signing, the family gathered around Alex, the warmth of their support enveloping him. "You were amazing," Eden said, kissing him on the cheek.

Alex smiled, pulling his family close. "I couldn't have done it without you all. This is our journey, and I'm so grateful for each of you. I'm going to need a new wrist now after all those signatures!"

"Yeah, Daddy! You signed so many books!" Isaac added, his eyes shining with pride.

They stepped out of the bustling bookstore and into the cool evening air. The city lights twinkled around them, casting a warm glow on the snowy streets. Alex, with his arm around Eden, felt a sense of accomplishment from the successful event, while Eden carried a tired but content Isaac in her arms. Abigail held Alex's hand, chattering excitedly about the people they had met and the stories she had overheard.

As they walked, the family enjoyed the serene atmosphere of the city at night. The streets, quieter now, were lined with softly lit shops and cafés. The crunch of snow under their boots added to the magical feel of the evening. They passed by familiar landmarks, each bringing back memories of their time in the city before moving to Everbrook.

Eden pointed out a park where she and her father used to spend time together, sharing a nostalgic smile with Alex. They walked past a charming ice cream parlor that Alex remembered for its unique flavors and whimsical decor, which he promised to visit the next day for a special treat with the kids.

Finally, they reached Maria's apartment building. The warm glow from the windows welcomed them as they entered the lobby and made their way up the elevator. Maria quickly went to the kitchen and started making hot cocoa.

Inside, the children promptly shed their coats and boots, eager to snuggle up on the couch with their grandmother. Alex and Eden felt a wave of relief wash over them as they settled in. The evening had been wonderful, but the comfort of family and the prospect of a restful night were exactly what they needed.

Maria handed out steaming mugs of cocoa, and the family sat together, recounting the highlights of the day. Laughter and warmth filled the room, creating a perfect end to an exciting day. As the night drew on, Alex and Eden tucked Isaac and Abigail into bed, promising them an exciting day of shopping and sightseeing tomorrow. With the children asleep, Alex and Eden finally allowed themselves to relax. They joined Maria in the living room, enjoying the peacefulness of the city night outside the window.

●

The following morning, snow continued to fall gently outside, blanketing the city in a serene white cover. The family sat around the breakfast table, savoring a hearty meal of French toast and sausage prepared by Grandma Maria.

Eden, sipping her coffee, looked around at her family and smiled. "Alright, everyone, I have a plan for today's shopping and sightseeing," she began.

Abigail's eyes lit up. "What are we going to do, Mommy?"

"First," Eden said, "we'll head to that toy store near the park. It's the biggest toy store you've ever seen! After that, we'll visit a few clothing stores nearby to pick up some new outfits. You kids are growing faster and faster, it seems."

Isaac, munching on a piece of toast, asked, "Can we go to the park too, since it's so close to the toy store?"

"Of course, Isaac," Eden replied. "We'll stop by the park for a quick walk after the toy store. It's all decorated for winter, and I bet the snow will make it look magical."

Maria nodded, smiling warmly. "Just make sure to bundle up— it's chilly out there."

Abigail chimed in, "And what about that ice cream parlor we passed last night? Dad said we could go there. I think it would be a great way to end the day."

Eden laughed. "I was just getting to that! Yes, we'll definitely stop by the ice cream parlor Dad mentioned for a treat before we head back to Grandma's apartment to warm up."

Abigail clapped her hands in delight. "Yay! I love ice cream!"

Eden continued, "We'll also do some sightseeing. There's a new dinosaur exhibit at the museum that I think you'll all enjoy. It's not too far from the toy store, so we can walk there after we finish shopping."

Alex winced and rubbed his neck. "Actually, can we rearrange that a bit? I must have slept funny because I've got this pain in my neck." He massaged the sore spot and grimaced. "I'd like to rest here for a bit before we head to the toy store. Maybe you can go there first and come back for me afterward?"

"Sure, honey. Are you sure you're okay?" Eden frowned, concern crossing her face.

"Yeah, it's probably just a pinched nerve or something. I'm not used to signing all those books. Nothing to worry about," Alex reassured her, though the pain in his neck was growing more intense by the minute.

As breakfast continued, Alex's discomfort seemed to worsen. He tried to keep up with the conversation, but it was clear he was in pain. By the time they were finishing their meal, he was wincing with every movement.

As they prepared to leave, Eden glanced at Alex again and noticed something alarming. "Alex, your ear... it's swelling up really bad. And you don't look well at all."

Alex touched his ear and winced. "It feels like it's on fire," he admitted, his face pale and strained.

Eden's concern deepened. "We need to get you to a doctor ASAP. This isn't just a stiff neck—it could be an infection or something serious. Your face shouldn't look like that, honey."

Maria quickly moved to Alex's side. "I'll call the clinic right away and see if they can fit him in. This doesn't look good."

Eden, with a sense of urgency, said, "I don't think the clinic is what he needs. We need to go to the ER. This is progressing too fast for my comfort."

Abigail, sensing the tension, asked, "Is Daddy going to be okay?"

Eden knelt down to reassure her. "Daddy's going to see a doctor, and they'll make sure he gets better, okay?"

Isaac looked worried but nodded, trying to be brave.

Maria gently placed a hand on Eden's shoulder. "I'll take care of the kids for the day. I'll take them to the toy store and maybe even the park. Hopefully, that will take their minds off the problem."

Eden looked relieved. "Thanks, Mom. That would be wonderful. The kids have been looking forward to today."

As they left the apartment, Eden kept a supportive arm around Alex. "We'll take care of this, Alex. Your health is the most important thing right now."

Eden helped Alex to the car, her mind racing with worry. The drive to the city hospital felt agonizingly slow, each minute stretching as Alex's condition worsened. By the time they arrived, his neck had swollen so much that his ear had turned into a massive cauliflower shape, and the pressure was beginning to push his eye out.

The ER at the hospital was a flurry of activity. Doctors and nurses moved swiftly, trying to understand Alex's rapidly escalating condition. Eden, though a doctor herself, felt a wave of helplessness wash over her.

"We're going to run some tests, but we need to stabilize him first," one of the doctors said, guiding them to a treatment room.

As they examined Alex, the severity of his condition became clear. The swelling was not only pushing his eye out but also putting intense pressure on his jugular, causing the blood flow in his body to stop moving correctly.

"We have no idea what's causing this," one of the doctors admitted, frustration in his voice. "The infection is spreading aggressively. If we don't stop it soon, the swelling could enter his brain within the next hour or two, and that would be disastrous."

"What are our options?" Eden asked, her voice steady despite her fear.

The doctor took a deep breath. "To stop the infection from spreading, we'll need to cut off his ear and possibly take out his eye."

Alex, who had been listening quietly, looked at the doctor with desperation. "Please, don't do that. Isn't there another way? I don't want people to call me Alex Van Gogh."

The doctor shook his head and laughed anxiously. "If the swelling continues, it will put even more pressure on your brain, and you will die. We have to act fast."

Eden's mind raced for a solution. Suddenly, an idea struck her. "What if we put him into a medically induced coma?"

The doctors looked at her, considering the suggestion. "Explain," one of them said.

"By inducing a coma, we can reduce the amount of energy those different brain areas need," Eden explained, her voice shaking with the weight of the decision. "If we can do that, then as the body heals and the swelling goes down, maybe those areas that were at risk can be protected, and the swelling won't enter his brain."

The doctors exchanged glances, then nodded. "It's a long shot, but it could work. We'll prepare for the procedure."

Before being put into a coma, Alex grabbed Eden's hand, his eyes filled with concern. "Eden, the bees... someone needs to take care of them if I'm... if I'm out for too long. They'll never survive in this weather."

Eden's composure cracked. Tears welled up in her eyes as she struggled to stay strong. "Alex, please... don't talk like that. We're going to get through this. I promise I'll get someone to take care of the bees, but I need you to fight, okay?"

Alex managed a weak smile. Noticing the tears in her eyes, he said, "There's no crying until the end."

Eden nodded, her heart breaking as she fought to hold back her tears. "Okay, Alex. I promise, no crying until the end."

As the doctors administered the sedative, Alex's grip on Eden's hand relaxed. His eyes fluttered closed, and the room was filled with the soft hum of medical machines. Eden stood there, feeling the weight of his fate on her shoulders, her heart heavy with fear and uncertainty.

●

Alex felt the world around him dissolve into a whirl of colors, shapes, and geometric patterns. It was as if he were floating in a kaleidoscope, each twist and turn of the mandala of colors pulling him deeper into a vivid, disorienting experience. The colors pulsated with life, shifting and morphing into new forms.

He struggled to find his bearings in this swirling chaos, his mind grappling with the surreal landscape. The colors danced and spiraled around him, faster and faster, until they began to merge. Slowly, they coalesced into a single, blindingly bright light. The intensity of the light grew until it consumed everything around him, leaving him standing in a vast, white room.

In the center of the room, a surgical table materialized. On the table lay a body, surrounded by intricate rods and machinery that seemed to be holding the body in place.

"Why are you here?" a voice crackled over what sounded like a loudspeaker, the sound cutting through the stark silence.

Alex turned, searching for the source of the voice, but saw only the endless expanse of white. "I don't know. I was going to ask you the same question. Who are you, where are you? Is that my body on the table over there?" he called out, his voice echoing in the emptiness.

"That is your body, and it's also your universe," the voice responded calmly, as if explaining something obvious.

"How can my body be the universe?" Alex asked, confusion and frustration mingling in his voice.

"We created it to understand where we came from," the voice explained, its tone detached and almost mechanical.

"Well, what did you learn?" Alex demanded, his fear rising as the sterile room seemed to close in on him.

"We learned that through your creation, someone, in turn, created us," the voice replied, the words reverberating through the vast, white space.

"Well, who are you then?" Alex shouted, feeling more disoriented and desperate.

"I am you," the voice answered simply, the words hanging in the air like an unspoken truth.

Alex's frustration boiled over. "I don't understand. I don't want to be here anymore, this is starting to freak me out."

"Then go," the voice said, almost tauntingly.

"Go where?" Alex asked, feeling the ground beneath him shift and warp.

"You can go anywhere. Just imagine it, believe it, and live it. What is your first memory? Start there. The further back you trace it, the easier it will become," the voice suggested, the words visibly swirling around him like a gentle command.

Alex closed his eyes, trying to block out the overwhelming sensory overload. Slowly, a memory began to form around him. He saw himself as a small child, in his crib, his mother tickling him while he giggled. He then saw himself unsteady on his feet, taking his first steps in his childhood home. The memory was more vivid this time.

Suddenly, the sterile white room began to fade, and Alex found himself transported back to that moment. He was in his childhood home, the familiar smells and sounds surrounding him. He felt a sense of comfort and safety as he relived those early moments of his life. His parents, George and Cindy, watched him intently, their faces radiating encouragement and love. George knelt a few feet away, arms outstretched, ready to catch his son. Cindy, holding a camera, aimed to capture this monumental moment.

"Come on, Alex, you can do it!" George's voice was gentle but filled with excitement. Alex's chubby hands grasped at the air for balance as he looked at his father's reassuring face. He could feel the softness of the carpet beneath his tiny feet, giving him just enough confidence to take that first crucial step. With a deep breath and a look of pure concentration, Alex lifted his right foot and placed it shakily in front of him.

He swayed a little, but George's soothing voice kept him steady. "That's it, buddy! One more step!"

Encouraged, Alex shifted his weight and brought his left foot forward. The world around him seemed to hold its breath as he took those first, hesitant steps.

"You did it, Alex! You walked!" Cindy clapped and laughed, tears of joy sparkling in her eyes. "Our little boy is growing up so fast," she said, capturing the moment on film.

●

Isaac and Abigail could hardly contain their excitement as they stood before the grand entrance of the Big City Toy Store with their Grandma Maria. The doors loomed large and inviting, adorned with colorful lights and a giant, playful sign that read, "Welcome to the Big City Toy Store!" Life-sized toy soldiers stood guard at the entrance, adding to the festive atmosphere.

"Are you ready?" Maria asked, her eyes twinkling with anticipation. Isaac and Abigail nodded eagerly, their hands clutching Grandma Maria's tightly. With a deep breath and wide-eyed wonder, they took their first steps into the toy store.

As they crossed the threshold, they were greeted by a world of magic and delight. The inside of the toy store was a sensory overload of colors, sounds, and delightful chaos. Shelves upon shelves were filled with every toy imaginable, from classic dolls and action figures to the latest gadgets and games. The air was filled with the cheerful sounds of children laughing and toys whirring.

The store's layout was a maze of wonders, with different sections dedicated to various types of toys. There was a train set village with miniature trains chugging along tracks, a giant stuffed animal forest, and a building block kingdom where children were busy constructing imaginative creations. Isaac and Abigail's eyes sparkled as they took in the sights and sounds. They were drawn first to the giant robot display in the center of the store, its mechanical arms moving and lights flashing in a mesmerizing dance.

"Look at that robot, Isaac!" Abigail pointed, her face aglow with excitement.

"It's amazing!" Isaac replied, equally enthralled.

Maria watched with joy as her grandchildren explored the store.

Isaac found a section filled with model cars and tracks. "Grandma, look! They have the race car set I've always wanted!"

Abigail, meanwhile, was captivated by a display of dolls and accessories. "Oh, Grandma, can we look at the dolls? They have everything here!"

"Of course, my dears," Maria said, guiding them through the aisles. She let them take their time, knowing how special this moment was for them. As they wandered through the arts and crafts section, Maria's eyes landed on a shelf filled with pet rock kits. She picked one up, her face lighting up with an idea.

"Isaac, Abigail, how about we decorate a pet rock for your daddy? It could be a fun present for him."

The twins looked at the kit curiously. "A pet rock?" Isaac asked, tilting his head.

"Yes, a pet rock," Maria explained, showing them the kit. "We can paint it, give it eyes, and even add some fun decorations. Your dad would love it because it's something you made yourselves."

Abigail grinned. "That sounds like so much fun! Let's do it!"

Isaac nodded enthusiastically. "Yeah, let's make a pet rock for Daddy!"

With the pet rock kit in hand, they continued exploring the store. After what felt like hours of exploration, they finally selected a few treasures to take home. Isaac clutched a shiny red race car and a set of tracks, while Abigail hugged a beautiful doll and a collection of outfits. Maria carried the pet rock kit, excited to start the project with her grandchildren.

As they made their way to the checkout, Maria looked down at her grandchildren, their faces glowing with happiness. "Did you have a good time?"

"It was the best day ever, Grandma!" Abigail exclaimed, and Isaac nodded in enthusiastic agreement.

"I'm so glad," Maria replied, her heart full. "Now, how about we take this stuff home, and then I'll show you two some more of the secrets the Big City has?" The twins nodded their heads in agreement as they cheerfully left the toy store.

●

While the children were busy with their grandma exploring the city, Eden was in the hospital, consumed with worry and determination. She studied Alex's medical charts, analyzing his blood results and the rapid spread of the infection. Her mind raced with possibilities and theories, each more alarming than the last. Though this area was not her medical specialty, she worked diligently to find an answer.

"It must've been a microscopic cut that got infected," she muttered to herself. "But how could it be so aggressive?" She leaned back in her chair, rubbing her temples. The constant stress and lack of food were taking their toll, but she couldn't afford to rest. Not when Alex's life hung in the balance.

Eden's thoughts were interrupted by the sound of footsteps approaching. She looked up to see Dr. Virgilio, one of the leading specialists, entering the room. His expression was grave, and Eden felt a knot tighten in her stomach.

"Any progress?" she asked, her voice barely above a whisper.

Dr. Virgilio shook his head. "I'm afraid not. We've run every test we can think of. I'm calling in some other specialists for their input. My fear is that the infection will enter his bloodstream. We need to consider more aggressive treatments. It seems like the coma is working in our favor for now, but how much longer he can hold on, we don't know."

Eden put her head in her hands, feeling the weight of the world pressing down on her. "What could have caused this? It's unlike anything I've ever seen."

Dr. Virgilio sighed. "That's what's so baffling. It's as if his immune system is overreacting to something, but we can't pinpoint what it is."

Eden's phone buzzed, breaking the tension. It was a call from Sarah, Alex's sister.

"Eden," Sarah's voice was shaky but determined. "I'm at the hospital. Where are you?"

Eden replied, "I'm in the lab. I'll meet you in the waiting room."

She gathered her notes and made her way to the waiting room, where she found Sarah pacing nervously.

"Sarah, thank you for coming," Eden said, pulling her into a hug.

Sarah clung to her, tears in her eyes. "How is he?"

Eden took a deep breath, trying to steady herself. "It's bad, Sarah. The doctors are doing everything they can, but the infection is spreading so fast. They're not sure what to do."

Sarah nodded, wiping her tears. "George and Cindy are on vacation. They're trying to come back early to visit him."

Eden nodded, grateful for the support. "I hope they get here soon."

Sarah took a deep breath, trying to compose herself. "I finally got a divorce from Tom today. We decided to tough it out until the kids turned 18 and graduated from high school. It's been hard, but... it was the right decision. And now Alex is sick, my world is falling apart! I don't know how much more I can take."

Eden squeezed her hand. "I'm so sorry, Sarah. But you're strong, and you'll get through this. Things always get worse before they get better." The two women sat together in the quiet room, drawing strength from each other. The weight of their shared struggles and the hope for Alex's recovery bound them together.

Sarah's tears fell freely now, mixing with the overwhelming emotions she had been holding back. "I thought I'd feel relieved after the divorce, but I just feel... empty."

Eden wrapped her arms around Sarah, holding her tightly. "I'm so sorry you had to go through that alone. You're not empty, Sarah. You have so much love and strength inside you. You're just tired and hurt right now."

Sarah nodded against Eden's shoulder, her sobs subsiding into soft whimpers. "I thought staying together for the kids was the right thing to do, but it only made things worse. They saw the fights, the distance between us. I felt like such a failure."

Eden pulled back slightly, looking into Sarah's eyes. "You're not a failure. You did what you thought was best at the time. And now you're making a new start for yourself. It's never too late to find happiness."

Sarah wiped her tears, taking a deep, shuddering breath. "Thank you, Eden. I needed to hear that. I just wish... I wish I could be as strong as you."

Eden shook her head. "I'm not strong. I'm terrified. Every moment I feel like I'm falling apart. But we have to keep going. For Alex, for the kids, for ourselves. We can't give up."

Sarah nodded, her resolve strengthening. "You're right. We can't give up. We'll get through this together."

Eden stood up, her movements slow and deliberate, and turned to Sarah.

"Come on, Sarah," Eden said gently. "Let's go see Alex."

Sarah stood up, her face pale and tense. Eden led her through the quiet halls, their footsteps echoing softly against the polished floors. The soft hum of machinery and the occasional murmur of voices were the only sounds breaking the stillness.

They reached the ICU, where Eden paused outside Alex's room. She pushed the door open gently, revealing Alex lying in the hospital bed, surrounded by an array of monitors and medical equipment. The room was sterile and cold, but Eden had placed a family photo on the bedside table, a small reminder of home.

Sarah stepped inside, her eyes filling with tears as she approached her brother. "Alex," she whispered, her voice breaking.

Eden touched Sarah's shoulder reassuringly. "I'll leave you two alone for a bit. I need to continue my research."

Sarah turned to Eden, her eyes pleading. "Eden, please take care of yourself too, you look exhausted. Alex wouldn't want you to wear yourself out."

Eden offered a faint smile, her eyes reflecting a mixture of fatigue and determination. "I will. I'll be nearby if you need me."

With a final hug, Eden left the room and walked down the hallway to the small office she had been using. The office was cluttered with medical journals, case studies, and her laptop. She sat down at the desk, her mind buzzing with possibilities and questions that needed answers.

As the hours ticked by, Eden immersed herself in her research. She looked over every piece of information she could find, hoping to uncover something that could help Alex. The night stretched on, the hospital growing quieter as the world outside darkened. Eden's eyes burned from the strain, but she refused to let fatigue take over. She leaned back in her chair for a moment, rubbing her temples, then took a sip of cold coffee from a nearby cup. The bitter taste kept her alert, driving her to continue.

Working through the night, fueled by love and the desperate need to help Alex, she found a few promising leads, but there was still so much to uncover. The weight of responsibility pressed heavily on her shoulders, but she knew she couldn't stop now.

As dawn approached, the first light of the new day filtering through the frosty hospital windows, Eden finally leaned back in her chair, exhaustion etched into her features. She glanced at the clock, noting the time, and knew she needed to update the rest of the family soon. For now, Eden allowed herself a brief moment of rest, closing her eyes and taking a deep breath. She looked out the hospital window, staring at the vast expanse of the city, praying for an answer.

●

Gabriel sat at the kitchen table, a steaming cup of coffee in his hands. The rich aroma filled the room. He gazed out the window, watching as the snow began to fall gently. The morning was quiet, with only the occasional chirp of a bird breaking the silence.

His son, Jacob, played with his new train set on the living room floor, the sound of the toy train chugging along its tracks adding a comforting background noise. Gabriel took a sip of his coffee, savoring the warmth, and continued to watch the street.

Suddenly, movement caught his eye. He leaned forward slightly, peering through the frosty glass. A car was pulling into Alex's driveway. Gabriel squinted, recognizing the familiar vehicle. It was Leo, Alex's brother-in-law.

"Looks like Leo's here," Gabriel murmured to himself, curiosity piqued. He wondered what had brought Leo over so early in the morning.

Jacob looked up from his train set, following his father's gaze. "Is someone visiting Alex, Dad?"

Gabriel smiled at Jacob's curiosity. "Yeah, buddy. It looks like Leo is visiting Alex. Maybe we'll see what they're up to later."

Leo stepped out of his car, bundled up against the cold. He

waved at Gabriel through the window, and Gabriel returned the gesture with a nod. Leo then turned and headed toward Alex's front door, his steps purposeful. Gabriel couldn't shake the feeling that something important was happening. He set his coffee mug down and stood up, contemplating whether to go over and see if everything was alright.

"Jacob, how about we get dressed and go say hi to Leo?" Gabriel suggested.

Jacob's face lit up with excitement. "Yes, Dad! Let's go!"

Gabriel quickly helped Jacob into his coat and boots, then put on his own winter gear. They stepped out into the chilly morning, the snow crunching under their feet as they made their way across the street to Alex's house.

As they approached the front door, Gabriel could hear Leo talking to himself inside. He knocked lightly, and after a moment, the door opened to reveal Leo, who greeted them with a warm but tired smile.

"Hey, Gabriel, Jacob. Come on in," Leo said, stepping aside to let them enter. Gabriel and Jacob stepped into the warmth of the house, shaking off the cold.

Gabriel noticed the slight tension in Leo's expression. "Hi, Leo. It's good to see you. Is everything alright?"

Leo's smile faded, replaced by a look of concern. "Actually, Gabriel, there's something I need to tell you. Alex, he... he's in the hospital, in a coma."

Gabriel felt his heart drop. "What happened?"

Leo sighed, rubbing his eyes. "His whole head started to swell up, and to stop it from getting worse, they put him in a coma. They're not sure what's wrong yet. Eden's with him, trying to figure things out. She asked me to come over to take care of the bees and look after the house while they're at the hospital."

Gabriel nodded, his mind racing with concern for his friend. "Oh my God, that's crazy! Is there anything I can do to help?"

Leo gave a small, grateful smile. "Actually, yes. I have no idea what to do with these bees, and I could use some help with them. Alex put so much effort into his beekeeping. I'd hate to see it all fall apart."

Gabriel chuckled. "Don't worry, Leo. I'll help you with the bees. I've watched Alex work with them over the years. We'll make sure everything is taken care of."

Jacob, sensing the seriousness of the conversation, looked up at his dad. "Is Alex going to be okay, Dad?"

Gabriel knelt down to Jacob's level, his voice gentle. "I hope so, buddy. Alex is getting the best care he can, and we'll do everything we can to help him. After we take care of the bees with Leo, we'll go see Alex to give him our support."

Leo nodded, his expression softening. "Thank you, Gabriel. It means a lot. Let's get started with the bees. You can show me what needs to be done."

The trio made their way to the greenhouse, the crisp winter air nipping at their cheeks. Inside, the warmth was a welcome relief from the cold outside. The greenhouse was filled with the hum of bees, busy despite the season.

Gabriel began explaining the process to Jacob and Leo, both of whom watched with wide-eyed fascination. "Bees are amazing little creatures. They work hard all year round, and it's important to take good care of them."

Leo listened closely, nodding along. "So, what do we need to do, big guy?"

Gabriel handed Leo a pair of gloves and a netted hat. "We're going to check on their food supply and make sure the hive is healthy. Winter can be tough on bees, so we have to be extra careful."

As they worked, the mood lightened. Gabriel's son laughed and asked questions, his curiosity a welcome distraction from the worries about Alex. The scene took a humorous turn when Leo, in his eagerness to taste some honey, lifted his mask and forgot about the bees buzzing around. Within moments, his suit was filled with bees, and he danced around trying to shake them off.

Gabriel laughed, shaking his head. "Leo, you need to be more careful!"

Outside, Jacob was playing in the snow, making snow angels. As Gabriel and Leo worked, they talked about Alex, sharing memories, and expressing their hopes for his recovery. The conversation was filled with both laughter and somber moments, reflecting the complex emotions of the situation.

Leo sighed, pausing to adjust his mask properly this time. "I just hope he pulls through. He's a fighter, but this... I don't know what to say, it's pretty rough."

Gabriel nodded, his face serious. "We all do. He's got a lot of people pulling for him. And we'll keep things running smoothly here until he gets back on his feet." Gabriel looked out at his son, now busy piling snow to make a snowman.

•

Alex found himself outside in a small clearing. He sat on a solitary tree stump surrounded by snow-tipped pines. The landscape was eerily still, the silence interrupted only by the occasional crunch of snow as it fell from the pine trees. The cold air made his cheeks rosy, but he felt strangely detached from the chill, as if he were merely an observer in this frozen world.

He looked around, trying to grasp where he was and how he had gotten here. The memory of being in the hospital, the pain, and the swelling all seemed distant and unreal. Here, in this snow-covered clearing, everything felt timeless and serene.

After a few moments, Alex decided to lie down. He stretched out on the snow, feeling its cold embrace as he moved his arms and legs to create a snow angel. The act felt familiar and comforting, like a childhood ritual. As he lay there, staring up at the sky, he felt a sense of peace wash over him.

When he rose, brushing the snow off his clothes, he was surprised to see a snowman standing in front of him. The snowman was simple, yet perfectly formed, with coal eyes, a carrot nose, and a wide, welcoming smile made from small pebbles. It looked at Alex with an almost knowing expression.

"I melted away one warm winter day," the snowman said, its voice soft and sad, "but I'll always remain in your memories."

Alex felt a sting of recognition, a bittersweet mixture of loss and fondness. He reached out his hand, but before he could touch it, the snowman began to melt. It didn't dissolve naturally; rather, it melted away like a wet oil painting, its form distorting and flowing into abstract shapes and colors.

As the snowman disappeared, vibrant flowers began to spring up from the ground where it had stood. The flowers were unlike any Alex had seen before, their petals shimmering with iridescent hues. They swayed gently, as if moved by an unseen breeze, and began to sing in harmonious voices.

"Let's all look at the light, let's all face the light, let's all put smiles on our faces," the flowers continued to sing, their melody soothing and uplifting.

Alex turned his gaze towards a bright light that seemed to emanate from above. The light was warm and inviting, growing in intensity as he focused on it. He squinted, trying to make out what lay beyond the brilliance, feeling a pull towards it.

The clearing around him began to blur and fade, the bright light enveloping everything until it was all he could see. The sounds of the singing flowers merged with a steady beeping, the cold air with a sterile scent.

Eden sat in the hospital room beside Alex, her eyes heavy with exhaustion. The rhythmic beeping of the monitors was the only sound in the otherwise silent room. She watched over Alex, her heart aching with worry and fatigue. Every breath he took, every movement he made, she noticed, her own breath catching each time there was a change.

Suddenly, the steady beeping turned faster and faster, and then it stopped. The sound was deafening, slicing through the silence like a knife. Eden's heart stopped, and she jumped up, her chair clattering to the floor.

"Alex!" she screamed, her voice filled with panic and desperation.

The room erupted into chaos as doctors and nurses rushed in. Eden was pushed aside, but she refused to leave. Her eyes were locked on Alex's still form, her mind racing with fear.

Dr. Virgilio took charge, barking orders to the medical team. "Get the crash cart! Start compressions!"

Eden couldn't tear her eyes away from Alex. She felt helpless, useless. She had to do something, anything. She pushed past the nurses and grabbed a flashlight, her hands shaking.

"Let me check his pupils," she said, her voice trembling.

Dr. Virgilio glanced at her, recognizing the desperation in her eyes. He nodded, allowing her to proceed. Eden leaned over Alex, her hands unsteady as she opened his eyes and shone the flashlight into them. She held her breath, praying for a response. For a moment, there was nothing. And then, miraculously, Alex's pupils reacted. The flatline changed to a slow, but steady beep. His pulse was weak, but it was there.

"He's got a pulse!" Eden screamed loudly.

Relief flooded her, making her knees weak. She clung to the edge of the bed, her heart pounding in her chest. The doctors exchanged puzzled looks but were visibly relieved. Dr. Virgilio stepped forward, his expression a mix of concern and curiosity.

"That was close," he said, his voice low. "In all my years, that is the strangest thing I've ever seen. Eden, you need to rest," he said gently. "You're not doing yourself or Alex any favors by running yourself into the ground. You look absolutely terrible."

Eden shook her head, her exhaustion making her defiant. "I can't leave him. He needs me."

Dr. Virgilio's expression softened. "I understand, but you're not in any condition to help anyone right now. You're exhausted, stressed, and I'd bet you haven't eaten or slept properly since you got here."

Eden opened her mouth to protest, but Dr. Virgilio held up a hand. "Eden, you're a doctor. You know how important it is to take care of yourself. If you collapse, who will be here for Alex and your children?"

The words hit Eden hard, and she felt a wave of guilt wash over her. She knew he was right, but admitting it felt like a betrayal. She nodded slowly, her shoulders slumping.

"What should I do?" she whispered.

Dr. Virgilio smiled gently and handed her a small card. "There's a special retreat just a block away. They specialize in helping people relax and rejuvenate. Go there, take the rest of today and as much time as you need tomorrow to rest and rejuvenate. Trust us to take care of Alex. The owner is a close friend of mine. I'll arrange for your stay tonight. When you feel content, you can come back. You'll only be a few minutes' walk from the hospital. Everything will be fine."

Eden took the card, staring at it as if it were a lifeline. The thought of leaving Alex, even for a short time, was terrifying, but she knew she had no choice. She couldn't help him if she was a wreck.

"Thank you," she said softly, looking up at Dr. Virgilio.

He nodded, giving her a reassuring hug. "Go get some rest, Eden. We'll take good care of him. If we need to get in contact with you, I know where to find you."

Eden took one last look at Alex, her heart aching with love and fear. She leaned down and kissed his forehead.

"I'll be back soon," she whispered. "Please, keep fighting." The thought of a day of rest was both a relief and a torment. But she knew deep down that she needed to do it, for Alex, for their children, and most importantly, for herself.

•

The next morning, the atmosphere in Maria's apartment was wild. Abigail and Isaac were full of energy, their excitement and worry about their father creating a blizzard of activity. Maria, already drained from the emotional toll of the past few days, struggled to keep up with their boundless enthusiasm.

"Grandma, can we have pancakes for breakfast?" Isaac shouted from the kitchen, where he was already pulling out ingredients.

"Abigail, don't jump on the couch! You might get hurt!" Maria called out, trying to keep an eye on both children at once.

"Look, Grandma, I made a drawing for Daddy!" Abigail said, running over with a colorful picture in her hand.

Maria smiled wearily. "That's beautiful, sweetheart. I'm sure he'll love it."

Just then, the phone rang. Maria wiped her hands on a dish towel and answered it. "Hello?"

"Mom, it's Eden. How are the kids?" Eden said.

Maria sighed, relieved to hear her daughter's voice. "They're full of energy, but they miss Alex. It's a lot to handle."

Eden's voice was filled with exhaustion. "I know, Mom. Listen, I'm going to be unavailable today. I talked with Sarah, and she said she could help with the kids for a bit. She is going to take them back to the cottage with Leo. They need some space to run around, and you could use a break."

Maria nodded, glancing at the children. "That sounds like a good idea."

A short while later, Sarah arrived at the apartment. She was greeted by the sight of Abigail and Isaac racing around, their boundless energy in stark contrast to her weary expression.

"Hey, Sarah," Maria said, giving her a tired smile. "Thank you for coming."

Sarah hugged her briefly. "Of course. Eden called and explained everything. How are you holding up?"

Maria sighed. "It's been tough, but we're managing. The kids have been making things for Alex. They even made a pet rock to cheer him up."

Sarah's face softened as she looked at the children. "That's sweet. I'll take them to see Alex and then head back to the cottage. They'll have more space there, and you can get some rest."

The kids, overhearing the conversation, ran over to them excitedly.

"Are we going to see Daddy?" Abigail asked, her eyes wide with anticipation.

"Yes, we are," Sarah replied, smiling. "We need to take your gifts to the hospital to give them to Daddy. I think it will cheer him up."

Abigail and Isaac's faces lit up. "Yes! Let's do that!" Isaac exclaimed.

With the pet rock carefully wrapped in a small blanket, Sarah and the children made their way to the hospital. The drive was filled with chatter about their plans at the cottage but underlying it all was a shared sense of purpose. They wanted to make Alex smile, even if just for a moment.

When they arrived at the hospital, the kids were unusually quiet, their earlier excitement tempered by the seriousness of their mission. Sarah held their hands as they walked through the corridors, feeling the weight of their hopes and fears.

They reached Alex's room, and Sarah gently knocked before pushing the door open. Alex lay in the bed, surrounded by monitors and medical equipment. His stillness was a stark contrast to the vibrant energy of the children.

"Daddy, we brought you something!" Abigail said softly, approaching the bed with Isaac by her side.

Sarah helped them place the pet rock on the bedside table. "The kids made this for you, Alex. They thought it might make you feel better."

Abigail reached out and touched Alex's hand gently. "We miss you, Daddy. Please get better soon."

Isaac nodded, his eyes wide and serious. "We made the pet rock with lots of love. It's to keep you company."

In the depths of his coma, Alex found himself standing in a vast, barren landscape. The crimson ground beneath him was hard and unyielding, dotted with strange, colorful rocks that seemed to pulse with an inner light. He walked forward cautiously, each step echoing in the eerie silence.

As he approached one particularly large rock, it suddenly shifted, revealing eyes that glowed with an otherworldly light. He paused as he approached the peculiar rock, an odd feeling washing over him. He could've sworn he heard it speak. Dismissing the thought, he was about to continue when the voice came again, clear and unmistakable.

"Halt," the rock said, its tone both commanding and ancient.

Alex stared, bewildered. "Did you just... speak?"

The rock's surface seemed to shimmer slightly, its eyes narrowing as if scrutinizing him. "Indeed, I did. I have no patience for people who interrupt me when I'm doing nothing, but I will make an exception for you. Listen closely, for what I have to say is of great importance."

Alex felt a strange familiarity with the entity, something he couldn't quite place. "What are you?" he asked, half expecting to wake up from some strange dream.

The rock's expression softened, its voice calm but firm. "I am no ordinary rock. I am a reflection of the Earth's ancient wisdom, a guardian of truths hidden from most. And now, I am here to guide you."

Alex blinked, trying to make sense of it all. "Guide me? Why me?"

"Because," the rock replied, "you have a destiny, Alex. One that is not just yours, but that of the whole universe. The path you walk will ripple across time and space. Embrace it, for it is your calling."

Intrigued yet still confused, Alex took a step closer. "What destiny? What am I supposed to do?"

The rock's eyes seemed to pierce through him, its voice echoing with a profound weight. "There will come a time in which all of you in the universe will overlap each other, but you shouldn't worry about that right now."

Alex frowned, trying to grasp the cryptic message. "Overlap?

What in the world are you talking about?"

The rock continued, its tone growing more intense. "There is a monster you are protecting, influenced by the power of this place. Now get out of here, I have things to do that involve nothing."

Before Alex could respond, the ground beneath him began to shift and tremble. He felt himself being lifted off the scorched earth beneath him, transported through a whirlwind of colors and sensations. His surroundings blurred and changed until he found himself in a tiny rowboat, floating on a sea that shimmered with a deep, purple hue.

The boat rocked gently on the waves, and Alex could see an island in the distance with a large tree looming from its center. He picked up the oars and began to row, the motion soothing yet surreal. The purple sea reflected the strange, twirling darkness of the atmosphere surrounding him, creating a landscape that seemed to stretch into infinity. As he rowed towards the island, the sound of the oars dipping into the water transformed into the soft murmur of children singing.

●

Sarah drove carefully through the snow-covered roads, the car filled with the cheerful voices of Abigail and Isaac as they sang, "Row, row, row your boat, gently down the stream, merrily, merrily, merrily, merrily, life is but a dream."

Sarah glanced at them in the rearview mirror, a small smile tugging at her lips. She was grateful for their innocence and the simple joy they found in singing, even in such difficult times.

As they neared the cottage, she could see Gabriel and his son in the driveway. Gabriel and his young son were just leaving, bundled up against the cold. Gabriel noticed their arrival and waved, lifting his son into the car before walking over to greet them.

"Hey, Sarah. How's everything going?" Gabriel said with a smile, his face turning red.

Sarah returned his smile, feeling a flutter of warmth at his presence. "We're managing. Just came to get the kids settled. How about you?"

Gabriel's eyes softened with understanding. "Doing our best. Leo's been a big help. We've been taking care of the bees and keeping the place in order."

Sarah's gaze lingered on Gabriel's for a moment, a silent connection passing between them. "Thank you for everything, Gabriel. It means a lot."

Gabriel nodded, a hint of something unspoken in his eyes. "Anytime, Sarah. We're all in this together."

Just then, Leo emerged from the cottage, his face lighting up at the sight of the kids. "Hey there, you two! How's my favorite pair of troublemakers?"

Abigail and Isaac ran over to him, their excitement bubbling over. "Leo! We missed you!" Abigail said, hugging him tightly.

Isaac grinned up at him. "We gave Daddy the pet rock. Do you think it will help him get better?"

Leo chuckled, ruffling Isaac's hair. "I'm sure it will, buddy. I've been keeping everything in order here. The bees are doing well, and I've even had some time to relax a bit. I built a little bonfire in the backyard fire pit, wanna roast some marshmallows?"

Sarah smiled, relieved to hear that everything was under control. "Thank you, Leo. I don't know what we'd do without you."

Leo waved off her gratitude with a laugh. "It's nothing. Just doing my part. Now, how about we get you all inside and warmed up?"

As they settled into the warmth of the cottage, Leo turned to Sarah with a thoughtful expression. "How's Eden holding up?"

Sarah sighed, her concern evident. "She's exhausted. Dr. Virgilio convinced her to take a day off and go to a spa. She needs it."

Leo nodded approvingly. "Good. She deserves a break. I think I'll give her a call and check on her, make sure she's doing alright."

Leo stepped outside to call Eden, dialing her number and waiting as the phone rang several times, but Eden didn't answer.

Leo sighed, leaving a brief message. "Hey, Eden, it's Leo. Just checking in to see how you're doing. Give me a call when you can. I hope you're taking some time to relax and not busy reading medical jargon. Talk to you later."

He wondered how her day was going, picturing her at the spa, wrapped in a plush robe, with a serene expression on her face. The thought brought a small smile to his lips, knowing that even in the midst of their worries, she deserved a little peace and comfort.

●

Eden had woken up in her room earlier that day at the Peruvian spa. The air was filled with the faint scent of lavender and eucalyptus, immediately soothing her senses. She stretched lazily, feeling the plush comfort of the bed beneath her. Today was a day dedicated to her well-being, and she was determined to make the most of it.

She sat up and reached for the small card on the bedside table. It was a list of affirmations provided by the spa, designed to start the day with positivity and intention. Eden read through the affirmations quietly, letting each one sink in:

"I am strong and capable."
"I am worthy of love and care."
"I embrace peace and serenity."
"I trust in my ability to heal."

Repeating the affirmations out loud, Eden felt a sense of calm wash over her. She closed her eyes, taking deep, steady breaths, allowing the words to resonate within her. This simple practice set the tone for the day, grounding her in a positive mindset.

Feeling more centered, Eden slipped out of bed and dressed in the spa's soft, comfortable robe. She made her way to the dining area, where a healthy breakfast awaited her. Fresh fruits, yogurt, and herbal teas were laid out in an inviting display. She chose a selection of vibrant berries, a bowl of creamy yogurt, and a cup of calming chamomile tea.

As she enjoyed her breakfast, Eden's mind wandered to Alex and the children. She felt a pang of worry in her stomach but reminded herself of the affirmations. She needed to take care of herself to be strong for them. After finishing her meal, she headed to the first session of the day.

The massage therapist, Lucia, greeted Eden with a warm smile. "Good morning, Eden. Ready to start your day of relaxation?"

Eden nodded, feeling the tension already beginning to melt away. "Yes, I really need this."

Lucia led her to a dimly lit room filled with calming music and the faint aroma of essential oils. "We'll start with a Swedish massage to help you relax, and then we'll move into some deeper tissue work. How does that sound?"

"That sounds perfect," Eden replied, lying down on the massage table.

As Lucia began to work on her muscles, she explained the benefits of the techniques she was using. "Swedish massage helps with overall relaxation, increases blood circulation, and can improve flexibility. It's great for relieving stress and tension."

Eden listened, fascinated by the detailed knowledge and care Lucia put into her work. "I can already feel the tension melting away. It's incredible."

Lucia smiled. "I'm glad to hear that. Just breathe deeply and let yourself relax."

As the session progressed, Eden felt the tension in her neck and shoulders gradually dissipate, replaced by a warm, soothing sensation. She marveled at how effective and immediate the relief felt, realizing that she had been carrying more tension than she had acknowledged.

After the massage, Eden was led to a room dedicated to Reiki, a practice she had heard of but never experienced. The Reiki practitioner, Miguel, greeted her with a serene smile.

"Good morning, Eden. Have you experienced Reiki before?" he asked.

Eden shook her head. "No, but I'm curious about it."

Miguel nodded. "Reiki is a form of energy healing that aims to balance the body's energy flow and promote healing. It involves channeling universal life energy through the practitioner to the recipient. Let's get started."

Eden lay on the treatment table, feeling a bit skeptical but open to the experience. Miguel placed his hands gently above various points on her body, beginning with her head and moving down to her feet.

As he worked, he explained, "I'll be focusing on your chakras, the energy centers of your body. Each chakra corresponds to different physical and emotional aspects of your being."

Eden felt a subtle warmth and tingling sensation as Miguel's hands hovered over her heart chakra. "I can feel the warmth. Is that normal?"

"Yes, that's the energy flowing through you," Miguel replied. "Reiki helps to remove energy blockages and restore balance. Just focus on your breath and let the energy flow."

By the time the session ended, Eden felt lighter, more balanced, and deeply relaxed.

"Thank you, Miguel. That was incredible," Eden said.

Miguel smiled warmly. "I'm glad you enjoyed it. Reiki can be a powerful tool for healing and relaxation."

After her Reiki session, Eden enjoyed a light lunch, savoring the fresh, healthy food that seemed to rejuvenate her weary body. Following lunch, she soaked in the soothing waters of a hot spring, feeling the tension melt away from her muscles once more. The warmth enveloped her, providing a much-needed respite from the stress she had been under.

Next, Eden was introduced to Pranayama, a series of breathing exercises designed to control the flow of prana, or life force energy, within the body. The instructor, Hector, greeted her with a serene smile and led her to a tranquil space with cushions and soft lighting.

Hector explained, "Pranayama is the practice of breath control. It helps to calm the mind, reduce stress, and improve overall well-being. We will start with Nadi Shodhana, or alternate nostril breathing."

Eden sat comfortably, following Hector's instructions. He demonstrated the technique, closing his right nostril with his thumb and inhaling deeply through his left nostril. He then closed his left nostril with his ring finger and exhaled through his right nostril. Eden mimicked his movements.

"Now, close your left nostril and inhale through your right," Hector instructed. "Then close your right nostril and exhale through your left. This completes one cycle."

Eden repeated the process, feeling a sense of calm wash over her. "This is very relaxing."

After several minutes, Hector introduced Kapalabhati, or skull-shining breath. "This technique involves short, powerful exhales and passive inhales. It energizes the body and clears the mind. Watch me first."

Hector demonstrated the technique, taking a deep breath in and then exhaling forcefully through his nose in rapid succession. Eden followed along, finding the practice invigorating. She felt a rush of energy with each breath, animating her entire being. The practice was both challenging and rejuvenating, leaving her feeling more alert and centered.

As the day progressed, Eden was introduced to Emotional Freedom Techniques (EFT), also known as tapping. The EFT practitioner, a compassionate woman named Claudia, explained that EFT involved tapping on specific meridian points on the body while focusing on negative emotions or physical sensations. This process was designed to release blockages in the body's energy system and promote healing.

Eden watched as Claudia demonstrated the technique, tapping lightly on points along her face, collarbone, and hands. Claudia encouraged Eden to follow along, tapping on the same points while repeating affirmations. Initially, Eden felt a bit self-conscious, but as she continued, she noticed a subtle shift in her emotional state. The repetitive tapping and affirmations seemed to calm her mind and ease her anxiety.

Claudia explained, "EFT works by addressing the emotional roots of physical symptoms and stress. It's a way to acknowledge and release negative emotions, allowing the body's energy to flow more freely."

Eden, tapping along with Claudia, repeated the affirmations quietly. "Even though I'm overwhelmed, I deeply and completely accept myself. Even though I'm worried about Alex, I choose to feel calm and peaceful."

As Eden continued tapping, her thoughts inevitably drifted back to Alex. The rhythmic tapping seemed to create a bridge between her conscious mind and the depths of Alex's unconscious state.

•

Alex was on the rowboat, now approaching the shore of the mysterious island. As the boat touched the shore, Alex stepped out, his feet sinking into the rough, uneven ground. The air was thick and warm, filled with the faint scent of sulfur.

In the distance, he heard a loud tapping noise, echoing through the stillness. The sound drew him toward a small, crude building made of rough stone. Inside, he found a classroom, oddly out of place among the surreal, otherworldly surroundings. Alex stood outside the classroom, listening in on the conversation taking place.

Inside the classroom, a younger version of himself sat at a desk, surrounded by other children. The younger Alex was tapping his pencil loudly, his expression one of frustration and discontent.

The other kids were singing, "If you're happy and you know it, clap your hands," their cheerful voices contrasting sharply with the younger Alex's sour mood.

The teacher, an older woman with angry eyes, noticed younger Alex's reluctance to join in. "Well, if you don't want to clap your hands, Alex, you can always stomp your feet!" she snarled.

Younger Alex frowned, his small face scrunching up in defiance. Without a word, he stood up and stomped his feet angrily, the sound reverberating through the classroom. He continued stomping out of the classroom, his footsteps heavy with anger.

As he stepped outside, he noticed the older Alex standing nearby. Younger Alex's eyes widened in recognition, finding joy in the surprise of seeing his older self. Suddenly, the classroom and the crude building disappeared, leaving them both standing next to large red rocks with small dead bushes scattered around the dry dirt.

"Hey! It's me... I'm you when you were younger," he said, his voice a mix of curiosity and disbelief. He magically picked up a ball lying on the ground and tossed it to the older Alex. "Hey, let's play ball."

Older Alex caught the ball reluctantly, feeling a strange mixture of nostalgia and unease. "Do you prefer reading comics or playing games?" younger Alex asked, his eyes shining with the innocence and curiosity of childhood.

Older Alex looked toward the center of the island, where he noticed the outline of a large, gnarled tree, its branches reaching out like skeletal arms.

"What? You're busy?" younger Alex interrupted, his voice painfully filled with hurt. His face twisted into a deep look of sadness, his small body shaking with sobs. "You don't have time for me...?"

Before older Alex could respond, younger Alex's form began to waver and blur, as if dissolving into the air. His tear-streaked face and the look of abandonment etched into his features were the last things older Alex saw before the younger version of himself disappeared completely.

The landscape around Alex began to shift and change colors, jagged cliffs and glowing lava pools morphing into being. It was as if the island itself was responding to the intense emotions of the encounter. Alex felt disoriented, yet strangely, he noticed that he had somehow gotten closer to the center of the island, nearer to the gnarled tree. Alex stood still for a moment, absorbing the transformation of his surroundings. The colors around him were more vivid, the atmosphere charged with a sense of foreboding. The twisted tree at the center of the island loomed larger, its branches reaching out to him, casting unusual shadows on the ground.

He felt a deep sense of regret and sorrow for his younger self. The unresolved emotions left a heavy weight on his chest, but there was no time to dwell on it. The island seemed to pulse with a life of its own, urging him to continue his journey.

●

The elevator doors slid open with a soft chime, and Gabriel stepped out, holding his son's hand. Gabriel's mind was preoccupied with thoughts of his friend Alex, his anxiety growing with each step he took toward the intensive care unit.

"Dad, look at this!" his son tugged at his sleeve, holding up a colorful drawing. Gabriel barely glanced at it, his thoughts consumed by the seriousness of the situation.

"Not now, buddy. We need to find Alex's room," Gabriel said, his voice distant.

"But Dad, it's important!" his son insisted, his small face scrunching up in determination.

"Later, okay?" Gabriel replied, walking briskly down the corridor. He felt a pang of guilt but pushed it aside, focusing on finding Alex's room.

Finally, they arrived at the ICU. Gabriel approached the nurse's station, where a young lady glanced up from her desk.

"I'm here to see Alex. Alex Freeman," Gabriel said, trying to keep his voice steady.

The nurse nodded, checking her chart. "Room 314. But visiting hours are almost over. You've got about 20 minutes, okay?"

Gabriel thanked her and hurried down the hall, his son still trailing behind him. As they reached the room, Gabriel hesitated for a moment before pushing the door open. The sight of Alex lying motionless on the bed, surrounded by monitors and IV lines, hit him hard. He swallowed, trying to hold back the surge of emotions.

His son tugged at his sleeve again. "Dad, look at my picture." Gabriel sighed, finally turning his attention to the drawing. It was a vibrant depiction of the two of them, with a big red heart in the center. His son had written in shaky letters, "I love you, Dad." Gabriel's eyes welled up with tears.

He knelt down, pulling his son into a tight hug. "I love you too, buddy. This is beautiful. Thank you, thank you so much."

The moment of tenderness brought a much-needed sense of relief. Gabriel stood up, still holding the drawing, and walked over to Alex's bed. He placed the picture on the bedside table next to the pet rock, hoping it would bring some light into the sterile room.

Just then, the door opened, and Dr. Virgilio walked in, holding a small vial. He nodded at Gabriel and glanced at the chart on the end of Alex's bed.

"I'm trying a new antibiotic," Dr. Virgilio explained. "It's not typically used for his condition, but it might help with some of the symptoms in his ear. At this point, we need to try every possible option."

Gabriel nodded, appreciating the doctor's determination. "Thank you, Doctor. All we can do is pray for the best."

Dr. Virgilio injected the antibiotic into Alex's IV line, his expression focused and intense. Gabriel pulled a chair next to Alex's bed, sitting down with his son on his lap. The room was filled with the soft beeping of monitors and the hum of machinery. Gabriel's thoughts wandered to the past, remembering all the good times he and Alex had shared. The laughter, the adventures, and the support they had given each other over the years.

Jacob snuggled closer, resting his head on Gabriel's chest. The warmth and innocence of his child's presence brought a bittersweet comfort. Gabriel held him close, feeling the steady rise and fall of his breathing.

"Alex is going to be okay, right?" his son asked, his voice small and uncertain.

Gabriel squeezed him gently. "Everybody is doing everything they can to make sure he gets better. We just have to keep hoping and praying."

They stayed by Alex's side for a little longer, Gabriel occasionally glancing at the monitors, willing them to show some sign of improvement. The minutes passed slowly, each one feeling like an eternity.

Finally, Dr. Virgilio returned. "I'm sorry, but it's time to go. You can come back tomorrow. You should go rest—it looks like you've had a long day."

Gabriel stood up, lifting his son into his arms. "Thank you, Doctor. We appreciate everything you're doing."

Dr. Virgilio nodded, his expression kind but firm. "Have a good evening and take care."

Gabriel carried his son out of the room, feeling the weight of the day pressing down on him. They walked down the corridor and out of the hospital. They found a nearby hotel, checked in, and settled into their room. Gabriel tucked his son into bed, his mind still racing with worry and fatigue.

"Goodnight, buddy," he whispered, brushing a kiss on his son's forehead.

"Goodnight, Dad. I love you," his son murmured sleepily.

"I love you too," Gabriel replied, feeling a sense of peace wash over him.

●

The morning light dazzled through Alex's hospital windows, highlighting the delicate snowflakes clinging to the glass. Outside, the world was wrapped in a fresh blanket of snow. Eden walked briskly down the hospital hallway, her heart pounding with a mixture of hope and anxiety. The spa retreat had given her a much-needed respite, but the weight of Alex's condition still hung heavily on her shoulders.

As she approached Alex's room, she took a deep breath, steadying herself. She pushed open the door and stepped inside, immediately noticing a change in the atmosphere. The oppressive tension that had gripped her the last time she was here seemed to have eased slightly.

Eden's eyes fell on Alex, lying peacefully in the hospital bed. The swelling on his face and around his ear had noticeably gone down, and the redness that had spread across his neck and head was beginning to fade. Her heart soared with cautious optimism. She approached the bed, her footsteps light and careful, as if afraid to disturb the fragile progress.

"Alex," she whispered softly, reaching out to gently touch his hand. The warmth of his skin reassured her, a stark contrast to the cold fear that had gripped her heart for so long. She leaned down, pressing a tender kiss to his forehead, her lips lingering as if willing him to wake up and smile at her.

Eden's eyes filled with tears, but she blinked them back, not wanting to let her emotions overwhelm her. She pulled a chair close to the bed and sat down, taking his hand in hers. She closed her eyes, her thoughts a whirlwind of prayers and hopes.

"Please, God," she murmured, her voice barely a whisper. "Please let him get better. Let him come back to us. The kids need their father, and I need him too. We've been through so much together, and I can't imagine life without him."

She squeezed his hand gently, her mind filled with memories of their journey together... their honeymoon in Egypt, the adventures and challenges they had faced, and the love that had carried them through the toughest times. Her heart ached with the longing for him to wake up, to see his eyes open and hear his voice again.

The door opened quietly, and Dr. Virgilio stepped in, a reassuring smile on his face. "Good morning, Eden. How are you feeling?"

Eden looked up, taking a deep breath. "Better. Thank you, Dr. Virgilio. I needed that time to recharge."

Dr. Virgilio nodded, his gaze shifting to Alex. "I have some good news. The new antibiotic seems to be working. The infection is retreating, and his vital signs are improving. We're not out of the woods yet, but this is a positive step."

Eden's heart leapt with relief. "Thank you, Doctor. Thank you so much for everything you're doing."

Dr. Virgilio gave her a reassuring nod. "It's our job, Eden. We'll continue to monitor him closely. I've started reducing the sedation, and he should wake up soon."

Eden nodded, feeling a surge of hope. "I'll be here, right by his side."

After Dr. Virgilio left, Eden settled back into her chair. She kept a steady vigil, her eyes never leaving Alex's face. Time seemed to blur as she watched the subtle signs of improvement, his breathing becoming more regular, the color returning to his skin. Hours passed, but Eden hardly noticed. She was lost in her thoughts and prayers, her heart filled with a deep, unwavering love for the man who had been her rock through so many storms. She thought about their children, Abigail and Isaac, and the joy they would feel when Alex finally woke up and came home to them.

Eden leaned forward, resting her head on the bed next to Alex's hand. She felt a sense of calm wash over her, a quiet assurance that everything was going to be alright. Her prayers were not just words; they were a lifeline, a connection to the hope that had kept her going through the darkest moments.

"Alex," she whispered, her voice filled with love and determination. "We're waiting for you. We need you. Please, come back to us."

●

Alex found himself standing at the center of the island, the twisted, gnarled tree looming over him like a silent sentinel. The trunk of the tree began to split and open. Suddenly, in front of him stood a large mirror, its surface rippling as if alive.

He hesitated for a moment before stepping closer, peering into the reflective surface. At first, he saw his own face, haggard and weary from the ordeal. But as he stared, the image began to distort, twisting into a grotesque, demonic version of himself. Horns sprouted from his forehead, and his eyes glowed with a malevolent light. The reflection sneered at him, its voice a chilling echo of his own.

A voice coming from the reflection in the mirror said to him, "I am the evil part of your mind. You can't beat me. Because you are the one who forced me into being."

Alex recoiled, feeling a surge of fear and anger. "No, that's not true. I didn't create you."

The evil version of himself laughed, a harsh, scratchy sound. "Oh, but you did. Every doubt, every fear, every moment of anger and hatred... I'm a part of you, and you can't get rid of me."

Alex felt a wave of despair wash over him. The island around him seemed to darken. The ground beneath his feet began to tremble, the twisted branches of the tree reaching out like skeletal fingers.

Suddenly, a voice from a loudspeaker echoed through the air, cutting through the darkness. "Know yourself, free your mind, and know what you must do. Your destiny has already been decided. You... I... Us... Where should we go?"

Alex felt a surge of defiance. He clenched his fists, his resolve hardening. "I want to go home! I want to be back with Eden and my children!"

With a primal scream, he lashed out at the mirror, his fist connecting with the glass. The mirror shattered, shards flying in all directions. The reflection of the evil, horned version of himself disintegrated, vanishing into the ether.

As the mirror shattered, the island began to dissolve around him, the colors blending into a surreal, psychedelic swirl. The ground beneath his feet seemed to melt away, and Alex felt himself being pulled into the vortex of light and color.

His body spun, the vivid nightmare breaking apart piece by piece, shimmering in the reflective shards of glass surrounding him. He could feel himself waking up, the surreal landscape fading into the background. The sensations of the real world started to seep in... the beeping of monitors, the soft murmur of voices, the warmth of a hand holding his.

With a final burst of willpower, Alex pushed through the remnants of the nightmare, his consciousness rising to the surface. He opened his eyes, blinking against the bright light of the hospital room. Eden was there, her face filled with relief and joy.

She squeezed his hand. "Alex, you're awake!"

He smiled weakly, his voice a hoarse whisper. "I'm back... I'm home."

Eden leaned down, kissing his forehead, her heart overflowing with gratitude. "Thank you, God. Thank you for bringing him back to us."

As Alex looked around the room, he saw the faces of his loved ones... Eden, Abigail, Isaac, Sarah, Leo, Gabriel, and his son, all standing around him with hopeful expressions. The nightmare was over, and he was surrounded by the people who mattered most.

He took a deep breath, feeling the warmth and love of his family envelop him. The journey had been long and arduous, but he had found his way back. Together, they would face whatever challenges lay ahead, their bond stronger than ever.

Eden held Alex's hand tightly, her eyes never leaving his. "You did it, Alex. You came back to us."

Alex smiled, his strength slowly returning. "I had to. I couldn't leave you all behind."

Abigail and Isaac climbed onto the bed, wrapping their small arms around their father. "We missed you, Daddy," Abigail said, her voice filled with emotion.

"I missed you too, sweetheart," Alex replied, hugging them both tightly. "More than you can imagine."

Gabriel stepped forward, his son at his side. "We've been praying for you, Alex. You're a fighter."

Alex nodded, feeling the weight of the journey lift from his shoulders. "Thank you, Gabriel. Thank you for everything."

Dr. Virgilio entered the room, a warm smile on his face. "It's good to see you awake, Alex. You've made remarkable progress. We'll continue to monitor you, but I'm optimistic you'll make a full recovery."

"Thank you, Doctor," Alex said, his voice filled with gratitude. "I owe you all my thanks."

"How long was I out?" Alex asked, his voice still weak but filled with curiosity.

Eden brushed a lock of hair from his forehead. "A little over four days. It felt like an eternity."

Alex nodded, absorbing the weight of her words. "It feels like I've been gone for much longer. I was living in a nightmare."

Eden smiled gently. "But you're back now, and that's all that matters."

Suddenly, the door opened, and in walked Alex's parents, George and Cindy, followed closely by Eden's mother, Maria. The room filled with warmth as the grandparents rushed to Alex's bedside, their faces a mixture of joy and relief.

"Alex, thank God you're alright," Cindy said, tears streaming down her cheeks as she embraced her son.

George, always the stoic one, placed a firm but loving hand on Alex's shoulder. "You gave us quite a scare, son, but I was irrefutably confident that you would recover."

Maria hugged Eden tightly before turning to Alex. "We were all so worried, but we never lost hope. We're here for you, all of us."

The room was filled with a sense of completeness, the family united once more. Abigail and Isaac, caught up in the joy of the reunion, excitedly shared their experiences from the past few days with their grandparents.

As the conversations flowed and laughter filled the room, Eden felt a profound sense of peace. "Do you remember when you told me there's no crying until the end?" Eden asked, a small smile playing on her lips.

Alex chuckled softly. "I remember."

"Well," she said, her eyes glistening with unshed tears, "this isn't the end. It's just the beginning, we have every moment moving forward to create a new life together."

Alex squeezed her hand, his heart full. "You're right. We have so much to look forward to."

Abigail and Isaac, sensing the moment, hugged their parents tightly. "We love you, Mom and Dad," they said in unison.

As the rest of the family and friends left the hospital, snow still falling gently outside, Eden remained with Alex through the night. Eden kicked off her shoes, sinking into the couch with a satisfied groan.

"So, what's next for us?" she said.

Alex sat up in his bed, grinning. "Whatever we want. Adventure's never been something we've shied away from."

Eden raised an eyebrow. "Adventure, huh? Sounds like trouble."

Alex winked. "The best kind."

※

<u>Lesson 9:</u>
<u>Holistic Well-being</u>

In this lesson, we explore the concept of holistic well-being, understanding that true vitality encompasses both physical and mental aspects. Within the realm of holistic well-being, we delve into three key areas: physical well-being, mental and emotional well-being, and energy management. Each of these facets plays a crucial role in nurturing health and vitality, and together, they form a comprehensive approach to holistic well-being.

First, we'll focus on physical well-being. We'll delve into strategies for exercise, nutrition, and self-care that promote optimal health. Through practical tips and guidance, you'll become empowered to create a personalized fitness and self-care plan. By embracing physical well-being, you'll discover the beautiful power of movement, nourishment, and self-care in enhancing your vitality and overall quality of life.

Next, we explore the realm of mental and emotional well-being. You'll recognize the importance of managing stress, enhancing mental resilience, and promoting emotional well-being. Through various techniques such as mindfulness and relaxation exercises, you will be equipped with practical tools to navigate life's challenges, cultivate inner peace, and foster emotional well-being. By nurturing your mental and emotional health, you'll discover a greater sense of clarity, balance, and joy in your daily life.

Finally, we'll explore the realm of energy management. Understanding the ebb and flow of our energy levels is key to maintaining vitality. We explore strategies for identifying energy-draining activities and making necessary adjustments to optimize our energy. By cultivating awareness of our energy levels and aligning our actions with our natural rhythms, we can sustain high levels of energy, productivity, and overall well-being.

Note: It is important to consult with healthcare professionals or certified experts for personalized advice on exercise, nutrition, and self-care practices based on individual needs and circumstances.

Physical Well-being

Physical well-being is a cornerstone of holistic health and vitality. In this section, we delve into strategies for exercise, nutrition, and self-care that contribute to optimal well-being. By understanding the importance of regular physical activity, balanced nutrition, and self-care practices, we can cultivate a foundation of vitality and longevity.

<u>Regular Physical Activity</u>: Regular physical activity is vital for maintaining physical health, boosting energy levels, and improving overall well-being. Engaging in exercise not only strengthens our muscles and cardiovascular system but also releases endorphins that enhance mood and reduce stress.

Experts recommend that adults aim for at least 150 minutes of moderate-intensity aerobic activity or 75 minutes of vigorous-intensity aerobic activity per week, along with muscle-strengthening activities at least twice a week. To incorporate exercise into your daily life, consider the following practical tips:

1. Find activities you enjoy: Choose exercises that align with your interests and preferences. Whether it's brisk walking, cycling, dancing, or playing a sport, engaging in activities you enjoy increases motivation and makes exercise more enjoyable.

2. Set realistic goals: Start with small, achievable goals and gradually increase intensity and duration. This approach helps you build momentum and maintain consistency in your exercise routine. You won't see results in a day or a week—it takes time, so don't be discouraged if you don't see immediate progress. It's a marathon, not a race.

3. Create a schedule: Consistency is key. Block out dedicated time for physical activity in your daily or weekly schedule. Treating exercise as a non-negotiable appointment with yourself increases the likelihood of following through. Be committed!

4. Stay active throughout the day: Look for opportunities to incorporate movement into your daily routine. Take the stairs instead

of the elevator, go for short walks during breaks, or engage in active hobbies like gardening or dancing.

Balanced Nutrition: Nutrition plays a fundamental role in supporting overall health and well-being. A balanced diet provides the necessary nutrients for optimal physical functioning, energy levels, and mental clarity.

Emphasize the importance of consuming a variety of whole foods, including fruits, vegetables, whole grains, lean proteins, and healthy fats. Consider the following guidelines for maintaining a balanced diet:

1. Portion control: Be mindful of portion sizes to avoid overeating. Listen to your body's hunger and fullness cues, and aim for a balanced distribution of macronutrients (carbohydrates, proteins, and fats) in your meals.

2. Hydration: Stay adequately hydrated by drinking plenty of water throughout the day. Water supports various bodily functions and helps maintain optimal energy levels. Avoid excessive caffeine, as a cup of coffee at 10 AM can linger in your system until 10 PM.

3. Mindful eating: Practice mindful eating by savoring each bite and paying attention to your body's hunger and satiety signals. Chew your food thoroughly and enjoy the process. By the end of the meal, you'll feel full and satisfied.

4. Limit processed foods: Minimize consumption of processed and sugary foods, as they often lack essential nutrients and can contribute to health issues when consumed in excess. Sugar is especially problematic, so aim to reduce your intake and be mindful of its presence in many processed foods.

Self-Care Practices: Self-care is a vital component of physical well-being. It involves nurturing your body, mind, and spirit to restore balance and promote overall health. Engaging in self-care activities allows you to recharge, reduce stress, and enhance your overall well-being.

Consider the following self-care practices to incorporate into your daily life:

1. Adequate rest and sleep: Prioritize getting enough sleep to support physical and mental rejuvenation. Establish a regular sleep routine and create a relaxing sleep environment. Aim for 6-8 hours of sleep per night. Avoid screens late at night, as the blue light emitted from devices can interfere with sleep. Instead, try reading, journaling, or meditating before bed.

2. Stress management: Develop stress management techniques that work for you, such as practicing mindfulness, deep breathing exercises, or engaging in activities that bring you joy and relaxation.

3. Time for relaxation: Carve out time for activities that bring you joy and relaxation, such as reading, listening to music, taking baths, or practicing hobbies.

4. Prioritize self-reflection: Engage in activities that promote self-reflection and self-awareness, such as journaling, meditation, or engaging in creative outlets.

By incorporating regular physical activity, balanced nutrition, and self-care practices into your daily life, you nourish your body, enhance your energy levels, and foster optimal physical well-being. Remember, small and consistent steps toward a healthier lifestyle can lead to significant long-term benefits. Take care of your body, and it will reward you with vitality and resilience.

Mental and Emotional Well-being

Stress is a universal experience—an inevitable part of life that touches us all. While some stress can be motivating, chronic stress is harmful, eroding both our mental and physical health over time. Without proper management, stress can spiral out of control, increasing the risk of anxiety, depression, cardiovascular issues, and even compromising our immune system. Essentially, unmanaged stress can be life-threatening. However, by learning how to manage stress effectively, we can safeguard our well-being and build resilience to face life's challenges with greater ease.

<u>Mindfulness</u>: Mindfulness is the art of being fully present in the moment, observing our thoughts, emotions, and bodily sensations without judgment. It's about living with intention rather than being on autopilot, allowing us to respond thoughtfully to situations rather than react impulsively. Practicing mindfulness helps us gain a deeper understanding of ourselves and our surroundings, promoting a sense of calm and clarity that can buffer the effects of stress.

Research has demonstrated that mindfulness can significantly reduce stress, enhance focus and attention, and improve overall well-being. For example, mindfulness-based stress reduction (MBSR) programs have been shown to lower cortisol levels, the hormone associated with stress, and increase gray matter in areas of the brain linked to learning and memory. By incorporating mindfulness into our daily lives, we can develop a heightened sense of self-awareness, which in turn fosters compassion and acceptance toward ourselves and others.

However, mindfulness is just one piece of the puzzle. To truly manage stress, we must also incorporate various relaxation techniques that activate the body's natural relaxation response. This response is the opposite of the stress response and involves slowing the heart rate, reducing blood pressure, and promoting a state of deep rest. Practicing these techniques daily can help us create a buffer against the stresses of modern life.

Here are some proven relaxation and self-care practices that you can easily incorporate into your daily routine:

1. Deep breathing exercises: Also known as diaphragmatic or belly breathing, this technique involves taking slow, deep breaths that engage the diaphragm. Inhale deeply through your nose, allowing your abdomen to expand, and then exhale slowly through your mouth. This practice slows down your heart rate, calms the nervous system, and promotes a sense of peace. It's a simple yet effective way to instantly reduce stress and center yourself.

2. Progressive muscle relaxation: This technique involves systematically tensing and then relaxing different muscle groups in

your body. Start at your toes and gradually work your way up to your head. As you tense each muscle group, hold the tension for a few seconds before releasing it completely. Pay close attention to how your body feels as the tension melts away. This practice not only helps reduce physical tension but also fosters a deep sense of relaxation and presence.

3. Guided imagery: This technique involves visualizing a peaceful and serene environment, engaging all your senses to create a vivid mental image. Close your eyes and imagine yourself in a calming setting, such as a beach, forest, or cozy cabin. Engage your senses—hear the sound of the waves, feel the warmth of the sun, smell the fresh air. Let this visualization transport you away from your stressors and into a state of tranquility.

4. Mindful movement: Engaging in gentle physical activities such as yoga, tai chi, or even a leisurely walk can help reduce stress and promote relaxation. These practices combine movement with breath awareness, helping to release tension, improve flexibility, and enhance overall well-being.

5. Journaling: Writing down your thoughts and feelings can be an excellent way to process emotions and gain perspective. Journaling allows you to express what's on your mind, providing clarity and helping you identify patterns or triggers that contribute to your stress.

6. Nature connection: Spending time in nature has been shown to reduce stress and improve mood. Whether it's a walk in the park, a hike in the woods, or simply sitting in your garden, being in nature helps us disconnect from the hustle and bustle of daily life and reconnect with the natural world.

Remember, everyone's path to mental and emotional well-being is unique. What works for one person may not work for another, so it's important to experiment with different techniques and practices to find what resonates with you. Don't be discouraged if something doesn't work right away—developing a stress management routine takes time and practice. It's also essential to seek professional guidance when needed, whether through therapy, counseling, or medical support. Most importantly, be patient and compassionate with yourself as you navigate this journey. By integrating stress management techniques, mindfulness practices, and self-care strategies into your life, you can create a foundation for mental and emotional well-being. These tools not only help you manage stress but also empower you to live a more balanced, fulfilling life. Embrace these practices as part of your daily routine and watch how they transform your relationship with stress and enhance your overall quality of life.

Energy Management

In this final section, we will explore the concept of energy management and its impact on our overall vitality and productivity. Understanding how to effectively manage our energy levels is crucial for maintaining a balanced and fulfilling life. Let's learn strategies for optimizing our energy. Energy is the fuel that drives our physical, mental, and emotional well-being. It affects our ability to focus, make decisions, and engage in various activities. It's important to recognize that energy is not solely dependent on sleep or physical rest but encompasses a broader spectrum of factors.

<u>Sources of Energy</u>: Our energy derives from various sources, including physical exercise, nutrition, sleep, relaxation, social interactions, and engagement in activities that bring us joy and fulfillment. These sources contribute to our overall energy levels and influence our vitality.

<u>Energy Patterns</u>: Energy levels fluctuate throughout the day, often following patterns commonly known as circadian rhythms. Recognizing these patterns can help us optimize our energy management. For example, many people experience a natural dip in energy levels in the afternoon, which can be mitigated with appropriate strategies. Life is full of patterns—look back at your life over time and see if you can identify any patterns. Do certain times of year make you feel certain ways? How did you feel 5 years ago, 10 years ago, 20 years ago? Life changes, but it always follows a cycle.

Here are some strategies for managing your energy effectively:

1. Identifying energy-draining activities: Start by reflecting on your daily routines and activities. Notice which ones leave you feeling drained, fatigued, or disengaged. These may include spending excessive time on social media, engaging in negative self-talk, or engaging in tasks that do not align with your passions or values.

2. Making necessary adjustments: Once you've identified energy-draining activities, explore ways to reduce or eliminate them from your routine. This may involve setting boundaries with technology, reevaluating commitments that no longer serve you, or delegating tasks that drain your energy. By making these adjustments, you create space for activities that replenish and uplift you.

3. Seeking energizing activities: Identify activities that boost your energy and bring you joy. These may include physical exercise, hobbies, spending time in nature, practicing mindfulness, engaging in creative pursuits, or connecting with loved ones. Make a conscious effort to incorporate these activities into your daily or weekly routine to sustain your energy levels.

4. Balancing rest and recovery: Just as physical exercise is essential for building strength, adequate rest and recovery are crucial for replenishing energy. Prioritize quality sleep, take breaks throughout the day, and engage in relaxation practices such as meditation or deep breathing exercises. By allowing yourself proper rest and recovery, you create space for renewed energy and vitality.

5. Listening to your body: Pay attention to the signals your body provides regarding energy levels. Notice when you feel fatigued or when you experience a surge of energy. Adjust your activities accordingly, taking breaks when needed and capitalizing on moments of high energy to tackle important tasks.

By understanding the concept of energy management and implementing these strategies, you can maintain high levels of energy, enhance your overall well-being, and maximize your productivity. Remember, energy management is a dynamic process that requires self-awareness, adaptability, and consistent practice. Take some time to reflect on your current energy levels and the activities that either drain or replenish your energy. Consider implementing the strategies discussed to optimize your energy management and experience a greater sense of vitality in your daily life.

Activity: Create a Personalized Fitness and Self-Care Plan

Now that we understand the significance of physical well-being, mindfulness, and energy management, let's embark on an exciting activity to create a personalized fitness and self-care plan. This plan will be tailored to your individual needs and preferences, allowing you to prioritize activities that promote your overall well-being. Are you ready? Let's go!

Step 1: Assess Your Current Lifestyle and Needs

Take a moment to reflect on your current lifestyle, including your daily routine, work commitments, and personal responsibilities. Consider the following questions:

1. How much time can I realistically allocate to physical activity, mindfulness, and self-care practices each day or week?

2. What are your current fitness levels and any specific areas you would like to improve?

3. Are there any physical limitations or health considerations that need to be taken into account?

By understanding your starting point, you can better design a plan that suits your lifestyle and helps you achieve your desired goals.

Step 2: Set Goals and Priorities

Identify your fitness, mindfulness, and self-care goals. Do you want to improve cardiovascular health, increase strength and flexibility, reduce stress, or achieve a better work-life balance? Setting clear and specific goals will provide direction and motivation throughout your journey. Use the SMART system from Chapter 4 if you need help getting organized.

Once you have your goals in mind, prioritize them based on their importance to you. This will help you focus your efforts and allocate your time effectively.

Step 3: Choose Activities that Bring Joy and Fulfillment

Think about the types of physical activities, mindfulness exercises, and self-care practices that resonate with you. It's important to choose activities that you genuinely enjoy, as it increases the likelihood of consistency and enjoyment.

Consider activities such as:

1. Physical exercise: Explore options like walking, jogging, swimming, dancing, yoga, or strength training. Choose activities that align with your interests and can be incorporated into your daily routine.

2. Mindfulness and relaxation exercises: Include practices like mindful breathing, progressive muscle relaxation, and guided imagery to support your mental and emotional well-being.

3. Energy-boosting activities: Identify hobbies, passions, or environments that uplift your spirits and increase your energy levels.

Step 4: Create a Schedule and Action Plan

Now, let's bring your personalized plan to life. Start by creating a weekly schedule that outlines when and how you will incorporate your chosen activities into your routine. Consider the following tips:

1. Be realistic: Set achievable goals and allocate time slots that fit well with your existing commitments. Avoid overwhelming yourself with too many activities at once.

2. Mix it up: Include a variety of activities to keep your routine exciting and prevent boredom. This can also help target different aspects of fitness, mindfulness, and well-being.

3. Be flexible: Recognize that life can sometimes throw curve balls, and it's okay to adjust your plan as needed. Be adaptable and find alternative ways to stay active and practice self-care during

challenging times.

Step 5: Track Your Progress and Adapt

As you embark on your fitness and self-care journey, keep track of your progress and make adjustments when necessary. Monitor how you feel physically, mentally, and emotionally after each activity. Reflect on the positive changes you notice and areas where you may need to tweak your plan. Remember, this is your personal journey, and the most important thing is to listen to your body and honor your needs.

Note: It's always a good idea to consult with healthcare professionals or certified experts before starting any new exercise or self-care program, especially if you have any underlying health conditions or concerns.

●

Throughout this lesson, we have explored the importance of prioritizing physical and mental well-being in our lives. We have delved into strategies for maintaining optimal physical health, managing stress, and promoting emotional well-being. Additionally, we have examined the concept of energy management and its impact on our overall vitality and productivity.

By incorporating the practices and techniques discussed in this lesson, we can cultivate a lifestyle that supports our well-being on multiple levels. Taking care of our physical bodies through regular exercise, balanced nutrition, and self-care practices lays a strong foundation for overall health.

Managing stress and promoting emotional well-being through mindfulness and relaxation techniques helps us navigate life's challenges with resilience and inner peace. Finally, by understanding energy levels and making necessary adjustments, we can optimize our vitality and productivity throughout the day.

Remember, the journey to nurturing health and vitality is a continuous one. It requires ongoing commitment, self-reflection, and adaptability. By prioritizing our well-being and incorporating these practices into our daily lives, we can experience the benefits of a balanced and vibrant existence.

As we conclude this lesson, I encourage you to take the knowledge and insights gained and apply them in your own life. Embrace the power of physical and mental well-being and let it serve as a solid foundation for your journey toward a fulfilling and joyful life. Remember, you hold the power to nurture your own health and vitality. So, make a commitment to yourself to continue this journey, knowing that every step you take toward nurturing your well-being is a step toward a more vibrant and fulfilling life.

Chapter 10: Old School

Everbrook was buzzing with excitement as summer vacation began. Sunlight filtered through the leafy oaks, casting playful shadows on the cobblestone streets. Birds sang cheerfully, and children's laughter filled the air. It was a peaceful morning, one of those rare, perfect days that seemed to promise endless possibilities.

Alex's alarm buzzed insistently, pulling him from a deep slumber. He groaned, reaching out to silence the noise, then lay still for a moment, savoring the quiet. Today was a big day. He and Eden were about to embark on a new adventure, each of them teaching a summer college course in the Big City.

He turned to see Eden already up, bustling around the room. She was zipping up the last of their suitcases, a focused look on her face.

"Morning," Alex said, stretching.

"Good morning," Eden replied with a smile. "Are you ready for this?"

"As ready as I'll ever be," Alex said, heading to the bathroom to freshen up. When he returned, Eden was setting their suitcases by the door.

In the next room, Isaac and Abigail, now ten years old, were engrossed in their devices, oblivious to the activity around them. Alex paused in the doorway, watching his children for a moment. They were so absorbed in their screens that they barely noticed their parents preparing to leave.

"Hey, you two," Alex called. "Come give us a hand, will you?" Isaac looked up briefly, his eyes barely focusing on Alex before returning to his game. Abigail didn't even glance up. Eden joined Alex at the doorway, shaking her head with a sigh.

"They're so hooked on those gadgets," she said softly. "It's like they're in their own little world."

Alex nodded thoughtfully. "Maybe it's time for a change," he said. "What if we have a tech-free summer?"

Eden raised an eyebrow. "You think they can handle it?"

"It'll be good for them," Alex said.

Eden smiled, nodding in agreement. "Alright, let's do it."

As Alex and Eden finished their final preparations, they moved to the kitchen, where the smell of fresh coffee filled the air. Eden poured them each a cup, and they sat down at the table.

"Alright," Alex said, taking a sip of his coffee. "How do we break the news to the kids?"

Eden thought for a moment. "We need to explain why we're doing this," she said. "It's not just about taking away their gadgets; it's about giving them a different kind of summer experience."

Alex nodded. "Agreed. We need to focus on the positives. All the activities they can do, the things they can learn, and the fun they'll have."

With a plan in mind, Alex and Eden called Isaac and Abigail into the living room. The kids shuffled in, eyes still glued to their screens.

"Hey, we need to talk," Eden said, gently taking the tablet from Abigail's hands. Isaac reluctantly put down his game controller.

"What's up?" Isaac asked, a hint of annoyance in his voice.

"We have something important to tell you," Alex began. "Your mom and I have decided that this summer is going to be different. We're going old school, baby! You two are going to have a tech-free summer." Isaac and Abigail stared at their parents, their faces a mix of confusion and disbelief.

"What do you mean, tech-free?" Abigail asked.

"That means no screens, no tablets, no video games, no smartphones," Eden explained.

"But how will we survive!?" Isaac exclaimed, his voice rising in panic.

"You'll survive just fine. Your mother and I survived without them growing up, and so can you," Alex said calmly. "Besides, there is so much more to the world you're missing out on with your heads stuck in those machines. Plus, we have a lot of fun activities planned. Your grandparents are coming to stay with you, and they have some great ideas for things to do over the summer."

Abigail crossed her arms, a pout forming on her lips. "This is so unfair," she muttered.

"I know it seems tough, and it's because you two are addicted to it," Eden said, "but we believe this will be good for you. It's a chance to try new things and spend more time together as a family."

"But all summer?" Isaac whined. "What if we get bored?"

"You won't," Alex assured him. "Your grandparents are going to make sure you have a great time. Trust us, you might even enjoy it."

The kids exchanged doubtful glances but said nothing more. Alex and Eden knew it would take time for them to adjust, but they were determined to make this summer memorable.

Later that morning, the sound of tires crunching on gravel announced the arrival of the grandparents. George and Cindy were the first to step out of their car, followed by Maria, who pulled up in her small blue hatchback. The kids ran outside to greet them.

"Grandkids!" George called out, sweeping Isaac into a bear hug while Cindy did the same with Abigail.

"Look how much you've grown!" Cindy exclaimed, ruffling Abigail's hair.

"As beautiful as ever," Maria remarked, giving each child a kiss on the cheek.

Isaac and Abigail's earlier gloom seemed to lift slightly at the sight of their grandparents. The excitement of seeing them softened the blow of the tech-free summer news. Inside, Alex and Eden finished packing the last of their bags. The grandparents helped carry the suitcases to the car, their presence filling the house with chatter and laughter.

"Alright, kids," Alex said, kneeling to their level. "We're heading out now. Remember to listen to your grandparents and have fun."

"We'll miss you," Eden added, hugging them tightly. "But we'll be back before you know it." Isaac and Abigail clung to their parents, the reality of their departure finally sinking in.

"We'll miss you too," Abigail whispered.

"Take care of each other, and try to get along!" Alex said, giving them one last hug before standing up.

As Alex and Eden drove away, the kids stood with their grandparents, waving until the car disappeared down the tree-lined road. George put a reassuring hand on Isaac's shoulder.

"Don't worry, buckaroo," he said with a twinkle in his eye. "We've got some great plans for this summer."

Back inside, the grandparents began to settle in. George immediately started talking about his big project. "I've always wanted to build a treehouse," George said, his eyes sparkling with excitement. "And this summer, we're going to do it."

Isaac's eyes widened with interest. "A treehouse? That sounds awesome!"

"Absolutely," George said. "It'll be a fun project, and we'll learn a lot along the way."

Cindy chimed in, "And while your grandpa is building the treehouse, I'm going to teach you all about beekeeping. We'll take care of the bees and learn how important they are to our environment."

Maria smiled warmly. "And we're going to have a beautiful garden this summer. We'll grow all sorts of plants and vegetables. You'll see how amazing it is to watch something grow from a tiny seed." The kids looked at each other, their eyes filled with a shared understanding, and then both let out a heavy sigh.

●

That afternoon, Isaac and Abigail decided to visit their Aunt Sarah, Uncle Gabriel, and cousin Jacob's house across the street. They needed to vent about the tech-free summer and hoped to find some solace with their favorite cousin. After Alex's stay in the hospital, Sarah and Gabriel had hit it off and started dating. In just a year, they were married, and now Sarah sings with Gabriel's band, quickly becoming a rising star in the industry.

When they arrived, Sarah greeted them with a smile. "Hey, kiddos! What brings you here?"

"We're here to see Jacob," Isaac said. "Is he around?"

Gabriel stepped out, wiping his hands on a rag. "Actually, we're just about to leave for the summer. We're going on tour with the band, singing all over the place."

Isaac and Abigail's faces fell. "So, Jacob's going too?" Abigail asked.

"Yep," Jacob said, coming out of the house with his backpack. "We're going to be performing all summer with Dad's band, The Runaway 6. I'm even learning to play the accordion for the polkas!"

Isaac and Abigail tried to hide their disappointment. "That sounds really cool," Isaac said. "We'll miss you, though."

"I'll miss you too," Jacob said, giving them each a hug. "But I'll tell you all about it when I get back."

As they got on their bikes, the weight of the summer ahead seemed a little heavier. But they were determined to make the best of it.

Instead of going home right away, they decided to take a bike ride down Old Dirt Hill Road. The road was known for its winding paths and steep hills, providing a bit of adventure, though the kids' spirits were low.

"This summer is going to be so boring without our gadgets," Isaac complained, pedaling hard up a hill.

"And now Jacob's gone too," Abigail added, panting slightly. "We don't even have him to hang out with."

They continued riding, bickering about the unfairness of their situation.

"You're always so negative!" Abigail snapped. "Maybe if you tried to have fun, it wouldn't be so bad."

Isaac glared at her. "Yeah, right, like you're Miss Sunshine yourself."

As they approached the top of a particularly steep hill, Abigail smirked. "Let's race. First one to the bottom wins."

"Fine," Isaac said, determined to beat her.

They took off, racing down the hill, the wind whipping through their hair. Abigail, seeing Isaac gaining on her, decided to take a shortcut through the grass, cutting him off.

"Hey, that's cheating!" Isaac shouted.

"All's fair in a race!" Abigail called back, laughing.

Distracted by his anger, Isaac hit a loose patch of gravel and lost control of his bike. He tumbled to the ground, scraping his knees on the rough road.

"Ouch!" he cried out, tears springing to his eyes as he inspected the small rocks embedded in his knees.

Abigail, realizing what had happened, skidded to a stop and turned back. "Quit whining, Isaac! You're fine!"

"Do I look okay?" Isaac snapped, trying to hold back his tears.

When they returned to the house, Isaac limping slightly, George, Cindy, and Maria were waiting for them on the porch. They quickly noticed Isaac's injuries.

"What happened?" George asked, concerned.

"We were racing," Abigail admitted, looking down. "And I... I might have cheated."

George guided Isaac to a chair and began cleaning his wounds. "Looks like you took quite a spill. But don't worry, these will heal up in no time."

As he worked, George settled into his storytelling mode. "Let me tell you about the time I confronted the legendary Chad the Rooster," he began, pausing for dramatic effect.

The kids leaned forward, captivated. They had heard tidbits of this tale but never the full story.

"Now, Chad was no ordinary rooster," George continued conspiratorially. "He was a massive bird with fiery red plumage, a crooked beak, and a personality as prickly as a porcupine."

George described Chad's taste for mischief... chasing terrified mailmen down the road, pecking incessantly at his own reflection, and crowing at ungodly hours.

"But for some reason, Chad reserved his spiciest sauce for none other than me!" George paused for a few seconds before saying, "Every morning, Chad would crow at the crack of dawn, right outside my window. And if that wasn't enough, he'd chase me every time I stepped outside," George said, rolling his eyes.

The kids giggled at the thought of their grandfather being chased by a rooster.

"One time," George continued, "Chad even managed to sneak into the house. I found him in the kitchen, pecking at the bread on the counter. It was a disaster!"

George recounted tales of being ambushed on the way to the bus and stared down with Chad's beady, unblinking glare. "But the worst was when Chad decided he didn't like me collecting the eggs. He'd wait until I reached into the coop, then peck at my hands until I dropped them."

The kids were in stitches, envisioning the scenes.

"Did you ever catch him?" Isaac asked, wincing as George dabbed at his knees.

"The day finally came," George said with a smile. "I finally had enough. Armed with nothing but a loaf of uncut bread and my quick wit, I approached Chad, who was sunbathing audaciously in the yard. When Chad caught sight of me, his feathers flared out menacingly like a deadly flower blooming." George demonstrated, puffing out his arms. "He let out a bone-rattling crow and came charging!"

The kids gasped.

"What did you do?" Abigail asked, eyes wide.

"I stood my ground," George said, "and held out a piece of bread. Chad stopped, eyeing it suspiciously. After a tense moment, he snatched the bread and strutted away, as if he'd won some great battle."

George grinned, imitating Chad's cocky head bob. "And from that day on, Chad and I had an understanding. Whenever he saw me coming, he'd give me a little nod, and I'd toss him a piece of bread."

The kids burst into laughter, imagining the proud rooster and their grandfather's antics.

"See," George said, making eye contact with Isaac and Abigail, "sometimes our fears seem scarier than they really are. With a little humor and courage, you can face anything."

Isaac, feeling the sting of his scraped knees lessen, looked at Abigail.

"I guess we can try to get along," Abigail said reluctantly.

Isaac nodded. "Yeah, I guess we can."

George smiled at them both. "That's the spirit. Now, let's get started on that tree house."

As the family gathered on the porch, George looked up at the sky, noticing the heavy clouds gathering in the distance.

"Looks like we might be in for some heavy rain this summer," he remarked. "Remember the big flood we had years ago? We should keep an eye on the weather, especially downtown."

Cindy nodded. "That flood caused quite a bit of damage. It reached the first floor of most of the major buildings. Let's hope it doesn't get that bad again, but it's always good to be prepared."

Isaac and Abigail exchanged curious glances.

"What happened during the flood?" Isaac asked.

George sighed. "It was quite the ordeal. The river overflowed, and downtown Everbrook was underwater for almost a day. A lot of businesses were affected, and it took a long time to recover. With all this rain coming, we need to be vigilant."

●

The following day dawned bright and clear, a perfect day for a trip to the market. George had already headed to the hardware store to pick up supplies for the treehouse, leaving Cindy and Maria to take the kids to the local market.

"Alright, everyone," Cindy called, gathering Isaac and Abigail in the kitchen. "We're heading to the market to get some plants and supplies for our garden."

Isaac and Abigail exchanged curious glances. The idea of a trip to the market sounded interesting, and it was a chance to do something different.

When they arrived, the local market was bustling with activity. Stalls brimming with fresh produce, vibrant flowers, and handmade goods lined the streets. The air was filled with the scent of baked bread, spices, and blooming flowers.

"Wow, look at all this," Abigail said, her eyes wide with wonder.

"Stick close," Cindy said, holding out a list. "We have a lot to get today."

Maria led the way, pointing out various stalls and explaining what they were looking for. "We need to get everything planted before the storm hits next week," she said. "The weatherman says it's going to last for about two weeks, so we want to make sure everything is well-established by then."

Isaac and Abigail nodded, understanding the urgency. They followed their grandparents through the market, taking in all the sights and sounds.

Maria led them to a stall overflowing with seedlings and young plants. "First, we need to pick out some plants for our garden," she said. "What do you think we should grow?"

Isaac and Abigail looked over the options, excitedly discussing the possibilities. They chose a mix of vegetables and herbs, envisioning the garden they would create. As they moved through the market, they heard vendors calling out their wares, and the kids marveled at the variety of goods on display. The bustling atmosphere was filled with energy, and the children felt a sense of excitement about their gardening project.

At the far end of the market, they came across a stall decorated with colorful peppers of all shapes and sizes. A short man with a bushy beard and a somewhat angry expression stood behind the table, his eyes scrutinizing the passersby.

"Welcome to Mark's Pepper Paradise," he said in a gruff voice. "What can I interest you in today?"

Maria began to explain their plan to grow peppers, but Mark interrupted, his stern face softening slightly as he listened.

"Growing peppers, huh?" he muttered, rubbing his chin. "Not a bad idea. But if you're going to do it, you should do it right. How about a little competition?"

Isaac and Abigail's eyes lit up with interest. "A competition?" Abigail asked.

"Yeah," Mark said, leaning forward with a mischievous look. "Each of you will grow your own pepper plants. We'll see who can grow the best peppers by the end of the summer. The winner gets a special prize from me."

Abigail looked at Isaac, her excitement growing. "That sounds awesome!"

"Deal," Isaac said, shaking Mark's hand.

Mark's eyes, though still stern, held a hint of amusement. "Alright then. You'll need these." He handed them a variety of pepper seedlings, already sprouting. "Take good care of these, and you'll have a real contest on your hands."

Isaac and Abigail looked at the pepper sprouts with determination, imagining the contest at the end of the summer.

"Since we want to grow our own peppers," Isaac said, "can we get some pots for ourselves?"

Cindy smiled, pleased to see their enthusiasm. "Of course!"

As they picked out the pots, Mark leaned in, lowering his voice. "Growing peppers is an art," he said. "They need just the right amount of sunlight and water. But if you do it right, you'll have the best peppers in town. Heck, they might even turn out to be better than mine, and mine are the third-best in the world!"

Isaac and Abigail hung on his every word, determined to grow the best peppers for the contest.

"Remember," Mark added, his voice taking on a serious tone, "peppers need patience. You can't rush them. Give them time, and they'll reward you."

As they finished their conversation, the kids felt a mix of excitement and determination. The idea of the contest added a new layer of interest to their gardening project.

Loaded with their new plants and supplies, the family headed back home. The kids chattered excitedly about their plans for the garden and the pepper contest.

"Today was fun," Isaac said, a hint of surprise in his voice.

"Yeah," Abigail agreed. "I can't wait to see our garden grow."

George returned from the hardware store just as they arrived, his truck filled with lumber and tools. "Looks like you had a successful trip," he said, glancing at their haul.

"We did," Cindy replied. "We got everything we need for the garden and more."

The family spent the afternoon preparing the garden beds and planting the seedlings. Isaac and Abigail carefully planted their pepper sprouts in their pots, taking Mark's advice to heart. As they worked, the anticipation of the upcoming storm added a sense of urgency to their efforts. They knew they had limited time to get everything in place before the weather turned.

"Let's get these last few in the ground," Maria said, her voice determined.

With the final plants in place, they stood back to admire their work, the garden beds neat and orderly, the pots arranged in a row.

"We did it," Abigail said, a sense of accomplishment in her voice.

"Now we just need to keep them watered and watch them grow,"

Cindy said.

As they cleaned up and headed inside, the kids felt a growing sense of anticipation and excitement, looking forward to the summer's challenges and adventures.

●

While the family settled into their routine back at the cottage, Alex and Eden had embarked on their own adventure in the Big City. The drive from their country home took a couple of hours, the scenery shifting from rolling hills to the bustling urban landscape. The city's skyline came into view, bringing with it a wave of nostalgia.

"This place hasn't changed much," Alex remarked as they navigated the familiar streets. "Remember when we used to come here every weekend?"

Eden smiled, her eyes scanning the buildings and parks they had once frequented. "I do. It feels like just yesterday we were exploring every corner of this city, dreaming about the future."

They pulled into the parking lot of the college where they would be teaching for the summer. The campus was vibrant with students milling about, and the air buzzed with academic energy. Alex and Eden stepped out of the car, taking in the sight of the ivy-covered buildings and the expansive quad.

"It's good to be back," Eden said, linking arms with Alex as they walked towards the administration building. "I can't wait to start this new chapter."

After meeting with the college administration and receiving their schedules, Alex and Eden made their way to Maria's apartment. She had graciously offered her city apartment for them to stay in while they taught.

"Mom's place hasn't changed a bit," Eden commented as they entered the cozy apartment. The walls were decorated with family photos, and the shelves were filled with books and mementos from their travels.

"It feels like home," Alex agreed, setting their bags down. "I think this will be a good home base for us this summer."

The first day of classes arrived with a mix of excitement and nerves. Eden, with her years of experience in medicine, had always been confident in her field. But standing in front of a classroom full of eager students was a new challenge. In her classroom, Eden began her lecture on "Innovative Approaches to Functional Medicine and Holistic Healing." She spoke passionately about her experiences and research, engaging the students with real-life examples and interactive discussions. Despite her initial jitters, she found herself enjoying the dynamic exchange of ideas.

Meanwhile, Alex was across campus, preparing for his first creative writing class. His love for storytelling had led him to write several successful novels, but teaching was an entirely new venture. He took a deep breath as he entered the classroom, greeting the students with a warm smile.

"Welcome to Creative Writing 101," he began, his voice steady despite the butterflies in his stomach. "I'm Alex, and over the next few weeks, we're going to explore the art of storytelling together. You may have read some of my books, like *The Nile's Redemption*, or my new hit series, *My Secret Life, Volumes 1-3*. I hope you're ready to have some fun this summer!"

As the week progressed, both Alex and Eden settled into their roles as educators. They spent their evenings discussing their classes, sharing triumphs and challenges over dinner at local restaurants. The experience of teaching brought them closer, reminding them of the early days of their relationship when they had dreamed of making a difference in the world together.

Eden's classroom became a hub of lively debates and thoughtful discussions. She encouraged her students to think critically about healthcare practices, pushing them to consider innovative solutions. Her passion for the subject was contagious, inspiring her students to delve deeper into their studies.

Alex's creative writing class was equally engaging. He fostered an environment where students felt free to express their ideas and hone their craft. They explored different genres, experimented with narrative techniques, and critiqued each other's work in a supportive atmosphere. Alex reveled in seeing his students grow as writers, their stories becoming more compelling even in just a few days.

One afternoon, as Eden crossed the quad, she was struck by a vivid memory. She paused near a bench under a large oak tree, remembering a pivotal moment in her past. This was where she had discovered the truth about Monica, who had tearfully admitted to having an affair with Eden's boyfriend at the time.

Although Monica had died during childbirth, the memory was a blunt reminder of how far Eden had come. She shook off the sadness and continued walking, feeling a renewed sense of purpose. Her life had changed so much since then, and now, with Alex by her side, she felt stronger than ever.

Despite the long days and the challenges of teaching, Alex and Eden found joy in their new roles. They reconnected with the city they loved and discovered new facets of each other through their shared experiences. Their first two weeks of teaching had brought them closer together, rekindling their love and reminding them of the dreams they had once shared. The summer was just beginning, and there were many more adventures to come.

●

The bright morning sun signaled the start of a productive day at the cottage. Cindy gathered Isaac and Abigail in the backyard near the beehives. The rhythmic hum of bees filled the air, creating a soothing backdrop.

"Today, we're going to dive into the world of beekeeping," Cindy announced, her face alight with enthusiasm. "Bees are fascinating creatures, and there's so much we can learn from them."

Isaac and Abigail listened attentively as Cindy began her introduction. She explained the role of bees in pollination and their crucial importance to the environment.

"Without bees, many of the foods we love wouldn't exist," she said. "They're nature's tiny workers, ensuring plants can reproduce and bear fruit."

Cindy led them to a small table where beekeeping suits and equipment were laid out. "Safety first," she said, helping the kids into the suits. The protective gear felt strange but comforting, and the kids couldn't help but feel a sense of adventure.

As they approached the hives, Cindy spoke about the structure and society of bees.

"A beehive is a marvel of nature," she said. "Each bee has a specific role, and together, they create harmony."

She carefully opened one of the hives, revealing the intricate honeycombs.

"Look at the geometry," Cindy pointed out. "Each cell is a perfect hexagon, the most efficient shape for space and storage. It's like nature's blueprint for perfection."

Isaac and Abigail leaned in closer, marveling at the precise patterns. Cindy's voice took on a more philosophical tone.

"The hexagon is a symbol of balance and harmony," she said. "Just as bees work together to build these structures, we too can create something beautiful when we work in unity."

Cindy's words resonated with the kids as she explained the roles within the hive.

"The worker bees, the drones, and the queen each have their purpose. The queen, though she doesn't rule in the way a monarch might, is central to the hive's function."

She pointed to the queen, larger and more distinct than the other bees.

"The queen's primary role is to lay eggs and ensure the hive's continuity. Her presence influences the behavior and harmony of the entire colony."

Isaac watched, fascinated.

"So, she's like the heart of the hive?"

"Exactly," Cindy replied. "And just as a heart must be healthy for the body to thrive, the queen's well-being is vital for the hive's success."

The philosophical musings deepened as Cindy discussed the bees' industrious nature.

"Bees are symbols of hard work and diligence. They toil tirelessly, each small action contributing to the greater good. There's a lesson in that for all of us."

Cindy then guided the kids through a hands-on lesson. She showed them how to gently handle the frames, check for honey, and inspect the health of the bees.

"Always be calm and deliberate," she advised. "Bees sense our energy. If we're calm, they're calm. Bees rely on the flowers for nectar, and flowers rely on bees for pollination. It's a beautiful cycle of give and take, reminding us of the balance in nature."

Isaac carefully held a frame, watching the bees move methodically.

"It's like they're all connected, part of something bigger," he observed.

Cindy nodded. "That's right. And just like the bees, we're all part of something larger. Every action we take impacts the world around us."

The afternoon passed in a blend of technical instruction and philosophical reflection. Cindy's passion for beekeeping was infectious, and the kids felt a growing respect for the tiny creatures and their intricate world.

As they finished their lesson, Cindy closed the hive and led the kids back to the garden table.

"Beekeeping teaches us patience, precision, and humility," she said. "It's a reminder that even the smallest beings have a crucial role to play."

Isaac and Abigail looked at the beehives with newfound appreciation.

"I never knew bees were so amazing," Abigail said, her eyes wide with wonder.

"They are," Cindy agreed. "And there's always more to learn. Beekeeping is a journey of discovery, much like life itself."

The kids felt a deep sense of satisfaction as they removed their beekeeping suits. They had not only learned about bees but also about the deeper connections that bind all living things.

Later that afternoon, Isaac and Abigail joined George in the backyard, surrounded by lumber and tools. George was meticulously measuring and cutting wood for the tree house frame.

"Hey, Grandpa! How's it going?" Isaac called out as they approached.

George looked up with a smile. "Just in time. I could use some extra hands."

Isaac and Abigail eagerly joined him, ready to assist. George handed them each a small task, explaining the basics of carpentry as they worked.

"Hold this piece steady while I hammer it in place," George instructed, showing Isaac how to position the board. "And always make sure your measurements are precise. A little error can throw off the whole structure."

As they worked, George shared stories about his own childhood.

"You know, I grew up in this cottage. I always wanted a tree house right here when I was your age, but my parents wouldn't allow it," he said. "Building one now feels like a dream come true."

The kids listened intently, their excitement growing as the tree house started to take shape. George's enthusiasm was contagious, and they felt a sense of pride in contributing to the project.

"Carpentry is all about patience and precision," George explained. "Just like with the bees, every small action contributes to the bigger picture."

Isaac and Abigail took turns holding tools, passing materials, and helping with the construction. With each piece they added, the tree house became more real, fueling their anticipation for the final product. By the end of the day, the tree house had a solid frame and was beginning to look like a true structure. Isaac and Abigail couldn't wait to see the finished product.

A couple of days later, Maria decided it was time to focus on the garden. She called Isaac and Abigail to join her near the garden beds, where the seedlings they had planted at the market were waiting to be tended.

"Today, we're going to learn about caring for our plants," Maria said, her voice warm and inviting. "Gardening teaches us about patience and nurturing."

They walked through the garden, discussing the various types of plants and their needs. Maria pointed out the vegetables, herbs, and flowers they had planted, explaining how each one contributed to the garden's ecosystem.

"The peppers you planted in the pots are looking good," Maria said, inspecting the small sprouts. "Remember what Mark said about taking care of them?"

Isaac nodded. "He said they need the right amount of sunlight and water, and we have to be patient."

"Exactly," Maria replied. She led the kids to a sunny spot indoors where the pepper pots had been set up.

"We'll take care of them here until the storm passes. This way, they'll be safe and still get the light they need."

As they worked on caring for the pepper plants, Maria shared her wisdom about growth and patience.

"Plants take time to grow," she said. "You can't rush them. But if you care for them and give them what they need, they'll flourish."

Abigail looked at the tiny pepper sprouts with determination.

"I want mine to be the best."

"They will be," Maria assured her. "As long as you put in the effort and care."

They spent the afternoon tending to the garden, pulling weeds, checking for pests, and making sure the plants were healthy. Maria's gentle guidance and the kids' eager participation created a peaceful and productive atmosphere.

"Gardening teaches us that growth is a slow and steady process," Maria said. "It's about nurturing and believing in the potential of each tiny seed. If you treat life the same way, you'll be amazed at the things you can achieve."

Isaac and Abigail felt a deep sense of connection to the garden. The act of caring for their plants became more than just a task; it was a lesson in life.

As the sun began to set, Maria gathered the kids for a final reflection.

"Remember, everything in nature is connected," she said. "Just like the bees and the plants, we all play a part in creating harmony."

The kids nodded, feeling a sense of accomplishment and a deeper understanding of the natural world. The lessons they learned in the garden, combined with their experiences in beekeeping and carpentry, were shaping their summer into a journey of growth and discovery.

●

Alex and Eden had found their rhythm at the college, settling comfortably into their roles as professors. The days passed swiftly, marked by the steady hum of lectures, grading papers, and mentoring students. Both were passionate about their work but they also knew how easy it was to get lost in the routine.

Despite the whirlwind of their new responsibilities, they made it a point to carve out time for each other. They often spent quiet evenings together, sharing the small details of their day, enjoying the simple pleasures of a life built on mutual respect and deep affection. Even as they juggled their careers, they remained each other's anchor, never letting the demands of their work pull them too far apart.

One afternoon, after a particularly busy week, Eden received a message from Maya, an old friend who was visiting the city. Eden smiled as she read the message, feeling a sense of excitement at the thought of reconnecting. It had been too long since they'd all been together. With a glance at Alex, who was focused on a stack of essays, she decided it was time to break the routine. She walked over, placed her hand on his shoulder, and suggested they meet Maya at the Midnight Bakery.

The day of the meeting with Maya arrived, and the air was thick with the kind of tension that always precedes a storm. Dark clouds gathered slowly on the horizon, casting a muted glow over the city as Alex and Eden prepared to leave. Eden noticed the slight chill in the air as she pulled on her coat, the wind beginning to pick up, carrying the scent of rain.

"Looks like we might get caught in a downpour," Alex remarked, glancing out the window. There was a certain electricity in the air, a quiet energy that seemed to heighten everything.

Eden smiled, zipping up her jacket. "Perfect weather for reminiscing over coffee and pastries," she said with a wink. "I'm looking forward to seeing Maya again. It's been too long."

"Yeah, it has," Alex agreed, slipping his arm around her waist as they walked to the door. "And the Midnight Bakery… feels like we're stepping back into a time capsule. Remember when we used to talk about how close we came to meeting there before we actually met?"

Eden nodded, her eyes softening with the memory. "It's funny how things work out. I think that's why I wanted to meet Maya there —it feels right, like coming full circle."

As they stepped outside, the wind tugged at their clothes, the sky darkening further. Alex looked up, squinting at the clouds. "We should probably bring an umbrella, just in case. Something tells me we'll need it."

Eden laughed lightly, taking his hand. "Let's take our chances. Besides, a little rain never hurt anyone. It might even add to the nostalgia."

Alex grinned, squeezing her hand as they began their walk. "You always find a way to make things more interesting, don't you?"

Eden leaned into him slightly as they walked, a comfortable silence settling between them for a moment. "I try," she said softly. "Let's just enjoy today. Who knows what the storm might bring?"

As Alex and Eden approached the Midnight Bakery, the familiar glow from its windows welcomed them, a comforting contrast to the darkening sky. The sign above the door, slightly weathered, still bore the name that held so many memories for them. The air was cool, with just a hint of something brewing in the distance, but that wasn't what occupied their thoughts. They were here, together, ready to reconnect with an old friend and relive the warmth of a place that had always felt like a quiet refuge.

The moment they stepped inside, Alex and Eden were greeted by the familiar scent of freshly baked pastries. The bakery was just as they remembered—cozy, inviting, with warm lights casting a soft glow over the rustic wooden tables. As they took it all in, Alex spotted a familiar face at a corner table.

"Alex! Eden!" Emmanuel's voice rang out with the same warmth it always had. He stood up, beaming as he approached them. "It's been far too long!"

The three embraced, and for a brief moment, it felt as if no time had passed at all. Emmanuel, with his ever-present twinkle in his eye, was just as they remembered—full of life and stories waiting to be told.

"It's so good to see you, Emmanuel," Alex said, feeling a wave of nostalgia. "We've missed you."

"And I've missed you both," Emmanuel replied, guiding them to his table. "Come, sit. Let's catch up properly."

They settled in, the bakery's warmth wrapping around them as they began to reminisce about old times. The conversation flowed easily, with laughter and fond memories filling the space between them. Despite the years apart, it felt like no time had passed at all.

Just as they were settling into their conversation, the bakery door swung open, and a burst of energy entered the room. Maya, with her ever-radiant smile, spotted Alex and Eden immediately and made a beeline for their table.

"There you two are!" Maya exclaimed, her voice full of warmth. "I've missed you both so much!"

"Maya!" Eden stood up to embrace her, laughter in her voice. "It's been way too long."

Maya hugged Alex next, her smile never faltering. "I'm so glad we could meet up. It feels like ages since we've all been together."

They pulled up another chair, and Maya joined the conversation seamlessly. The atmosphere was light and joyful, filled with updates on life, work, and family. Maya's stories brought a fresh energy to the table, her presence a perfect complement to the nostalgia that

Emmanuel's had stirred.

"You'll never guess who I ran into recently," Maya said with a mischievous grin. "Nate."

Eden raised an eyebrow, exchanging a quick glance with Alex. "Nate? How's he doing?"

"Still the same," Maya replied with a shrug. "It's strange to see how much we've all changed, and yet some people just… don't."

Alex nodded thoughtfully. "It's true. Growth is everything. It's what keeps us moving forward."

As they talked, Emmanuel leaned back, his expression thoughtful. "You're right, Alex. Life is about growth," he began, his voice calm and reflective. "But it's also about knowing when to embrace change. Sometimes, it's the unexpected twists that lead us to where we need to be."

Maya smiled, but this time it was softer, more contemplative. "That's true. Change is important, but so is not taking everything too seriously. I mean, who would've thought we'd all end up here today, in this bakery, years later? Sometimes, life's little detours are the best part."

Eden nodded, squeezing Alex's hand gently. "It's those unexpected moments that remind us of what really matters—like being here, with the people who know us best."

Alex glanced at Emmanuel and then at Maya, a smile tugging at the corners of his lips. "And it doesn't hurt to have good friends along the way to share those detours with."

Emmanuel raised his coffee cup slightly, his eyes twinkling. "To growth, change, and the company of friends who've been with us through it all."

Maya clinked her cup against the others, adding, "And to the unexpected moments that make life interesting."

The mood at the table was perfect—a blend of reflection, warmth, and just the right touch of humor. The conversation flowed naturally, a reminder of how deep their bonds ran and how far they had come together.

As the evening wore on, the conversation eventually slowed, transitioning from shared memories to a comfortable silence. The warmth of the bakery, combined with the rich history they all shared, left them feeling content and connected. Emmanuel finally rose, signaling the time had come to part ways.

"It's been wonderful catching up," Emmanuel said, his voice full of warmth. "Don't be strangers, you two. Keep in touch."

"Absolutely," Alex replied, giving him a firm handshake, followed by a hug. "Take care, Emmanuel."

Maya hugged both of them tightly. "We'll do this again soon. No excuses."

With final goodbyes exchanged, Alex and Eden stepped out of the bakery and into the cool evening air. The sky was now a deep, velvety blue, the city lights flickering on one by one. The storm still loomed, but it remained a distant threat, allowing the night to feel serene and full of possibility.

Hand in hand, they walked through the quiet streets, the glow of the city reflecting off the damp pavement. The sounds of the city softened around them, leaving them in their own little world. As they approached a small plaza with a view of the skyline, Alex suddenly stopped.

"Eden," he said, turning to her with a playful grin. "How about a dance?"

She laughed softly, looking around at the empty plaza. "Here? Now?"

"Why not?" he replied, pulling her closer. "No one's watching but the city."

Without another word, he guided her into a slow dance, their steps in sync as they moved together. The city lights twinkled around them, the skyline a stunning backdrop. In that moment, it was just the two of them—lost in the rhythm, the world fading away. Their silhouettes merged with the cityscape, a timeless image of love and connection.

They danced as if the night would never end, holding onto the moment, the memories, and each other. The city stood as a silent witness to their story—a story still unfolding, with many more dances yet to come.

●

Dark clouds gathered ominously on the horizon, and the wind began to howl through the trees around the cottage. The air grew heavy, and the distant rumble of thunder signaled the approaching storm.

George called out to the family, "It's time to batten down the hatches! This storm is going to be a big one."

Everyone worked together to secure the house. Windows were shuttered, loose items in the yard were brought inside, and extra supplies were stocked up. The first drops of rain started to fall just as they finished their preparations, quickly turning into a heavy downpour.

The family huddled inside, listening to the wind howl and the rain lash against the windows. The power flickered once, then twice, before going out entirely, plunging the house into darkness.

"Well, looks like we're in for an adventure," Cindy said, lighting a few candles and placing them around the room. The warm glow cast comforting shadows on the walls.

With the storm raging outside and the power out, the family had to find ways to entertain themselves without technology. The sound of rain pattering against the windows created a cozy backdrop as they pulled out board games and puzzles.

"Let's start with some checkers," suggested Cindy, setting up the board. As they played, laughter and friendly competition filled the room. They moved on to puzzles, piecing together intricate scenes of landscapes and animals. In the evening, they gathered around to read books and share stories by candlelight.

The following afternoon, as the rain beat steadily against the house, George decided it was the perfect time to go over the blueprints for the tree house. He spread the plans out on the dining table.

"Alright, let's see what ideas you two have for our tree house," he said, looking at Isaac and Abigail. Isaac pointed to a section of the blueprint.

"We need a fireman's pole!" Isaac continued. "It'll be so much fun to slide down."

"No way, a rope ladder is cooler!" argued Abigail. "We should hang seahorse lanterns inside too!" she said. "They're so whimsical and pretty."

Isaac shook his head. "Seahorse lanterns are too girly! We need dinosaur lights instead. Much cooler."

They bickered back and forth about which lights to use. A smile crossed George's face as a forgotten memory surfaced.

"Hearing you mention seahorse lamps reminds me of the time when Grandma Cindy and I had our disagreement in Italy," he chuckled. The kids paused, glancing over curiously. George rarely told traveling tales. He leaned back in his chair, eyes twinkling with the memory.

"It was on the Amalfi Coast in Italy. We were admiring the charming seahorse lamps that lined the clifftop shops when we got into a silly spat about which route to take," George began.

"Your grandmother and I had just arrived for a romantic getaway. We planned a seaside dinner that evening on the cliffs. But that afternoon, we couldn't agree on the walking route. Cindy wanted to take the scenic route through the village, while I thought the coastal path would be faster and more fun."

Cindy, walking up from the basement with a load of laundry, chuckled softly. "Ah yes, the 'unexpected detour.'" She set the laundry down all over the blueprints and took over the story. "George was convinced his way was quicker, but I wanted to explore the charming village streets. We argued for a bit and then, out of sheer stubbornness, decided to go our separate ways."

George continued, "I took the coastal path, thinking I'd beat Cindy to the restaurant. But the path turned out to be much rockier and winding than I expected. I ended up taking a few wrong turns and got completely lost."

Cindy laughed. "Meanwhile, I was wandering through the village, getting distracted by the little shops and stalls. I thought I'd have plenty of time, but I got so turned around that I couldn't find my way back to the main road."

George and Cindy shared a look, their eyes sparkling with the shared memory. "After hours of wandering in circles, we finally stumbled into each other at the same place we started," George recalled, chuckling. "The sun was nearly set by then. But looking into each other's eyes, all the frustration melted away."

"We were both exhausted and hungry," Cindy added, "but we couldn't help but laugh at how ridiculous we'd been. So, we started walking in a completely different direction, and we stumbled upon this charming, off-the-path village square. And to our surprise, there was a film crew setting up for a scene."

George interrupted, "The director saw us, two flustered tourists, and approached us. He said they needed a couple to fill in the background, just a simple scene of two people talking at a café while eating dinner. And he asked if we'd be interested."

Abigail laughed. "So, you two became movie stars for a day?"

Cindy smiled. "Something like that. We didn't know who the lead actor was, but judging by the crew's excitement, he was someone famous. He chatted with us during breaks, such a genuine soul, interested in our love story and journey together."

George nodded. "There, sitting next to the camera and under the delicate glow of seahorse lamps, we found ourselves reminiscing about our early days, our challenges, our disagreements, and our undying commitment to each other. The actor mentioned how real love stories, like ours, have so much depth."

Cindy looked toward the heavens. "It reminded us of how we've navigated through stars and storms in our relationship. And that evening, under the Amalfi skies, we learned that the key is open communication, understanding, and growing together."

The kids listened, captivated by the story and the lessons it carried.

Isaac asked, "So, you two just made up after getting lost?"

George nodded. "We realized that the journey was more important than the destination. Sometimes, taking different paths can lead to the same beautiful place."

The storm in Everbrook continued for a few more days, and the family found comfort in their indoor activities. The power came back on, but the kids were still without technology. Isaac and Abigail adapted by finding joy in simpler things. They played more games, read books, and shared stories. Each day, the storm seemed to intensify, with howling winds and relentless rain, but there were brief reprieves, allowing for the sun to shine from time to time.

Isaac and Abigail, still glowing from the stories their grandparents had shared during the blackout, found themselves more attuned to each other. Instead of arguing over the tree house additions, they began to approach the project with a newfound spirit of collaboration. The lessons learned in the darkness carried over into the light, turning what could have been conflicts into opportunities for teamwork and compromise. The excitement for their shared project grew, now fueled by a deeper understanding of what it meant to work together.

"Maybe we can have both a rope ladder and a fireman's pole," Isaac suggested one evening. "And we can find a place for both the seahorse lanterns and the dinosaur lights."

Abigail nodded in agreement. "Yeah, that sounds like a good idea."

George and Cindy exchanged proud glances, seeing the growth and maturity in their grandchildren.

After nearly two weeks, the storm finally began to calm. The clouds parted, and rays of sunshine broke through, casting a warm glow over the drenched landscape. The family gathered on the porch, watching as the last raindrops fell. They reflected on the experience, appreciating the time spent together and the lessons learned.

"We made it through the storm," George said, wrapping an arm around Cindy. "And we're stronger for it."

The kids nodded, feeling a sense of accomplishment and unity. The storm had tested them, but it had also brought them closer together. With the storm now behind them, the family looked forward to the next phase of their summer adventure.

George, Isaac, and Abigail gathered in the backyard, ready to complete their project. The tree house had come a long way from its initial stages, and the children were excited to see it finished.

"Alright, let's get to work," George said, rolling up his sleeves. "We're almost there. Just a few more touches, and it'll be perfect."

They climbed up to the tree house, each carrying tools and materials. The frame was sturdy, and the walls were up, but there were still a few features to add. Isaac and Abigail had finally agreed on incorporating both a fireman's pole and a rope ladder, combining their ideas into a single masterpiece. George started by installing the fireman's pole behind the tree house. "Hold this steady, Isaac," he instructed as he positioned the pole. Isaac held it in place while George secured it with bolts.

"Perfect," George said, stepping back to admire their work. "Now for the rope ladder."

Abigail eagerly helped to attach the rope ladder to the other side of the tree house. It dangled invitingly, ready for climbing adventures.

"We should hang the seahorse lanterns outside," Abigail suggested. "It'll make it look magical at night."

George nodded. "Good idea. Let's add those next."

They spent the afternoon adding the final touches: a small table and chairs, colorful curtains, and even a small shelf for books and games. The tree house transformed into a cozy retreat, a perfect hideaway for summer adventures.

As George was hammering in the last nail on one of the supports, he accidentally swung the hammer too hard and lost his grip. The hammer flew out of his hand at an awkward angle and struck him in the ribs. George winced and staggered back, clutching his side.

"Grandpa! Are you okay?" Abigail asked, her voice filled with concern.

George gritted his teeth and nodded. "I'm fine, it's just a flesh wound," he said, though his face was contorted with pain.

Cindy heard the commotion and came running. "George! What happened?"

"He hurt his ribs," Isaac explained, his eyes wide with worry.

Cindy knelt beside George, examining his side. "You need to rest and put some ice on that." With Isaac and Abigail's help, they carefully supported George and guided him into the house. Cindy fetched an ice pack and handed it to George.

"You're going to need to take it easy for a while," Cindy said, her tone firm but gentle. "No more heavy lifting."

George sighed. "I guess the tree house will have to wait a bit longer for those final touches."

Isaac and Abigail exchanged determined looks. "We can finish it, Grandpa," Isaac said. "You've taught us well. We can handle the rest."

George smiled, pride shining in his eyes. "I know you can. Just be careful, alright?"

While George rested inside, Maria and the kids turned their attention to the garden. The pepper plants they had been nurturing indoors had grown considerably, and it was time to prepare the garden for planting them outside.

"Let's check on our peppers," Maria said, leading the way to the indoor garden setup.

Isaac and Abigail carefully examined their plants. The leaves were vibrant green, and beautiful peppers had formed. They were proud of how well the peppers had grown under their care.

"They look great," Abigail said, beaming.

"They do," Maria agreed. "But we need to prepare the garden beds before we plant them outside." They spent the next few hours weeding the garden beds, turning the soil, and adding compost. By the time they finished, the garden beds were ready, and they transplanted the pepper plants from their pots to the garden.

With the garden prepared and the tree house nearly complete, the family decided to visit the market one last time to pick up some final decorations and supplies for the tree house. As they walked through the market, Isaac and Abigail spotted Mark's pepper stand. They had brought a few peppers from their plants to show him.

"Mark! Look at these peppers we grew!" Isaac exclaimed, holding up the peppers proudly. Mark, with his gruff exterior and kind heart, inspected the peppers with a critical eye. He picked up one pepper, examined it closely, and then took a small bite. His eyes widened, and he nodded approvingly.

"Not bad, not bad at all," he said, a slight smile breaking through his stern facade. "This one's the third best pepper I've ever tasted."

Isaac and Abigail exchanged confused glances. "The third best?" Abigail asked. Mark picked up another pepper and took a bite. He nodded again.

"Yep, this one too. Third best," he said with a grin.

The kids laughed. "What about this one?" Isaac asked, handing him a third pepper.

Mark repeated the process and declared, "Third strongest pepper." Isaac and Abigail couldn't help but laugh at the amusing consistency of Mark's evaluation.

"So, they're all the third best?" Isaac asked, still chuckling.

Mark's eyes sparkled with mischief. "Absolutely. Every one of them. You know, if you keep this up, you might just put me out of business!"

Abigail giggled. "Maybe we should start our own pepper stand."

Mark eyed the kids with a labored smile. "Tell you what, as a prize for your hard work, I'll let you sell some of these peppers from my stand. How does that sound?"

Isaac and Abigail's eyes widened with excitement.

"That sounds like fun!" Isaac said. "We're in!"

Mark nodded and then reached under his table, pulling out a small box of seedlings. "And here's something special. These are my prized pepper seedlings. Take good care of them, and you'll have some of the best peppers around." The kids accepted the seedlings with wide smiles, eager to continue their pepper-growing adventure.

They spent the rest of the afternoon picking out decorations for the tree house. Abigail chose a colorful carpet, while Isaac picked out a few interesting trinkets and games. They also bought some snacks and drinks to enjoy in their newly completed hideaway.

Back at the cottage, the family gathered around the tree house for a final inspection. George, with his ribs bruised and propped up on a stool, watched with pride as Isaac and Abigail added the finishing touches.

"It looks amazing," Cindy said, admiring the tree house. "You've done a wonderful job." Isaac and Abigail climbed up to the tree house, looking out over the yard. The view was breathtaking, and they felt a deep sense of accomplishment.

"We did it," Abigail said, smiling at her brother.

"Yeah, we did," Isaac agreed. "And we've got a lot more to look forward to."

As they sat around the dinner table that evening, they talked about their favorite moments from the summer and the lessons they had learned. The anticipation for Alex and Eden's return and the upcoming pepper tasting contest added an extra layer of excitement.

"I can't wait to show Mom and Dad everything we've done," Isaac said.

"They'll be so proud," Cindy replied. "And I'm proud of all of you. This summer has been an incredible journey, and we've all grown so much."

●

The week flew by, and soon it was time for Alex and Eden to wrap up their teaching assignments. They stood in front of their respective classrooms for the last time, addressing their students with a mix of pride and nostalgia.

Eden smiled at her students. "I've enjoyed every moment teaching you about medicine. Your dedication and curiosity have been inspiring. Remember, the key to success in this field is continuous learning and compassion."

Alex echoed similar sentiments to his writing class. "Seeing your stories come to life has been an incredible journey. Writing is a powerful tool, and I hope you continue to use it to express yourselves and explore the world."

After heartfelt goodbyes and a round of applause, they left their classrooms, feeling accomplished and fulfilled. That evening, Alex and Eden decided to celebrate with a romantic dinner at a quaint restaurant they had discovered earlier in the summer. They sat by the window, watching the city lights twinkle as they reflected on their journey.

"This summer has been incredible," Eden said, gazing at the city skyline. "We've learned so much, and it's brought us closer."

Alex nodded. "I agree. It feels like we've reconnected with our younger selves and with each other. But I'm also excited to see the kids and hear about their adventures." They toasted to their achievements and the memories they had made, savoring the last moments of their city adventure.

The following morning, Alex and Eden packed their bags, ready to return to the cottage. With the car packed, they began the drive back to Everbrook. The journey was filled with discussions about their future, the new friends they'd made, and their anticipation of reuniting with the family.

As they pulled up to the cottage, they saw Isaac and Abigail waiting eagerly by the front door. The kids ran up to the car, their faces beaming with excitement.

"Mom! Dad!" Isaac shouted, running up to the car.

"We missed you so much!" Abigail added, her arms wide open for a hug.

Alex and Eden stepped out of the car, their faces lighting up at the sight of their children. They embraced them tightly, feeling the warmth and love that only family can bring.

"We missed you too!" Eden said, her voice full of emotion.

"How have you two been?" Alex asked, ruffling Isaac's hair.

"We have so much to show you!" Isaac said, practically bouncing with excitement. George, Cindy, and Maria joined them, smiling warmly.

"Welcome back," George said, his voice filled with pride.

"It's good to be home," Alex replied, shaking George's hand.

The kids led their parents to the backyard, eager to show off their summer accomplishments. The tree house stood proudly, a testament to their hard work and creativity. The garden, now lush and thriving, was a vibrant display of their dedication.

"This is amazing," Eden said, her eyes wide with admiration.

"You've all done such a wonderful job," Alex added, his voice filled with awe.

"We had a lot of help from Grandpa and Grandma," Abigail

admitted, grinning.

"And we learned so much," Isaac said proudly.

After catching up and sharing stories, it was time for the much-anticipated pepper tasting contest. The family gathered around a table in the backyard, which was decorated with an array of colorful peppers. Alex and Eden took their place as judges, their expressions a mix of curiosity and excitement. The kids had carefully nurtured their pepper plants, and the results were impressive.

"Alright, let's see what you've got," Alex said, eyeing the peppers. Isaac and Abigail each presented their peppers, their faces glowing with pride. There were sweet peppers and hot peppers, each variety showcasing their hard work.

Eden picked up the first pepper, a sweet variety, and took a bite. Her eyes widened with delight. "This is delicious! So sweet and crisp."

Alex nodded in agreement as he sampled the same pepper. "You've done an excellent job with these."

Next, they moved on to the hot peppers. Eden cautiously took a small bite, her face immediately flushing red. She reached for a glass of milk, laughing. "Wow, that's got quite a kick!"

Alex, not to be outdone, took a bite of the hot pepper. His eyes watered, and he fanned his mouth. "These are definitely strong! Great job, kids."

The family laughed together, enjoying the playful competition and the varying reactions to the peppers. The pepper tasting contest turned into a joyful celebration of their hard work and the fun they had shared throughout the summer.

Isaac grinned. "So, who wins?"

Eden smiled. "I think you both win. These peppers are fantastic, and the effort you put into growing them is what really matters."

Alex nodded. "You've shown dedication and teamwork. That's more important than anything."

As the sun set, casting a warm glow over the cottage, the family gathered around the dinner table for one last meal together before the end of summer. The atmosphere was filled with a sense of accomplishment and togetherness.

"I can't believe how much we've done this summer," Isaac said, his eyes shining with pride.

"We've had so many adventures," Abigail added, smiling at her brother. Alex and Eden exchanged proud glances.

"You both have grown so much," Eden said, her voice filled with emotion. "Not just in size, but in what you've learned and how you've worked together."

George nodded in agreement. "This summer has been a testament to the power of teamwork and resilience."

Cindy raised her glass. "To all the lessons we've learned and the memories we've made."

"To family," Alex said, clinking his glass with everyone. "And to a summer we'll never forget." As the dinner wound down, Alex and Eden brought out a box from the living room. They set it on the table, and the kids looked at it curiously.

"What's that?" Isaac asked.

Alex smiled. "It's all your gadgets. We said you'd get it back at the end of the summer." Abigail and Isaac looked at each other.

"We made it through the whole summer without it," Abigail said, a hint of pride in her voice.

Alex nodded. "And we're very proud of you both. You've shown that you can do so much more than you ever thought possible." Eden opened the box and handed Isaac and Abigail their devices. They took them hesitantly, looking at the screens they hadn't seen in months.

After a moment, Isaac set his device down. "I think I'll go to the tree house instead," he said.

Abigail nodded in agreement. "Yeah, me too. The tree house is way more fun." Alex and Eden looked at each other in confusion as they watched their children run outside. They followed them to the tree house, where Isaac and Abigail were already climbing up, laughing and talking excitedly. As the family gathered around the tree house, the kids sat on the floor, looking out over the yard.

"This summer has been amazing," Isaac said. "I feel like we've done so much and learned so many new things."

Abigail nodded. "Yeah, it's been the best summer ever. I'm kind of glad we didn't have our devices. We got to do so much more."

Alex and Eden climbed up and joined them, sitting on the floor of the tree house. "We're so proud of you both," Alex said.

"And we know you'll continue to do great things," Eden added, hugging them tightly.

Isaac suddenly looked thoughtful. "Do you think we'll have to grow up soon?"

Eden smiled softly. "Growing up is a part of life, but don't rush it. Enjoy being kids. It's more fun that way."

Alex nodded. "There's plenty of time for responsibilities. Right now, focus on enjoying your childhood and the adventures it brings."

As they sat together, reflecting on the summer and looking forward to the future, the family felt a profound sense of connection and love. The lessons learned had not only made their summer unforgettable but had also strengthened their bonds in ways that would last a lifetime.

※

<u>**Lesson 10:**</u>
<u>**Growth Mindset**</u>

A growth mindset is the belief or attitude that individuals can develop and improve their abilities and intelligence over time through dedication, hard work, and learning. At its core, a growth mindset is not just a psychological theory; it's a way of life—a philosophy that challenges us to perceive difficulties as opportunities, embrace failures as stepping stones, and see setbacks as mere detours on the road to mastery.

Understanding the concept of a growth mindset and its impact on personal success is a foundational step toward achieving your full potential. In this lesson, we will delve deeper into what a growth mindset entails and how it can shape your journey toward success. By learning how to adopt a growth mindset, your abilities, intelligence, and talents can be developed and improved over time through dedication, effort, and learning. Unlike a fixed mindset, which assumes that traits are static and unchangeable, a growth mindset fosters a love for learning and resilience in the face of challenges.

Key Characteristics of a Growth Mindset

<u>Embracing Challenges</u>: People with a growth mindset see challenges as opportunities to learn and grow. They are more likely to take on new and difficult tasks because they view them as a chance to develop their skills.

<u>Persisting in the Face of Setbacks</u>: Instead of giving up easily when they encounter obstacles or failures, individuals with a growth mindset persevere. They see setbacks as a natural part of the learning process.

<u>Effort as the Path to Mastery</u>: A growth mindset emphasizes the importance of effort. It suggests that putting in hard work and dedication is the way to master new skills and achieve success.

<u>Learning from Criticism</u>: Constructive feedback and criticism are seen as valuable opportunities for improvement, not as personal

attacks. People with a growth mindset are open to learning from others' insights.

Inspired by Others' Success: Rather than feeling threatened by the success of others, individuals with a growth mindset are inspired by it. They see it as evidence that their own efforts and learning can lead to success.

Embracing Learning: Lifelong learning is a core value for those with a growth mindset. They continuously seek to expand their knowledge and skills, believing that personal development has no limits.

The Impact on Personal Success

When you embrace a growth mindset, your entire approach to success transforms in remarkable ways. Challenges, once daunting, begin to feel like thrilling opportunities. You stop seeing obstacles as roadblocks and start viewing them as stepping stones toward your goals. The idea of facing something difficult no longer intimidates you; instead, it sparks a sense of excitement because you understand that every challenge is a chance to improve.

Failures and setbacks, which once might have felt like the end of the road, become merely bumps along the way. You come to realize that stumbling is part of the process. Rather than being discouraged, you dig in, knowing that perseverance will eventually lead to success. With this mindset, your resilience grows stronger with every hurdle you overcome.

Hard work takes on new meaning. You begin to see effort as the true driver of achievement. Success isn't something reserved for the naturally gifted; it's the result of dedication and persistence. This realization fuels your motivation, pushing you to give your all, no matter how difficult the journey may be.

Criticism, once something to avoid, becomes a valuable tool. You start to welcome feedback, recognizing it as a guide for your growth. Rather than taking it personally, you see it as a map pointing you toward areas where you can improve. Each piece of advice, every bit of constructive criticism, becomes another opportunity to refine your skills.

And then there's the success of others. Instead of feeling envious or threatened, you find inspiration in their achievements. If they can reach great heights through effort and learning, you believe you can too. Their stories become fuel for your own journey, reminding you that growth is possible for anyone willing to put in the work.

Ultimately, a growth mindset turns life into an endless adventure of learning. You become eager to expand your knowledge and skills, understanding that there's always room to grow. The pursuit of personal development becomes a lifelong journey, one that brings continuous fulfillment and endless possibilities.

Lifelong Learning and Skill Development

Adopting a growth mindset creates a passion for lifelong learning and self-improvement. There are many strategies to continually expand one's knowledge and develop new skills. Setting learning goals in areas of interest is crucial. This could involve taking a class, reading books, watching tutorial videos, or seeking a mentor. As discussed earlier in the book, breaking larger goals into measurable steps with deadlines brings structure and accountability.

Trying new hobbies frequently exercises creativity and neural plasticity. Photography, pottery, coding, painting, gardening, and exploring unfamiliar domains stretch the mind. Learning basic skills lays a foundation, and incremental progress over time leads to mastery.

Exposing oneself to new experiences, people, and cultures expands perspectives. Traveling, volunteering in one's community, networking outside one's field, and reading diverse media foster open-mindedness. Reflecting on knowledge gained through all experiences cements learning. Journaling about insights, discussing progress with others, and applying emerging skills reinforces growth.

Pursuing formal education like degrees, certificates, conferences, and seminars builds credentials. Professional training opportunities through one's workplace are invaluable. Routinely assessing personal knowledge and skill gaps guides growth. Reevaluate your goals over time. Growth requires lifelong effort, but the rewards are limitless.

Fostering a Growth Mindset in Everyday Life

Fostering a growth mindset in children is not just about specific activities or isolated moments; it is about infusing everyday life with the principles of growth and learning. In this section, we will explore practical strategies to embed a growth mindset into various situations, highlighting the importance of praising effort and modeling a growth mindset ourselves.

Encourage Effort and Emphasize the Process:

Children thrive when they understand that effort and the process of learning are instrumental in their growth. By praising their efforts and highlighting their progress, we can instill in them a belief that they can improve and achieve their goals through dedication and hard work.

Imagine your child working on a challenging puzzle. Instead of focusing solely on whether they solved it correctly, take a moment to acknowledge the effort they put into it. Comment on their persistence and problem-solving skills, recognizing the strategies they employed to tackle the puzzle. This way, you are reinforcing the value of effort and the process, teaching them that it's not just about the outcome but the journey of learning and growth.

Provide Opportunities for Learning and Growth:

Everyday activities can be transformed into opportunities for learning and growth. Engaging in open-ended discussions, offering challenging tasks, and exploring new interests and hobbies can foster a growth mindset in your child.

During family conversations, encourage your child to express their thoughts and opinions freely. Engage them in discussions that promote critical thinking, asking open-ended questions that encourage them to consider multiple perspectives and come up with creative solutions. By creating an environment that values curiosity and questioning, you are nurturing their natural inclination to explore and learn.

Incorporate challenging tasks into your child's routine. Present them with activities that stretch their abilities, tasks that require problem-solving and persistence. When they encounter difficulties, provide guidance and support, reminding them that mistakes are not failures but stepping stones to progress. Encourage them to embrace the challenge, to persevere, and to learn from their mistakes.

Introduce your child to new interests and hobbies that require learning and skill development. Encourage them to explore various activities, whether it's playing a musical instrument, learning a new sport, or engaging in creative arts. Help them set goals, monitor their progress, and celebrate their achievements along the way. By exposing them to different pursuits, you are fostering their love for learning and encouraging a growth mindset.

<u>Model a Growth Mindset:</u>

Children learn by observing those around them, particularly their parents and caregivers. As you strive to foster a growth mindset in your child, it's essential to model the behaviors and attitudes you want them to adopt.

Share stories of your own learning experiences, both past and present. Talk about the challenges you have faced and how you overcame them. Be open about your mistakes and failures, highlighting how you used them as opportunities for growth. By sharing these experiences, you are demonstrating that learning is a lifelong journey and that setbacks are natural and valuable learning moments.

Incorporate growth mindset language into your conversations with your child. Use phrases and statements that emphasize the importance of effort, perseverance, and learning from mistakes. Encourage them to embrace challenges with a positive attitude, reminding them that their abilities can be developed through practice and dedication.

Finally, demonstrate resilience in your own life. When faced with setbacks or obstacles, approach them with a growth mindset. Show your child how you handle difficulties by maintaining a positive attitude and persevering in the face of adversity. By modeling resilience, you are teaching them that setbacks are temporary and that they have the power to overcome any obstacles they encounter.

By consistently implementing these strategies in your everyday interactions with your child, you create an environment that nurtures a growth mindset. You are instilling in them the belief that they have the ability to learn, grow, and achieve their goals through effort and perseverance. Through your guidance and modeling, you are setting them on a path of lifelong learning and personal development.

Remember, fostering a growth mindset is a journey that requires patience, consistency, and continuous reinforcement. By integrating these strategies into your daily life, you are providing your child with the tools and mindset necessary to thrive and succeed, not only academically but also in all areas of their life.

Activity: Identifying and Embracing Growth

Change is a constant in life, and with the right perspective, it can be a powerful catalyst for personal growth. In this activity, you will reflect on both past and anticipated changes, identifying opportunities for growth and taking inspired actions to embrace them.

Part 1: Reflecting on Past Changes

Select a Significant Change: Think about a major change or transition you experienced in the past year. It could be related to your career, relationships, health, location, or personal habits. Choose one that had a notable impact on your life.

Reflect on the Change: Take a moment to reflect on this past change and consider the following questions:
- What specific challenges did this change present?
- What opportunities emerged as a result of this change?
- How did you adapt to navigate these challenges and seize opportunities?
- What valuable lessons or insights did you gain from this experience?

Document Your Reflection: Write down your thoughts and insights in a journal or notebook. This will help you consolidate your understanding of how you've grown through past changes.

Part 2: Anticipating Future Changes

Identify Potential Changes: Now, think about changes you anticipate in the coming year. These could be related to your career goals, new commitments, external shifts in your environment, or personal development aspirations.

Acknowledge Your Initial Reactions: Consider any fears, uncertainties, or resistance that come up as you contemplate these impending changes. Write down these initial reactions without judgment.

Reframe Changes as Opportunities: Challenge yourself to reframe these anticipated changes as opportunities for personal growth. Ask yourself:
- How can I leverage these changes to learn and develop new skills?
- What knowledge or abilities would be beneficial in navigating these changes effectively?
- How might embracing these changes lead to personal and professional advancement?

Part 3: Taking Inspired Action

Identify Inspired Actions: Based on your reflections, pinpoint 1-2 concrete actions you can take to proactively prepare for the anticipated changes and promote self-improvement. These actions should align with your growth mindset and may include:
- Enrolling in a relevant course or workshop.
- Starting a journal or self-reflection practice to process emotions and insights.
- Setting specific goals for personal development.
- Joining a group, network, or community that supports your growth objectives.

Commit to Your Actions: Make a commitment to follow through with the actions you've identified. Set clear timelines and goals for each action to ensure accountability.

Part 4: Embracing Growth (Ongoing)

Continuous Reflection: As you navigate both past and future changes, continue to reflect on your experiences. Consider how your mindset and actions contribute to your personal growth journey.

Adapt and Expand: As you achieve your initial actions, repeat this process to set new objectives and explore additional areas of interest. Embrace change as an ongoing opportunity for growth.

By engaging in this activity, you'll not only identify opportunities for personal growth within the context of change but also proactively take steps to embrace these opportunities. Remember that maintaining a growth mindset allows you to approach the evolving future with optimism, wisdom, and purpose.

●

In this lesson, we embarked on a journey of cultivating a growth mindset in ourselves and our children, whether they be your children or another person's. Understanding the concept of a growth mindset serves as the foundation for personal growth and achievement.

We explored the importance of nurturing a growth mindset from a young age and the positive impact it can have on their personal and academic development. Through the story of Alex and Eden, we witnessed their dedication to fostering a love for learning, adaptability, and embracing challenges in their children.

By instilling a growth mindset in our children, we are equipping them with a powerful mindset that can propel them toward success and personal fulfillment.

Throughout this lesson, we discussed the importance of nurturing a growth mindset in everyday life. Practical strategies were provided for parents to foster a growth mindset in their children, such as using growth mindset language, praising effort and the process, and modeling a growth mindset through their own actions and attitudes.

By nurturing a growth mindset in not only ourselves but our children, we become empowered to embrace challenges, persist through obstacles, and continuously strive for improvement. The benefits extend beyond academic achievement, as a growth mindset equips everyone with essential life skills such as adaptability, resilience, and a passion for lifelong learning.

As we conclude this lesson let us remember that our role as human beings is pivotal in cultivating a growth mindset in ourselves and our children. By implementing the strategies and activities presented in this lesson, we lay a strong foundation for personal and academic success. Let us continue to foster a growth mindset in ourselves and our children, guiding us on a path of self-discovery, resilience, and limitless potential.

Chapter 11: Big Time

Monday, December 2nd, arrived with a crisp, frosty morning, and Alex and Eden's cottage was already full of excitement. The scent of Alex's famous Holiday French toast, heavy on the nutmeg, wafted through the air, mingling with the cheerful sounds of holiday music playing softly in the background. Alex was in his element, flipping slices of French toast on the griddle.

"Breakfast is ready!" he called out, his voice carrying a warm, inviting tone.

Isaac and Abigail, both seventeen years old, barreled down the stairs, drawn by the irresistible smell. Abigail slid into her seat, eyes wide with anticipation.

"Morning, everyone," Alex greeted, setting a plate piled high with French toast on the table. "Big day ahead. Lots to discuss."

"Morning, Dad!" Abigail chirped, her eyes sparkling. "Are you going to start decorating downtown today?"

Alex nodded, a smile spreading across his face. "That's right. As the Executive Oak Master, I've got a lot of responsibilities, and decorating the town square is top of the list. We're going to make it the most magical Christmas Everbrook has ever seen."

Isaac, who had been rummaging through a closet, appeared in the doorway, looking frustrated. "Has anyone seen my Santa hat? I swear I left it here last year."

Eden chuckled, shaking her head. "Did you check the attic, Isaac? That's where we store all the holiday decorations."

Isaac sighed and turned back toward the stairs. "I'll go look. I can't start the season without it."

Eden placed a stack of plates on the table and sat down. "While you all are busy with the decorations, I'll be at the clinic. We've got a lot of people to help this season, and I'm also working on raising money to feed the hungry. It's going to be a busy few weeks, but I know we can manage it all."

Abigail tilted her head, curiosity gleaming in her eyes. "How do you think the free clinic is gonna go, Mom? Are you expecting a lot of donations?"

Eden nodded, her expression serious yet hopeful. "We are. The demand is higher this year, and I want to make sure no one goes hungry during the holidays. It's a lot of work but seeing the relief on people's faces makes it all worth it."

Alex reached over and kissed Eden's cheek. "You're doing an amazing thing, babe. We'll make sure to lend a hand whenever we can."

Eden smiled, feeling the support of her family. "Thanks, honey. You know, starting my own practice was a big step, but running the free clinic during the holidays has become a tradition I cherish. People donate whatever they can, and we use that money to feed the hungry. It's our way of giving back."

Abigail, ever the eager helper, leaned forward. "I want to help at the clinic too, Mom. Maybe after we finish decorating downtown, I can come by and assist."

Eden's eyes softened. "That would be wonderful, Abby. I could always use an extra pair of hands."

Isaac, now wearing his Christmas hat, rejoined the table. "I found it! And count me in to help at the clinic too, Mom. Just let me know what you need."

Eden smiled at her children. "Thank you, both of you. It means a lot to me."

"Alright, let's get this day started," Alex said, clapping his hands together. "We've got a lot to do, and I want to make sure we get a head start."

Abigail jumped up, grabbing her coat. "I'm ready! We'll be down to help after school. Let's make Everbrook sparkle!"

Isaac chuckled, following his sister's lead. "Speaking of sparkling, don't let Abby near the glitter. Last year, we were finding it in the house for months."

Eden laughed, shaking her head. "Oh, I remember. Let's try to keep the glitter contained this time."

With breakfast wrapping up, the family dispersed to their respective tasks. Alex headed out to gather supplies for the day's decorations, while Eden began organizing her materials for the clinic. Isaac and Abigail, full of enthusiasm, prepared to join their father downtown after school, eager to contribute to the town's holiday magic.

●

The Tall Oaks Organization was a cornerstone of Everbrook's community spirit, dedicated to fostering a sense of togetherness through free year-round events. Housed in a towering four-story building in the heart of downtown Everbrook, it was a hub of activity, especially during the holiday season.

Alex parked his truck in front of the Tall Oaks building, taking a moment to admire its festive facade. The massive brick structure was decorated with twinkling lights and garlands, a testament to the hard work and dedication of the organization's members.

Inside, the atmosphere was just as lively. Members of the Tall Oaks Organization bustled about, carrying boxes of decorations and setting up displays. The lobby was filled with the sounds of cheerful chatter and the occasional burst of laughter.

"Morning, Alex!" called out Mr. Watkins, the head of the volunteer committee. He was directing a group of volunteers as they assembled a massive Christmas tree in the lobby.

"Morning, Mr. Watkins!" Alex replied, giving him a wave.

"Looks like we're off to a great start."

Mr. Watkins nodded, his face lighting up with a warm smile. "We sure are. The wreaths are ready, and the garlands are being prepped. We should have the lobby done by noon."

Alex smiled. "That's fantastic. I'll be outside with the team, setting up the lights and the big tree in the square. We've got a lot of ground to cover today."

He stepped outside and was immediately greeted by a crisp winter breeze. The town square of Everbrook was on its way to becoming a winter wonderland. Alex, with a vision of festivity and joy, stood in the center, directing volunteers from the Tall Oaks Organization. The air was filled with the sound of laughter and the sight of twinkling lights being strung across trees and lampposts.

Alex took a deep breath of the crisp winter air, feeling invigorated. "Alright, team! Let's start with the lights on the big tree in the center. We want it to be the focal point of the square." Volunteers hustled around, stringing lights, and hanging garlands. The sense of camaraderie was infectious, and everyone seemed to be in high spirits.

"Hey, Alex!" called out Mr. Driscoll, one of the long-standing members of the Tall Oaks Organization. "Where do you want these wreaths?"

"Hang them on the lampposts, please. They'll look great there," Alex replied, smiling as he watched the transformation begin.

As the day went on, more townspeople gathered to help. The atmosphere was one of shared joy and community spirit. Everyone was contributing in their own way, coming together to create something magical.

"Alex, this looks amazing!" Mrs. Thompson exclaimed, pausing to admire a newly decorated tree. "You've really outdone yourself this year."

"Thanks, Mrs. Thompson," Alex replied, beaming with pride. "We're trying to make this the best holiday season Everbrook has ever seen."

Mr. Adams, the local baker, approached with a tray of freshly baked cookies. "Thought you all could use a snack," he said, offering the tray to the volunteers.

The atmosphere was festive and lively. Laughter rang out as people worked together, sharing stories, and enjoying the process of decorating their town. It was clear that the community spirit was strong, and everyone was invested in making the holiday season special.

"Alex, where do you want the nativity scene?" another volunteer called out.

"Right by the fountain, Dan. It'll be the perfect spot," Alex responded, directing traffic like a conductor leading an orchestra.

"Great job, everyone," Alex said, his voice filled with pride. "Everbrook has never looked more beautiful."

The volunteers cheered, their faces glowing with accomplishment. It was moments like these that made all the hard work worthwhile, reminding them all of the true meaning of the season.

•

Later that morning at Everbrook High School, the excitement of the holiday season was evident among the students. The hallways were decorated with tinsel and lights, and the festive spirit was infectious. Isaac and Abigail walked to their lockers, discussing their plans for the weekend.

"So, what's the plan for Friday night?" Abigail asked as she spun her combination lock.

Isaac shrugged, trying to sound casual. "I'm not sure yet. I was thinking about going to the new ice rink downtown after the Tree Lighting Ceremony."

Abigail raised an eyebrow, a playful smile on her lips. "Going ice-skating alone, or do you have someone in mind?"

Isaac blushed, focusing intently on his locker. "Maybe I'll ask Jenny. We've been talking a lot in chemistry class, and I think she might be interested."

Abigail smirked. "You've been crushing on her for months, if not years by now. Just ask her already!"

Isaac sighed. "Easier said than done. What about you and Max? Any plans?" he asked, changing the subject.

Abigail's smile softened. "Not yet, but we're planning to do something special soon. He's been so sweet. I'm really lucky to have him."

Just then, their cousin Jacob appeared, a guitar case slung over his shoulder. He gave them a quick nod as he approached.

"Hey, guys. What's up?" Jacob asked.

"Hey, Jake," Isaac greeted. "Just talking holiday plans. How's the band going?"

Jacob grinned, his eyes lighting up. "Busy, but good. We've got a bunch of gigs lined up for the holidays. My parents are really excited about the Gala. Dad's been rehearsing some new songs nonstop."

Abigail laughed. "I bet. Uncle Gabriel takes his music seriously. Are you going to be playing at the Gala too?"

Jacob nodded. "No, I mean, I don't know. My parents haven't asked me yet, but I wouldn't mind being a part of the opening act. They tend to wait until the last minute to tell me these things."

The bell rang, signaling the start of the third period. The three cousins grabbed their books and headed to their respective classes, the conversation shifting to schoolwork and upcoming exams. But even as they focused on their studies, the excitement of the holiday season lingered in the air.

During lunch, Isaac spotted Jenny sitting at a table with her friends. Gathering his courage, he walked over, trying to ignore the butterflies in his stomach.

"Hey, Jenny," he said, his voice only slightly wavering.

Jenny looked up, a smile spreading across her face. "Hey, Isaac. What's up?"

Isaac opened his mouth to speak but hesitated, losing his nerve. "Nothing much. Just wanted to say hi."

Jenny's smile widened. "Hi."

Isaac chuckled nervously, feeling his cheeks heat up. "So, are you going to the Christmas market this weekend?"

Jenny nodded while nervously twisting her hair. "Yeah, I'm planning to, but I don't really have anyone to go with. It should be fun though."

"Cool. Maybe I'll see you there," Isaac said, mentally kicking himself for not asking her out.

"Maybe," Jenny replied with a wink. As Isaac walked back to his table, he couldn't help but feel a mixture of relief and frustration. Abigail, who had been watching from a distance, gave him an encouraging nod.

Later that afternoon the final bell rang and the students flooded out of the school. Isaac and Abigail met up with Jacob again as they headed to the parking lot.

"You should have just asked her," Abigail teased, nudging Isaac playfully.

Isaac rolled his eyes. "I know, I know. Maybe next time."

Jacob chuckled, slinging his guitar case into the back of his car. "Hey, you guys heading downtown? I'm going to help set up for the Gala with Dad inside the Tall Oaks building."

Abigail's eyes lit up. "Yeah! We were going to help our Dad with the decorations, let's all go down together."

Isaac nodded. "Yeah, let's roll."

The three of them piled into Jacob's car, the anticipation of helping with the town's decorations adding to their excitement. As they drove towards downtown Everbrook, the festive spirit seemed to grow stronger with each passing minute.

When they arrived, the town square was bustling with activity. Volunteers from the Tall Oaks Organization were hard at work, transforming the square into a winter wonderland. Alex was in the thick of it, directing the placement of the giant snow globe.

"Hey, Dad!" Abigail called out as they approached. "We're here to help!"

Alex looked up, a wide smile spreading across his face.

"Great timing, you two! We've got plenty to do." Together, they joined the volunteers, stringing lights, hanging ornaments, and setting up festive displays.

As they hung the final ornament on the towering tree in the center of the square, Alex took a step back, admiring their work. The town square was now a breathtaking display of colors and lights, a testament to the power of community and the magic of the holiday season.

"Alright, everyone," Alex began, his voice carrying across the square. "I wanted to take a moment to talk about the Gala and the events leading up to it." Isaac, Abigail, the small crowd of volunteers, and the townspeople listened intently, their curiosity piqued.

"The Gala is scheduled for December 13th," Alex continued. "It's in two weeks from today, and the festivities will continue until Christmas Day. The Gala itself will be a big dance and dinner held downtown at the Tall Oaks building. It's a large charitable event, Santa Claus will be there, and the famous band the Runaway 6 will be playing some new unreleased songs. It's the biggest Christmas party this side of the Mississippi."

Abigail's eyes widened with excitement. "That sounds amazing, Dad! I can't wait to see everything."

Isaac nodded in agreement. "Yeah, it sounds like a lot of fun. What else is planned?"

Alex smiled warmly at his children's enthusiasm. "Well, before the Gala, we have a whole series of events planned. There will be an ice-skating rink, a massive outdoor snow globe, ice sculptures, a Christmas market, and a live nativity scene. Also, this Friday, December 6th, we'll have the tree lighting ceremony to kick off the festivities. It's going to be a fantastic start to the holiday season."

Abigail grinned. "The tree lighting is always my favorite. I love seeing everyone come together."

Isaac's thoughts drifted to Jenny for a second. "And the ice-skating rink sounds awesome. I'll definitely be there. Can I be part of the live nativity?" asked Isaac.

Alex nodded. "Yes, you can do that. It's a great opportunity to get involved and meet new people. Go see Mr. Watkins inside to sign up." Isaac grinned, already thinking about Jenny. He would finally get a chance to talk to her.

Mrs. Thompson, who had been listening, chimed in, "The Gala sounds wonderful, Alex. I'm sure it's going to be a magical evening for everyone."

Alex nodded. "That's the plan. We want to make this a holiday season to remember for all of Everbrook." Alex smiled, turning towards Isaac and Abigail. "However, because the night of the Gala is going to be a late night, your mom and I will be staying at a hotel downtown after the event. Don't expect us home until late the next day, we'll have a lot of cleaning up to do."

The sense of anticipation and excitement among the townspeople was evident. The Gala was shaping up to be a spectacular event, and everyone was eager to be a part of it. As the volunteers began to disperse, Abigail pulled Isaac aside, her eyes gleaming with excitement.

"Did you hear what Dad said?" asked Abigail. "They'll be staying at a hotel the night of the Gala and won't be home until later the next day!"

Isaac raised an eyebrow, catching on to her enthusiasm. "Yeah, I heard. What are you thinking?"

Abigail glanced around to make sure no one was listening. "We should throw a party. A big holiday party while they're gone. It's the perfect opportunity!"

Isaac's eyes widened with a mix of surprise and excitement. "Are you serious? That could be epic. But we'd have to be really careful. If they find out, we'll be in big trouble."

Abigail nodded, a mischievous grin spreading across her face. "Of course. We can invite just a few friends, keep it low-key but fun. And guess who could help us with the music?"

Before Isaac could respond, Jacob strolled over, having noticed their hushed conversation.

"Hey, what are you two scheming about?" asked Jacob.

Abigail quickly filled Jacob in on their idea, her excitement bubbling over. "You're in, right? We need your DJ skills and your equipment."

Jacob grinned, clearly intrigued by the idea. "A secret holiday party? I'm definitely in. I can bring my sound system and set up a killer playlist."

The three of them huddled together, their voices low but filled with excitement as they began to strategize.

"Okay, first things first," Abigail said. "We need to make a guest list. Only people we trust not to spill the beans. Make sure they know to keep it quiet and not post anything on social media."

Isaac nodded, pulling out his phone. "Agreed. This has to stay under wraps until the last minute. I'll start texting a few friends. We'll keep it small and manageable."

Jacob added, "I'll handle the music and lights. We can set up in the living room and maybe even have a mini dance floor. Your outside patio would be perfect for a bonfire and s'mores making station."

Abigail grinned. "Perfect. And we should make it a themed party, like everyone wear an ugly Christmas sweater!"

As they hashed out the details, their excitement grew. The idea of a secret holiday party was thrilling, and they were determined to make it a night to remember.

●

The sound of laughter and holiday cheer from the town square seemed distant as Eden worked diligently in her practice. Her free clinic had become a beacon of hope for the less fortunate, and during the holiday season, the need for care was greater than ever. Eden's dedication to her patients was unwavering, but the strain of balancing her responsibilities was beginning to show.

The clinic was a modest building situated near the center of the town square. Eden had managed to hang a wreath on the entrance door, giving it a mediocre festive feel. She moved from room to room, checking on patients and offering words of comfort and reassurance.

In one room, she knelt beside a young boy with a bandaged arm. "How are you feeling today, Kevin?" she asked, her voice gentle.

The boy looked up at her with wide eyes. "It hurts a little, but not as much as yesterday."

Eden smiled, ruffling his hair. "That's good to hear. You're very brave. Let's get you some more pain medicine, and you'll be back to playing in no time."

As she exited the room, she was greeted by Ms. Palmer, a local medical student who frequently volunteered at the clinic to gain experience in the field.

"Eden, thank you so much for your help. You're a blessing to this community. You're an inspiration to me. I want to be just like you when I graduate!"

Eden gave Ms. Palmer a hug. "It's my pleasure, Ms. Palmer. Your words are so kind, bless your heart. I'll teach you as much as I can."

Despite the satisfaction she felt in helping everyone, Eden couldn't ignore the nagging worry about balancing her clinic duties with family time. The upcoming holiday events and the preparations at home weighed heavily on her mind. Just then, the clinic door opened, and Sarah walked in, her arms full of holiday decorations.

"Hey, Eden! I thought I'd come by and help you decorate," Sarah said. "We need to get this place looking more festive."

Eden's face lit up with relief and gratitude. "Sarah, you have no idea how much I appreciate this. I've been so overwhelmed."

Sarah set down the decorations and gave Eden a hug. "I can see that. Let's get to work. We'll make this place shine."

As they hung garlands and lights, Sarah glanced at Eden. "You're doing an amazing job here, you know. It's not easy, but you're making a real difference."

Eden sighed, stepping back to admire their handiwork. "I just wish I could find a better balance. The clinic needs me, but so does my family. I know Alex isn't going to be at home much, and the kids are always off doing their own thing. Nothing is going to get done at the house."

Sarah nodded. "I get it. But remember, it's okay to ask for help. We're all here for you. I've got some free time—just tell me what you need me to do."

Eden smiled, feeling some of the weight lift from her shoulders. "Thank you, Sarah. I don't know what I'd do without you."

As they continued decorating, the conversation turned to the upcoming festivities. "Gabriel and I are really looking forward to performing at the Gala," Sarah said. "We'll be playing Christmas songs outside during the evening festivities too. The Runaway 6 is ready to bring some holiday cheer to Everbrook."

Eden's eyes sparkled with excitement. "That sounds wonderful! The town is going to love it. And it's just what we need to lift everyone's spirits."

Sarah grinned. "It'll be great. Music has a way of bringing people together, especially during the holidays."

The clinic began to take on a festive glow as they finished the decorations. The patients who came in were greeted by twinkling lights and colorful garlands, a small but meaningful touch that brightened their day.

"Thanks for your help, Sarah," Eden said, giving her sister-in-law a warm hug. "You've made a big difference today."

Sarah hugged her back. "Anytime, Eden. That's what family is for."

With the clinic looking festive and her spirits lifted, Eden felt ready to take on the challenges ahead. The holiday season was in full swing, and despite the struggles, the love and support of her family and friends made everything seem possible.

Later that evening, after a long day of decorating and running the clinic, Alex, Eden, and the kids gathered in their cozy living room. The fire crackled in the hearth, casting a warm glow across the room. Abigail and Isaac were sprawled on the couch, while Alex and Eden sorted through a pile of mail on the coffee table, enjoying a rare moment of relaxation.

"Bills, bills, and more bills," Alex muttered, sifting through the envelopes. "Isn't there anything cheerful in here?"

Eden picked up a brightly colored envelope from the pile and held it up. "What about this? It looks like it's from Leo."

Alex chuckled, taking the envelope from Eden. "Oh boy, I can only imagine what he's come up with this time."

He opened the envelope and pulled out a card decorated with cartoon-looking aliens and spaceships. As he read the message inside, a smile spread across his face. Clearing his throat, he began to read aloud:

"Greetings Star-crossed friends! I have charted a course across the Milky Way to beam down and spread intergalactic holiday cheer with my favorite Earthlings. Get ready for a sleigh full of supernatural hijinks and paranormal cheer when Cosmic Kringleo teleports to your world... Merry Christmas!"

Isaac burst out laughing. "Cosmic Kringleo? That's definitely Uncle Leo."

Eden shook her head, smiling. "He always knows how to add a unique twist to the holidays. Remember last year's card about the time-traveling shrimp and their Shrimpsmas tree?"

Abigail giggled. "And the year before that, when he claimed to be sending presents from an underwater kingdom?"

Alex nodded, reminiscing. "Uncle Leo's cards are always the highlight of the season. He sure knows how to keep things interesting."

Eden took the card from Alex and admired the quirky drawings. "It's sweet, though. He always puts so much effort into making us smile."

Abigail leaned over to look at the card again. "Do you think he's planning something special for us this year?"

Isaac shrugged. "With Uncle Leo, you never know. But it's bound to be fun."

Alex placed the card on the mantel, where it joined the other holiday cards they'd received. "Whatever he's planning, we'll be ready. It's part of the holiday magic, after all."

Eden nodded in agreement. "Uncle Leo's surprises always bring us closer together. It's his way of reminding us to embrace the unexpected and find joy in the little things."

The family settled back into their evening, their spirits lifted by the whimsical message from Uncle Leo.

The following week, the town of Everbrook buzzed with anticipation as holiday preparations continued in full swing. Alex, the ever-diligent Executive Oak Master, was overseeing the setup of the downtown ice rink, the ice sculpture park, and the finishing touches on the massive Christmas tree.

The sound of laughter and holiday music filled the air as volunteers test skated on the freshly laid ice, and children watched in awe as the ice sculptures took shape. The festive spirit was infectious, and Alex couldn't help but smile as he directed the final touches.

Later in the afternoon, Alex decided to take a short break. He strolled over to a nearby vendor selling hot cocoa and bought a cup to warm his hands. As the vendor handed him his change, something caught Alex's eye—an old dollar bill with faded, familiar handwriting on it. Curious, he looked closer and saw a message written on the bill:

"April 14. Eden + Alex We'll meet again."

His heart skipped a beat as memories flooded back. He recalled that beautiful April evening when they passed each other on the street near the Midnight Bakery. Holding the dollar bill, Alex felt a wave of nostalgia and love wash over him. It was as if the universe had given him a gentle reminder of the beautiful journey he and Eden had shared.

He remembered their first date, the laughter, the connection, and the promise of forever. Inspired by the discovery, Alex knew he wanted to do something special for Eden this holiday season. An idea began to form in his mind—a scavenger hunt that would take Eden on a trip down memory lane, reliving their first date and other cherished moments.

Determined, Alex started to plan the scavenger hunt. He made a list of meaningful locations and mementos, envisioning how each clue would lead Eden to the next spot. As he mapped out the details, Alex felt a renewed sense of excitement. This scavenger hunt would be a way to show Eden just how much she meant to him, a gesture of love and gratitude for all the years they had shared.

With the plan taking shape, Alex couldn't wait to see the look on Eden's face as she followed the clues, rediscovering their love story one step at a time. The holidays were about to become even more magical, filled with love, memories, and the promise of forever.

After school, Abigail, Isaac, and Max decided to go shopping for their ugly sweaters. They piled into Max's car, laughter filling the air as they drove to the local thrift store downtown near Eden's clinic. Inside, they split up to hunt for the most ridiculous sweaters they could find. Isaac held up a sweater decorated with blinking lights and a giant reindeer face.

"What do you think? Hideous enough?" Isaac asked.

Max laughed. "That's perfect. I found one with a 3D Santa and elves. It's so bad, it's good."

Abigail, giggling, held up a sweater covered in colorful pom-poms and jingling bells. "This one's got to be the ugliest."

As they continued browsing, Abigail noticed a particularly outrageous sweater that she knew would be perfect for Isaac. It was bright red with a huge, fluffy snowman on the front. She grinned, holding it up for everyone to see.

"This one's for you, Isaac!" she said with a mischievous smile.

Isaac rolled his eyes but couldn't help laughing. "Very funny, Abby. I'm not wearing that."

Abigail's eyes sparkled with a new idea. "Hey, what if you give a sweater to Jenny? It could be a funny way to break the ice with her."

Isaac's eyes widened. "Are you serious?"

Max chuckled. "That's actually a great idea. You can make it into a joke and finally get the jingle balls to ask her out."

Isaac laughed, then shrugged. "Alright, I'll do it. But if she hates it, I'm blaming you."

Abigail grinned, handing him the sweater. "Deal. Just be yourself, and she'll love it."

The group continued shopping, laughing and joking as they picked out their own ugly sweaters. All the while, they couldn't wait to see how Isaac would handle giving the outrageous sweater to Jenny.

As they continued to talk about the secret party while waiting to check out, Eden, who was on a break from the clinic, was carrying a few items herself.

"Mom!" Abigail exclaimed, trying to hide the sweaters behind her back. "What are you doing here?"

Eden smiled, surprised to see them. "I'm just picking up some things for myself and a few decorations for the clinic. What about you?"

Abigail thought quickly. "We're, um, just getting some last-minute things for the tree lighting ceremony."

Eden raised an eyebrow, noticing the laughter and the conspicuous bags. "It looks like you're having fun. Are you planning something special?"

Isaac and Max exchanged nervous glances. Abigail tried to keep her composure. "Oh, you know, just trying to get into the holiday spirit with some ugly Christmas sweaters."

Eden nodded, seemingly satisfied with the answer. "Well, don't let me interrupt your fun. Just remember, we have a lot of work to do around the house. The dishes need to be done, and..."

"Of course, Mom," Abigail said abruptly, interrupting Eden. "We'll go home soon to take care of everything."

As Eden walked away, Abigail let out a breath she didn't realize she had been holding. "That was close. I don't think she heard us talking about the party."

Max chuckled. "I don't think so either, but that was too close. We need to be more careful." Isaac nodded in agreement. With their mission accomplished and their secret still safe, they left the store and headed home to take care of their chores.

●

The night of the tree lighting ceremony arrived, and the town square was alive with festive energy. The massive Christmas tree stood proudly in the center, its branches adorned with twinkling lights and colorful ornaments. Families and friends gathered around, sipping hot cocoa and chatting excitedly as they waited for the main event.

Alex stood by the tree, making sure everything was in place. He had worked tirelessly to ensure this moment would be perfect for Everbrook. The twinkling lights reflected in his eyes as he looked around at the bustling square, filled with townspeople enjoying the festivities.

Eden was nearby, talking with a few townspeople about her free clinic. Her eyes sparkled with enthusiasm as she explained the services they offered and the difference it was making in the community. Despite the busy season, she always found time to give back. Sarah and Gabriel, both dressed festively, were setting up their equipment for a special performance.

"Gabriel, can you hand me that cable?" Sarah asked, adjusting a microphone stand.

"Sure thing," Gabriel replied, passing her the cable. He paused to look out at the crowd, a smile spreading across his face. "This is going to be great. Look at how many people are here!"

As the mayor stepped up to the podium, the crowd hushed in anticipation. "Good evening, everyone! It's time to light up our beautiful Christmas tree and officially kick off the holiday season!" The crowd cheered as the mayor flipped the switch. The tree burst into light, casting a warm, golden glow over the square.

Nearby, Max and Abigail were wandering through the Christmas market, enjoying the festive atmosphere. They sampled holiday treats, admired the handcrafted ornaments, and soaked in the holiday spirit.

"This is wonderful," Abigail said, taking a sip of hot cider. "I love spending time like this."

Max smiled, wrapping an arm around her. "Me too. It's moments like these that make the holidays special." They strolled hand in hand, taking in the sights and sounds of the market, and found Isaac at the live nativity near the manger, dressed as a shepherd and guiding visitors through the scene.

Abigail waved him over. "Hey, Isaac!"

Jenny stood nearby, smiling warmly. Isaac felt a surge of confidence as he saw her watching him.

"Hi, Jenny," Isaac said, walking over with a bright red package in hand. "I wanted to ask you something."

Jenny's eyes lit up with curiosity. "Sure, what's up?"

Isaac took a deep breath. "We're having a secret holiday party, and I'd really like it if you came. It's going to be a lot of fun."

Jenny's smile widened. "I'd love to come to your party, Isaac. Thanks for inviting me!"

Isaac grinned, his confidence growing. "Great! And, well, it's actually an ugly sweater party. I saw this and thought it would be perfect for you." He handed her the package. Jenny opened it and burst into laughter.

"Wow, this is... definitely ugly!" Jenny said, her face turning red.

Isaac laughed along with her. "Yeah, it's pretty outrageous. But I thought it might be fun."

Jenny looked at the sweater with amusement. "I'll wear it. Thanks, Isaac."

Isaac's excitement bubbled over as he continued, "Awesome. And, um, my shift at the nativity scene is over in a few minutes. I was wondering if you'd like to go ice-skating with me afterward?"

Jenny's smile widened even more. "I'd love to go ice-skating with you, Isaac."

Isaac's heart raced with excitement. "Great! I'll meet you at the rink in a little bit then." As Jenny walked away, clutching the sweater, Isaac turned to Abigail and Max, who were watching with approving smiles.

"Well done, bro," Abigail said, giving him a playful nudge. "You've got this."

Isaac smiled, feeling a mix of relief and excitement. "Thanks, Abby."

A few minutes later, Isaac and Jenny laced up their skates and stepped onto the ice, joining Max, Abigail, and other skaters in the packed rink. As they glided across the ice, Isaac felt a sense of magic in the air. The lights, the music, and the laughter created a perfect backdrop for this special moment.

"You're pretty good at this," Jenny said, smiling up at Isaac.

Isaac grinned. "Thanks. I used to come here a lot when I was younger. It's been a few years, though."

Jenny's eyes sparkled. "I went skating here last year with my sisters. It was awful; they teased me the whole time because I couldn't skate too well. I feel so much better here with you, thanks for inviting me!"

Isaac felt a surge of happiness. "I'm glad you came. This is perfect. We can skate as slow as you want."

As they continued skating, they passed by Alex, who was helping a few younger kids learn to skate. He looked up and saw Isaac and Jenny, a proud smile spreading across his face. He gave Isaac a thumbs-up, which Isaac returned with an awkward grin. Eden, meanwhile, was chatting with Sarah and Gabriel, who were preparing to start their performance.

"You two ready to spread some holiday cheer?" Eden asked.

Gabriel nodded. "Absolutely. We've got a great set list lined up."

Sarah smiled. "We can't wait to get started. This is one of our favorite events of the year."

As the first notes of "Jingle Bell Rock" filled the air, the crowd gathered around the stage, clapping and cheering. Sarah's voice rang out, clear and melodious, as Gabriel played the guitar with contagious energy. The Runaway 6 had everyone dancing and singing along in no time.

Isaac and Jenny skated to the music, the festive tunes adding to the magic of the evening. They shared stories, laughed, and enjoyed each other's company, feeling a connection that was growing stronger with each moment. Max and Abigail found a spot near the stage, joining in the dancing and singing.

"They're amazing!" Abigail said, her eyes shining with excitement.

Max nodded. "Yeah, they really know how to get the crowd going."

As the evening continued with more music, laughter, and holiday cheer, Alex and Eden found a moment to themselves, watching the festivities unfold around them.

"This is fantastic," Eden said, leaning into Alex. "You've done an impressive job with everything."

Alex wrapped an arm around her. "I couldn't have done it without everyone's help. Seeing the town come together like this—it makes all the hard work worth it."

Eden smiled, looking out at the twinkling lights and the happy faces. "It really does. This is what the holidays are all about."

As the night ended, the Runaway 6 played a final song, and the crowd gathered for a group sing-along of "Silent Night." The voices of friends, family, and neighbors filled the air, creating a moment of pure holiday magic. Isaac, Jenny, Max, and Abigail stood together, joining in the song and feeling the warmth of the season. The anticipation for their secret party added an extra layer of excitement, but for now, they were content to soak in the joy of the moment.

●

The week after the tree lighting ceremony was a whirlwind of activity and excitement in Everbrook. The town square remained a hub of festive energy, with ongoing events and preparations for the upcoming Gala.

The ice rink was constantly filled with skaters, young and old, gliding gracefully under the twinkling lights. The giant snow globe attracted families who marveled at the enchanting winter scene inside. The Christmas market buzzed with activity as vendors sold handcrafted gifts, holiday treats, and warm beverages.

Sarah, Gabriel, and Jacob, along with their band, the Runaway 6, performed Christmas songs every evening for an hour, drawing crowds who swayed and sang along to the familiar tunes. Their performances added a magical ambiance to the town, making the evenings feel even more special.

Alex spent his days ensuring everything was perfect for the Gala. He coordinated with volunteers, checked on the decorations, and made sure all the logistics were in place. He found joy in seeing the town come together, the community spirit shining brightly through every aspect of the festivities.

Eden balanced her responsibilities at the clinic with the holiday preparations she was doing at home. She continued to provide free care for those in need, her dedication unwavering. The donations from the community helped accomplish her goal of feeding the hungry during the holidays, and Eden felt grateful for the support. During her breaks, Eden enjoyed walking through the festive town square, soaking in the holiday atmosphere. The lights, music, and laughter were a welcome respite from her busy schedule.

Isaac and Abigail juggled their schoolwork with the excitement of the upcoming events. Isaac participated in the live nativity, enjoying the camaraderie with his close friends. Jenny frequently came to see him at the nativity, their budding romance adding a layer of excitement to his days.

Abigail spent time with Max, their relationship growing stronger with each passing day. They enjoyed watching holiday movies together, going to the ice-skating rink, and frequenting the Christmas market, making memories that would last a lifetime. The siblings also kept their secret party plans under wraps, eagerly awaiting the night of the Gala when they could finally celebrate with their friends.

By the end of the week, Everbrook was ready for the Gala, and the townspeople were full of excitement. Alex woke up early, his mind filled with anticipation for the evening's events and the special surprise he had planned for Eden. He had spent the past week carefully preparing a scavenger hunt that would take her on a nostalgic journey through their most cherished memories.

Alex carefully wrapped a small Christmas present and placed the first clue inside. He drove to Eden's clinic, feeling a mix of excitement and nerves. As he walked in, he saw Eden busy with her patients, her dedication shining through as always.

"Hey, love," Alex greeted, handing her the package. "I thought you might like an early Christmas present."

Eden smiled, a curious spark in her eyes. "What's this? You're up to something, aren't you?"

Alex chuckled. "You'll have to open it and find out. But you can't open it until three o'clock this afternoon, alright? I'll see you later tonight, babe!"

With that, he gave her a kiss and left the clinic. Alex headed to the Italian restaurant where he planned to meet Eden later. He arranged for their favorite table to be beautifully decorated, the perfect setting for a romantic dinner before the Gala.

A few hours later, with all the patients attended to, Eden decided to close up early. Glancing at the clock, she realized it was time to open the package. Inside, she discovered a beautifully handcrafted card with a heartfelt message:

"To my dearest Eden,
Our love story has been the greatest adventure of my life. Follow these clues to relive some of our most treasured moments.
Your first clue: Go to the café where we had our first coffee date."

Eden's heart fluttered with excitement as she read the clue. She quickly locked the doors at the clinic and made her way to the café. When she arrived, the café was bustling with holiday cheer. She walked up to the counter, and the barista handed her a steaming cup of her favorite cappuccino, with a heart-shaped foam art on top, along with a small envelope.

"Here you go, Mrs. Freeman. Alex asked me to give this to you."

Eden smiled and opened the envelope:

"We've traveled so far since the first day we met. Do you

remember how our journey started with you pounding at my door? I couldn't have been happier to meet you than on that fateful day. On our journey, we have walked, thought, and fought.

Yet through all of this, you've never lost your love for me, even though you've experienced pain many times. I am thankful that I am never alone with you by my side. You are not an ordinary person; you have an amazing destiny to fulfill, and I want to be there with you, always and forever. When you finish this cup of coffee, go to the place where we first kissed."

Eden's eyes filled with tears of joy as she sipped her coffee, savoring the moment and the thoughtful message. Once she finished, she made her way to the gazebo. It was nestled in the town park, beautifully decorated with ice sculptures, twinkling lights, and garlands. As Eden approached the gazebo, she spotted another Christmas present with her name on it sitting under the bench where they had first kissed.

She carefully unwrapped it to find the dollar bill she had written on for Alex, a pair of exquisite ceramic earrings, and this note:

"Like a great tapestry, our memories together have created one large, beautiful image. I received this dollar the other day and realized how much we have grown since passing each other on that beautiful April evening. There's no telling what will happen from here on out, but if one thing is for certain, it's that I believe in you, and I know everything will be alright. Put on this pair of earrings and go to the restaurant where we had our first dinner. I'll be waiting for you."

Eden felt a rush of emotions as she gently put on the earrings. She remembered wanting them on their first trip to the market together. The memories of their journey together filled her heart with warmth and love. She made her way to the Italian restaurant, eager to see Alex and share this special moment. When she arrived at the Italian restaurant, her heart was racing with anticipation.

The hostess greeted her with a warm smile and handed her another envelope. "Alex wanted me to give this to you."

Eden opened the envelope and read the heartfelt message inside:

"Wake up in the morning, fall in love. At lunch, fall in love. And in the evening, fall in love again. That's my dream life. You've made it all possible. Meet me at our favorite table."

Eden followed the hostess to their table, which was beautifully decorated with candles, flowers, and twinkling lights. Alex stood by the table, his eyes filled with love and adoration. He pulled out a chair for Eden, and she sat down, her heart overflowing with emotion.

"This is incredible, Alex. Thank you for reminding me of all these beautiful moments," Eden said.

Alex took her hand, his eyes shining. "You've made my life a dream, Eden. I wanted to give you a night to remember before we head to the Gala."

They ordered their meal, then began reminiscing about their journey together and the love that had grown stronger with each passing year.

Back at the cottage, Abigail and Isaac were putting the final touches on their secret holiday party. The living room was decked out in festive decorations, complete with a garland-draped staircase and a mistletoe disco ball. The room was filled with the sound of holiday music and the scent of freshly baked cookies.

"Everything looks perfect," Abigail said, adjusting a string of lights around the fireplace.

Isaac nodded, checking the sound system one last time. "Yeah, we're all set. This is going to be epic."

As the first guests arrived, the house quickly filled with laughter and excitement. Friends came dressed in their ugliest holiday sweaters, each one more outrageous than the last. The atmosphere was electric, and the party was in full swing.

"Hey, nice sweater, Isaac!" one of his friends called out, pointing to the ridiculous snowman sweater he had on.

"Thanks," Isaac replied with a grin. "Yours isn't too shabby either!"

The living room buzzed with energy as more friends arrived. They danced on the makeshift dance floor, shared stories, took selfies, and enjoyed the merry atmosphere. Holiday-themed games, snack tables piled high with treats, and a lively playlist kept everyone entertained. Suddenly, a loud CRASHING BOOM BANG sounded from outside. Red and blue lights flashed.

Abigail's stomach dropped as kids yelled, "Cops!"

Teens scrambled in a panic, ducking behind furniture, or fleeing toward the back door patio.

"Wait, hold on!" Isaac shouted, peering out the window. "It's not the police, it's...an alien spaceship?!"

Suddenly, the front door banged open. In strode Uncle Leo, wearing an over-the-top ugly alien Christmas sweater, complete with tinsel tentacles and flashing lights.

"Greetings, Earthlings!" he yelled in a robotic voice. "Your interstellar party crasher has arrived to bring some cosmic holiday cheer!"

The teens froze, then erupted in laughter at the sight of Uncle Leo. He cranked up the music again and started break dancing in his galactic getup, his moves as outrageous as his outfit.

Abigail sighed with relief, then started giggling next to Max. "Leave it to Uncle Leo to make a supernatural flashy entrance!" she said. "Uncle Leo, you're unbelievable!"

Uncle Leo continued to dance, encouraging the teens to join in. "Come on, everyone! Let's make this the best party in the galaxy!"

The initial panic transformed into excitement as the teens embraced the fun. They joined Uncle Leo on the dance floor, laughing and mimicking his exaggerated moves. The party atmosphere shifted from secretive to exuberant, with Uncle Leo's unexpected arrival adding a new layer of joy and hilarity.

The house echoed with music, laughter, and the occasional alien sound effect from Uncle Leo's costume. The teens took turns posing for pictures with him, making memories that would last long after the holiday season ended.

Abigail and Isaac looked at each other from across the room and exchanged excited glances. Their secret party had faced a surprise twist, but it turned out even better than they had planned. The spirit of the holidays, with its unexpected moments and joyful surprises, was alive and well in their home.

●

Alex and Eden were thoroughly enjoying their date night at the cozy Italian restaurant downtown. Over steaming plates of pasta and red wine, they chatted and laughed, relishing this rare night out without the kids.

"This is exactly what we needed," Eden said, twirling her fork in the pasta. "Just the two of us, good food, and no interruptions. I feel so much more relaxed here."

Alex smiled, reaching across the table to fix her hair. "Absolutely. And you know, the nice thing about this place is, they'll never ask if you'd like some fries with that shake, but I will." He winked, causing Eden to burst out laughing.

They continued to share stories and laugh, savoring each other's company. The ambiance of the restaurant, with its soft lighting and gentle music, made the evening feel even more special.

"We should stop by the Gala later so you can make an appearance," Eden said. "I bet they're missing their star organizer."

"They don't need me more than I need you," Alex replied, though he knew she was right. He just didn't want this precious time alone with her to end. Just then, the busboy walked by, chatting with a server.

"Man, I wish I was at that huge party instead of working," the busboy said with a dramatic sigh. "I heard Isaac and Abigail's parents aren't home for the night. It's supposed to be the rager of the year!"

The server chuckled in agreement. "Right? I bet it's insane over there."

"Man, I'd take that ugly sweater party over these dishes any day," the busboy said.

The server chuckled again. "For real, sounds way more fun than this."

Eden froze, her drink halfway to her lips. Alex stared blankly with a forkful of tiramisu halfway to his mouth. Slowly, they turned to each other with widening eyes.

"Ugly sweater party?" she said slowly. "You don't think… Abigail and Isaac?"

Alex groaned, already signaling for the check. "I can't believe our kids would take advantage of our absence. If they're throwing a party, they'll be in trouble, Big Time!"

In a panic, the couple rushed from the restaurant, speeding home to bust the party they now felt sure their teenage children were throwing. Gone were thoughts of dancing and romance as parental duties called.

Downtown at the Christmas Gala, the energy in the ballroom was off the charts as Gabriel, Sarah, and the Runaway 6 took the stage at the city's annual Christmas Gala fundraiser. Decked out in jeweled dresses and sharp suits, the band kicked off an upbeat jazz number that immediately got the crowd dancing.

Couples swung and twirled across the dance floor as the band's lively trumpet and saxophone solos rang out. The atmosphere was festive and lively, with huge smiles all around. It was clear this performance was a big hit. After a few more jazzy tunes, the band slowed it down for a romantic ballad. Couples swayed in close embrace as Sarah's smooth vocals filled the room with comfort and joy.

As the set wound down, the Master of Ceremonies grabbed the mic.

"Let's hear it for Runaway 6!" he said as the crowd erupted into wild cheers and applause. "And now, a few words from the man who put this all together, Alex, our Executive Oak Master!" the Master of Ceremonies announced. But Alex was nowhere to be found, leaving the crowd murmuring in confusion. Had he forgotten?

After an awkward pause, a nervous man in a chef's apron shuffled below the stage, trying to avoid the spotlight but inadvertently getting tangled in the microphone cord. He tripped, knocking the microphone stand over. The room fell silent as the mic clattered to the floor in front of him.

The crowd, already in high spirits, saw the humor in the situation and started to chant, "Speech! Speech! Speech!"

The chef, blushing and flustered, picked up the mic. "Uh, sorry about that," he stammered, straightening his apron. "You know, this isn't the first time I've knocked over a microphone and been forced to give a speech."

The crowd laughed and cheered him on. Emboldened by their support, he took a deep breath and began, "Tonight is about abundance. Not just in the food we enjoy or the decorations we see, but in the love, community, and generosity that fills this room. Abundance isn't just about having a lot; it's about appreciating and sharing what we have with others."

The chef's voice grew steadier as he continued, "In Everbrook, we see abundance in the way we come together, in the way we

support each other, and in the way we celebrate. This Gala is a
testament to our shared spirit and the joy we find in being a part of
something bigger than ourselves."

The crowd began to nod and smile, the chef's unexpected speech
resonating with them. "So, let's continue to embrace the abundance
in our lives. Let's share our blessings, support one another, and
create memories that will last a lifetime. Thank you, and enjoy the
rest of the evening."

The room erupted in applause, the chef grinning sheepishly as he
handed the microphone back. The Master of Ceremonies, relieved,
took over again. "Well said! Let's give another round of applause for
our wonderful chef!"

Meanwhile, Alex and Eden rushed home, their concern growing
as they noticed flashing blue and red lights on the hilltop. The sight
of what appeared to be cop car lights in their driveway filled them
with worry. As they turned the corner, the flashing lights became
even more pronounced, and they felt a growing sense of dread.

Eden's voice quivered as she spoke, "Alex, this doesn't look good
at all. What do you think is happening?"

However, as they got closer, they began to hear a strangely
festive and otherworldly tune emanating from their own house. The
flashing lights were not coming from a police car, but from Uncle
Leo's car, which was parked sideways in their driveway and
completely transformed into a UFO-themed spectacle.

Alex and Eden exchanged perplexed and then amused glances. It
was as if their quirky Uncle Leo had taken holiday decorations to a
whole new level. The car looked like a giant acorn with metallic foil,
glowing lights, and strange symbols. As they approached the front
door, it swung open to reveal Uncle Leo, grinning from ear to ear,
dressed in his over-the-top alien-themed holiday sweater.

"Greetings, Earthlings!" Uncle Leo declared with a dramatic
flourish. "Welcome to the UFO Gala!"

Alex blinked in surprise. "Leo, what's going on here?"

"Everything is under control," Uncle Leo said with a confident
nod. "Just spreading some interstellar holiday cheer."

Eden tried to peer past him into the house. "Are the kids...?"

Uncle Leo stepped in front of her line of sight, holding up his
hands. "The kids are fine. They're just having a little holiday fun.
You two should go back to the Gala and enjoy your night."

Alex raised an eyebrow. "Are you sure everything's alright? We don't want to come home to a disaster."

Uncle Leo chuckled. "Trust me, Alex. I've got this."

Alex sighed, then gave a half-smile. "Alright, but can you at least park your car correctly in the driveway and turn off those crazy lights?"

Uncle Leo saluted. "Understood. Now go on, have a magical night. I'll handle everything here."

Reluctantly, Alex and Eden exchanged a look and then headed back to their car. "Well, that was unexpected," Eden said, shaking her head.

Alex chuckled. "It certainly was. But I trust Uncle Leo to keep things under control. Let's head back to the Gala and make the most of our night."

As they drove back to the Gala, they couldn't help but laugh at the absurdity of the situation. The holiday magic was alive and well, reminding them that sometimes the best memories are made in the most unexpected ways.

※

Lesson 11:
Abundance

Financial prosperity isn't just about accumulating wealth; it's about achieving a state of financial well-being where money supports your life goals, provides security, and grants you the freedom to pursue what truly matters. Understanding how to manage your finances is the first step toward this goal. Whether you're just starting out or looking to get your financial life back on track, this chapter will guide you through the essentials of financial literacy, wealth creation, and developing a mindset of abundance.

NOT FINANCIAL ADVICE: The information provided in this lesson should not be understood or construed as financial advice. I am not an attorney, accountant, or financial advisor, nor am I holding myself out to be. The information contained hereafter is not a substitute for financial advice from a professional who is aware of your individual situation. The following should be understood as educational and for research purposes only.

Understanding Financial Education and Literacy

Financial literacy is the foundation upon which financial prosperity is built. It involves understanding the basics of money management—how to budget, save, invest, and make informed financial decisions. If you're new to this, don't worry. The key is to start with the basics and build from there.

Budgeting is the cornerstone of financial management. It's the process of creating a plan for how you'll spend your money each month. A budget helps you ensure that you're living within your means, saving for the future, and not overspending on things that don't align with your goals.

To start, track your income and expenses for a month. This will give you a clear picture of where your money is going. Once you have this information, you can create a budget that allocates your income toward different categories:

1. Needs: These are your essential expenses, such as housing, utilities, groceries, transportation, and insurance. The goal is to keep

your needs to about 50% of your income.

2. Wants: These are the things you enjoy but don't necessarily need, like dining out, entertainment, and hobbies. Aim to keep these expenses to about 30% of your income.

3. Savings and Debt Repayment: The remaining 20% of your income should go toward savings and paying off debt. This is crucial for building wealth and financial security.

You can also try the **Envelope System** of budgeting. In this system, you physically or digitally allocate your budgeted amounts to different categories, using only what's in each "envelope" for that specific purpose. By sticking to a budget, whether it's the 50/30/20 rule or the Envelope System, you'll have a clear plan for your money each month, which helps reduce stress and allows you to focus on your financial goals.

An **emergency fund** is money set aside to cover unexpected expenses, such as medical bills, car repairs, or job loss. This fund acts as a financial safety net, preventing you from going into debt when unexpected costs arise. Aim to save three to six months' worth of living expenses in your emergency fund. Start small if you need to —saving even $500 can make a difference when an emergency occurs.

Keep your emergency fund in a separate, easily accessible savings account that earns interest. A high-yield savings account is a good option because it offers a higher interest rate than a regular savings account while still allowing you to access your money quickly when needed.

Debt can be a significant obstacle to financial prosperity, but it's also a tool that, when managed correctly, can help you achieve your financial goals. There are two main types of debt:

Good Debt: This is debt that's used to invest in your future, such as student loans, mortgages, or business loans. These types of debt typically have lower interest rates and the potential to increase your earning power or build wealth.

Bad Debt: This is debt used to purchase things that don't increase in value, such as credit card debt, payday loans, or car loans. Bad debt typically comes with high-interest rates and can quickly become unmanageable if not paid off promptly.

To manage your debt effectively, start by listing all your debts, including the balance, interest rate, and minimum monthly payment. Then, choose a debt repayment strategy:

Debt Snowball Method: Pay off your smallest debts first while making minimum payments on larger debts. Once the smallest debt is paid off, move on to the next smallest. This method gives you quick wins and keeps you motivated.

Debt Avalanche Method: Pay off your debts with the highest interest rates first while making minimum payments on others. This method saves you more money in interest over time.

Investing: Making Your Money Work for You

Investing is the process of putting your money into assets like stocks, bonds, real estate, or mutual funds with the expectation that it will grow over time. Unlike saving, which is about preserving your capital, investing is about generating returns and building wealth. Here's an overview of some common types of investments:

Stocks: When you buy a stock, you're purchasing a share in a company. Stocks have the potential for high returns, but they also come with higher risk. Stocks are best suited for long-term investing, as they can be volatile in the short term.

Bonds: Bonds are loans you make to a government or corporation in exchange for regular interest payments and the return of your principal at maturity. Bonds are generally considered lower risk than stocks, making them a good option for more conservative investors.

Mutual Funds and ETFs: These are collections of stocks, bonds, or other securities that you can buy into. They offer diversification, which reduces risk, and are managed by professionals. ETFs, or Exchange-Traded Funds, trade on stock exchanges and can be bought and sold like stocks.

Real Estate: Investing in real estate involves purchasing property to rent or sell for a profit. Real estate can provide a steady income stream and appreciates over time, making it a solid long-term investment.

Retirement Accounts: 401(k)s, IRAs, and Roth IRAs are tax-advantaged retirement accounts that allow you to invest in a mix of stocks, bonds, and mutual funds. These accounts are crucial for building a nest egg for retirement.

One of the most powerful concepts in investing is **compounding**. Compounding is the process by which your investment earnings generate their own earnings. Over time, compounding can turn even small investments into significant wealth. For example, if you invest $10,000 at a 7% annual return, after 10 years, your investment will grow to approximately $19,670. The longer you invest, the more powerful compounding becomes.

To take full advantage of compounding, start investing as early as possible, even if you can only contribute a small amount. The key is consistency—regular contributions, even small ones, can lead to significant growth over time.

Diversification is the practice of spreading your investments across different assets to reduce risk. By diversifying, you ensure that no single investment can have a disproportionately large impact on your portfolio. For example, if one stock performs poorly, the other investments in your portfolio can help offset the loss.

A well-diversified portfolio typically includes a mix of stocks, bonds, and other assets like real estate or commodities. Your asset allocation—the percentage of your portfolio invested in each type of asset—should be based on your risk tolerance, time horizon, and financial goals. As you approach retirement, for example, you might shift your allocation toward more conservative investments to preserve your wealth.

Building Wealth: Long-Term Strategies for Prosperity

Building wealth is about making consistent, informed decisions over time. It's not about getting rich quickly, but about creating a solid financial foundation that supports your long-term goals. Here's how to approach wealth-building in a sustainable way.

The first step in building wealth is setting clear financial goals. Your goals will guide your financial decisions and help you stay focused on what's most important. Consider both short-term and long-term goals:

Short-Term Goals: These are goals you want to achieve within the next one to five years, such as saving for a vacation, buying a car, or building an emergency fund.

Long-Term Goals: These are goals that will take longer to achieve, such as buying a home, funding your children's education, or saving for retirement.

Once you've set your goals, break them down into smaller, actionable steps. For example, if your goal is to save $20,000 for a down payment on a house in five years, you'll need to save $333 per month. By breaking your goals down into manageable steps, you'll make steady progress without feeling overwhelmed.

Investing for the Long Term

Investing is one of the most effective ways to build wealth over the long term. The key is to invest consistently and let your money grow over time. Here's how to approach long-term investing:

Start Early: The earlier you start investing, the more time your money has to grow. Even if you can only invest a small amount, starting early allows you to take full advantage of compounding.

Invest Regularly: Make investing a regular habit by contributing to your investment accounts on a monthly or bi-weekly basis. Automating your investments ensures that you stay consistent, regardless of market conditions.

<u>Stay the Course</u>: The stock market can be volatile in the short term, but history shows that it tends to grow over the long term. Don't let short-term market fluctuations derail your long-term investment strategy. Stay focused on your goals and resist the urge to make impulsive decisions based on market movements.

Real Estate as a Wealth-Building Tool

Real estate can be a powerful tool for building wealth. Whether you're investing in rental properties, flipping houses, or buying land, real estate offers the potential for both income and appreciation. Here's why real estate is a valuable part of a diversified portfolio:

<u>Steady Income</u>: Rental properties provide a steady income stream that can supplement your other investments. The rent you collect can be used to pay down the mortgage, cover expenses, or reinvest in other opportunities.

<u>Appreciation</u>: Real estate tends to appreciate over time, meaning that the value of your property increases. This appreciation, combined with the income generated from rentals, can significantly boost your net worth.

<u>Leverage</u>: Real estate allows you to use leverage—borrowing money to increase your potential return on investment. For example, if you purchase a property with a 20% down payment, you control 100% of the property's value. If the property appreciates, your return on investment can be substantial.

However, real estate also comes with risks, such as property market fluctuations, maintenance costs, and tenant issues. It's important to thoroughly research the real estate market and consider working with a real estate agent or financial advisor before making any investment decisions.

Shifting the Money Mindset: Cultivating Abundance

Your mindset around money can profoundly impact your financial success. Shifting from a scarcity mindset—where money is something to be feared or hoarded—to an abundance mindset—where money is seen as a tool for creating opportunities—can change everything.

Limiting beliefs about money are often ingrained from childhood. Maybe you've always heard that "money doesn't grow on trees" or that "wealth is only for the lucky few." These beliefs can create mental barriers that hold you back from achieving financial prosperity. But they don't have to.

Start by identifying these limiting beliefs. Ask yourself what thoughts come up when you think about money. Are they empowering, or do they make you feel stuck? Once you've identified them, challenge and reframe these thoughts. Instead of thinking, "I'll never be good with money," start telling yourself, "I'm learning to manage my money effectively." The shift might seem small, but it can have a profound impact on your financial decisions.

Developing a positive relationship with money involves seeing it as a tool to achieve your life's goals, not as a source of stress. Keep a money journal where you explore your thoughts and feelings about money. Celebrate your financial wins, no matter how small, and set clear intentions for what you want your money to do for you.

Visualization and affirmations can also be powerful tools in reshaping your mindset. Spend a few minutes each day visualizing your financial goals as if they've already been achieved. This not only increases your motivation but also helps you stay focused on the path to prosperity.

Surround yourself with people who have a positive relationship with money. Community and mentorship are invaluable in your journey toward financial abundance. Being around others who are also committed to financial growth can provide encouragement, share insights, and keep you accountable.

A positive relationship with money means viewing it as a tool, not an end in itself. It's about understanding that money can enhance your life and the lives of those around you. Start by practicing gratitude for what you have, and then focus on what money can do for you. Whether it's providing security, enabling experiences, or supporting causes you care about, money should be seen as a means to achieve your broader life goals.

Here's how to nurture this relationship:

Money Journaling: Keep a journal where you explore your thoughts and feelings about money. Track your financial goals and celebrate your progress.

Set Financial Intentions: Be clear about what you want to achieve with your money. Whether it's financial independence, supporting your family, or contributing to a cause, having clear intentions helps you stay motivated.

Visualization and Affirmations: Regularly visualize your financial goals and use positive affirmations to reinforce your belief in your ability to achieve them.

Mindset Practices for Abundance

To cultivate a mindset of abundance, incorporate these practices into your daily routine:

Affirmations: Use statements like "I am worthy of financial success" or "Money flows to me easily and abundantly" to reinforce a positive mindset.

Visualization: Spend a few minutes each day visualizing your financial goals as if they've already been achieved. This can increase your motivation and focus.

Community and Mentorship: Surround yourself with people who have a positive relationship with money. Join groups or communities that support financial growth, and seek out mentors who can guide you on your journey.

Financial prosperity is more than just accumulating wealth—it's about creating a life that reflects your values, provides security, and allows you the freedom to pursue your passions. By understanding your finances, implementing smart wealth-building strategies, and cultivating a positive money mindset, you can build a life of abundance and fulfillment.

Activity: Taking Control of Your Financial Future

This activity is designed to help you apply the concepts from the lesson to your own financial situation. It will guide you through setting up a budget, starting an emergency fund, managing debt, and beginning your investment journey. By the end of this exercise, you'll have a clearer understanding of your financial situation and a plan to move forward.

Step 1: Assess Your Current Financial Situation

1. Track Your Income and Expenses:
 - For the next month, track every dollar that comes in and goes out. Use a notebook, spreadsheet, or a budgeting app to record your income and expenses. Include everything—rent, groceries, entertainment, transportation, and even those small, seemingly insignificant purchases.
 - At the end of the month, review your spending. Categorize your expenses into three main areas: Needs, Wants, and Savings/Debt Repayment. This will give you a clear picture of your financial habits.

2. Calculate Your Net Worth:
 - Make a list of all your assets (what you own) and liabilities (what you owe). Assets might include cash, savings accounts, investments, and property. Liabilities include all your debts—credit card balances, student loans, mortgages, etc.
 - Subtract your total liabilities from your total assets. The result is your net worth. This number will give you a starting point and help you set financial goals.

Step 2: Create a Budget

1. Choose a Budgeting Method:
 - Based on your tracking, create a budget using the method that feels most comfortable to you. The 50/30/20 rule is a good starting point: allocate 50% of your income to Needs, 30% to Wants, and 20% to Savings/Debt Repayment.
 - Alternatively, try the Envelope System. Physically or digitally

allocate your budgeted amounts to different categories and spend only what's in each "envelope" for that specific purpose.

2. Set Financial Goals:
   - Define your short-term and long-term financial goals. Short-term goals might include paying off a credit card or saving for a vacation. Long-term goals could be buying a home, funding education, or saving for retirement.
   - Break down your goals into actionable steps. For example, if you want to save $1,000 for an emergency fund in six months, aim to save about $167 per month.

3. Adjust Your Spending:
   - Use your budget to identify areas where you can cut back on spending, particularly in the Wants category. Redirect this money toward your Savings/Debt Repayment or emergency fund.
   - Ensure that you're living within your means and saving for the future.

Step 3: Start an Emergency Fund

1. Open a High-Yield Savings Account:
   - If you don't already have one, open a high-yield savings account that offers a higher interest rate than a regular savings account. This will allow your emergency fund to grow while remaining easily accessible.

2. Set Up Automatic Transfers:
   - Automate your savings by setting up a monthly transfer from your checking account to your emergency fund. Even small amounts, like $25 or $50 per month, can add up over time.
   - Aim to save three to six months' worth of living expenses in your emergency fund. If that feels overwhelming, start with a smaller goal, like $500, and build from there.

Step 4: Manage Your Debt

1. List Your Debts:
   - Write down all your debts, including balances, interest rates,

and minimum monthly payments. This will give you a clear overview of what you owe and help you prioritize repayment.

2. Choose a Debt Repayment Strategy:
- Decide whether to use the Debt Snowball Method (paying off the smallest debts first) or the Debt Avalanche Method (paying off the highest interest rate debts first). Both methods have their advantages—choose the one that feels right for you.
- Focus on paying down your debts consistently, using the money you've freed up from budgeting and cutting unnecessary expenses.

3. Automate Payments:
- Set up automatic payments for your debts to ensure you never miss a payment. This will help you avoid late fees and reduce the mental burden of managing multiple due dates.

Step 5: Begin Investing

1. Educate Yourself:
- Before you start investing, spend some time learning about different investment options. Read books or articles about investing from reputable sources.
- Consider taking an online course in investing to build your knowledge and confidence.

2. Start Small:
- Open a brokerage account or a retirement account (like an IRA) and start with a small investment in a diversified index fund or ETF. These funds spread your money across many companies, reducing risk.
- Set up automatic contributions to your investment account, even if it's just a small amount each month. The key to investing is consistency and taking advantage of compounding over time.

3. Diversify Your Portfolio:
- As you become more comfortable with investing, consider diversifying your portfolio by adding different types of investments, such as bonds, real estate, or individual stocks.

- Monitor your investments regularly, but avoid the temptation to make impulsive changes based on short-term market fluctuations. Investing is a long-term strategy.

Step 6: Cultivate an Abundant Money Mindset

1. Identify Limiting Beliefs:
   - Reflect on your thoughts and beliefs about money. Write down any negative or limiting beliefs you have, such as "I'll never be wealthy" or "Money is the root of all evil."
   - Challenge these beliefs by reframing them into positive affirmations. For example, replace "I'll never be wealthy" with "I am capable of building wealth through smart financial decisions."

2. Practice Gratitude:
   - Keep a gratitude journal where you write down things you're thankful for each day, including financial blessings, no matter how small. This practice helps shift your focus from scarcity to abundance.
   - Regularly acknowledge and celebrate your financial progress, whether it's paying off a debt, saving a certain amount, or sticking to your budget.

3. Visualize Your Financial Success:
   - Spend a few minutes each day visualizing your financial goals as if they've already been achieved. Imagine the peace of mind that comes with having a solid emergency fund, the excitement of investing for your future, and the satisfaction of living within your means.
   - Use positive affirmations to reinforce your belief in your ability to achieve these goals, such as "I am in control of my financial future" or "I am worthy of financial success."

4. Surround Yourself with Positive Influences:
   - Join a community of like-minded individuals who are also focused on improving their financial situation. This could be a local group, an online forum, or even a few friends who share similar goals.
   - Seek out a financial mentor or advisor who can provide

guidance and support as you work toward your financial goals.

At the end of the month, review your progress. Reflect on what you've learned about your financial habits, the steps you've taken toward your goals, and any challenges you faced. Adjust your budget, savings, and investment strategies as needed to keep moving forward.

This practical activity is designed to help you take control of your finances step by step. By following these actions, you'll build a solid financial foundation, reduce stress, and create a path toward financial prosperity that supports your life goals and values.

•

Throughout this lesson, we have embarked on a journey exploring the principles of financial management, wealth creation, and abundance. We delved into the importance of financial education and literacy, examined various wealth-building strategies and investment opportunities, and focused on cultivating a mindset of abundance and prosperity.

Financial prosperity is not merely about accumulating wealth; it encompasses a holistic approach to managing our finances, making informed decisions, and embracing a mindset that attracts abundance. It is about creating a solid foundation for financial well-being, nurturing healthy money habits, and aligning our beliefs and attitudes towards money with our desires for a prosperous life.

In our exploration of financial education and literacy, we learned the importance of understanding personal finance, budgeting, and investing. By equipping ourselves with knowledge and tools, we can make informed financial decisions, create effective budgets, and develop sound investment strategies.

Building wealth is another crucial aspect of financial prosperity. We explored various strategies and investment opportunities that can help grow wealth over time. From saving and investing to exploring different asset classes, we discovered the importance of diversification and long-term planning. Building wealth requires discipline, patience, and a willingness to adapt to changing market conditions. By setting personalized wealth-building plans and exploring investment options, we position ourselves for long-term financial success.

Lastly, we delved into the realm of shifting our money mindset. Cultivating a mindset of abundance and prosperity opens up new possibilities and attracts positive financial experiences. Through practicing gratitude and affirmations, we harness the power of positive thinking and align our thoughts and emotions with financial abundance. By embracing a mindset of abundance, we break free from limiting beliefs and create a fertile ground for attracting opportunities, wealth, and prosperity into our lives.

As we conclude this lesson, remember that financial prosperity is a lifelong journey that requires dedication, discipline, and self-awareness. It is not solely about the accumulation of money but also about living a fulfilling and purposeful life, making a positive impact, and achieving financial freedom that allows us to pursue our passions and dreams.

Stay committed to your financial goals, continue expanding your financial knowledge, and embrace a mindset of abundance. With these principles in mind, you are well on your way to creating a life of financial prosperity and fulfillment.

> "I am a spark from the Infinite. I am not flesh and bones. I am light. In helping others succeed I shall find my own prosperity. In the welfare of others I shall find my own well-being. I am infinite. I am spaceless, I am tireless; I am beyond body thought, and utterance; beyond all matter and mind. I am endless bliss."
>
> -Paramahansa Yogananda

Chapter 12: The Show Must Go On

The rain outside was ferocious, pouring down in relentless sheets and creating a steady drumbeat against the roof and windows of the Tall Oaks building. The sky above was a dark, swirling mass of clouds, occasionally lit by jagged streaks of lightning, followed by the deep rumble of thunder. Despite the storm having only begun the day before, it had stalled over Everbrook, dropping nearly 12 inches of rain in less than twenty-four hours.

Inside the Tall Oaks building, however, was a different world entirely. The large hall was brightly lit and decorated for the pancake breakfast and polka party that had drawn the entire community together.

Tables covered in colorful tablecloths were adorned with vases of fresh flowers, adding a touch of spring to the otherwise stormy Sunday morning. The room was filled to capacity, with every table occupied by families and friends who were sharing stories and soaking in the lively music.

Children weaved through the crowd, their giggles mingling with the lively conversations around them. Elderly couples sat side by side, reminiscing about past polka parties and pancake breakfasts, while younger families created new memories.

The lively sound of polka music, played by Jacob's band, filled the air. The upbeat melody danced through the hall, blending seamlessly with the laughter and chatter of the guests. The clinking of cutlery and plates added to the festive atmosphere. Occasionally, the deep bass of a tuba or the bright notes of a clarinet would rise above the general hum of conversation, drawing cheers and applause from the crowd.

The scent of butter melting on hot griddles, sizzling bacon, and freshly made pancakes mingled with the sweet scent of maple syrup and the rich fragrance of freshly brewed coffee. The warm, comforting smells permeated the air, inviting everyone to indulge and enjoy the hearty breakfast being served by volunteers. Despite the weather outside, the Tall Oaks building was a place of joy, music, and community, where people could momentarily forget the storm and savor the company of friends and family.

In the center of the hall, a space had been cleared for dancing. Couples twirled and swayed to the lively polka music, their movements synchronized with the cheerful rhythm. Among them, Alex and Eden danced together, their steps light and joyful. Despite their age, they moved with grace and ease, their faces glowing with happiness.

Sarah, her bright smile lighting up the room, stood on stage and sang along with the music, her melodic voice blending beautifully with the instruments. Beside her, Gabriel played his accordion with enthusiasm, his eyes often drifting toward Sarah, filled with love and admiration.

At a table near the dance floor, Isaac and Jenny managed their energetic triplets with practiced ease. Jenny cradled one baby, gently rocking him in her arms, while Isaac focused on feeding another with a bottle. The third triplet lay on a blanket spread out on the table, gurgling happily, and reaching for a colorful toy.

Abigail and Max were nearby, helping their children, eight-year-old Emma and nine-year-old Liam, with their pancakes. Abigail carefully cut up Emma's pancakes into bite-sized pieces, while Max poured syrup over Liam's plate, making sure to get it just right. Their movements were quick and synchronized, a dance of parental teamwork honed over years.

Uncle Leo moved from table to table, making jokes and telling animated stories. Dressed in his usual colorful attire, his white hair and quick wit made him a favorite among the children. He made jokes and told animated stories, causing bursts of laughter to echo through the room. Children followed him eagerly, captivated by his animated gestures and the magic of his tales.

Alex and Eden walked off the dance floor toward Isaac and Abigail's table, mingling with guests along the way. Older now, Alex exuded a dignified yet approachable aura, while Eden's gentle smile and kind eyes radiated warmth. They moved through the crowd, sharing smiles and warm conversations, their connection with each person genuine and heartfelt.

Alex paused near Emma and Liam, who were eager to talk to him. Kneeling down to their level, he listened intently as Emma's eyes sparkled with curiosity.

"Are you going to write another book, Grandpa?" Emma asked, her voice filled with wonder.

Liam looked up at him, eyes sparkling with curiosity. "We love your stories!"

Alex's expression turned reflective. "The older you get, the more stories there are for you," he said, his voice gentle. "But when it's time to put an end to something, it's best you just leave it alone."

Alex picked up Emma and sat her on his knee. "You know, you have a wonderful imagination, Emma. Why don't you write a story?"

Emma's eyes lit up. "Me? But I'm just a kid."

"That's the best time to start," Alex said, his voice filled with encouragement. "You have the power to create amazing stories with your imagination. All you need is a bit of paper and a pencil. Who knows? Maybe one day, people will be asking you about your stories."

Emma beamed at the idea. "Okay, Grandpa, I'll try!"

Satisfied with their conversation, Emma and Liam decided to play hide and seek. They darted off, giggling, and soon disappeared among the tables and chairs, their laughter blending with the music and chatter.

The ferocious rain pounded against the windows of the Tall Oaks building, each droplet a relentless hammering that drowned out the lively sounds inside. The warmth and cheer of the pancake breakfast and polka party continued, but a crack of thunder suddenly turned the power on and off, plunging the room into brief, startled silence. The lights flickered back on, and a murmur of concern rippled through the crowd.

From the kitchen, the steady voice of a news reporter cut through the airwaves of the radio. "This just in: the river is swelling rapidly, and water levels are beginning to rise. Authorities are advising residents to seek higher ground as storm drains are becoming blocked and the possibility of flash floods threatens the downtown and surrounding low-lying areas of Everbrook."

As the report continued, the front door of the Tall Oaks building swung open, letting in a gust of wind and rain. A drenched man stumbled in, his shoes squelching with every step, with water streaming off his clothes. His pants were rolled up to his knees, revealing his soaked ankles. He held the fabric high, trying to keep it dry as much as possible.

"Water's starting to trickle inside," he announced, his voice tinged with urgency. "It's rising fast out there!"

People began to glance outside worriedly, the reality of the storm settling in. Isaac, trying to maintain a calm demeanor, turned to Abigail and placed a reassuring hand on her shoulder.

"There's nothing to worry about," he said confidently. "If Everbrook didn't flood back when the big storm hit when we were kids, it won't flood now."

Abigail gave him a faint smile, but her eyes betrayed her concern. The atmosphere inside the building shifted as the community realized the seriousness of the situation. The lively chatter and laughter that had filled the room moments ago were replaced by a murmur of worried voices. People began to gather their things, casting anxious glances outside. A woman near the window checked her phone, her face paling as she read the screen.

"There's a severe weather alert," she announced, her voice shaking slightly. "They're saying it could turn into a major flash flood."

Meanwhile, in a corner of the hall, Emma and Liam continued playing hide and seek, their laughter a stark contrast to the growing tension among the adults. Liam tiptoed through the hall, his eyes scanning for any sign of his sister.

"Emma, where are you?" he whispered, a grin spreading across his face.

He moved past tables and chairs, his heart racing with the thrill of the hunt. Suddenly, he spotted a small foot peeking out from behind a curtain.

"Got you!" he exclaimed, pulling the curtain aside to reveal Emma, who burst into giggles.

"Okay, you found me," Emma said, still laughing. "Now it's your turn to hide, but let's make it more fun. Let's go to a different room. It'll be more challenging!"

Liam's eyes sparkled with mischief. "Alright, let's do it," he agreed.

The two of them quietly slipped out of the main hall, careful not to draw any attention from the adults. They made their way down a dimly lit corridor, the sound of the storm outside still audible but slightly muffled. The corridor led to a smaller room on the first floor, which was usually used for storing tables and chairs.

Emma found a spot and began to count, her voice soft but clear. "One... two... three..."

Liam hurried to find a hiding place, his mind racing. He found an old antique armoire and quickly slipped inside, closing the door just enough to leave a small crack for him to peek through.

"...eight... nine... ten! Ready or not, here I come!" Emma called out.

As she began her search, the tension in the room started to build. The faint sound of trickling water reached her ears, but she was too focused on the game to pay much attention. She moved around the room, checking behind boxes and furniture.

A crack of thunder echoed through the Tall Oaks building, the lights flickering ominously once more. The Executive Oakmaster, a young man named Lorenzo, jumped up on the stage and grabbed the microphone. He addressed the crowd with a firm voice that cut through the disturbance of the storm.

"Everyone, we need to move to the second floor for safety!"

The cheerful atmosphere evaporated as a wave of concern churned through the room. People began to gather their belongings, eyes wide with worry. Near the stage, Sarah and Gabriel quickly began packing up their instruments.

"We need to hurry, Gabriel!" Sarah urged, her voice tight with anxiety.

Gabriel nodded, securing his accordion and gathering their music sheets. "I've got everything, let's go!"

At a nearby table, Isaac and Jenny scrambled to gather their triplets. Jenny carefully placed each baby into a large stroller, making sure they were secure, while Isaac grabbed their diaper bag and a few essentials.

"Isaac, make sure the stroller is locked!" Jenny said, her voice trembling.

"It's secure. Let's get to the stairs!" Isaac replied, pushing the heavy stroller towards the stairwell.

The triplets, sensing the change in atmosphere, started to fuss, their cries adding to the growing tension.

Panic set in as Abigail and Max realized Emma and Liam, who were playing hide and seek, were missing. Abigail frantically looked around the dance hall, her heart pounding.

"Where are Emma and Liam? They were just here!" she exclaimed.

Max called out their names, "Emma? Liam?" His voice rising above the noise. "They were playing hide and seek. We have to find them!"

Uncle Leo, ever the calming presence, moved through the crowd, trying to maintain order. "Stay calm, everyone! Follow the person in front of you and keep moving! We'll get everyone to safety if we move in a calm and orderly fashion."

"Alex, Eden," he called out, "help me keep things orderly. We need to get these folks upstairs quickly."

As Alex and Eden joined Uncle Leo in organizing the move, Abigail and Max continued their desperate search for Emma and Liam, their hearts pounding with fear for their children's safety.

Isaac and Jenny, struggling with the stroller and their belongings, realized the stairs would be too difficult to navigate. Isaac looked at Jenny with concern.

"We can't carry all of this up the stairs. The elevator is our best option," he said.

Jenny nodded, worry etched on her face. "But what if the power goes out again? We can't risk getting stuck."

Isaac sighed, knowing the risk but feeling they had no choice. "It's too much to handle otherwise. Let's just get to the elevator quickly."

Isaac, Jenny, the triplets, and several elderly and disabled individuals entered the elevator, hoping to reach the second floor safely. The once lively and festive Tall Oaks building was now a hive of urgent activity, with everyone working together to ensure that no one was left behind as the floodwaters threatened to rise.

People moved quickly to the second floor, guided by the calm but firm directions of the volunteers. The second-floor rooms, usually spacious and used for holding meetings, were now crowded with people seeking refuge. Large windows lined the walls, offering a grim view of the rising water levels and the storm's fury outside.

Isaac and Jenny managed to get the stroller into the elevator, cramming in with several elderly and disabled people. Isaac tried to offer a reassuring smile to Jenny.

"We'll be okay," he said, more to convince himself than her. Jenny nodded, holding one of the triplets close.

"We have to be," she whispered, her eyes fixed on the numbers of the elevator panel as she repeatedly pressed the number two. As the elevator doors closed and began its ascent, Isaac and Jenny braced themselves for what lay ahead.

Emma and Liam, caught up in their game of hide and seek in the storage room, were blissfully unaware of the growing chaos around them. Liam, hidden in the armoire, felt a chill as he noticed water seeping in under the door. It started as a small trickle but quickly began to spread across the floor. His excitement turned to apprehension as the water continued to rise.

Emma, still searching, finally turned towards the armoire. "Liam, I know you're in there!" she declared, her voice echoing slightly in the now eerie silence of the room. She pulled the wardrobe door open just as the water reached her ankles. Both children stared at each other, their eyes wide with fear.

"Emma, the water! It's coming in fast!" Liam shouted, stepping out of the wardrobe.

Emma looked around, the rising water now an undeniable threat. "We need to get out of here, Liam! Now!"

They turned to leave, but the water was already making it difficult to move quickly. Panic set in as they struggled to make their way back to the corridor. The once playful game of hide and seek had turned into a desperate race against the rising floodwaters.

"Emma! Liam! Where are you?" Abigail called, her voice cracking with anxiety.

She left the dance hall and moved quickly from room to room, her eyes scanning every corner. Max followed closely, his own anxiety mounting.

"They couldn't have gone far. We need to check all the rooms on this floor," he said, trying to keep his voice steady.

As they searched, the water on the first floor began to rise more rapidly, seeping under doors and creeping up the walls. Abigail's heart pounded in her chest.

"Emma! Liam! Answer me!" she shouted, her voice echoing off the walls.

Max moved quickly through the room, checking under tables and behind chairs. "Come on, kids, this isn't funny anymore!" he shouted, his worry mounting with each passing second.

Meanwhile, Isaac, Jenny, the triplets, and a few other people packed into the elevator. Isaac held the large stroller tightly, ensuring the triplets were secure. Jenny stood close by, trying to soothe the fussing babies. The other individuals leaned against the walls, their faces etched with concern.

As the elevator began its ascent, Isaac suddenly muttered, "Oh no!" He then quickly added with a forced smile, "Don't stand too close to me, I just farted."

A few nervous chuckles filled the small space, briefly brightening up the mood. But as if on cue, the elevator jolted to a stop right after his joke. The lights flickered, and a collective gasp filled the small space. Isaac's attempt at humor faded quickly.

"What's happening? Are we stuck?" Jenny asked, her voice trembling.

"It looks like it," Isaac replied, trying to stay calm. "Everyone, stay calm. We'll get this sorted out."

Panic began to spread among the elevator occupants. An elderly woman clutched her chest, while a man in a wheelchair looked around helplessly.

Isaac took a deep breath, trying to project confidence. "I'll call for help," he said, pulling out his phone and quickly dialing Jacob's number. "We need help, Jacob! We're stuck in the elevator with babies and some other people."

The backup emergency lights flickered in the stalled elevator, and the sound of water trickling underneath them added a new layer of fear. Isaac and Jenny exchanged worried glances as the soft but unmistakable sound of rising water reached their ears. The triplets, sensing the tension, began to whimper, their tiny faces scrunching up in distress.

"We can hear water," an elderly man in the corner whispered, his voice trembling. "It sounds like it's getting closer."

Isaac, determined to keep the panic at bay, put on a brave face. "We'll be fine. Help is on the way," he said, though his own anxiety was evident in his eyes.

Meanwhile, on the second floor, the community had gathered in small groups, trying to comfort one another as they waited for news about those still downstairs. Uncle Leo, always one to lighten the mood, decided to take action.

"Alright, folks," he said, clapping his hands to get everyone's attention. "Let's see if we can distract ourselves a bit. Who's up for a quick game of charades?"

A few hesitant laughs followed, and someone in the back shouted, "Sure, why not? Better than just sitting here worrying."

Uncle Leo smiled and mimed pulling an invisible object out of his pocket. "Guess what I am!" he announced, wiggling his eyebrows.

"An idiot!" someone called out, and the room erupted in laughter, a welcome release of tension.

Back in the elevator, Isaac's phone buzzed with a text message from Jacob, who was coordinating efforts upstairs. Isaac read the message out loud, hoping to reassure everyone.

"They're working on getting us out. They're getting a crowbar to open up the elevator shaft. Just a bit longer," he said, trying to keep his voice steady.

Outside, the storm raged on, relentless and unyielding. The river, swollen to monstrous proportions, lapped hungrily at the foundations of nearby structures. Rain fell in heavy sheets, and the wind howled through the streets, carrying with it the ominous creaks and groans of strained trees.

A particularly fierce gust tore through near the stone bridge, and a massive oak tree, its roots weakened by the saturated ground, began to sway dangerously. It stood on a small rise near the river just beyond the stone bridge, its ancient roots gripping the soil desperately. The wind intensified, and with a final, mighty push, the tree gave way.

With a deafening crack, the oak was uprooted. Its thick trunk and sprawling branches, once a symbol of strength and stability, were now at the mercy of the storm. The tree teetered for a moment before the wind carried it into a violent descent. Branches snapped and leaves scattered as the tree plummeted down the slope, crashing through the underbrush and tearing up chunks of earth in its path.

The tree's journey was a destructive force of nature, ripping through anything in its way. Smaller trees and shrubs were flattened, their broken remains adding to the debris. The roots, now exposed, looked like gnarled fingers clawing at the air. The wind roared, and the tree gained momentum, hurtling quickly through the streets. It began heading towards downtown Everbrook with unstoppable force.

Inside the building, the sudden, intensified, howling roar outside drew everyone's attention. Eyes turned towards the windows just as the massive oak came into view, a dark, menacing silhouette against the stormy sky.

The tree violently struck the Tall Oaks building with terrifying speed. It pierced through a window on the first floor where Emma and Liam were hiding, sending heavy stone blocks and glass shards flying in all directions. The force of the collision didn't stop there; its momentum carried it forward, tearing a large, gaping hole in the side of the building. A substantial chunk of the wall crumbled away, creating a wide, jagged breach. The tree spun around with the churning, fast-moving current of the river, and it continued its destruction as it floated down Main Street, carrying part of the Tall

Oaks building with it.

Water surged in through the breach and into the room where Emma and Liam had been playing hide and seek, flushing them out into the hallway. The floodwaters, propelled by the storm, carried them rapidly toward the stairs where Alex, Max, and Abigail were taking refuge. Alex and Max sprang into action, their faces set with determination.

Alex's voice cut through the panic. "There they are, they're headed right for us! Max, help me get Emma and Liam!"

Abigail was frantic, her eyes wide with fear as she screamed for her children's safety. "Emma! Liam! Grab onto something!" she called out desperately, her voice breaking with panic.

Alex and Max saw the children being swept away by the floodwaters. Without a moment's hesitation, they dove into the water, fighting against the powerful current. The water was turbulent, cold, and fierce, but their determination drove them forward.

"I've got you, Emma! Hold on tight!" Alex shouted as he reached for his granddaughter. He wrapped his arms around her, pulling her to safety.

"Liam, don't let go!" Max yelled as he grabbed hold of his son, lifting him out of the water and carrying him to a dry area up the stairs. The children clung to them, shivering and terrified.

Emma, safe in Alex's arms, screamed. "Aiiieeee... I screamed... I don't know what else to do!" She began to cry, her voice echoing through the chaos, the fear and relief overwhelming her. Abigail and Sarah were ready with blankets, quickly wrapping the shivering children and comforting them.

Abigail's voice was calm and soothing. "You're safe now, sweethearts. Everything's going to be alright."

On the second floor, the impact of the oak tree was felt immediately. The entire building shook violently, causing furniture to topple and people to be thrown off balance. The once orderly evacuation had turned into a frantic scramble for safety. Panic erupted as screams filled the air. People scrambled to get to safety, some trampling over others in their desperation. Shouts and cries mingled with the sound of the storm, creating a scene of pure pandemonium.

"Did you hear that? The building's going to collapse!" someone shouted, their voice rising above the commotion.

"We need to get out of here!" another voice screamed, the fear rising.

Among the chaos, Lorenzo, with a defiant stride, pushed his way through the crowd. His face was set with determination as he tried to restore order. "Everyone stay calm!" he shouted, his voice firm and commanding. "The Tall Oaks building was built by master builders. It was made to withstand the attack of storms like this. It's the safest building in Everbrook!"

Suddenly, a bookshelf toppled, pinning a woman's leg beneath it, breaking and exposing part of her bone.

"Help! Someone help me!" the woman cried out in terror, trying to free herself from the heavy bookshelf.

Leo and Lorenzo rushed to her side, working together to lift the heavy piece of furniture and pull her to safety. "It's going to be alright," Leo assured her, his voice calm and steady. "We've got a doctor here who can help you."

Nearby, a man clutched his bleeding arm, cut by flying debris. Eden began tending to the injured man, tearing strips from her dress to use as makeshift bandages.

"Hold still," she instructed, her hands deftly wrapping the wound. "We need to keep pressure on this."

Meanwhile, Jacob and Gabriel were working furiously to pry open the elevator doors. The faint sound of water trickling from under the elevator added to the urgency of the situation.

"Jacob, put your back into it! We need to get these doors open!" Gabriel shouted, his voice strained with effort.

"I'm trying! Just a little more!" Jacob grunted, their combined strength finally forcing the doors open with a crowbar, revealing the frightened faces of Isaac, Jenny, the triplets, and other individuals inside.

"Hang on, folks," Gabriel said, his tone steady and calming. "We're going to get you out of there." Isaac and Jenny, holding their triplets close, were pulled to safety.

"It's okay, we've got you," Jacob reassured her. Next, they helped an elderly woman, guiding her gently through the narrow gap. The man in the wheelchair was more challenging, but with coordinated effort, they managed to lift him safely out.

The elevator group was guided to safety on the second floor, where Eden was ready with warm blankets and comforting words. Isaac and Jenny, clutching their triplets, were visibly relieved to be out of the water and safe.

•

The second-floor meeting rooms at the Tall Oaks building buzzed with activity as Eden began transforming the space into a makeshift hospital. Her voice rang out with clear instructions, cutting through the lingering panic.

"We need to set up makeshift beds over here! Jacob, help me move these tables. Sarah, start distributing blankets and medical supplies. Leo, make sure everyone has water and is comfortable."

In one corner of the room, a woman named Anne lay on a blanket, her leg crushed and broken from a heavy bookshelf that had fallen during the initial chaos of the flood. The bookshelf had already been moved, but Anne's leg was in a dire state. The bone was protruding through the skin, and she was in excruciating pain.

Eden approached Anne with a reassuring smile. "Anne, I'm Eden. I'm going to take care of you."

Anne nodded weakly, tears streaming down her face. "It hurts so much," she whispered.

"I know," Eden said gently, kneeling beside her. "But I'm here now, and we're going to get you fixed up. Jacob, I need clean cloths, disinfectant, and a splint."

Jacob returned with the requested items, and Eden set to work. She cleaned the wound as best as she could, the makeshift supplies barely adequate for such a severe injury. The exposed bone and torn flesh made it clear that Anne needed professional medical attention, but Eden knew she had to do everything possible to stabilize her until help arrived.

"This is going to sting a bit, but it's important to prevent infection," Eden explained as she applied the disinfectant. Anne winced but remained still, her breathing heavy.

"You're doing great, Anne. Just keep focusing on your breathing," Eden encouraged, her voice steady and calm. Once the wound was clean, Eden prepared to set the bone.

"Jacob, I need you to hold her leg steady while I apply the splint," Eden instructed. Jacob complied, his face pale but resolute.

Eden carefully aligned the bone, causing Anne to cry out in pain.

"I'm sorry, Anne, but this is necessary," Eden said, her voice calm and firm. She worked quickly, securing the splint and wrapping the leg tightly to minimize movement.

"There, the worst part is over," Eden said, wiping her brow. "We've stabilized the leg, but you need to stay still and keep it elevated. We'll get you to a hospital as soon as we can."

Anne nodded, her breathing heavy but more controlled. "Thank you," she whispered, tears of relief mingling with the sweat on her face.

"You're very brave, Anne," Eden said, giving her hand a comforting squeeze. "Just hang in there. We're going to get through this."

Eden glanced around the room, ensuring that the other injured were being attended to. As she passed by a group of people huddled together, she heard a voice filled with panic.

"We came here to die, we're never going to make it!" the person said, their voice trembling.

Eden stopped and turned to face them, her eyes steady and reassuring. "We didn't come here to die," she said firmly, her voice carrying an untroubled strength. "We came here to be alive! And we will make it through this, together."

Her words seemed to have a calming effect on the group. They nodded, some wiping away tears, as they drew strength from her conviction. Eden moved from person to person, her hands steady and her voice soothing.

"We need more blankets here," she called out, pointing to an empty spot where a makeshift bed had been set up. "And someone bring more water and towels."

Isaac, seeing the need for more hands, took charge of gathering additional supplies. He led a group of volunteers to search through all the rooms on the second floor to retrieve anything that could be useful.

"Let's move quickly but carefully," he urged, his voice carrying a reassuring tone. "We don't want anyone getting hurt."

As they returned with armfuls of blankets, towels, and other necessities, Eden continued to coordinate the setup. The room began to take on the appearance of a well-organized triage center, with medical supplies laid out neatly and volunteers tending to the injured. Eden knelt beside an elderly woman who had been carried up from the elevator. She checked the woman's pulse and offered her a reassuring smile.

"You're going to be fine," Eden said softly, wrapping a blanket around her shoulders. "We're taking good care of you."

Nearby, a young volunteer was bandaging a child's scraped knee, her hands gentle but efficient. "There you go, all better," she said, giving the child a comforting pat on the shoulder.

Isaac returned with another load of supplies and caught Eden's eye. "We've got more blankets and some extra medical kits," he reported, his face showing both exhaustion and determination.

"Good work," Eden replied, her voice filled with gratitude. "Let's keep it up. We need to make sure everyone is warm, dry, and comfortable."

Uncle Leo, ever the calming presence, moved among the people, cracking jokes and sharing stories to lighten the mood. "Did I ever tell you about the time my grandparents got caught in a flood back in '66?" he began, his voice carrying a note of humor. The laughter that followed was a welcome sound amidst the tension.

Uncle Leo grinned as he started the story. "During the Everbrook Flood of '66, my grandparents were stuck on the second floor of their house. The flood was at its peak when my grandfather, ever the innovator, decided they should have a bit of fun and organized a 'raft regatta' in their living room."

He paused, seeing the curiosity in everyone's eyes. "They fashioned different rafts out of anything that would float—sofa cushions, planks of wood, even an old door. My grandmother, competitive as ever, insisted on decorating her raft with curtains and flowers. She even found an old umbrella to use as a makeshift sail, convinced it would give her an edge."

Leo chuckled, "My grandfather, not to be outdone, decided his raft needed a name. He christened it 'The Good Ship Lollipop,' saying that it was the fastest ship in the fleet and would bring him a sweet victory. They paddled around using broomsticks, and the goal was to navigate from the kitchen to the fireplace without tipping over."

Leo leaned in, his voice lowering as if sharing a secret. "Things started off smoothly enough. They were paddling along, laughing and shouting encouragements. But then, my grandmother's umbrella sail caught a draft from an open window, and her raft started spinning in circles. She was so dizzy she almost fell off, but she managed to hang on, shouting, 'Giovanni, close that window!'"

The crowd laughed, and Leo continued, "Meanwhile, my grandfather was doing quite well until 'The Good Ship Lollipop' hit a snag—literally. It got caught on the chandelier, and he ended up tipping over into the water, splashing everywhere. He came up sputtering and laughing, but my grandmother was determined to win. She paddled furiously towards the fireplace, but the current from the water was stronger than she anticipated."

Leo's grin widened. "Just when it looked like she might actually reach the finish line, the family cat, Mr. Poochyfud, decided to join the fun. He leapt onto her raft, startling her so much that she lost her balance and toppled into the water with a scream. Mr. Poochyfud, of course, landed gracefully on a floating cushion and proceeded to groom himself as if nothing had happened."

The room erupted in laughter, the tension easing as people enjoyed the humorous story. "In the end," Leo said, "neither of them won the race, but they had the time of their lives. They were soaked but happier than ever. My grandmother always said that little regatta kept their spirits afloat, quite literally. The waters receded shortly thereafter, and they spent the rest of the evening drying off by the fireplace, drinking hot cocoa, and planning their next adventure. And Mr. Poochyfud? He stayed dry and smug on his cushion, the real winner of the day."

As the laughter died down, a sense of calm and resilience filled the room. Eden continued to tend to the injured, the warmth and support of the community surrounding her. Outside, the water was reaching dangerous levels, threatening to overwhelm their makeshift sanctuary.

●

Alex, Lorenzo, and Gabriel decided it was time to head to the third floor to find more supplies and assess the situation better. They moved carefully through the building, the floors creaking under the force of the storm outside. The path to the stairs was treacherous, with debris scattered everywhere from the impact of the oak tree.

As they climbed, Alex broke the silence. "We need to figure out a way to signal for help. The roads are probably washed out, and who knows how long the power will be out."

Lorenzo nodded, his face grim. "I agree. The old bell in the watchtower could work but it's been years since it was used. Do you think it'll still ring?"

Gabriel chimed in, his voice tense but trying to lighten the mood. "Well, if it doesn't, we'll just have to yell really loud. I've got a pretty good set of lungs."

Lorenzo chuckled despite the tension. "We might need more than that, Gabriel. But let's check out the third floor first. Maybe we'll find something useful."

Reaching the third floor, they were greeted by a collection of decorations used for the various events held by the Tall Oaks throughout the year. Banners, lights, and other festive items were stored neatly, a stark contrast to the chaos below. Alex and Gabriel moved towards a large storage area, while Lorenzo checked another smaller room.

Gabriel opened a door and stepped back, surprised. "Hey, look at this! A boat. It's small, but it might be useful."

Alex joined him, inspecting the find. "It's not perfect, but it could help. Let's get it downstairs. If the water keeps rising, we'll need every bit of help we can get."

Meanwhile, in another room, Lorenzo found a large stash of canned food. "Anyone hungry?" Lorenzo yelled from the room. "These could come in handy," Lorenzo said, lifting a box of canned pork and beans.

The three men regrouped, their findings piled beside them. Alex turned to Lorenzo. "I think it's time we try the bell. If we can get it ringing, maybe someone will hear us and send help."

Lorenzo agreed. "Let's do it. Gabriel, you coming up with us?"

Gabriel shrugged, afraid to admit he was scared of high places. "I'll take these supplies downstairs and get Jacob. We'll come back up to grab the boat and see if we can find anything else. You guys go ahead without me."

Alex and Lorenzo made their way to the narrow spiral staircase leading to the watchtower. As they climbed, the passage became more difficult. The room became narrower with each step, the sound of the howling wind outside beating against the massive stone structure was deafening.

Reaching the top of the stairs, Lorenzo pushed open the heavy door to the watchtower. The wind howled through the open area, carrying the scent of rain and earth. The sight that greeted him was sobering. The entire first floor of the Tall Oaks building was underwater, and some of the smaller stores throughout downtown Everbrook were completely submerged. The water wasn't flowing fast; there was a stillness to everything, a quiet devastation.

"We need to ring that bell," Alex said, grabbing the rope attached to the bell. He gave it a hard pull, and the bell rang out, its clear, resonant sound cutting through the storm. Lorenzo stood behind him, looking out over the town, bracing himself on a nearby railing.

Again and again, Alex pulled the rope, the bell's toll echoing into the distance. He continued until his arms ached, refusing to stop until he was certain that the sound had carried far enough to be heard. As he paused to catch his breath, Alex looked out over the flooded landscape next to Lorenzo. The town, usually so vibrant and full of life, was now a sea of water and debris.

"Look over there!" Lorenzo said, pointing to an adjacent building. Alex squinted through the rain and saw people on the roof, waving frantically and screaming for help. The water was rising quickly, nearly covering the rooftop they were stranded on.

"We have to do something," Alex said, his voice urgent. "If the water rises any higher, the current is going to overtake them, and they'll be swept away."

Lorenzo nodded. "We can use the boat we found. It's small, but it might be enough to get them out of there." Returning to the third floor, Alex and Lorenzo quickly shared their plan with Isaac and Gabriel.

"We found people stranded on a rooftop," Alex explained. "The water is almost over the rooftop. We need to use the boat to get them out."

Gabriel's face turned serious. "Then let's move. We don't have much time."

Gabriel, Alex, Jacob, and Lorenzo quickly prepared the small boat, securing it to the central pillar on the second floor of the building with sturdy ropes. The pillar, sturdy and reliable, would keep the boat from being swept away by the powerful currents.

"Make sure it's tight," Lorenzo instructed, his authoritative voice cutting through the noise. "We can't afford to make any mistakes."

Jacob double-checked the knots, ensuring they were secure. "It's good to go," he confirmed, his hands steady despite the rising tension. The boat, an old but reliable rowboat used during community events, now stood as their only means to save the stranded people on the adjacent rooftop.

"Are you sure this thing will hold?" Alex asked, eyeing the boat with skepticism.

Lorenzo grinned, trying to lighten the mood. "Well, it's held plenty of rowdy festival-goers. It should hold us."

Alex joined in, his tone half-joking, half-serious. "I don't know about this. I think we're going to need a bigger boat! You're crazy if you think I'm getting on that thing. I'll stay here and pull you guys back." The group chuckled, despite the seriousness of the situation.

"Better crazy than leaving those people out there. Let's do this," Jacob said, his expression turning serious again.

They carefully navigated through the crowd, making their way to an exit that led to the rising floodwaters. The group worked together to carefully lower the boat into the rising waters. The current was deceptively strong, and the boat rocked precariously as it hit the surface. Jacob and Lorenzo climbed into the boat, and with a final tug to ensure it was secure, they pushed off from the second floor, navigating the turbulent waters.

"Remember, keep it steady and stay low," Gabriel instructed. "We'll be here to pull you back if needed."

Alex watched as Jacob and Lorenzo paddled away, the small boat moving slowly but surely towards the stranded group. The rain lashed against their faces, and the wind threatened to push them off course. Despite the adverse conditions, the two men pressed on, their focus unwavering. Lorenzo took the lead, steering the boat with skill and precision.

As they neared the adjacent building, the cries for help grew louder. The sight was serious: a group of four people huddled together on the roof, the water nearly covering it completely. Fear and desperation were etched on their faces as the ruthless tide could take them at any second, but hope sparked as they saw the boat approaching.

"We're here to get you out!" Jacob shouted, his voice barely audible over the storm. "Everyone, stay calm and follow our instructions."

Lorenzo steadied the boat as best as he could, reaching out to help the first person climb aboard. The process was slow and nerve-wracking, each movement needing precision to avoid capsizing. One by one, the stranded people were brought onto the boat, their relief noticeable despite the harrowing conditions.

"We're almost there," Jacob encouraged, his grip firm as he helped another person into the boat. "Just a little bit more."

With the boat now heavily laden with people, the return journey was even more treacherous. The added weight made it difficult to navigate the strong currents, and the boat rocked dangerously with each stroke of the paddles.

"We're gonna make it," Lorenzo said repeatedly, trying to keep spirits high. "Just hang on tight."

Back at the Tall Oaks building, Alex and Gabriel watched anxiously, ready to pull them back. The tension was thick as the boat slowly made its way back, each moment feeling like an eternity.

"Come on, come on," Alex muttered under his breath, his hands gripping the rope tightly.

Finally, the boat reached the building, and Alex and Gabriel pulled it in, securing it firmly. The rescued people scrambled out, their expressions a mix of exhaustion and profound gratitude.

"Thank you," one of them said, tears mingling with the rain on their face. "You saved our lives."

Jacob and Lorenzo, soaked to the bone and visibly relieved, shared a weary smile. "Just doing what we had to do," Jacob replied, his voice hoarse from the effort.

Eden, with unwavering diligence, moved to help the new arrivals, her hands gentle but efficient. "Let's get you all warm and dry," she said, guiding them to the makeshift beds.

Suddenly, the steady voice of a news reporter on the radio cut through the tense silence. "This just in: The storm appears to be losing strength. Meteorologists predict a significant reduction in rainfall over the next few hours. Residents are advised to remain in place until further notice."

A wave of cautious optimism swept through the room. The news brought a collective sigh of relief, but also a sense of uncertainty about what to do next.

"Alright, folks," Lorenzo said, standing up to address the crowd. "It looks like the worst might be over and the storm might break soon. But we still need to stay put until it's safe to leave."

Gabriel glanced around, the tension still evident in his eyes. "So, what do we do in the meantime? Just sit around and wait?"

As if on cue, the lights in the Tall Oaks building flickered, causing everyone to pause. A collective breath was held as the room plunged into brief darkness. Then, with a sudden surge, the power returned, the overhead lights blazing to life. The room erupted in cheers, the sudden return of power lifting the spirits of everyone present. The darkness that had loomed over them was vanquished, replaced by the warm, bright light that filled every corner of the room.

Uncle Leo, always quick to lift spirits, clapped his hands and grinned. "Alright, everyone!" Uncle Leo's voice boomed over the crowd. "Let's prove to this storm that we won't be beaten! We came here to party, didn't we? So, let's get this polka party started again! The show must go on!"

There was a moment of stunned silence, followed by a murmur of agreement and a few tentative smiles. The idea of resuming the party, even in the midst of chaos, was both absurd and comforting.

"You know what? Leo's right," Jacob said, a smile spreading across his face. "We've got to keep our spirits up. Let's get the band back together."

With a renewed sense of purpose, the community began to set up for the polka party once more. Tables were rearranged, a small stage was put together, and an area was cleared out to make room for a dance floor. Jacob and his bandmates retrieved their instruments, checking them for damage and tuning up.

"Let's do this," Sarah said, adjusting her microphone. "We need it now more than ever."

As the lively melody of polka music filled the air, the atmosphere in the Tall Oaks building began to shift. The festive sounds blended with the dying storm, creating a surreal but uplifting ambiance. People who had been sitting in worried silence moments before now found themselves tapping their feet and smiling.

"This is just what we needed," Eden said to Alex, who was watching the scene with a mixture of amusement and admiration.

"It's amazing how resilient everyone is," Alex replied, shaking his head in wonder. "We've been through so much, but here we are, dancing and laughing."

The dance floor quickly filled with couples and families. Children, still wet from their earlier adventures, giggled as they twirled around. Even the elderly, who had been resting and recuperating, found the energy to join in, their faces lighting up with joy. Isaac and Jenny, holding their triplets, watched from the sidelines.

Isaac shook his head with a chuckle. "I can't believe we're having a polka party in the middle of a flood."

"Sometimes you just have to dance, even when it rains," Jenny replied, smiling at the babies in her arms.

Abigail and Max joined the dance floor with Emma and Liam, who had recovered from their earlier fright. The children's laughter mingled with the music, creating a sense of normalcy amid the chaos.

Suddenly, the radio crackled to life again. "This is an emergency broadcast. The storm is officially downgraded, and the floodwaters are receding. Authorities advise residents to stay indoors for a few more hours until it's safe to assess the damage and begin cleanup operations."

The news was met with a mixture of cheers and tears. The worst was over, and while there was much to do, the immediate danger had passed.

"Looks like we'll be able to head out soon," Alex said to Eden, relief evident in his voice.

"We'll need to start planning the cleanup, but for now, let's enjoy this moment," Eden replied, a soft smile on her lips.

As the community danced and celebrated, the sense of unity and resilience grew stronger. They knew there were challenges ahead, but they faced them with renewed hope and determination.

"Ladies and gentlemen, may I have your attention, please!" Uncle Leo shouted, his eyes twinkling rascally. "I know we've had quite the adventure today, but remember, we're Everbrook strong! And if there's one thing we do best, it's turning a bad situation into a great story. So, let's keep this party going until the cows come home —or until the floodwaters recede, whichever comes first!" The crowd laughed and cheered, their spirits lifted by his infectious enthusiasm.

"Leave it to Uncle Leo to keep everyone's spirits high," Eden said, watching the scene with admiration.

"He's a gem. We're lucky to have him," Alex replied, nodding in agreement.

As the music played on and people danced, the storm outside seemed a distant memory. The Tall Oaks building, a beacon of hope and resilience, stood strong against the elements, filled with the sounds of laughter, music, and the unbreakable spirit of its community.

•

The afternoon turned to dusk, and the storm clouds began to break apart. The once ferocious storm had passed, leaving behind a quiet, eerie calm. The air was thick with the scent of rain and mud, and the only sounds were the distant drip of water and the occasional creak of the Tall Oaks building settling.

The floodwaters receded quickly, revealing the extent of the damage. Streets were littered with debris and mud, remnants of what had once been normal life. The Tall Oaks building, though battered, stood tall as a testament to the community's resilience. People began to emerge from buildings throughout the town, their faces a mix of relief and sorrow as they surveyed the destruction.

"Look at this place," someone murmured, surveying the damage.

"This town has been through worse," another replied, trying to muster some optimism. "We'll rebuild."

Isaac stood with Jenny, cradling one of the triplets while the other two slept in the stroller. Abigail and Max were nearby, Emma and Liam clinging to their legs. The chaos of the past twelve hours had taken its toll, and it was clear that the children were exhausted and overwhelmed.

Isaac exchanged a glance with Jenny, then looked over at Abigail and Max. "I think it's time we leave this behind," he said softly. "The cottage is still standing. It's high enough on the hilltop to be away from any flood damage."

Jenny nodded, her expression one of quiet agreement. "We need some peace, some normalcy," she added, glancing down at the sleeping babies. "The kids need it too."

Max put a reassuring hand on Abigail's shoulder. "It's a good idea," he said. "We could all use a break from this chaos."

Abigail looked at Emma and Liam, who were clinging to her, their eyes wide with uncertainty. "The cottage sounds perfect right now," she agreed. "Let's go."

As they made their way outside, the air was cool and fresh, and the streets were a mix of mud and debris, with the occasional car or piece of furniture wedged in awkward positions. People were everywhere, some hugging each other in relief, others beginning the arduous task of cleaning up.

Alex, Eden, and Uncle Leo were among the crowd, helping wherever they could. Alex spotted the family and walked over, his face a mixture of weariness and relief.

"Heading to the cottage?" he asked, glancing at the packed bags.

Isaac nodded. "Yeah, we need to get the kids somewhere safe and quiet."

"Good idea," Alex said. "We'll be here helping with the cleanup and rescue efforts. Take care of each other. We'll be back home later when the stars come out."

Eden joined them, giving each of the children a reassuring hug. "Stay safe, and we'll see you soon after things settle down," she said, her eyes glistening with emotion.

As the family walked away from the Tall Oaks building, they could hear the sounds of their community coming together. People were working side by side, clearing debris, setting up makeshift shelters, and distributing food and water. The spirit of Everbrook was strong, undaunted by the storm that had tried to break it.

Reaching the edge of town, they saw the path to the cottage was clear. The sky above was now a soft orange and pink, the last remnants of daylight giving way to night. The journey to the cottage was quiet, each family member lost in their thoughts.

When they arrived, the sight of the familiar, cozy structure brought a sense of peace. The cottage was untouched by the flood, a safe haven on a hilltop. Inside, they lit candles and settled in. The children, finally free from the chaos, played quietly, their laughter a soothing remedy to the adults' frayed nerves. The triplets, content and curious, crawled around the living room, exploring their new surroundings.

Isaac broke the silence, his voice thoughtful. "It's hard to believe how quickly everything changed. One moment, we were enjoying breakfast, and the next, we were fighting for our lives."

Jenny nodded, her gaze distant. "It's a humbling reminder of how fragile everything is. But it's also amazing how we managed to come together and get through it."

Abigail sighed, looking at her children playing nearby. "I kept thinking about the kids the whole time. How they'll remember this. What they'll take from it. It's like the seasons. There's a time for everything—a time to grow, a time to endure, and a time to heal."

Max added, "And just like the seasons, we cycle through these phases over and over again. Each time we face a challenge, we learn something new about ourselves and about each other."

Isaac leaned back, his eyes reflecting the last rays of the sun. "I think that's what makes us resilient. It's not just about surviving the storm; it's about understanding that the storm is part of the journey. We grow through what we go through."

Jenny squeezed Isaac's hand. "I kept thinking about how we don't really appreciate the calm until we've weathered the storm. It's like we take so much for granted until it's almost taken away. Every end is just a new beginning. The flood washed away so much, but it also cleared the way for something new. We have a chance to rebuild, to create something even stronger."

The family fell into a comfortable silence, each lost in their own reflections. The events of the past few hours had left them physically and emotionally exhausted, but there was a sense of peace in knowing they had faced the storm together. They had survived, and they had each other.

As the evening sky deepened into twilight, Alex and Eden walked down the debris-strewn streets, helping their neighbors where they could. At the edge of town, they passed the Italian restaurant where they had shared so many memories. Eden stopped to look at the damage and noticed a faint glow.

"Look, Alex," she said, pointing towards the patio. "There's a light on."

Intrigued, they made their way over. The patio, usually alive with diners, was empty except for a few candles flickering in the gentle breeze. They cast soft, dancing shadows across the cobblestones.

Alex pushed open the gate, which creaked in protest. The familiar scent of garlic and herbs filled the air, bringing a wave of happy memories. They stepped onto the patio, their footsteps echoing softly on the cobblestones.

As they approached the door, which was slightly ajar, Alex hesitated for a moment before gently pushing it open. The interior was dimly lit, the warm glow of candlelight creating an inviting, nostalgic atmosphere despite the disarray left by the flood. Chairs were overturned, and there were traces of mud on the floor, but the restaurant still retained its charm.

"Hello?" Alex called out softly, unsure if anyone was there.

From the back of the restaurant, a figure emerged—Cosimo, the kind older gentleman who had owned the restaurant for as long as they could remember. His face lit up with a warm smile despite the weariness in his eyes.

"Alex! Eden!" Cosimo exclaimed, coming forward with a broad smile. "How are you both holding up?"

Alex nodded, a tired but genuine smile on his face. "We're managing, Cosimo. It's been tough, but the community is pulling together."

Eden added, "We've set up a makeshift hospital at the Tall Oaks building. People are hurt, but they're resilient."

Cosimo's face showed concern. "And my son, Lorenzo? Have you seen him? Is he alright?"

Eden smiled reassuringly. "Yes, Cosimo. Lorenzo has been incredible. He's been coordinating the rescue efforts and keeping everyone calm."

Alex chimed in, "He was there when we needed him most. Lorenzo's leadership has been vital in getting everyone to safety. We couldn't have done it without him."

Cosimo's eyes glistened with relief and pride. "Thank God. I knew he had it in him. The flood may have taken a lot from us, but with Lorenzo's help, I know our community will undergo a renaissance."

Eden nodded, placing a comforting hand on Cosimo's arm. "Absolutely. With his guidance and the strength of everyone here, we'll rebuild and come back stronger than ever."

Cosimo smiled, a glimmer of hope in his eyes. "Thank you both. It's good to know we have such strong, caring people in our town."

Eden smiled back, a sense of comfort washing over her. "Cosimo, it's so good to see you made it through this too. We were helping with the cleanup and saw the light."

Cosimo nodded, his eyes twinkling. "Ah, yes, I thought the light might bring some hope. It felt wrong to let the darkness take over completely."

Alex and Eden stepped inside, the familiar ambiance enveloping them like a warm embrace. Soft strains of an Italian love song played from an old wind-up record player in the corner, adding to the nostalgic atmosphere. Despite the disarray, the tables were set with simple vases of fresh flowers.

"I can't offer you a full meal," Cosimo said, "but I can pour you a glass of our best wine and share some bread and cheese."

"That sounds perfect," Alex replied, grateful for the gesture.

Cosimo led them to a table on the patio. As they sat down, he brought over a bottle of red wine and two glasses, followed by two small plates of bread and cheese.

As they raised their glasses, Cosimo said, "Let us eat, drink, and be merry, for tomorrow we may die."

"Let us eat, drink, and be merry," Alex and Eden echoed, clinking their glasses together.

As they sipped the wine, Alex and Eden reflected on the events of the past few hours. "It's incredible how much has changed," Eden said softly. "But being here, it feels like a part of our life is still intact."

Alex nodded, his hand resting on hers. "This place holds so many memories. It's a reminder that no matter what happens, we have each other and the moments we've shared."

The conversation flowed naturally, touching on old memories and new hopes and dreams. The flickering candlelight, the gentle music, and the warmth of the wine created a space where they could relax and reconnect.

After a while, Cosimo approached them with a gentle smile. "When you're ready to leave, just blow out the candle," he said softly. "I need to head to bed and rest now."

"Thank you, Cosimo," Eden said, giving him a warm hug. "For everything."

Cosimo nodded, smiling warmly. "Take care, my friends."

As the night deepened, the air grew still, wrapping Alex and Eden in a comforting silence. The last song from the old record player began to play. Alex turned to Eden, his eyes reflecting the flickering candlelight.

Taking her hand, he asked softly, "Shall we dance?" Alex blew out the candle, casting them into darkness. "In the dark?" he whispered in her ear.

Eden looked into his eyes, her heart swelling with love. "Always and forever, my love," she replied with a tender smile.

They stepped onto an open space on the patio, the cobblestones cool beneath their feet. Above them, the night sky stretched out, a vast expanse of twinkling stars. Alex pulled Eden close, and they began to dance, their movements slow and graceful.

Meanwhile, outside the cottage, Emma and Liam were playing under the calm night sky, the air filled with the soft sounds of nature and the distant echo of the storm's aftermath. Emma looked up, her eyes widening in wonder.

"Liam, look at that! I've never seen those stars before."

Liam squinted, trying to make out the shapes. "It looks like... two people dancing. Do you see it?"

Emma nodded excitedly. "Yeah, I do! It's beautiful. Let's tell Mom and Dad."

They rushed inside, their faces alight with excitement. "Mom! Dad! Come outside, quick!" Emma called, tugging on Abigail's hand.

Abigail and Max exchanged curious glances before following the children outside. "What is it, sweetie?" Max asked, lifting Liam into his arms.

"Look up there!" Emma said, pointing to the sky. "There's a new constellation. It looks like people dancing!"

Abigail and Max looked up, their eyes scanning the night sky. "I don't see anything different," Max said, shaking his head.

Abigail squinted, trying to see what Emma and Liam were so excited about. "I don't either. Are you sure, kids?"

Emma and Liam exchanged puzzled looks. "But it's right there," Emma insisted, pointing again. "Two people dancing. Can't you see it?"

Liam tugged on Max's sleeve. "It's really there, Dad. They're right above us."

Abigail knelt down to their level, her eyes soft with understanding. "Sometimes, kids can see things that grown-ups can't," she said gently. "Maybe it's a special constellation just for you."

Max smiled and ruffled Liam's hair. "Yeah, maybe it's a gift for the two of you. A reminder of something magical."

Emma's eyes sparkled with wonder. "You really think so?"

Liam looked up at the sky, a sense of awe in his voice. "It's like they're dancing together, forever."

As the family stood together, Emma and Liam gazing up at the sky, they felt a profound sense of connection and love. The constellation, unseen by the adults, shone brightly in the children's eyes.

Eden looked up into Alex's eyes, a soft smile on her lips. "Do you remember when you told me, 'No crying until the end'?" she whispered, her voice filled with emotion.

Alex's gaze softened, his expression tender. "How could I forget?" he said, a gentle smile tugging at the corners of his mouth. "It was our way of holding on to every moment together until the end."

As the memory washed over them, Eden felt her eyes welling up. Despite the promise they had made to save the tears for the end, the weight of their shared journey brought emotions to the surface. A single tear escaped.

"You promised," Alex teased gently, brushing his thumb against her cheek, wiping the tear away.

Eden laughed through her tears, leaning into him. "I know, but I guess we've reached the end, haven't we?"

As they continued to sway together, the world around them seemed to fade away, leaving only the two of them, lost in their shared rhythm. Their steps were synchronized, each movement a testament to their deep bond and enduring love.

The air around them shimmered as their movements grew lighter, more ethereal. A soft glow began to emanate from their intertwined forms, and the stars above twinkled in response, their light mingling with the gentle glow surrounding Alex and Eden.

Their transformation wasn't one of departure but of becoming—gradually merging with the night sky. As they moved together, they didn't just become part of the night—they became the night, their souls entwined with the stars, a love story written in the heavens, destined to shine for eternity.

※

<h1 style="text-align:center"><u>Epilogue</u></h1>

When does a dream begin?
With a kiss on a summer night,
When two hearts softly spin?
Or in a moment of pure delight,
When reality fades from sight?

Is it born in a whispered wish,
Or when our minds start to stray?
Does it start in a moment of bliss,
Or when night turns into day?
When does a dream begin?

Once upon a time,
staring up at the stars,
wondering why they seem so far

Away, in the distance,
my heart beats faster,
I hear your laughter.
The universe breathes,
I see your face, bright smile, loving joy.
We look at each other and embrace.

There is only one person. And it is you.
There is only one place. And it is here, with you.
There is only one time. And it is now, in this moment.
There is only one reason. And it is why we are here.
There is only one way. And it is meant for you and I.
We hold hands and dance, the world begins to spin,
ascending upwards into the heavens we begin,
to create music, divine and sublime.
Our bodies sparkle in the night sky,
two star-crossed lovers,
together, forever,

Dancing In the Dark

That in our wake, we shall find that
which we desire the most, and after finding it,
we lose it, only to remember its joy.

Sigh.

One day I was thinking,
And my thoughts became words.
Every word became common shapes,
Until the world of which I thought,
I knew, became a surreal text.

It started with "Once upon a time," and ended with, "Sigh."

<u>**The Final Lesson:**</u>
<u>**The Fundamental Truths**</u>

As we reach the culmination of our journey together, it's time to distill the wisdom from the eleven lessons we've explored into a set of Fundamental Truths—concepts that can guide you toward a more fulfilling, purposeful life. These truths are not just a summary of what we've covered; they are the essence of a life well-lived, derived from understanding your past, mastering your emotions, making thoughtful decisions, and cultivating resilience and growth.

Throughout this book, we've delved into the complexities of childhood experiences, the power of emotions, and the art of decision-making. We've discussed personal growth, the impact of language, the importance of breaking bad habits, and the strength found in resilience. Relationships and holistic well-being have been highlighted as pillars of a balanced life, while a growth mindset and an attitude of abundance have shown us the potential for limitless success.

Now, we bring it all together in seven guiding truths. These are not rigid rules but flexible truths that can adapt to your unique journey. They are meant to serve as a compass, helping you navigate the complexities of life with clarity, confidence, and purpose. As you embrace these truths, you'll find that they resonate with the lessons you've learned, empowering you to live in alignment with your values and aspirations.

In this final lesson, we will explore these seven truths in depth, offering insights on how to integrate them into your daily life. Whether you're just beginning your journey or looking to refine your path, these truths will provide the foundation for a life of fulfillment, growth, and lasting happiness. Let's take this final step together as we unlock the timeless wisdom that can guide you toward your highest potential.

The Universal Mind

Imagine that the universe, in all its vastness and complexity, is like a giant, cosmic brain—a boundless mind that encompasses everything we know and everything we have yet to discover. In this view, everything we experience, from the physical world around us to our innermost thoughts and feelings, is not just happening to us but is being co-created by us. We are not merely passive observers of reality; we are active participants in its formation.

This perspective invites us to recognize the incredible power of our thoughts. Our minds are not isolated entities but integral parts of this grand, universal consciousness. Every thought, every intention, every belief we hold has the potential to shape our reality. The world we perceive and experience is, in many ways, a reflection of our inner mental state. When we understand that the universe is mental in nature, we realize that our thoughts are not just fleeting, inconsequential activities—they are powerful tools for creation.

Consider this: every invention, every masterpiece, every significant achievement in human history began as a thought in someone's mind. The airplane, the light bulb, the internet—all were once ideas, mere figments of imagination, that were brought into physical reality through focused intention and persistent action. This is the creative power of the mind at work.

Let's take the example of an artist. Before the first stroke of the brush touches the canvas, the entire image already exists within the artist's mind. This mental creation is not just a blueprint; it's a vibrant, living concept that guides the artist's hand. In the same way, the universe can be seen as a vast mental canvas where every experience, every interaction, is a result of the thoughts and intentions projected onto it.

This concept also explains phenomena like the placebo effect in medicine. When a patient believes in the efficacy of a treatment, even if that treatment is inert, the mere belief can lead to real, measurable improvements in health. This is not just a trick of the mind—it's a demonstration of how powerful our thoughts and beliefs can be in shaping our physical reality.

Let's delve even deeper. Think about how your mood or mindset can change the way you perceive the world. On a day when you're feeling confident and positive, challenges seem manageable, and opportunities seem abundant. But on a day when you're feeling down or stressed, those same challenges can feel overwhelming, and opportunities might seem out of reach. The external circumstances haven't changed—what's changed is your mental state, and with it, your perception of reality.

This understanding brings a profound responsibility. If our

thoughts have the power to shape our experiences, then it's crucial to cultivate a mindset that aligns with the reality we wish to create. This is where the practice of positive thinking, visualization, and focused intention comes into play. By consciously directing our thoughts and focusing on what we desire, rather than what we fear, we tap into the creative power of the universal mind to bring those desires into being.

However, this principle is not about denying reality or ignoring challenges. It's about recognizing that the way we think about our challenges can influence how we respond to them and, ultimately, how we overcome them. It's about understanding that we have the power to choose our thoughts, and by choosing thoughts that are aligned with our highest goals and aspirations, we set the stage for those goals to manifest in our lives.

Cause and Effect

Nothing in the universe happens by chance. Every event, every action, has a cause and leads to an effect. Imagine life as a giant domino setup, where each piece, when set in motion, influences the next. This intricate web of causation is the underlying structure of the universe, connecting every aspect of existence in a vast, interwoven tapestry. By understanding and recognizing the relationships between our actions and their outcomes, we gain the power to consciously shape our lives.

This concept teaches us that everything we experience is the result of a specific cause. Whether it's the success we achieve, the challenges we face, or the seemingly random occurrences in our lives, each is tied to a preceding action, thought, or decision. This understanding shifts our perspective from seeing life as a series of unrelated events to recognizing the deep interconnectedness of all things.

By acknowledging that our thoughts, words, and deeds have far-reaching consequences, we become empowered to take control of our own destiny. Instead of feeling like passive participants in our lives, we become proactive agents, capable of influencing the direction and quality of our experiences. This realization is both liberating and sobering—it means that we are responsible for the outcomes we create, for better or for worse.

Consider the idea of cause and effect in the context of personal development. Let's say you want to improve your physical health. The first step in this journey is to recognize that your current state of health is the result of past actions—your diet, exercise habits, sleep patterns, and even your stress levels. This awareness empowers you to make deliberate changes. By choosing healthier foods, incorporating regular exercise into your routine, and prioritizing rest, you create positive effects that enhance your well-being. This proactive approach demonstrates how understanding causation can lead to meaningful changes in our lives.

This idea extends beyond personal health to every area of life. Think about your relationships, for instance. The quality of your relationships is influenced by how you communicate, the time and energy you invest, and the respect and understanding you offer. If a relationship is strained, recognizing the causes—whether they stem from miscommunication, neglect, or unresolved issues—allows you to take steps to heal and improve the connection. By addressing the root causes, you can change the trajectory of the relationship, creating a more positive and fulfilling dynamic.

The same applies to your career or personal goals. Success in these areas is not random; it's the result of consistent effort, strategic planning, and the decisions you make along the way. Understanding the causes behind your successes and setbacks enables you to refine your approach, learn from your experiences, and make better choices moving forward. This understanding transforms challenges into opportunities for growth, as you learn to see setbacks not as failures, but as valuable lessons that inform your future actions.

Cause and effect also teaches us about the power of intention. When we set an intention—whether it's to achieve a specific goal, improve our relationships, or enhance our well-being—we set into motion a series of causes that will eventually lead to the desired effect. However, this process requires consistency and patience. Just as a seed doesn't become a tree overnight, our intentions take time to manifest. By staying committed to our intentions and taking consistent, aligned actions, we create the conditions for our desired outcomes to unfold.

Moreover, this concept reminds us of the importance of mindfulness in our daily lives. Every action we take, no matter how small, has an effect. A kind word can lift someone's spirits and create a ripple of positivity, while a thoughtless comment can cause harm and spread negativity. By being mindful of our actions and their potential impacts, we can choose to create positive effects in the world around us. This mindfulness extends to our thoughts as well— our internal dialogue shapes our perceptions, which in turn influence our actions and the results we achieve.

Understanding cause and effect is also crucial when navigating life's challenges. When faced with difficulties, it's natural to feel overwhelmed or powerless. However, by examining the situation through the lens of cause and effect, we can often identify the factors that led to the challenge and determine what actions we can take to change the outcome. This approach encourages a proactive mindset, where we focus on what we can control and take responsibility for our role in shaping our experiences.

Everything is in Constant Motion

Another fundamental truth of the universe is that everything is in a state of constant motion and vibration. Nothing rests—everything, from the smallest atom to the largest galaxy, vibrates at different frequencies. This perpetual motion is the very essence of life, the heartbeat of existence that drives the universe forward.

Imagine a vast dance floor where every being, every object, every thought, is moving to its own unique rhythm. Some move quickly, others more slowly, but all are in motion, contributing to the symphony of the universe. This dance of life is not random but governed by the principle that everything vibrates. The differences we observe in the world—whether in physical objects, energies, or even our thoughts—are a result of these varying rates of vibration.

Understanding this fundamental truth allows us to recognize that by tuning into higher vibrations, we can elevate our consciousness and experience more refined states of being. Just as a musician tunes their instrument to achieve harmony, we can tune our minds and bodies to resonate with the higher frequencies of the universe. This awareness becomes a powerful tool for personal growth and transformation, aligning us with the natural flow of life.

For instance, practices like meditation, gratitude, and compassion help us raise our vibrational frequency. Meditation quiets the mind, allowing us to tune into the subtle energies that surround us. Gratitude shifts our focus from what we lack to what we have, elevating our emotional state and aligning us with the abundance of the universe. Compassion opens our hearts, connecting us to others on a deeper level and fostering a sense of unity and harmony.

This fundamental truth of vibration also reminds us that change is an inherent part of life. Nothing remains static; everything is in flux, constantly evolving and transforming. Consider the process of learning a new skill. At first, it may feel awkward and unfamiliar, as if you're out of sync with the task. But as you practice, something remarkable happens—your mind and body begin to adapt, to vibrate in harmony with the new skill. Over time, what once felt difficult becomes second nature, a seamless part of your being. This transformation is a direct result of embracing the discomfort of change and persevering through the learning process.

Major life transitions, such as moving to a new city or changing careers, operate on the same principle. Initially, the change can be daunting, pulling you out of your comfort zone and into unfamiliar territory. But these transitions also offer incredible opportunities for growth and new experiences. By embracing change, rather than resisting it, we open ourselves to the possibilities that lie beyond our current understanding. We align ourselves with the universal dance, moving in step with the rhythms of life.

However, this idea also teaches us the importance of balance between action and reflection. In our fast-paced world, it's easy to get caught up in the constant motion, forgetting the need to pause and reflect. Yet, just as a dance includes moments of stillness and grace, our lives must include time for reflection. Taking time to reflect allows us to gain insights, process our experiences, and make thoughtful decisions that align with our values and long-term vision.

For example, setting aside time each day for meditation or journaling can help clear the mind and provide clarity. These practices allow us to step back from the busyness of life and reconnect with our inner selves. In doing so, we create space for new ideas and perspectives to emerge, guiding our actions with greater intention and purpose.

Achieving our goals requires this balance between action and reflection. While action propels us forward, it is reflection that ensures our actions are aligned with our true desires and values. By integrating both, we create a harmonious and purposeful life, one that resonates with the rhythms of the universe.

Gratitude plays a crucial role in this process as well. By regularly acknowledging and appreciating the positive aspects of our lives, we shift our focus from what is lacking to what we have. This shift in perspective raises our vibrational frequency, fostering a sense of abundance and contentment. Simple practices like keeping a gratitude journal, expressing thanks to others, and reflecting on positive experiences can cultivate a habit of gratitude that transforms our outlook on life. This practice not only enhances our mood but also strengthens our relationships and overall quality of life.

Life is a Duality

Life is full of dualities: light and darkness, joy and sorrow, love and hate, hot and cold. These opposites are not separate entities but different degrees of the same thing. It's like looking at a thermostat where hot and cold are just points on a scale. As you move up or down the scale, the extremes start to blend—at some degree, cold can actually feel hot, and hot can feel cold. Understanding this concept allows us to see beyond apparent contradictions and recognize the unity underlying duality.

This fundamental truth, known as polarity, teaches us that everything exists on a continuum, and opposites are simply varying degrees of the same fundamental essence. Just as light and darkness are two extremes on the spectrum of visibility, so too are joy and sorrow on the emotional spectrum, and love and hate on the spectrum of human relationships. By grasping this truth, we begin to understand that life's dualities are not in conflict with each other but rather complementary forces that contribute to the richness of our experiences.

Embracing duality allows us to see challenges as opportunities for growth. Consider how the experience of sorrow can deepen our capacity for joy. When we go through difficult times, we often emerge with a greater appreciation for the good moments, having developed resilience and wisdom along the way.

Similarly, the presence of conflict in a relationship can lead to deeper understanding and stronger bonds when approached with a willingness to communicate and resolve differences. This recognition of duality encourages us to look at life's challenges not as obstacles, but as essential parts of our journey that contribute to our growth and development.

The concept of duality is particularly evident in our emotional experiences. Emotions like love and hate, joy and sorrow, are not distinct entities but points on a spectrum. For example, think about a relationship that has experienced both deep love and intense conflict. These emotions, though seemingly opposite, are part of the same continuum of human connection. By acknowledging that these feelings are interconnected, we can work to transform negative emotions into positive ones. This might involve open communication, forgiveness, and a shift in perspective, recognizing that the presence of conflict doesn't negate love—it can actually deepen it when resolved with care.

When we embrace both aspects of our emotions, we allow ourselves to grow and strengthen our connections with others. Instead of seeing negative emotions as something to avoid, we can view them as opportunities for introspection and healing. For instance, feeling anger or frustration in a relationship might prompt us to address underlying issues, leading to a healthier and more authentic connection. By working through these emotions, we not only resolve conflicts but also enhance the depth and resilience of our relationships.

The fundamental truth of duality also teaches us that we have the power to transform undesirable conditions by shifting their polarity. This means that through a change in perspective, we can turn negative experiences into positive ones. For example, a setback at work might initially feel like a failure, but by shifting your perspective, you might see it as a learning opportunity that paves the way for future success. This approach encourages us to embrace all aspects of life, knowing that each experience, whether positive or negative, contributes to our overall growth and understanding.

Just as the sun and moon balance each other in the sky, we too must balance our inner forces to achieve harmony. When we bring together action with reflection, strength with compassion, and ambition with contentment, we create a life that is both dynamic and serene.

Life is Cyclical

Everything in existence follows a natural rhythm and cycle. We see this in the changing seasons, the ebb and flow of tides, the phases of the moon, and even in the rise and fall of civilizations. These rhythmic cycles are the heartbeat of the universe, a constant reminder that life is in perpetual motion. Just as nature moves through its cycles of growth, decay, and renewal, so too do our lives follow these patterns, affecting our emotions, energy levels, and experiences.

Consider the rhythm of your daily life. Just as the seasons change, our lives naturally move through different phases—times of growth, rest, productivity, and reflection. These cycles are not random; they are intrinsic to our existence, guiding the flow of our experiences. Recognizing these cycles can help us manage our energy and expectations, allowing us to live in harmony with the natural flow of life.

In a work setting, for example, there are periods of intense activity—deadlines, projects, and high-pressure situations—followed by quieter times when the pace slows down, giving us a chance to recover and regroup. Understanding and respecting these rhythms can help us avoid burnout. Instead of pushing through every moment with the same intensity, we learn to ride the waves of productivity and rest, maintaining a sustainable pace that supports long-term success.

This concept of natural rhythms extends beyond the workplace. It manifests in every aspect of our lives—our relationships, our creative endeavors, and our personal growth. There will be times when everything seems to be flowing smoothly, when opportunities abound and progress feels effortless. Conversely, there will be times when things slow down, when obstacles arise, and when patience is required. By understanding and aligning ourselves with these natural rhythms, we can navigate the ups and downs of life with greater ease and resilience.

For instance, think about how your energy levels fluctuate throughout the day. Most people experience peaks of energy and focus in the morning, followed by a dip in the afternoon, and then another boost in the evening. By recognizing these natural cycles, you can schedule your most demanding tasks during your peak energy times and save less intensive activities for when your energy is lower. This way, you work with your body's natural rhythm rather than against it, enhancing productivity and well-being.

Similarly, our emotional lives are subject to cycles. There are times when we feel emotionally strong, able to handle challenges with grace and confidence. At other times, we may feel more vulnerable, needing rest and reflection to process our experiences. By tuning into these emotional rhythms, we can practice self-compassion, allowing ourselves the space to rest and recharge when needed, rather than pushing ourselves to be constantly "on."

The rhythms of life also teach us about the importance of balance. Just as nature requires a balance between day and night, growth and decay, activity and rest, so too do we need to balance the different aspects of our lives. This balance is crucial for our overall well-being. When we align our actions with the natural rhythms, we create a life that is both productive and fulfilling, one that honors the need for both action and reflection.

Moreover, understanding these rhythms helps us remain balanced and centered, even when confronted by change and uncertainty. Life is inherently cyclical—what goes up must come down, and what is down will eventually rise again. This cyclical nature means that no situation is permanent. Times of difficulty will eventually give way to times of ease, just as winter gives way to spring. This understanding can provide comfort and perspective during challenging times, reminding us that change is a natural part of life and that each phase has its own value.

By aligning ourselves with the natural rhythms of life, we tap into a deeper flow, one that supports our growth and well-being. This alignment doesn't mean that we won't face challenges or hardships, but it does mean that we'll be better equipped to handle them. When we move in harmony with the rhythms of life, we become more resilient, more adaptable, and more at peace with the ebb and flow of existence.

Masculine and Feminine Forces

At the core of all creation are the complementary forces of the masculine and feminine. These forces extend beyond physical sex and gender, representing fundamental aspects of all forms of creation, generation, and existence. The masculine embodies action, initiative, and expansion, while the feminine represents receptivity, nurturing, and contraction. Both are essential, and their interplay brings about balance, harmony, and the dynamic equilibrium necessary for the flourishing of life.

This balance of masculine and feminine energies is not about rigid roles or characteristics assigned to individuals based on gender; rather, it's about understanding the dual forces that exist within each of us and in all aspects of life. The masculine force is characterized by assertiveness, the drive to move forward, to create, and to make things happen. It's the energy that sets things in motion, taking bold steps, initiating projects, and pushing boundaries. On the other hand, the feminine force is characterized by receptivity, intuition, and the ability to nurture and sustain. It's the energy that allows ideas to grow, provides space for creativity, and ensures that what has been initiated is cared for and brought to fruition.

When these forces are integrated within ourselves, we achieve a dynamic equilibrium that fosters creativity, fulfillment, and a deeper engagement with the world. This balance allows us to express our full potential and navigate life's complexities with grace and effectiveness.

Consider the process of creation and problem-solving. Imagine you're working on a project that requires both analytical thinking and creative insight. The masculine aspect of this process involves setting clear goals, developing a plan, and taking decisive action. It's the force that drives progress and ensures that everything get done. The feminine aspect, however, is equally important. It involves tapping into intuition, allowing creative ideas to emerge, and nurturing the process as it unfolds. It's the force that provides the flexibility to adapt, the patience to let ideas develop, and the empathy to understand the needs of the project and the people involved.

When these masculine and feminine energies are in balance, the outcome is a harmonious and successful project. The masculine energy drives the project forward, while the feminine energy ensures that it's done with care, creativity, and responsiveness to the needs of the moment. This dynamic balance is essential not only in professional endeavors but also in personal relationships, where the interplay of action and receptivity, strength and compassion, and assertiveness and understanding creates deeper, more meaningful connections.

In personal relationships, for example, the masculine energy might express itself through taking initiative, setting boundaries, and providing support and protection. The feminine energy, on the other hand, might express itself through empathy, nurturing, and creating emotional intimacy. Both energies are necessary for a healthy, balanced relationship. When one dominates without the other, the relationship can become strained or unfulfilling. But when both are honored and integrated, the relationship becomes a source of growth, joy, and mutual fulfillment.

These universal forces are not just abstract concepts; they are practical tools for living a balanced and harmonious life. By recognizing and embracing the masculine and feminine energies within us, we can approach life with a sense of wholeness. For instance, in moments of stress or challenge, we might draw on our masculine energy to take decisive action and overcome obstacles. At other times, we might draw on our feminine energy to reflect, heal, and restore balance.

Moreover, this balance allows us to be more adaptable and responsive to life's changing circumstances. In a fast-paced world that often values constant action and productivity (masculine energy), it's easy to overlook the importance of rest, reflection, and nurturing (feminine energy). Yet, these feminine qualities are crucial for long-term well-being and success. They provide the space for creativity to flourish, for ideas to mature, and for individuals to recharge and reconnect with their inner selves.

By integrating both masculine and feminine forces, we become more effective in our endeavors and more fulfilled in our lives. We can transform our mental states, improve our relationships, and achieve our goals in a way that feels authentic and sustainable. This integration doesn't mean we always use both energies equally in every situation; rather, it means we have the awareness and flexibility to draw on the appropriate energy when needed, creating a life that is balanced, dynamic, and deeply rewarding.

Interconnected Patterns

As we delve deeper into understanding the nature of reality, we begin to notice a profound truth: the patterns and laws that govern one level of existence often mirror those on other levels. This concept is beautifully encapsulated in the ancient saying, "As Above, So Below." It suggests that the macrocosm reflects the microcosm and vice versa, meaning that the structure of the universe is mirrored in the tiniest details of life. To understand one is to gain insight into the other.

Imagine holding a set of Russian nesting dolls. Each doll is a smaller, yet identical, version of the one that encases it. Similarly, in a hologram, every fragment of the image contains the whole picture, regardless of how small the piece is. This is how the universe operates—each part reflects the structure and principles of the whole.

Take, for example, the structure of an atom. It's a miniature solar system, with electrons orbiting a nucleus just as planets orbit the sun. This similarity is not just a coincidence; it's a manifestation of the principle that the patterns in the universe repeat themselves on different scales. The atom, the solar system, and even the galaxy all follow similar structural laws, demonstrating the interconnectedness of all things.

This fundamental truth of interconnected patterns helps us make sense of complex concepts by relating them to familiar experiences. It fosters a sense of unity with the cosmos, reminding us that we are not separate from the universe but an integral part of it. By observing the world around us, we can gain insights into the workings of the universe at large.

Consider the act of gardening. When you plant a seed, you're not simply placing a single entity into the ground. You're engaging with a vast, interconnected system of life. The soil, rich with microorganisms, interacts with water, sunlight, and air to support the growth of the plant. This small act of planting reflects the broader ecosystem, where each element plays a crucial role in maintaining balance and promoting life. The health of the plant depends on the health of the entire system, just as the well-being of an individual is connected to the well-being of the larger community and environment.

This interconnectedness can also be seen on a global scale. Our planet's ecosystem is a complex web of interdependent relationships, where the actions of individuals and communities can have far-reaching effects. For instance, when a factory releases pollutants into the air, it affects not only the immediate environment but also contributes to global climate change. This, in turn, influences weather patterns, agriculture, and the health of ecosystems worldwide. Understanding this web of connections makes it clear that individual actions, such as reducing waste, conserving energy, and supporting sustainable practices, have a significant impact on the health of the planet.

The interconnected patterns also play out in our personal lives, especially in our social relationships. Think about the influence of a simple act of kindness. A kind word or gesture can uplift someone's spirits, creating a ripple effect that spreads positivity far beyond the initial interaction. This ripple effect strengthens the social fabric that connects us all, showing how deeply interconnected our lives are. The support we receive from family, friends, and community directly impacts our emotional and mental well-being, just as our actions can contribute to the well-being of others.

The idea that everything is connected and that patterns repeat on different levels of existence is a powerful reminder of our place within the universe. It shows us that our actions, no matter how small, can have far-reaching consequences. By recognizing this interconnectedness, we can make more informed and responsible choices, whether in our personal lives, our communities, or our relationship with the environment.

Activity: Integrating Fundamental Truths into Daily Life

In this final activity, we will synthesize the concepts discussed throughout the book, using them to enhance our daily lives. By reflecting on our experiences and aligning with universal truths, we can foster a deeper connection to ourselves and the world around us.

Step 1: Cultivate Mental Awareness (Everything is Mental)

1. Morning Mindset Check-In:
- Begin each day with a few minutes of mindfulness. Before getting out of bed, take a deep breath and bring your awareness to your thoughts. Notice any recurring thoughts or feelings—are they positive, neutral, or negative?
- Affirmation Exercise: Choose a positive affirmation that aligns with your goals for the day. For example, "I am in control of my thoughts and actions," or "Today, I will create positive outcomes."
- Journal Prompt: At the end of the day, write about how your mindset influenced your experiences. Reflect on any challenges and how your thoughts shaped the outcomes.

Step 2: Recognize and Apply Cause and Effect (The Web of Causation)

1. Action-Outcome Reflection:
- Throughout the day, consciously observe the relationship between your actions and their outcomes. For example, if you choose to start your day with exercise, notice how it affects your energy levels and mood.
- Cause and Effect Diary: Keep a small notebook with you and jot down a few actions you take during the day, along with the effects they produce. This practice will heighten your awareness of how your choices shape your reality.
- Journal Prompt: Reflect on a specific action you took today and its outcome. How can you use this understanding to make more deliberate choices in the future?

Step 3: Embrace the Flow (Constant Motion and Vibration)

1. Energy Flow Check-In:
    - Pay attention to your energy levels throughout the day. When you feel your energy dip, take a moment to reconnect with your body—stretch, take a deep breath, or go for a quick walk.
    - Raising Your Vibration: Engage in activities that uplift your mood and energy, such as listening to music you love, spending time in nature, or practicing gratitude. Notice how these activities affect your overall well-being.
    - Journal Prompt: At the end of the day, write about how your energy fluctuated. What activities helped you maintain or raise your vibration? How can you incorporate these into your routine?

Step 4: Balance Dualities (Embracing Duality)

1. Duality Awareness:
    - Reflect on areas in your life where you experience dualities—such as work and rest, joy and sorrow, or love and conflict. How do these opposing forces show up in your daily life?
    - Integrating Opposites: When faced with a challenging situation, consciously seek to balance the dualities. For example, if you're feeling stressed (an active, masculine energy), balance it with a calming activity like meditation or deep breathing (a receptive, feminine energy).
    - Journal Prompt: Write about a duality you encountered today. How did you manage to balance it? What did you learn from this experience?

Step 5: Align with Natural Rhythms (Understanding Natural Cycles)

1. Cycle Awareness:
    - Pay attention to the natural rhythms in your day—your energy peaks and dips, your productivity cycles, and your moments of reflection. Align your tasks with these rhythms to enhance efficiency and reduce stress.
    - Daily Rhythm Planning: Plan your day in a way that aligns with your natural cycles. Schedule demanding tasks during your

energy peaks and reserve quieter times for reflection and less intensive activities.

- Journal Prompt: Reflect on how aligning your activities with your natural rhythms affected your day. What changes can you make to better respect these cycles?

Step 6: Harmonize Masculine and Feminine Energies (Achieving Dynamic Equilibrium)

1. Energy Balance Practice:
- Throughout the day, notice when you're using more masculine energy (assertiveness, action) and when you're using more feminine energy (receptivity, reflection). Strive to balance these energies in your interactions and tasks.
- Balanced Action: If you find yourself overly focused on action and productivity, take a moment to slow down and engage in a receptive activity, like listening deeply to a colleague or nurturing a creative idea.
- Journal Prompt: Write about how you balanced masculine and feminine energies today. How did this balance impact your effectiveness and relationships?

Step 7: See the Unity of Life (As Above, So Below)

1. Correspondence Reflection:
- Reflect on the connections between different areas of your life. How do the patterns in your work life mirror those in your personal life? How do small changes in your daily habits influence larger outcomes?
- Micro-Macro Connection: Choose a small, positive change to make in your daily routine, such as practicing gratitude or improving communication. Observe how this small change ripples out to affect other areas of your life.
- Journal Prompt: Write about a pattern you observed today that connects different aspects of your life. How does understanding this connection help you make more conscious choices?

Step 8: Synthesize and Reflect

1. Integration Reflection:
- At the end of each week, review your journal entries and reflect on how you've integrated the seven concepts into your daily life. What changes have you noticed in your mindset, energy levels, relationships, and overall well-being?
- Personal Insights: Write down the key insights you've gained from this practice. How have these concepts helped you create a more balanced and fulfilling life?
- Journal Prompt: Summarize your week by noting how these concepts have influenced your life. What are your intentions for the upcoming week to continue this journey of personal growth?

2. Create a Daily Practice Plan:
- Based on your reflections, create a simple daily practice plan that incorporates the seven concepts. This plan could include morning affirmations, energy check-ins, balancing activities, and evening reflections.
- Ongoing Commitment: Commit to practicing this plan daily, adapting it as needed to fit your evolving needs and circumstances. Allow these concepts to become an integral part of your life, guiding you towards greater awareness, balance, and fulfillment.

●

In exploring these Fundamental Truths, we gain profound insights into the nature of reality and our place within it. These ideas remind us that we are not passive observers but active participants in the grand tapestry of existence. We are capable of shaping our destiny through conscious thought and action.

By integrating these concepts into our daily lives, we unlock our potential, foster deeper connections, and live in alignment with the universal laws that govern all things. This philosophical exploration encourages us to embrace the interconnectedness of all things, recognize the power of our minds, and align ourselves with the natural rhythms of life. As we journey through life with this understanding, we become more attuned to the infinite possibilities within the universe and within ourselves.

By applying these fundamental truths, we can transform our mental states, improve our relationships, achieve our goals, and contribute to the well-being of the planet. This holistic approach to life encourages us to cultivate mindfulness, resilience, and creativity. It reminds us that we are interconnected beings, capable of making a positive impact on the world. As we continue to learn, explore, and embrace these fundamental truths, we create a life of purpose, harmony, and fulfillment.

So, next time you find yourself pondering the mysteries of the universe, remember that you are an integral part of this grand, cosmic dance. Every thought, every action, every connection you make contributes to the entirety of all existence. Trust your intuition, embrace the journey, and let the wisdom you have learned along the way guide you toward a life of meaning, balance, and joy.

AΩ